I0660441

THE
DREAM
SPINNERS

A NOVEL ABOUT LOVE, LOSS AND SECOND CHANCES
WITH A LITTLE HELP FROM THE OTHER SIDE

EVELYN ROBERTS BROOKS

Copyright ©2011, revision ©2019 Evelyn Roberts Brooks

Born to Triumph logo copyright ©2012 Evelyn Roberts Brooks

All rights reserved. The use of any part of this publication reproduced, transmitted by any form or by any means, electronic, mechanical, photocopying, recording, or otherwise, or stored in a retrieval system, without the prior consent of the author, except in the case of brief quotations embodied in critical reviews and certain other noncommercial uses permitted by copyright law, is an infringement of the copyright law. This novel is intended to provide entertainment, and is not meant to prescribe, diagnose, treat, offer medical, psychological, or other professional advice. The author encourages you to explore this book if the material is of interest to you. You accept full responsibility for your own actions and choices. The author disclaims responsibility for what you might or might not do with ideas or information expressed in this book. Please use the information responsibly. This is a work of fiction. Names, characters, places, and incidents are a product of the author's imagination. Locales and public names are sometimes used for atmospheric purposes. Any resemblance to actual people, living or dead, or to businesses, companies, events, institutions, or locales is completely coincidental.

The Dream Spinners / Evelyn Roberts Brooks
ISBN 978-1-7322080-7-0 paperback

Would you like to learn how to dissolve guilt, reduce your stress, and stop letting regrets for the past and worry about the future tie your stomach in knots? Stop by today to claim free Instant Download Access to a powerful three-part gift at evelynbrooks.com

This book includes a **READER'S GUIDE** at the end. Whether you are reading the book alone or discussing it in your book club, the 21 questions will enhance your experience of *The Dream Spinners*.

Follow Evelyn at:
twitter.com/evelynbrooks
facebook.com/evelynbrooksauthor
youtube.com/evelynbrooks
pinterest.com/evelynRbrooks

Books by Evelyn Roberts Brooks

Keep up to date by visiting booksbyevelyn.com

When you finish the book, please take a moment to leave a review so other readers can find me, too. I really appreciate it. I love hearing from readers. Contact me at evelynbrooks.com or facebook.com/evelynbrooksauthor

Nonfiction:
AMERICA'S NEW BREED OF FREEDOM FIGHTERS: With Liberty and Justice for All
WHAT WERE THEY THINKING?: Inside the Minds of Trump's Voters [Political humor]
WHAT TRUMP'S VOTERS WERE REALLY THINKING: The Complete Report Unedited [Political humor]
WHEN THEY GO LOW WE GO HIGH: Tending Our Garden of Democracy
RESTORING TIBET: Global Action Plan to Send the Dalai Lama Home

Born to Triumph Series
YOU WERE BORN TO TRIUMPH: Activate Your Spiritual Awakening
FIVE PROVEN METHODS TO STOP SELF-SABOTAGE
DO'S AND DON'TS FOR RECOVERING PEOPLE-PLEASERS
SIX SECRETS FOR A HARMONIC MARRIAGE
CALLING ALL LIGHTWORKERS
CHOOSE HAPPINESS NOW
HEAL YOUR TOXIC FRIENDSHIPS
YOUR GRIEF RELIEF: Heal the Void

Other Personal Development Titles
FORGET YOUR TROUBLES: Enjoy Your Life Today
GET HAPPY TODAY: No More Excuses!

BE HEALTHY, BE RICH: Secrets of Wellness and Wealth (classics by Wallace D. Wattles, annotated)

Fiction: Adult and Young Adult
THE DREAM SPINNERS (a novel about love, loss, and second chances with a little help from the Other Side)
THE GYPSY TALISMAN
THE CALICO TAPESTRY
VAMPIRE MISCHIEF

Juvenile Fiction
PROFESSOR BUBBLES AND THE MISSING FORMULA: A Law of Attraction Mystery for Middle Graders
My Days of the Week Underwear: The Fast and Fun Way to Learn the Days of the Week (preschool)

CONTENTS

I think that a good many people,
here and everywhere,
have a feeling in their bones
that some sort of
large-scale reawakening
is in the cards for humanity.
E. B. White, author and poet

So what if we have to part...
Parting is not goodbye...
Try thinking with your heart,
We'll be together again.
from *We'll Be Together Again*
lyrics by Frankie Laine

I believe we need never feel pain
at the passing of a loved one,
that we need never fear our own "death."
Adela Rogers St. Johns, journalist and author

Goodbyes are hardest
when you are the one staying behind.
Jean Kirtley Roberts (1913-2001)
(the author's mother)

IN MEMORY OF
my three younger siblings
who never reached adulthood:
Maryanne, Philip and Charlene
(we'll be together again)

Introduction

The Dream Spinners is a novel about second chances. About hope, about love, about forgiveness. About the synchronicity of seeming coincidences in life. About people who are struggling with loss, regrets and self-recrimination, told from different perspectives so that, living vicariously through Jemma, Andy, Marybeth, Mike and others, you may, if desired, experience the full spectrum of grief, rage, confusion, despair... and, eventually, healing.

There's a lot of humor in the story as well, because isn't that how life is? Even in the midst of our tragic moments we find the antics of a toddler amusing, we appreciate the warm hug from someone who cares (even someone who is seemingly a stranger), we laugh in remembrance of things past, as Shakespeare put it.

Have you ever stopped to ask yourself if there is an emotional logic behind everything we do? I believe it's the inner call for peace, love, happiness. We seek unconsciously to fill the void created by the absence of love, but in our lack of awareness we inadvertently create problems, pain and sorrow instead of all the joy we really want.

Grief can enter our lives from many directions: when someone we love dies, or in the aftermath of severe illness, divorce, pet loss, unemployment, an empty nest, retirement, natural disaster or a devastation such as a fire or an accident, a significant lifestyle or health change, and other varieties of swift upheaval to our regular daily routine.

Other sensations of loss come from the slow steady erosion of happiness caused by an inner dissatisfaction you can't seem to cure, and from missed opportunities—those regrets over "what might have been" that haunt and impede our journey.

The result of any unhealed loss or grief is that we feel off-balance, uncertain who we are now that the familiarity of our days has been shaken, tossed, and tumbled out in disjointed pieces.

When someone you care about passes away, you may feel they are lost to you forever and that there is no more communication possible. However, you can learn to open yourself to visits with your loved ones by asking them to interact with you while you are sleeping.

A visitation from a deceased love one is not the same as having a regular dream about them, from which you awaken wondering what it was all about because some (or all) of it didn't make much sense. As you come more fully awake, the dream's details grow fuzzy and then fade, leaving a vague impression that you had some sort of interaction with the person who died. You might wonder if it meant anything, if you should look for symbols in why, for instance, they turned away in the dream or said something cruel or upsetting. If that is the sort of dream experience you've had, understand that's probably a dream created by your mind as it sorts your activities and uses the faces of familiar people to populate your nightly soap opera and to bring up issues from your subconscious mind for you to address in your waking hours.

The truly meaningful sleep time visits with relatives and friends who have passed over come about because, while deep in that unconscious state, you are open to connections that are more difficult for them to achieve within the mental static and distractions of your busy life.

Those who are in the nonphysical state find it easier to communicate with you while you sleep. The visit may be brief, an experience in which the person embraces you, stands silently smiling before you, or says "I love you" as if from behind you or just out of sight. You may find yourself speaking a few words to them even though they are not speaking, and you know they understand your loving message. They may give you a specific message in words or in symbols or in a type of "knowing" that is meaningful to you or that proves meaningful in the coming days or weeks.

In a dream visitation, you may experience a sensation of being cared for deeply, that stays with you when you wake up and you know without a doubt that your loved one was with you. You may see a symbol in your sleep such as a butterfly, and then see the same color of butterfly the next day in an unexpected place, confirming the visit.

The visit may be brief, and yet it will always be comforting.

After all, when your friend or family member was alive, you didn't have to spend all day together to know you were loved—often a quick hug or brief phone call or text was all you needed to affirm your connection. The same holds true even though you still have a physical body while they do not.

It's not the length of the visit that matters, it's how you feel about it.

Loved ones never come to harm or berate or threaten you, even if the relationship when they were alive was a troubled or abusive one, but rather to leave comforting and reassuring messages and lasting impressions of their continued love and affection for you. Often these communications will include a two-way forgiveness and releasing of problems that defined your relationship with them when they were alive.

If you feel uncomfortable about the idea of a dream visitation, perhaps you hold the residue of old beliefs from childhood, when you were taught that devils and demons have the power to grab and hurt you even if you struggle to get away. To release that notion, before you go to sleep, visualize a protective white bubble around you that only allows in those who wish you well.

Affirm this: I attract only peace, love and harmony into my life, whether awake or asleep.

When you awaken from a visitation, the episode will feel clear, and the memory of it will stay with you. Why? Because it was real, it was true, it actually happened. Dreams fade because if they occupied a slot in our memory bank, we'd all be walking around in a state of confusion, uncertain what we had really done the day before compared to what was dreamt.

The truth is, we all are eternal beings enjoying a physical experience here on earth to create more joy and expansion while we are here, however long or short this lifetime might be.

Today, with quantum physicists and other experts in the human mind delving into the relationships we share in our never-ending connectivity with each other and universal energy, controlled experiments have proven that skilled mediums do indeed communicate with people who have died. I'll leave you to explore this topic more if it interests you.

As an author and spiritual healer, I help you release grief and stress, and create happiness. I write personal development books to support change so you can heal what's important to you, and feel happier.

Long before I began writing nonfiction, I chose to create the story of a mother and child that would capture your imagination and make it easier to consider the idea of having your departed loved ones talk with you and visit with you while you sleep. Death is <u>not</u> the end of your relationships.

This new release includes a special bonus: the words in this novel have been spiritually energized to uplift and comfort. You don't have to believe in anything special to feel the shift in awareness, which may be gradual or sudden, but in the reading of this book you will be connected with the frequency that love resides on, and where all past, present and future events and relationships co-exist in joy.

I hope you enjoy *The Dream Spinners*. It's a novel with many interwoven subplots and seeming coincidences, an exploration of different experiences with loss and bereavement and despair, but even more, it is about opening your heart to love and second chances ... with help from the Other Side.

Evelyn

Evelyn Roberts Brooks

Prologue

1988...

In a cozy off-campus apartment in walking distance to Arizona State University in Phoenix, an alarm clock buzzed early one morning, the day after graduation. Groping towards it from the bed, a young woman's hand hovered over the snooze button again, but then firmly pressed the off switch.

It was Jemma Malotki's left hand, bearing a modest engagement ring. Her fingernails were sensibly manicured, short and unpolished, as befit a future scientist and astronaut.

Mike murmured in her ear, "Let's stay in bed all day, celebrate." He smiled sleepily. Everything was going great in his life. Maybe Jemmie would be open to the idea of getting married this summer before she got caught up in grad school, maybe they could even talk about starting a family. He'd continue giving her whatever support she needed behind the scenes to make her crazy schedule work. "Love you, babe," he whispered, drifting back to sleep.

Jemma lay in her beloved fiancé's arms, her dark brown eyes troubled by the knowledge of the upheaval the next few minutes would bring. She was overwhelmed by an intense longing to stay, to find a way to be with Mike. Her whole body, every cell, seemed to be filled with an unabashed yearning for him that brought an ache to her throat. And yet, she'd been over and over this ground already, arguing with herself, knowing that whichever side of the debate won, both would lose something intrinsic to her happiness.

But she'd made her decision, difficult as it had been to do so. She couldn't put off telling Mike any longer. Today was the day. She pulled away slightly, bracing herself to get up and into action.

Without waking fully, Mike drew her closer into his embrace, as if missing her for that brief interval.

She sighed almost imperceptibly, regretting that she would be causing him unfathomable pain. The window air conditioner droned steadily, keeping the desert heat at bay. She wished for something that would do the same for Mike's inevitable reaction.

Strewn across the floor were all the signs of their graduation the day before: her honor society sash and the purple lei of Dendrobium orchids that Mike had draped over her shoulders, their mortar boards and Sun Devil maroon satin gowns, as well as the clothes they'd worn beneath their graduation raiment.

On her nightstand, nestled within a cantaloupe-sized amethyst geode they'd bought as a souvenir on a hiking trek last summer, Jemma's Phi Beta Kappa key sparkled in a ray of light from a crack in the drawn curtains. She was a biochemistry undergraduate and fully intended to add more initials after her name like a string of pearls.

Mike had earned degrees in both English literature and history, but was content to stop his formal education to pursue his dream of being a novelist.

He fumbled for the remote on his nightstand and pressed a button. Music played softly from a boombox on the bookcase, looping a cassette of favorites he'd compiled--mellow jazz and rock classics, with Sinatra interspersed here and there to, as Mike put it, keep them grounded in the reality of their timeless love.

"Mike?" she whispered, without turning around.

"Hmmm?" He drowsily kissed the nape of her neck, inhaled the faint floral scent of the mimosa cologne she always wore.

"I got accepted into the graduate program."

"Hey, that's great, Jemmie. Good thing we signed another year's lease--"

She cut him off in a voice so unusually soft that he barely heard her. "Not here, Mike, not Arizona State."

He tensed, waiting. For years, he'd gently teased Jemma about her determination to make right one of space history's wrongs, but he had utter respect for what she was doing with her life and her plans that held the potential to heal decades-old wounds.

Mike was unabashedly in love with Jemma and devoted to creating a lifetime together that would be more precious and richly satisfying with each passing year. He knew their relationship was worth fighting for. It was worth honoring the silent vows he'd already made in his heart and tried to express in their life together each day, to love and cherish her forever.

Her intake of air was shakily audible before she spoke. "UCLA."

Suddenly wary, he said with forced cheer, keeping his arms tightly around her, "Just give me two weeks' warning and I'll quit my job at the bookstore and we'll–"

"I'm driving to L.A."

"When are you going?"

She didn't answer.

"Today?" He sat up as if jerked into awareness that his life was about to be turned on its head. "You're leaving now. Is that what you're saying?"

She nodded, still without turning to face him.

This conversation was so unusual it scared him. He never had to coax information from her. She was always one to speak her mind, to be direct and even outspoken. The fact that she could barely tell him what her plan was gave him hope that he had a chance to influence it.

"You're just going to take care of paperwork, right? Find us an apartment? And then I'll join you."

"No."

"Are you—are you saying...are you breaking up with me?" He rushed ahead, not giving her time to answer, not wanting to allow her to wedge her logical responses between them. "Just because you want to be in California? But

I can write anywhere, Jemmie. All I need is my insanely creative mind, and my beautiful, benevolent muse."

He kissed her silken, tanned shoulder, the one with the tattoo of a woman flying a biplane, the tattoo he'd dared her to get just after she'd earned her pilot's license at age sixteen, thus taking an irrevocable step toward her dream of being a spaceflyer.

"Mike, they don't take slackers in the Space Program."

"Slacker?" He turned her to face him. "You, honey? Since when?"

"I almost got a 'B' from Dr. Harrison, because of missing so many classes. I was lucky she let me submit other work for extra credit."

"What are you talking about? You never skipped any--"

"It was my only early morning class. And I was usually here...with you."

He couldn't help recoiling. "You blame me?"

She studied his face, so dear to her, and stroked his cheek, desperate to impress this final touch deep into her memory. "I don't want to ever blame you for anything. My coming schedule will be even more grueling than--"

"We'll put alarm clocks all around the room. That'll force us to get up. I'll even figure out how to disable the snooze buttons so--"

"I need to focus on my work." Not waiting for his response, she slipped out of bed, hurried into the bathroom, took a swift shower and returned in shorts and a knit top.

While she showered, he pulled on khaki shorts, made the bed and tossed their clothes from the floor onto the bedspread. Now he put his arms around her and wrapped her long straight black hair around his neck.

"You are bound to me, Jemmie. You are mine and nothing can change that. I'll get an apartment near you and we'll see each other whenever you–"

She put a finger on his lips, halting the words. Disentangling her hair, she took a step back. Tears streamed down her high cheekbones but her jaw tilted stubbornly. She opened the closet, grabbed her suitcase from the back and filled it with her personal belongings, already stacked in drawers as if awaiting this step.

"How long have you known?" he asked, not missing a detail.

Jemma zipped her bag, avoiding his eyes. "A while."

The music segued into Frank Sinatra's voice singing, "The Best Is Yet to Come."

"The piano player was singing this," he said, "when you said yes to me."

"I know." Her voice was not unkind.

"It wasn't a coincidence."

She nodded. "I saw you go up to him when I was coming out of the ladies room, so I backed up, stayed out of sight, waited a few moments."

"But you pretended—"

"I didn't expect the proposal that night but I knew you were in a really romantic mood for some reason, and I didn't want to spoil it by bursting whatever surprise you were planning. The whole evening was so typical of you, Mike, from start to finish. A charming restaurant, candles, my favorite menu, favorite dessert. And you, smiling across the table. Kissing me. Stammering out your proposal. Completely and utterly loving...and generous...and thoughtful. And dear to me. So very dear to me."

"Then why—" His voice broke in agony.

"You're the wordsmith, Mike. I don't know how to explain myself. This...this urge, this drive I feel inside. You know it's not—"

"It's not the typical ambition for acclaim or glory," he said, nodding, understanding her need to be clear on this point. "You're an explorer with a specific mission. Marco Polo. Captain Cook... Make that Captain Kirk. Your lodestar lies light years beyond the North Star. I know that. I've known it for years, Jemmie. Don't you understand that I love you because you are different from anyone else I've ever known, not in spite of your differences? You have such integrity of spirit, my love. I look back at history from the comforting vantage point of hindsight, and you dream of going off into the unknown without a safety net. You need me, to help you stay grounded in what matters most. Love."

Their eyes met and held for a long moment, Mike with luminous hope in his slate-blue eyes, Jemma with a sense of dread that she would be the one to permanently diminish that light.

"I don't have the right stuff, Mike. Not for marriage."

"But—" he paused, desperate for the right words, a clever turn of phrase that would convince her to stay long enough for him to demonstrate that he wouldn't be the distraction she feared. "Let me be your way station. Let me be the one you come home to from your journeys." Anger flared. "You can't just walk away from all we mean to each other!"

With a deep breath, she turned away from him, gently slid the engagement ring off her finger and set it on their shared dresser, next to the watch that was her graduation gift to him. She glanced around the room as if to be sure she wasn't leaving anything, but clearly storing the details of their life into her golden memories.

She tucked her Phi Beta Kappa charm into her wallet, and left the heavy geode she'd used as the charm's parking space for Mike to keep or discard.

Frantic to stop her from leaving, Mike rummaged in the sagging shelves of an overcrowded bookcase and withdrew a small volume.

She saw what he held: James Allen's influential work, *As a Man Thinketh,* originally published in 1902. She'd found a beautiful first edition for Mike's Christmas present last year, knowing he'd be more pleased with it than any sweater, tie, or wallet, no matter how expensive.

He opened the book to the inscription, and read it out loud, his voice choked with emotion. "Dearest Mike, You are my sheltering tree, my sturdy rock. I will love you forever. Your Jemmie."

"Please don't–" Her chest ached from the wrench of ripping their private world asunder, but she was determined to go forward with her plan. It was the only path that felt sure and unequivocal.

He flipped to the last chapter in the short book, and read the passage Jemma had underlined with a pencil, "'The strong, calm man is always loved and revered. He is like a shade-giving tree in a thirsty land, or a sheltering rock in a storm. Who does not love a tranquil heart, a sweet-tempered, balanced life?'"

She groped for words to explain herself in a way he might be able to comprehend later, after the initial shock dulled and he found his own way toward acceptance and healing. "I don't know how to balance it, Mike. I just don't know how. It's some kind of defect in me, that others like you seem to understand innately."

He tossed the book aside and strode to her. "So you kept all this to yourself and went through the motions and now you're doing the above-reproach thing with me, like you always do."

"I'm not–"

"I've tried to be that shade-giving tree, Jemmie, that rock in a storm for you to find refuge whenever you need solace. I haven't complained that ninety-nine percent of the time your schedule determines whether we hook up or not. I know you've got your sight on--"

"I can't help it, Mike." She met his gaze in agony. "I need to spend the next five, ten, fifteen years making sure I qualify for NASA. And if I don't make the grade, I don't want to have anyone but myself to blame."

He looked at her a long moment. His muscles were tense, filled with apprehension as he tried not to anticipate her next damning words. He'd talk her out of this. He would. Then they'd both relax and laugh together over her overreaction to a simple choice, and his groundless fears.

He took her hands in his, and she let him.

"I have to go," she said simply. "Please let me. I don't have the gall to ask for your blessing, but please—"

"Let's brainstorm, Jemmie. Okay? You owe me that."

"Bottom line, Mike, when I'm with you, I want to play. I want to make love and laugh and dance. Some people know how to have the whole triangle. Marriage, family, career. I envy them! But with you in my life, I'm so torn inside it's… it's killing me."

"I'll respect your study time."

She yanked her hands free and crossed her arms. "It's not fair to you--to us--to make you settle for crumbs, Mike. You deserve better."

He bit back a curse. "Don't tell me what I deserve. I want you. I love you, Jemmie. You've been mine since the day we met."

She winced at the pain in his eyes, the confusion and despair in his voice.

Deep within her soul glowed her intense love for Mike, an unquenchable flame that had grown stronger and brighter each year since they had met at age ten when his family moved across the street from hers in a suburb of Phoenix. They'd camped together, swum together, been buddies, then tennis rivals, then best friends, and then lovers.

He looked at her evenly, refusing to glance away as if he was wrong, as if he should be ashamed to fight for their love. Jemma had a vulnerability that was hidden now, but he'd known it for years, long enough to recognize when she was trying too hard to be brave. Now was such a time, and if he gave in, she'd be able to widen the crack between them that would destroy all they'd built together since childhood.

He knew her dream was too big to be limited by a practical goal plan that might suffice for countless others, and he also knew that when her determination shifted focus she would again reveal that vulnerability that only he could see, that only he knew how to cherish and protect from those who would take advantage of a seeming weakness in her.

The task before him was to show her that she could have it all, that she didn't have to limit herself to a single monastic path.

Jemma looked at him, knowing he was trying to figure out how to change her mind, knowing she couldn't let him. Steeling herself to recite the words she'd rehearsed in the mirror all week, and with the hot conviction of youth untempered by life's more complex emotional experiences, she said, "Don't wait for me, Michael. Go live your own dream. Find a sweet girl to watch 'Gone with the Wind' and 'Romeo and Juliet'—"

He cut in. "The only epic romance I've ever been interested in is ours, Jemma."

"Write your Great American Novel and..." She turned away, drained. "Create a wonderful romance and let them be our proxies and give them the happy ending we can't have."

"But we can!"

She slung her purse and a tote bag over one shoulder and then wheeled her suitcase to the door, more briskly on the outside than she felt within.

He snatched a framed photo from the bookshelf. "You almost forgot this." In the picture, young Jemma stood in front of a Cessna 172, her grin showing bright metal braces, holding her pilot's license, flanked by her flight instructor and Mike, who was beaming at her with love and pride. Mike had framed it after writing on it in his bold scrawl, "Hot Wings! You fly me to the moon. Love always, Mike."

Jemma silently slid the photo into the tote bag. Keenly logical and goal-oriented, Jemma knew instinctively that she had to abort this burning love before it consumed her passion for space travel. Toward that end, she unconsciously began forming a crust around her heart, as if diamond-hard crystals multiplied in a nucleation process, creating an impenetrable fortress to protect her from her own all-too-human desires.

At the door, she turned and looked at him, feasting on the thousand and one memories they had created over the years.

He stood in the center of the room, the early morning sunshine backlighting him. His shoulders were slumped and his eyes brimmed with tears.

For a moment, she almost lost her resolve, but she stayed steady, knowing that discipline was her only path to a seat on a space shuttle. "The truth is, Mike," she said evenly, by rote, "I just don't love you enough."

He flung out an arm, indicating the rumpled sheets on the bed and the two pillows snuggled close together, mute witnesses to their love. "What was that–a parting gift?"

"If we go any further, the hurt will be even worse." She opened the door, hesitated only briefly and then left him.

He reached towards her, but pride kept him rooted within the room where their love had bloomed but failed to mature the way he had assumed it would.

As if by their own volition, his bare feet stumbled after her into the open-air corridor of the two-story apartment complex. He watched her bump her suitcase down the outside stairs to the parking lot. He knew she would not welcome assistance, and so he stemmed the impulse to leap forward and grab her bags. A harsh laugh bubbled up. Grab them, and bring them back inside? She'd fight even harder for what she'd decided, she'd push back, she'd resist. He'd never win that way.

His sense of loss and devastation was overwhelming. His knees gave a slight shimmy, as if his whole body was begging him to simply collapse into the pain. With an effort of will, he remained upright but found himself leaning heavily against the outer wall of their apartment, its rough stucco support the only thing preventing him from falling to his knees.

It was as if something had swept in from the desolate outreaches of the desert and twisted his heart out of his chest. He felt engulfed by a sense of vast emptiness that would only grow larger with time.

She finished loading her car's hatchback, opened the hot car door handles with the hem of her shirt and let the car air out a few moments. Even with the windows cracked, the heat inside always built to scorching levels. She smoothed a beach towel on the driver's seat to protect her legs from the hot tan pleather.

Mike watched her every move, searing the sight of her into his soul.

He whispered softly, "Come back, Jemma. Come back to me. Please."

A hot breeze stirred around him in the open corridor and his whispered words seemed to boomerang in his face, mocking him. As she drove away, he felt a jolt, as if Phoenix had been visited by one of its rare earthquakes, only this one had the power to destroy all he held dear.

Jemma was taking his heart with her.

He began silently weeping, unable to control the tears.

You're the wordsmith, Mike.

Her words came back to him as if on that now benevolent desert breeze, her words carrying the reminder that there was still a chance to bypass her logic and fly straight into her heart.

I'll write her. I'll write her a letter. And another one. And then another, until she comes back to me.

Turning away from the dwindling sight of her white hatchback heading toward the L.A.-bound freeway onramp in the distance, he went inside their apartment, filled with a new steadying resolution, and softly closed the door behind him.

THE DREAM SPINNERS

Chapter 1

20 Years Later...

Jemma woke with a start, her heart racing from a dream that was already eluding capture. Her mind felt clotted with a sensation of impending doom but she couldn't grasp the fleeting images and make them hold still long enough to study them and interpret their significance. Even so, she felt it was the same dream that had been plaguing her sleep lately, like a second skin she was unable to slough.

Wide awake now, she lay in her assigned bed in the sleep quarters tucked in Houston's sprawling Johnson Space Center. When Jemma had learned she would not be on the final shuttle team, she did what she always did when an obstacle loomed in her path: she found a way around it, so that now Dr. Jemma Malotki Powell, renowned biochemist, was training with astronauts from other countries who hoped to be on an international launch in the near future.

The others might <u>hope</u> for it, Jemma reflected, but she held to an unwavering belief that she would get into space, somehow, some way.

She got up, stretched for a few moments and then showered. It was a hot, humid, sticky summer day, typical for Houston, and she was looking forward to returning to the dry heat of the Los Angeles suburb where her husband and teenage son awaited.

The deliciously cool water cascaded down her back and rippled around her toes, reminding her of summers camping at Apache Lake, Arizona when she was growing up. As she shampooed her glossy shoulder-length raven hair, Jemma's thoughts turned lightly to the personal sacrifices that had brought her to this point, but when those thoughts started to yield regrets over a certain path not taken, she shut the door on the past and reclaimed her boundless optimism and determination.

Dressing quickly, she packed for the flight home, leaving the room as sterile and hotel-like as it had been on her arrival.

She headed down a corridor toward the office of Fran Hastings, her cheerful advisor in the space program. Along the way, she greeted several staff members and fellow astronaut-candidates. Her confidence and expertise, combined with a natural friendliness and interest in others, earned warm greetings in return. Both well-liked and well-respected, Jemma felt completely at home in this realm of sky-high dreams. She couldn't imagine wanting or being satisfied with any other type of work.

Jemma parked her suitcase and carryon in the hall, tapped on Fran's half-open door and called in, "Hey, you. Time for a quick visit?"

Fran, graying, plump and near retirement, hoped to see Jemma succeed during her tenure. She beckoned. "Door is always open to you. Want to go get a coffee?"

"Some other time, Fran. Heading for the airport now."

Slender and physically fit, Jemma lounged against the door frame. The driving single-minded ambition of her youth had mellowed into a broader purpose. Jemma was comfortable and easy in her own skin. She still had a tendency to keep her troubles to herself, and to run her life in an orderly progression, but she was no longer a poster child for total self-sufficiency. Although she had many acquaintances and colleagues, she had few friends, none of them close. Her relationship with Fran was professional, but she did open up to the older woman now and then, and share some of her doubts and concerns about her dream of space flight in relation to the other demands in her life of family and home.

"By the way," Jemma said to Fran, "that rental house you lined up for us is perfect. Saved me a lot of footwork. I have the feeling even Hart will approve of the kitchen."

"Glad to hear that. What about Andy? Still getting a nudge every hour on the hour, trying to change your mind about moving? That kid is a superb campaigner. Probably be a politician when he grows up."

Jemma smiled in rueful agreement. Her fifteen-year-old son Andy had been spending a lot of time with an older high school buddy, Eric Blum, during summer vacation. The boys had cooked up a plan for Andy to live with Eric's family during senior year instead of moving to Houston with his own parents.

Andy promoted the idea to Jemma via frequent text messages, emails and calls, but Jemma was holding firm in her refusal. Still, a doubt kept creeping into her mind that her timing for the astronaut corps was off.

Fran noticed her hesitation. "What?"

"Maybe I should put this off a year or two, Fran."

The older woman gaped. "I know a lot of other candidates freaked out and left when the budgets were slashed, but I never expected to hear a four-letter-word from you."

Jemma looked at her in confusion, swiftly scanning what she'd just said to see if she'd let slip a curse word. "I—" she began to defend herself.

"I mean the word 'quit,'" Fran said dryly. "I've heard you swear like a longshoreman, coming out of a meeting in the administrator's office, but I never thought I'd hear that particular foul word come out of your mouth."

"Not quitting," Jemma clarified. "Postponing. Just until Andy is settled in college."

For years, Jemma had felt a strong sense of duty to a higher purpose. Before Andy's birth, she hadn't known how to reconcile the place for personal joy in her lonely equation that defined success. But things were different now. She wanted to put her son first. She'd long felt the touchstone of a person's character was honesty and forthrightness, and couldn't abide those who tried to evade a stern look at reality. Today her reality was being torn.

"We're alike in some ways, Jemma. Not many, but some. I never take anything at face value either. I delve beneath the surface, so I have to ask you bluntly. How long have you dreamed of this?" Fran got up and came around her desk. "Ten years? Fifteen? Or maybe you were born with it?"

"You're probably right," Jemma said with a self-deprecating laugh. "Even though I wasn't born with wings I was born for flight, the way Beethoven was born to compose music. I've always had my head tilted up, looking at the sky. When I'm flying that Cessna I borrow now and then, I'm fearless. The air is my real home, not this earth and its gravity. I guess I yearn for space flight the way other people dream about an all-expense-paid trip to Disneyworld."

"Hardly in the same category." Fran crossed to a wall of framed astronaut photos. "I've seen a lot of people come and go around here. Only a very few get on this special wall of mine. I've met a lot of ambitious people over the years, Jemma, both here and when I worked in the corporate world. Putting aside the cutthroat assholes, excuse my French, I've never known someone with your laser-focused drive and determination."

"Most people would call it being tough and bitchy." Jemma winked. "Thanks for your tactful word choices."

"Strong, ambitious women belong here. Your picture belongs here." Fran pointed to an empty space in the gallery. "The Mercury Thirteen women belonged here, but it's too late for them. Jerrie Cobb, Wally Funk. The others. You can be their proxy if you keep going with that top secret idea you shared."

"Truth is, Fran, I know Andy's going to be upset when I break the news about my trip to Kazakhstan."

"You didn't tell him yet?" Fran's face showed her surprise.

"I didn't have the heart to do it on the phone."

"Since when are you chicken about anything? I've never known you to keep quiet when you had something on your mind."

"But I've promised for years that I'd take him to see the reservation where my grandfather Qaletaqa grew up, and last month I told him to circle a date on his calendar."

"Now you're crossing it out." Fran shrugged philosophically. "You'll make it up to him at another time. Andy's a bright kid. He understands things have changed drastically here. Even people not connected with NASA know the program took a sharp turn away from business as usual and the last shuttle flight is less than two years off. It's not like it was before, when you applied and had a good shot at one of our own shuttle missions."

"Don't remind me." Jemma forced a laugh. "It's painful. I know I'm not the only one dismayed by the extreme budget cuts, but I keep thinking of that old saying--Where there's a will, there's a way."

"And you have plenty of will power. I know the public view of you is that you are unfailingly polite even as you push for what you believe in. You've always been above-reproach in your career. I know you don't need a pep talk, certainly not from me, but discipline and persistence have served you well and will continue to do so if you don't give up."

"I feel bad about disappointing Andy. Yet again. Not exactly the first time."

"Won't be the last, either. Part of life for any kid, especially one with a high-achiever mom. We all have to learn we aren't the center of anyone else's universe no matter how much love there is. You're a terrific role model for that kid, you and your ambition."

"Thanks. I think. Sounds like you've got something else to say I might not like."

Fran nodded. "You quit, you're giving him permission to quit on his own life. You've got a dream, Jemma. A huge one. And I want to help you make it come true. The meeting you finagled with the Russians is just the beginning of great things."

"I feel guilty about cancelling the trip to Arizona."

Jemma proudly claimed a mixed heritage of Irish-American and Hopi Indian, and had grown up in the suburbs of Phoenix with her parents and her younger sister, Lulu. Although Jemma had not been raised with tribal traditions, Andy was curious to learn about them first-hand and had been begging her to take him to the reservation in Arizona before she got even more involved with the space program.

"But, Jemma, surely he must realize your best options are to team up with other countries and seize whatever opportunity you can. How could you even think of turning down an invitation to a Cosmodrome to see a Russian launch, and meet with the very people who can make your idea work? It proves they're taking all your conference calls and emails seriously and not blowing you off."

"But am I being greedy?" Jemma felt the need for an objective opinion and knew that Fran could be trusted to give her one. "After all, my life is nearly perfect already."

"Admit you're entitled to better than a nearly perfect life. Live your dream—you can have it all. I know you can."

Jemma laughed. "I'm lucky to have you on my side, Fran. I'd hate to see what happens to someone when you're not."

"You've earned your bragging rights. Not every day someone approaches me with an idea to correct the history books. You're one in a million and it's an honor to know you. Seriously. I don't want you to go home for your time off without knowing I can't think of anyone else who deserves this more." She pointed to the gallery wall and the empty space waiting for Jemma's image.

"That means a lot," Jemma said, "especially coming from you."

"I'm a crusty old broad and I've seen it all." As Fran glanced out toward the corridor, she dropped her voice to a conspiratorial whisper. "If I were you, Dr. Malotki, I'd acquire a taste for Tang," Fran said, referring to the powdered orange drink that early astronauts re-hydrated and drank during space flights. Her keen blue eyes twinkled.

"It's been off the NASA shuttle menu for years."

"Maybe it's time you introduced it to the Russians?" Fran looked at her with an innocent air.

Jemma chuckled, eyeing Fran. "What do you know that I don't? Is there something in my file I need to sneak a peek at?"

Fran smiled. "Go on home and enjoy your family, Jemma. And stay in touch."

In Andy's bedroom in the Powell's two story suburban residence, track trophies, textbooks and vacation souvenirs crowded a wall of bookcases. Clusters of photos showed Andy at the starting block at track meets, building sand castles at the beach, or scuba diving.

Discarded shoes and clothes littered the floor along with old pizza boxes and empty water bottles. A framed poster of a yellow Ferrari dominated the wall behind the bed.

There were only two spaces where order reigned: his desk and his 55-gallon coral tank.

Andy opened a can of tropical fish food. He was almost sixteen, lean and dark-haired like his mother, and moved with the same compact grace. His well-kept coral reef aquarium was near the window but out of direct sunlight. Weighing over 800 pounds, the tank rested on a strong stand with cupboard doors which concealed shelved supplies and equipment.

After turning off the filter he sprinkled food across the water surface. Two orange clownfish darted out of their hiding place in a bubble-tip anemone. Angelfish, tangs and other small saltwater fish swam to feed on the drifting flakes.

"Hey, there, Dory," he said to a bright blue tang, named for the blue tropical fish in *Finding Nemo*.

Eric Blum took the last slice of mushroom and cheese pizza from a box open on the unmade bed. He was almost eighteen, a high school fullback.

"You didn't answer my question yet." Andy concentrated on the fish.

"You mean," Eric said, chewing, "how come you're such a loser?"

Andy shrugged, trying not to show how important this was to him.

For as long as he could remember, Andy had wanted his life to mean something. He looked around the world and saw that most people lived on the surface of life. He wanted to dive deep, to explore the magic of the universe, to forge a life purpose that would make him feel good while helping others climb out of their safe, predictable lives. Admittedly, he'd absorbed his worldview growing up in a household with two bright, ambitious and caring parents. He'd taken the route of following their example instead of feeling the need to sabotage himself by rebelling against an academic path.

Given all that, Andy had another purpose that had been welling up inside for months: he wanted his senior year of high school to be off-the-charts fantastic. He wanted to experience being part of the in-crowd. He wanted to have a once-in-a-lifetime blast that he could look back on and recall with a big fat self-satisfied grin.

And Eric was his ticket in.

"Well," Eric said, looking up as if wanting to give this issue his full attention, "first off it doesn't help you skipped a couple grades so you're younger than the rest of us. I mean, you'll be a senior at the end of summer and you don't even drive yet. How nerdy is that?"

"I'm a nerd with a capital N." Andy forced a smile, as if it was all a joke that didn't matter. But to him, it was utterly serious. He had chosen his course and he was determined to make it happen.

Andy's academic achievements got in the way of friendships his own age, and his age itself was a barrier with his classmates. Sometimes he wondered if he would ever find his right place. He looked at Eric. It felt like he was reaching out in desperation for a magical time of popularity and being admired as one of the coolest guys at El Camino High, instead of just the nerd most likely to lead the school's Acadecathlon team to another win.

But of course, Andy told himself swiftly, feeling an urge to soothe a protest from within, after graduation, he'd settle back into his perpetual nerdiness and pursue his university studies.

"The thing is, I kind of like you." Eric studied Andy with a level gaze. "You're a nerd. But a fun nerd. You've got potential."

Andy turned to look at his friend. "You're not just saying that because I'm helping with your summer school homework?"

"There's something likable about you. Just...try not to act so nerdy all the time." Eric reached in a pocket of his cargo shorts and put something on his wrist.

"Yeah. Got it. Thanks. I'll act cool.... Whatever that is." Andy noticed the watch Eric had just put on. "Whoa. You got a diver's watch?"

Eric held his arm up.

Andy approached and they admired the watch.

"Always wanted one," Eric explained.

"But you don't even dive."

"So what?" Eric shrugged. "Dig all the cool dials."

"Do you even know how to use them?"

Eric laughed, shaking his head. "I like the way it looks."

"I've seen that exact model at the store. Why would you buy something that expensive you won't even use?"

Eric shot him a challenging look. "We're entitled to a freebie now and then. It's not personal. They write it off to insurance."

Andy was taken aback. "You mean you–"

"Act casual when you go in the store." Eric shot him a look. "Don't draw attention to yourself. Be nerdy and no one will suspect anything. It's the cool guys they look out for."

"So now you're saying I shouldn't be cool?"

"Well, uh, no. I mean–"

"Just kidding." Andy smirked, not used to being the one pulling off a slick comment.

"Best part is we're underage." Eric shrugged. "No biggie if you're caught. But you won't be if you're careful."

"Nah. I don't think I could." Andy went back to the coral tank and used the magnet algae scrapers to clean the inside glass.

"Why are you so, like, obsessive about cleaning that?" Eric asked.

"So the fish can see out." Andy carefully removed a smear of green algae.

The water in the tank rippled.

Eric lounged on the bed and played with the dials of his stolen watch. "Stop being such a pussy.""I'm not a...a what you said," Andy mumbled, embarrassed.

"All the guys are doing it. Man up if you want to be a cool senior. The other guys don't even want me to let you hang with us. Not just 'cause you're a nerd. And not just 'cause you're younger."

"Then what?"

Eric frowned, as if trying to recall what else. He shrugged, giving it up as a lost thought. "Like I said, you're a nerd. I don't know why, you just are. Maybe because you're top of the class and you're not even sixteen yet."

"I get it." Andy nodded, considering everything Eric had said. More than anything, Andy wanted his senior year to be totally cool and awesome, and just hanging out with Eric the past few weeks had already made him feel special.

So what if the time they spent together was in private, never where the cool guys hung out, and the purpose was to help Eric with summer school homework? Eric said that he liked him, so Andy knew he could be part of the popular group when school started, and make his last year before college one to remember.

"I wish you didn't have to probably move away," Eric lamented. "If you're parents make you go to Houston, I'm shit out of luck. I'm going to need a lot of help to stay on the team and graduate. Coach said I can probably get a football scholarship to college. Like a stepping stone to go pro."

"That's cool."

Eric looked around, admiring the mess. "Wreck the whole room and your mom'll be thrilled to ditch you, leave you behind with the garbage when they move. My folks are always bugging me about being a slob and threatening to disown me. Maybe you could get them disgusted with you."

"I emailed my mom a bullet list of all the advantages for me staying here."

"That was a nerdy thing to do. But I guess it makes sense."

Andy nodded. "Made a pie chart and four graphs showing the pros outweigh the cons by a significant margin."

"Wow." Eric gave a low whistle. "Did it impress her? It sure would me."

"She pointed out seven mistakes in my logic. My dad says it's okay with him if I stay with you, but he said she has to agree, and I have to be the one to convince her. I don't know what to do next."

Eric finished the pizza. "Try crying. It always works with my mom."

"Yeah, but your mom is normal." Andy sighed, stymied. "Try impressing a scientist with phony tears. I know my mom. If she can't see something, it doesn't even exist. Some things are just totally outside her radar range."

"That sucks. Need any help packing for Houston?"

"I won't give up until the moving van is at the door and the guys are loading up my fish tank."

"What about a hunger strike? Tell your folks that you refuse to eat until they agree you can live with me, but then come up here and drop a rope out the window with a tote bag or basket or something tied to it. Send me a text and I'll sneak food up to you. You can pay me later."

Andy considered the idea, but shook his head. "She'd expect me to lose weight on a hunger strike." Andy thought a moment longer. "There's got to be something that'll convince her to let me stay in L.A. She gets home tonight and I feel like I'm running out of time. I keep dreaming about clocks lately for some unknown weird reason.... Wait."

"Wassup?"

"She's a scientist, right? Scientists love facts. I need to show her she's got nothing to fear."

"How're you going to do that?"

"It's so obvious, I can't believe I didn't think of it sooner. I'll introduce her to your family, so she'll be reassured that I'll be well taken care of and have all kinds of rules to live by."

"Meet my family?" Eric looked at him, startled.

"I've seen your sister Cara around school and she seems nice enough. It's the perfect plan. A summer barbecue."

Eric frowned doubtfully. "You sure that's a good idea?"

"Why? What's wrong with your folks?

While buckling up, Jemma noticed the young girl beside her on the Boeing 767 was struggling to adjust her seat belt. "Here, let me help. First time flying?"

The twelve-year-old girl nodded. "Going to see my dad in Los Angeles for the rest of the summer."

"I'm going there, too. We'll change planes in Denver, so stick with me."

As Jemma reached for her phone to turn it off, a call came in from Andy. "Hi, honey," she said. "We just boarded so I can't talk long."

"Can I invite Eric's family for a barbecue?"

Smiling, suspecting this was a new strategy in his campaign to live with Eric, she replied, "Check with your dad and set it up, but it's okay with me."

"Uh, Mom? I thought me and Dad could keep on staying here and you'd keep commuting to NASA."

Jemma sighed softly, wishing he hadn't introduced this wrinkle into her otherwise straight path. "Do we really need to keep going over the same ground, honey? I've been commuting for over a year and I want you two with me so we can be a family again. You and Dad will join me in Houston right before school starts. Fran found us a house to rent and your room has a sliding door to the pool and lanai. Later on, we'll move back to L.A. We'll rent out our house in the meantime, so it'll be waiting for us. It's all very do-able."

"But Eric's parents said it's cool. Why are you so against it? You act like they're going to adopt me. I won't call her 'mom.' That's for you--I'll still call you Mom."

"You know I need to be closer to JSC and I want us all to be together, like always. Andy, listen, you're not breaking up this family."

"Then put it off till I'm in college. Only another year."

Jemma reflected that if she hadn't pushed the school administration to let him skip a grade, not just once but twice because of his high scholastic scores, it would be two years until high school graduation and his case would be weaker. She felt a spurt of annoyance. "I thought you wanted me to be an astronaut--"

The girl looked at Jemma with interest, eavesdropping openly.

"I never realized we'd have to move–" Andy began.

Jemma cut in, "We've been talking about it for a long time. You'll make new friends in Houston, honey. It'll be a great adventure."

"Would you listen to me, Mom? I'm doing senior year here. With the friends I already have. I'll stay at Eric's and get a job after school to pay for my food and stuff. I'll visit you and Dad on holidays. I worked it all out. It's totally do-able!"

One of the flight attendants made an announcement to turn off all electronic devices.

"I've got to hang up now, Andy. I'm really sorry you're not happy about this, but I think you'll adjust once we make the change. We'll talk about it more when I'm home. Transitions can be hard, but look at the opportunities, okay? See you when I get in. Love you."

"Yeah. Love you, too, Mom. Safe flight."

Jemma turned off her phone and put it away.

The girl next to Jemma asked shyly, "Are you really an astronaut?"

Jemma never tired of this question. "I'm in final training, but I'm not in the spaceflyer program yet."

"My mom said there won't be any more shuttles for a long time, maybe not ever. A guy I go to school with says he'll probably be able to finish college and apply by then."

"That's all true, but there are international teams now. Astronauts from different places like Canada, Japan and Europe all train at NASA. My expectation is that I will get a mission to space, somehow. And I find that you generally get what you expect out of life."

Jemma reached in her carryon bag and brought out a copy of a young adult book she'd written about the history of women in the space program. "Would you like this? I often speak at schools to promote careers in science. I think you'll enjoy the stories."

With an eager nod, the girl asked, "Sign it for me? My name's Savannah."

Taking out a pen, Jemma autographed the book. "What kinds of things are you interested in, Savannah?"

"I love to paint. My art teacher says I'm really good at landscapes. I want to be an artist, but my mom says it's not practical."

"I'm sure she's trying to spare you pain and disappointment—that's what parents do--but if painting is your heart's desire, don't let anyone talk you out of it. Don't quit. Find a way to do something every day toward your goal, and don't be discouraged by setbacks. Will you promise me to do that?"

"Yeah. Okay, I will."

"My email address is in the back of the book, and I hope you'll send me photos of your landscapes. I'd love to hear how you're doing, so be sure to write. Will you do that, too?"

Grinning, the girl nodded.

After Eric left, Andy played a game of poker on his laptop computer, and then wandered downstairs to practice piano in the living room.

He was learning the Beatles' song *Hello, Goodbye* but had trouble with one of the notes, always forgetting it was an F-sharp. When he hit the wrong key, it sounded a sour note.

He played it a few times, singing the lyrics and enjoying himself, even though he hit that wrong note each time. His mother always teased him about that note, and they both got a good laugh out of it, so he decided maybe he shouldn't try too hard to remember the F-sharp after all. He enjoyed making people smile.

When she got home from Houston, Jemma took gifts from her suitcase. For her blond husband Hart, she'd unearthed a collector's edition of a NASA coffee mug for his shelved collection of over a hundred mugs, many brought to him from her travels around the world to science and space conferences, and for Andy, a NASA insignia baseball cap.

"This is perfect for our trip to Arizona." Andy admired the cap in his hands.

She looked at Andy warily.

He groaned softly. "No way, Mom. No. You're not backing out."

"She's been invited to see a Russian launch behind the scenes." Hart squeezed Andy's arm affectionately. "We'll have some more guy time and do something cool."

"What 'guy time'? You're always busy at the bistro."

"We'll reschedule the trip to the reservation," Jemma said, watching Andy's face, hoping he'd understand.

"That means never."

She ruffled his hair. "I promise, honey."

Hart gave her a kiss and held up the mug as if in a toast. "Have a good flight back?"

She nodded, and hugged him with the fleeting thought: In years past, we would've sent Andy to bed early or over to a friend's to spend the night, and then reconnected our lives by eating Hart's famous chocolate mousse in bed and talking long into the night about everyday things and how much we appreciated each other. But now...?

Jemma had to admit that her life with Hart, who was chef and owner of a popular local bistro, was not all bad, although she sadly recognized that it was decaying. It would be unfair to characterize the marriage as a mistake. But when had it changed? When had they made the tacit agreement to stay together primarily for Andy's sake and not their own?

Even though it had never been a great passion, they'd created a loving home for their son, and an atmosphere of support for each other's dreams.

It had started with a drifting apart over the past year or two. They never discussed the emotional distance between them, both of them busy with their careers and perhaps both preferring the easiness of denial. It pained her that she was his silent partner in this conspiracy against their own marriage, and yet she felt helpless to do anything differently because she felt there was a wall of resistance coming from Hart.

For years, while Andy was growing up, Hart was a model husband and father, devoted to his family, faithful and loving. But when she began making more frequent and more prolonged trips to the Johnson Space Center in Houston, the dynamics of the marriage shifted like tectonic plates jostling beneath the sea and sliding past one another. She didn't think he was being unfaithful, but suspected that he was probably tempted often and might succumb one day soon.

Whenever her thoughts drifted toward divorce, Jemma quickly retreated from that option. She'd witnessed far too many broken families, including her younger sister Lulu's divorce, and was determined that Andy would not pay the price for her own failure. What was the point? There wasn't another man she'd rather be with, although she had a permanent reminder of her first love in the form of the tattoo on her left shoulder, a woman flying an open cockpit biplane.

Twenty-five years ago, she had gotten the tattoo on a friendly dare from her then-boyfriend Mike McLeod after earning her private pilot's license. Mike was her childhood sweetheart, the man she almost married the summer after they graduated from college.

She'd loved Mike deeply all through high school and undergraduate school, and had relished being around his creative energy, but she couldn't figure out how to be that space explorer she wanted to be, with her focus on her lodestar, and also cherish and nourish a marriage and family. Heartbroken, realizing the high price she was paying for her dream of space flight, she'd broken their engagement.

Firm in her resolve to avoid derailing her career goals, she'd moved on to more degrees and a more practical marriage to Hartley Powell. Hart made few demands of her time, and that suited her well. Was the problem that she no longer felt needed in his life? Or she in his? She couldn't put her finger on what had gone wrong with them. Where had that feeling of compatibility and congeniality gone to? And when? Had it been so gradual a slipping away, an easing down a gentle slope of neglect, that she only noticed it now as she saw a void in her life where her marriage should be?

She had told Fran her life was nearly perfect, but she knew that was an exaggeration. She'd lost her chance for bliss when she turned Mike away years ago and then refused to open his letters. Her sister Lulu later found out when Mike got married, and told Jemma about it, but Jemma made it clear that she did not want to be informed of Mike's doings. That stage of her life was over, and there was no reason to torture herself with regrets. Her life was complete. It was satisfactory. It was more than what most people had.

Andy.

NASA.

An amicable, decent marriage to Hart, who was creative, successful, attractive, kept himself fit and trim, and gave her no reason to complain. Her life was richly fulfilling without demanding "true love" as if it were her due.

"Hey, look what else I brought." Jemma pointed to an insulated soft cooler tote she'd hidden behind her suitcase. The tote was labeled with a caution that it contained perishables and dry ice. "Four pounds of the biggest Gulf shrimp I've ever seen."

"Let me see!" Andy began opening the cooler.

Jemma smiled at Andy's eagerness. "Careful, honey. The dry ice is so cold, it'll burn you."

"The dinner menu just changed." Hart grinned. "I'll get right to work on butterflying them for the grill. I hope you're both hungry."

"Always." Andy laughed. "I'm still growing, you know."

"I ate a sandwich on the plane." Jemma looked at Hart, "but I won't say no to a salad, and a bite of your shrimp. If you'll share."

Hart's protest was automatic. "What are you talking about? I always share."

"At least you didn't say you'll be in your study doing paperwork." Andy looked at his mom hopefully. "So maybe that means we can all watch a movie together later?"

"Great idea. Pick out a DVD if there's nothing good on the recorder we haven't seen."

Hart looked at her quietly. "Maybe someday we'll actually have an entire meal together, start to finish?"

Seeing the wary wistfulness in his eyes and feeling the disconnect between them, she wondered whether it would be wrong to give him false hope, or if making an intention would actually lead them toward a firmer path in their marriage.

They both enjoyed their comfortable suburban life. They had a small circle of friends, other couples or singles they occasionally socialized with, although that part of the family calendar had been growing more and more barren as Hart was busy with his bistro and an idea for a television cooking show, and Jemma was, of course, snowed under with duties related to NASA.

Was Hart's request to eat dinner together unreasonable? Was there subtext beneath his simple comment that she should be trying to understand?

She was unsure of herself in this arena, and felt awkward about what to say to jumpstart their stalled relationship. A new habit of eating dinner together? "Yeah, maybe so...well, sure, why not? Of course we will!"

She bent over her suitcase and zipped it closed to take it upstairs.

Hart opened his mouth as if to say something more, but instead picked up the insulated cooler and strode toward the kitchen, whistling tunelessly.

Jemma straightened.

Andy plopped the NASA cap on his head backwards, gave Jemma a comic salute and shouted in a goofy imitation of Barney Fife, "My mom, the astronaut!"

With mock severity, she straightened the cap. "Don't you dare jinx it, young man. I plan to be on a space flight no matter what country I have to launch from. And nothing's going to stop me."

Chapter 2

The Hollywood Reservoir–known to locals as Lake Hollywood–lies nestled beneath the shadow of the famed Hollywood sign. The wide path around the water is closed to vehicles but popular with pedestrians, bicyclists and joggers.

Finishing his third lap, Mike McLeod slowed his run to a walk and stopped to drink from a bottle of spring water. Tall, dark-haired and lanky, his stance revealed an inner confidence and strength while the laugh lines around his slate-blue eyes spoke of his quick wit and good humor.

A troop of fourth-grade Girl Scouts approached on bicycles, chaperoned by several mothers. One of the women spotted Mike, and called to her daughter in a low tone, "Quick, Lauren, camera-ready! I read in the trades he's casting a new movie."

The little girl struck a pose, tossed her long brown hair back over one shoulder and smiled brightly, ready.

At a signal from the intrepid stage mother, the troop waylaid Mike as he tried to jog around them.

Lauren called out as if in surprise, "Oh, hi, Mr. McLeod! Remember me? Lauren Selkin. I auditioned for you last summer."

He smiled a bit warily. His time spent running around the reservoir was one of the few slots on his calendar he carved out to be alone and recharge from the demands of his career as a writer/director of indie films. "Hey there, ladies. Not casting any kids right now, Lauren, but I'll keep you in mind the next time. Beautiful day for a bike ride. I'll let you get back to it."

The stage mom pulled out her phone to take a picture and gestured for Lauren to get next to Mike. "You mind?" she asked Mike. "It's for her website."

"If you think my name will help you any." Mike amiably posed for the picture and then, with the ease of practice, detached himself from their eager questions about his new movie and broke into a run.

"He's so nice," Lauren said to the other girls, watching as he slowed to a jog. "I'd love to work with him."

Mike smiled to himself, wondering if she'd meant for him to overhear or was paying a sincere compliment. He'd learned early on in Hollywood to be wary of compliments and praise, and rely instead on his own inner compass and work ethic.

Not waiting for Mike to be out of earshot, the stage mother told the other moms, "He had a messy divorce a year ago. No surprise after he married another pea-brained *fashionista* so obviously not his type. Must've been lonely, or maybe delusional. Married three times. Hasn't found the right one yet. If I weren't married already, I'd seduce him. Then he'd have to give Lauren a part, even if he had to write it into the script for her."

Laughing, the women herded the wandering girls and continued their bike ride.

Mike was relieved to see the scouts turn and head back the other direction. He had seen two mini-vans on his arrival, and no doubt they were ready to get on to their next badge-earning activity.

At the bridge, he stopped to watch a blue heron. His running shoe kicked a pebble into the reservoir, startling the bird into flight.

Its movement rippled the water.

That afternoon, Mike met on a studio lot with Simon Tarzyn, producer of the screenplay Mike had written and would direct, and with their casting director, Penny Sheridan.

Since they wanted to fill the role of Cerise, the female lead in "Seven Funerals," the table was littered with headshots of actresses in their early- to mid-twenties, some well-known, others still hoping to get their big break.

Mike studied Marybeth Lacroix's headshot. She had long blonde hair and green eyes. "Very pretty. Something about her eyes that I like. That rare juxtaposition of strength and vulnerability that's perfect for Cerise. What's she done?"

Penny consulted her notes. "Not much, to be honest. She was in a low budget indie earlier this year. But you're right, she has a great look. Those eyes of hers are really compelling. Feels like she could look right through you and see something in your heart you didn't know was there. Put her in the possibilities stack?"

He tossed Marybeth's headsot in the short stack with a few others he thought had potential. "I'm invariably disappointed to meet the girl and find out that dewy-eyed look was from eye drops."

"You're turning into a cynic," Simon teased. "Watch out or you'll lose your own dewy-eyed innocence."

Mike laughed. "Never happen. I'm too much of an optimist."

Penny watched Mike's reaction as he pushed the final batch of photos aside, rejecting all of them. "Hold on before you make a hasty decision, Mike. Meet with a few of these actors. I'll put it together for next week."

"Okay, Penny." Mike got up. "Sorry to be so picky, but Cerise is in every scene. I need someone brave enough to carry the whole film on her back without wilting."

Mike's assistant, Rodney, a young black man, came in with bottles of water and passed them around. On a nod from Mike, he helped Penny gather the headshots into two piles, one considerably larger than the other.

She packed her briefcase and speed-dialed a talent agent on her cell as she left.

Mike tilted his head and drank from a bottle of water.

Marybeth woke with a deep sense of loss. She felt it in her throat first, as if a long cool drink of water would soothe her soul.

Marybeth Lacroix Garner, an actress aged twenty-three, felt a deep yearning to have a friend, not to replace her cousin Naomi, but to do some of the same things with. A friend she could call to go shopping together on the spur of the moment, to go see a romantic comedy or grab a to-go salad for lunch and eat it at the park. Someone special to chat with and hang out with like she had with Naomi most of her life.

Naomi's sudden death had left a void, and until this moment Marybeth had not even thought of attempting to fill it.

They'd been such compatible souls in every way, but surely there might be some other person she could feel close to, someone to create something good, something fine, something wonderful with? A seeming accident of birth into the same family had brought her and Naomi together as children, but that didn't mean she couldn't find someone new, did it? Not a substitute for Naomi, not someone to fill that void, but someone worthy in her own right of sharing a special reciprocity of affection.

She found herself wondering if the time was finally right to reach out and develop a new friendship with a woman her own age, someone who would have the same reference points she did with the TV shows they'd watched growing up, the shared dreams and hopes of someone who had already discovered that turning twenty-one was not the magical event that a teenager thought. You *didn't* suddenly have all the answers about life, and know exactly what your purpose was and what you should be doing.

She knew her husband would object to a friendship because it would take her attention and energy away from him. Cabot told her often, as if hammering home the point because otherwise she'd forget it, that they had an idyllic, exclusive marriage, and didn't need anyone else cluttering up their lives.

But Marybeth's therapist had told her Cabot was wrong, and no one should expect a spouse to fill every need. On this point, unlike most others, she agreed with the therapist.

He'd also said, having evaluated Cabot during their one and only joint therapy session, "Your husband is a narcissist. He'll never be able to give you the love you are looking for. He sees you as the great teat in the sky that will give him everything--the way a mother tends her baby's every need. So, Marybeth, what are you going to do with this information? What are you going to do about your marriage?"

She didn't have an answer then, and still didn't, but in the meantime she'd learned more about narcissism. She'd thought it meant ordinary vanity, which Cabot certainly exhibited, preening and strutting like a peacock every time they were in public. It turned out to be a personality disorder that could range from mild to severe. Cabot made everything all about him, and his bloated ego was exhausting to live with.

Now, standing in line at a sandwich shop, looked nervously at her watch, Marybeth realized she'd been gone too long already. It had probably been a mistake, she decided, to spend so long picking out the sleeping bag, but she felt good about it anyway.

No regrets!

She glanced around at other customers, disappointed there were no women her age. On the heels of her decision to have a new friend in her life, a secret fantasy was born that one day she'd simply look up and her brand new best friend would be there, waiting to fall in step and continue this journey side-by-side.

"Take your order?" The teen girl behind the counter yawned.

"Yes, thank you." Even though she already knew what she wanted, Marybeth glanced up at the menu board. It was easier than looking strangers in the eye. "I'd like a plain green salad to go, with diet Italian. And in a separate bag would you put a foot-long sub with everything, two bags of chips and a couple of those big sugar cookies? Oh, and also two cartons of milk."

The girl nodded and began putting the order together.

Marybeth paid with cash, so there'd be no record of her purchase, and put her change in the tip jar.

Grabbing the two bags, she hurried to her car. She put the salad and her purse on the front seat then locked the car and stood in the parking lot, turning in place as she searched the area. After a few moments, she saw him: a homeless man nudging a shopping cart loaded with his shabby possessions toward the sidewalk.

Marybeth opened her car trunk, grabbed a large plastic bag from Bed, Bath and Beyond and hurried to the man. "Excuse me?"

He turned, and his face broke into a grin. "My angel! I thought you forgot about me."

She thrust out the large bag. "I got you a sleeping bag to replace the one you said the other guys stole from you. You can put the plastic shopping bag on the ground under it, like a tarp, to keep you dry. And here's something to eat." She gave him the heavy lunch bag.

He peered in it. "Subs! Chips! Cookies! And fresh milk! God bless you, my angel."

Shaking her head to deflect his thanks, feeling it was a small thing to do for someone in such need, she hurried shyly to her car and drove away, only looking in the rearview mirror briefly to see the man open up the big bag and examine his new sleeping bag.

Glancing nervously at the car clock every few minutes, knowing she was late, Marybeth drove home and parked her white convertible in the driveway. As she got out with her salad, she heard hammering from the backyard and knew it was safe to sneak in the house through the garage.

She hurried into the kitchen and ate her lunch over the sink while watching her husband covertly from the window.

In the backyard, Cabot staked plants heavy with green tomatoes in the new bed he'd prepped for herbs and vegetables. He was middle-aged, of medium height and medium weight with a paunch he tried to disguise by tucking in his shirt and then blousing it over his belt, even when wearing jeans or shorts, as he was today. Marybeth decided with a suppressed giggle that he made up for being medium in looks and personality by strutting a size XXXL ego.

In the center of the yard, water in an old pond was stagnant. Nearby, the stone birdbath was empty and stained. A black and white Phoebe land hopefully on the rim of the birdbath, but then flew off.

Neatly stacked bags of mulch, flats of bold yellow and orange perennials, paper bags bulging with flower bulbs all spoke of plans to restore the unkempt yard to beauty. Pairs of shovels, small spades and bulb dibblers gleamed in two rows, shown to her by Cabot with the enticing declaration that they would garden together.

Marybeth hadn't joined him yet, not even to plan which flower should go where. Her thoughts rose to the defensive: *I try to care, but I just can't!*

She glared at the oversized cartons that had been delivered yesterday and were waiting by the pond. They contained a white garden gazebo and patio furniture she didn't want.

Cabot would have to hire day laborers to help him assemble it all. She wasn't going to do it, she wasn't going to be his little helper.

She decided to be firm on that point.

In the master bathroom Marybeth brushed her teeth, then filled the marble sink with cool water. She bent her head to splash her face, creating ripples in the basin.

Behind her on the dressing room wall, reflected in the wide mirror over the sink, was a collage of her wedding photos from two years ago. Other than one or two shots of the bridal couple, the collage featured herself and her maid of honor--her cousin Naomi, a college student at the time. These were the last photos the girls took together, their bond cut short by tragedy.

She stared at a smiling picture of Naomi while water trickled down her cheeks.

Determined to follow her therapist's advice... *Don't look back, Marybeth! Look forward!* ... she dried her face, put on fresh makeup and opened her agenda book, as if a new entry might have found its way there via spirit writing.

She studiously checked off the morning's completed events and activities, including the one marked for her therapist appointment even though she hadn't gone. Each thirty-minute period of the day held an entry. Her therapist had suggested what he called a "Controlled Task System," saying if she got organized, she'd avoid bouts of melancholy. So far, she did not feel any difference but remained hopeful that the meticulous system the man had invented and was so proud of would work if she kept at it.

Another glance at the wall clock. Twenty minutes before she needed to leave for an audition. She wiped down the sink and counter, erasing all traces of her presence.

In her side of the master closet, Marybeth dug beneath an artfully draped pile of lingerie and blouses in a round wicker laundry basket. It was a safe hiding place because Cabot would never deign to touch her soiled clothes.

She unearthed a glossy shopping bag and removed a bright tropical print dress. Using the only sharp thing she could find--Cabot's nail clippers--she snipped the dress's label and price tag then tucked that evidence of newness in her purse to dispose of later in a public trash bin.

No sense stirring the viper's nest by confessing she'd gone shopping Monday when she was supposedly at her therapist's, the same way she'd supposedly been at her therapist appointment just now.

It'd been over a month since she'd bothered making an appointment, but twice a week she dutifully told Cabot she was leaving the house for her grief therapy session.

Instead, she went shopping, buying clothes for her auditions, careful to watch the time. But then one day she'd noticed a homeless man eating from a trash bin and so she began buying lunch for him, and giving money to other homeless people she became aware of.

Upon returning home each time, however, she said nothing of these new adventures and instead reported to Cabot that the therapist said she was making excellent progress.

He'd nod then ask if she'd remembered to stop for half-and-half on the way home.

Behind her, the master bedroom suite was still cluttered with moving boxes she had not finished unpacking although they'd been living here for five weeks. The threadbare carpet was so filthy they wore slippers or shoes even for a bathroom trip in the middle of the night. Stained draperies in a hideous teal sagged at the windows.

Cabot said for her to choose what color the walls should be. She'd managed to get to the paint store after Cabot's nagging became unbearable, and then smeared swatches of various colors on one wall. Green, cream, blue and taupe.

She was no closer to a decision today. Thinking about the work needed to decorate each room exhausted her.

In all these matters related to the house and to her state of mental health, Cabot, nearing forty with a Damoclesian sword of middle age looming over him, forced his relentless patience upon her, heavy as cold syrup and as unwelcome.

Each time she caught him looking at her, he burdened her with the guilt of his long sad face.

According to Cabot, they had bought the house to be her special project, to occupy the hours of her days with something meaningful. Each night at dinner he presented her with an anecdotal reminder of how much she'd enjoyed decorating their old apartment, as if the Reader's Digest-style stories were daisies that would surely perk up her spirits.

One day, about two months ago, in a flash of insight, she'd blurted to her therapist that Cabot couldn't comprehend that the bright sunny girl he'd married had fallen into an abyss. His cheery coaxing wasn't strong enough to draw her out. Might as well try to climb up a length of dental floss when an industrial steel cable was needed.

She knew Cabot was frustrated by her detachment, but she couldn't share his determination to try again to create a family.

This place was no more home to Marybeth than a hotel. Theirs was the smallest house at the end of a cul-de-sac in an upscale hillside area in the San Fernando Valley area of Los Angeles, one they couldn't have afforded if the house had been in better shape when they'd made an offer on it.

In need of paint, repairs and landscaping, the house was a single story wood frame that had long been the neighborhood eyesore. After a string of careless owners failed in basic maintenance, the most recent had bought it as an investment and over the years didn't bother to repair damage done by serial tenants.

When the realtor showed it to them and explained the reason for the reduced price, Marybeth took one look and blurted that the house was bad luck.

Cabot ignored her comment and said the house had tremendous potential.

Listlessly, she'd signed the escrow papers and promised to help restore the house to its rightful place in this desirable West Hills neighborhood where Cabot said the schools were good.

And where Jemma, Hart and Andy Powell also lived, although Marybeth had never met them and did not yet know their names.

Suddenly aware of time passing, Marybeth slipped her feet into red pumps and brushed her long straight blonde hair again. She eyed herself critically in the mirror, then applied a brighter red lipstick.

She turned to go, and gave a small start to see Cabot in the doorway, his denim work-shirt darkened by sweat.

A live green parrot perched on his shoulder.

He fed the bird a sunflower seed from his pocket. To his pet, he said, "Look who decided to join us. My own precious bird of paradise." He looked at Marybeth. "How was your session? Seemed like you were gone longer than usual today."

"I just had a few errands–" she began, angry at herself for wobbling in the face of his stern look.

To the parrot, he commented, "Maybe I should clip her wings. Keep her home with us. "

Moving to the bedroom, he rummaged in a top bureau drawer filled with her collection of wide cuff bracelets, holding up one after another, slowly appraising each before tossing it back. "Going somewhere fancy?" he asked, as if needing to know which style would be more appropriate.

"An audition." She worried that her tone was too sharp. Nervous to deflect his questions, she rattled on, "They're doing a remake of *Kitty Foyle*. It's an old movie that starred Ginger Rogers. A drama. It's a great new script, or at least the pages I have are. And I've been rehearsing it while I unpacked our wedding china and crystal into the china cabinet. You'll be proud of me if I get this part, Cabot. It's a big one."

"But I thought you were going to start on the guest room today so Yolanda and Tom can stay with you when I go to Cleveland. It needs wallpaper. The crown molding needs paint. So do the window frames and closet doors."

"This audition is on the kitchen calendar." She tried to keep tears from welling up and spoiling her makeup. "I told you about it over a week ago. Dear. And I don't need a babysitter," she added in a low tone, muting her defiance but taking a stand nonetheless.

Cabot had been a million miles away from her thoughts while she was dressing.

Too bad he couldn't stay there!

He must have sensed that she was ignoring him. Her very lack of thinking about him had drawn him in like a homing pigeon, him with that parrot that unnerved her with its sudden squawking when she didn't realize it was near. Usually, Marybeth loved all birds and animals, but something about Cabot's parrot made her feel uneasy. Even though she knew it wasn't possible, it was hard to shake off the fantasy that the talking bird was spying on her every day and would later be whispering about her in Cabot's ear.

When Cabot saw her dart a glance uneasily at her agenda book and then at the clock, his movements slowed to a maddening crawl. She caught the tiny smirk on his face as he picked a shiny red cuff to match the ginger flowers on her dress, and then hunted slowly in the drawer for its mate.

"Another of your little subterfuges, Marybeth?"

"Wh—what do you mean?"

She spotted the mate right away–it was the only bright red bracelet in the entire drawer--but restrained her fingers from grabbing it to end this madness. Such an action would only prompt him to decide against the red and start a new search.

He glanced at her, frowning. "I don't remember that dress. "

Her mouth went dry.

"You love drama so much," he said. "You imagine villains lurking in every shadow. I'm not your enemy, Marybeth. I'm your husband. Have you been out shopping without me? You know I like to go with you and have you model the outfits before you pick anything."

She was afraid that if she admitted going shopping she would find herself confessing that she'd been giving away most of the money allotted for therapy to homeless people she encountered in the Valley. There was such a huge homeless population in L.A. and she found it incomprehensible that she'd never noticed them before. True, she'd only lived in Los Angeles for two years, since marrying Cabot, but it shamed her that she had been focused on her own troubles to the exclusion of others' woes.

"Yolanda found it at a garage sale for me," she lied. "It, uh, had a stain on the front but I got it out."

"Your cousin is a resourceful woman. Nice of her to mail it. I didn't know you'd gotten a package, Marybeth." Cabot found the red bracelet, removed the silver filigree cuffs she was wearing and tossed them aside on the bed even though her jewelry drawer was open in front of him. "I wish you'd stop going to these things, Marybeth."

His dulcet tone grated her nerves, but she said nothing.

"You know it'll just upset you," he added gently.

She lifted her chin. "My therapist thinks it'd be good for me to find work again."

Actually, the avuncular therapist had warned her to give up acting since the strain of rejection was overwhelming her delicate mind.

That was the day she'd decided never to return. On her next scheduled appointment, she'd gunned the engine and sailed past his office building–giddy and laughing out loud--and drove on to the mall. To reward her uncommon bravery, she bought a lace jacket with the funds earmarked for the therapy session, and sublimely-impractical gold strappy evening heels with money intended for the guest room wallpaper. She hadn't worn either the shoes or the lace jacket, but they waited patiently, mutely, sweetly, hidden in the closet at the very bottom of a carton filled with her winter-weight sweaters and scarves.

Since then, instead of buying more cosmetics, dresses and shoes for herself, most of her purchases were warm blankets and anoraks she distributed one by one to homeless women and men.

She discovered that most of the homeless people she encountered trolling the shopping centers and strip malls didn't want a handout, and would not take money or food directly from her. They would claim they didn't need it, and then wander away, sometimes shouting gibberish.

She was undeterred. Now that she'd recognized the homeless problem, she was determined to do her small part. She'd taken to creating care packages and sometimes slipped twenty dollar bills into a fast food bag or between the pages of the Bibles she bought and passed out, hoping to bring comfort to these lost souls. She usually set down the package in their vicinity then left, allowing them privacy to open her gifts.

Cabot snapped the red cuffs over the scars on her wrists, those hostile reminders of her two suicide attempts.

The abrupt noise sliced her thoughts like weeds in the garden. She stared at him.

Cabot smiled. "That boy you were living with before didn't know what to do the first time, did he?"

"We were both in shock. Robbie loved Naomi, too. "

His chuckle insinuated an unsavory element.

She flushed, hating his ongoing taunts that Robbie had cheated on her with her best friend and cousin. "It wasn't like that!"

"You're so gullible, Marybeth." He tucked a lock of hair behind her ear, judged the result, then flicked it back the way she'd combed it. "Can I tell you something without you getting all upset?"

"Yes." She braced herself, her mind awhirl with possibilities of what he might say, none of them pleasant.

"I don't feel appreciated lately," he said. "After all I've done."

"Oh! Of course I'm grateful. Dear. I...."

She yearned to finally blurt her true thoughts: *I can't breathe! You diminish everything I believe in, and berate me like a child when no one is around to bear witness. You fool everyone by pretending to care so much. I hate it that you work at home now so you can watch me night and day. I feel like I'm in prison. And you are my jailer.*

She was stressed from living on edge all the time, vigilantly awaiting the next outburst of Cabot's cool, rational anger. The effect of his tantrums and rants lingered long after a black eye or broken arm would have healed. Most

34

confusing of all was that she knew he loved her—he told her so, frequently--and he'd never acted this way during his whirlwind courtship that led to a wedding only weeks after they'd met.

Since she felt it must be something she was doing wrong, Marybeth tried even harder to make the marriage work. Out loud she said, with rehearsed earnestness, "I really appreciate everything you do for me, Cabot. You've been very generous and understanding."

"I'm a better husband than Robbie would've been."

"Yes indeed." She nodded firmly. "And I'm a very lucky girl."

After waiting an hour with other hopeful actresses, Marybeth auditioned for the lead role of *Kitty Foyle*. During the reading, Marybeth brought her own sensibilities to the complex role of a low-class working girl in love with a socialite. She felt proud of her portrayal and confident she'd done a beautiful job.

The director leaned toward her assistant. "Another Ginger Rogers copycat!"

Marybeth overheard the damning comment. She knew it was both unfair and untrue, but there was nothing she could do. The director's word was law. After she was officially told *No thank you*, she flashed a big bright fake smile, thanked everyone for their time and walked out with her head held high, her shoulders aching with stiffness.

In her convertible, Marybeth slumped against the driver's seat and fought back tears. She scolded herself for proving the therapist right: She couldn't handle rejection. Her biggest dream was to be a successful actress. While taking a class at the actors' studio or rehearsing lines at home, she got to be someone else. Acting was the escape route out of her own skin and into another woman's life where the script told her exactly how things would turn out in the end.

She could leave behind her own memories as if they belonged to some other person she had ceased to be, starting with Naomi's death early last year and compounded by that additional heartbreaking loss last fall.

Acting made her feel alive.

She couldn't give it up.

I won't quit!

Feeling more resolute, she started the car and steered toward home. Shaken by the audition, replaying the scene again and again in her thoughts, she fretted over how she could've been more perfect in the reading. She dreaded having to tell Cabot she'd failed, just as he'd predicted.

Up ahead, the traffic signal turned yellow. Marybeth zoomed through the intersection as the light went red, barely hearing the impatient honk of a driver who had started to cross on the green.

Eight months earlier, Marybeth had been given a part in a low-budget film that was shot locally. It didn't pay much, but she knew the credit would help her get noticed. Cabot told her she was foolish to accept a part that wasn't bigger, but for once she didn't let his disapproval sway her decision. In fact, her main worry during the ten-day shoot was that she might get a scolding from the makeup artist about the circles under her eyes.

"Been out drinking, eh?" the man asked the first time she came in looking hung-over, but truly from lack of sleep and the nightmares about events related to her two suicide attempts.

When she protested weakly, not wanting to confide in him, he got out a pot of under-eye concealer to match her fair skin tone. "Better take it easy. The camera won't be fooled if you keep on partying."

"I hardly ever go out, and I don't drink anything stronger than green tea." She paused, then admitted, "I–I have a hard time sleeping." There was something in her voice that rang true.

He took a bottle from his canvas tote bag and shook out a few pills into the palm of her hand. "One. With a full glass of water and only when you have seven or eight hours available for sleep. They're pretty strong. I don't want you driving to set half-groggy."

A small voice in Marybeth's head warned her to refuse the pills, or at the very least, if she felt compelled to be polite, to take the pills but then discard them at the first opportunity. But all Marybeth could think of as she looked at the small white pills was that here was the promise of a good night's rest. The thought of sleeping without waking up in a sweat almost made her whimper out loud with hope and longing. *What can it hurt? It's not like he's giving me an entire bottle of something illegal!* They were prescription tablets to help people who had trouble falling asleep or staying asleep.

She told herself it didn't mean she was now a druggie or that the makeup artist was a pusher. He was just being friendly and helpful, and she was being practical. She had to sleep, after all, especially to please the camera. With these thoughts encouraging her, she smiled her thanks and tucked the pills into a small mirrored lipstick holder in her bag.

Later, after she'd discovered the pills actually worked, she went online and ordered one prescription after another from various pharmacy sites that only required you to fill out a form stating your health history and why you wanted the prescription. Each time she paid extra for the online medical consultation that was in lieu of faxing a prescription from her own physician.

She didn't feel guilty lying on the form and claiming she needed the prescription in a rush because she was going on a cruise with her husband who snored so loudly she would not be able to sleep in their small cabin. It didn't feel like a lie, because Cabot talked often about going on a cruise someday, although he never took an action toward actually booking such a vacation for them. And he did snore, like a chainsaw. So she wasn't actually lying, just shifting time a bit when she mentioned the cruise.

Over the next few months, fear of sleeplessness grabbed hold of her in such a way that she only let out a breath of relief when she had squirreled away seven bottles of the pills inside an old purse on the top shelf of her closet. She didn't use the sleep aid often. The real relief came from knowing those pills were there in case of emergency, like a security blanket.

A nagging voice within kept telling her the sleeping tablets were a slippery issue for someone with her history of suicide attempts, but she ignored the warning and told herself she had the right to a good night's rest, and that was all she had in mind.

Now, as it approached one o'clock in the morning and Marybeth was still awake, she took a long hard look at Cabot to be sure he was sound asleep. Even though his snoring might indicate he was in the deepest stage of sleep, she knew from experience that he could startle awake at the slightest disruption. It was as if he had an internal radar, always turned on, always tracking her every movement.

She slipped out of bed, tiptoed across the bedroom and into the closet, silently got out the old purse and reached in blindly for one of the bottles, easing it out so the pills wouldn't rattle and alert Cabot. Standing in the dark, hesitating, she remembered the promise she'd made to herself that she wouldn't use these again. *I should get rid of temptation!* she thought desperately, but fear of not having help available when she needed it prompted her to put the bottle back, zip the purse and tuck it away again.

She padded back to bed, knowing her feet were dirty from the filthy carpet, but feeling that was the least of her worries. She lay awake all night, staring at the curtained window, her mind wildly alert like a spinning top, although her body craved sleep. All the while, she felt oppressed by the stuffy air as if someone was holding a thick gray blanket over her nose and mouth.

Marybeth longed to leap up and throw the window open, but knew that would annoy Cabot, who preferred running the air conditioner all night.

Her restless thoughts finally wore themselves out like little children playing too hard. Her eyelids drooped drowsily just as the room began to lighten from the rising sun, and she drifted into a heavy, unrefreshing sleep.

Chapter 3

Dressed in shorts and a white NASA t-shirt for a tennis lesson, Andy thundered down the stairs past a photo gallery in the stairwell. In family pictures, he was inevitably posed between his parents—as if he was the linchpin holding them together.

While loping toward the kitchen, he thumbed through a catalog, admiring a green lava lamp he had just circled while browsing it in his room. Leaving the catalog folded open to that page, he shoved it in his backpack.

Joining his parents at the kitchen table for breakfast, Andy took his usual seat between them.

They smiled and perked up, as if the sun had just come out on an overcast day.

"Saw something in a catalog I'd like for my birthday," he announced, pouring a bowl of homemade granola.

Jemma winked at Hart, thinking of the new golf clubs and bag that Hart had bought the day before and hidden in the garage. Andy didn't play golf, but had said he'd like to learn.

"Put it on your wish list, honey," Jemma said.

Hart chuckled. "Long as it's not a new Ferrari to match that poster in your room!"

Joining in the laughter, Jemma was reminded once again of why she stayed, why it was worth it to her general sense of well-being to keep this family intact.

She returned to the front page news, and Hart finished the crossword puzzle. Andy ate while scanning the sports section.

A car honked out front.

"That's Eric." Andy got up and grabbed his backpack.

"Have a good time, honey." Jemma tilted her head up for her son's customary kiss-on-the-cheek-before-leaving.

"Don't forget Eric's family's coming for the barbecue at five," Andy said.

"We're good to go," Hart said. "Menu is planned, shopped for and prepped."

Jemma shook her head, quietly amused at how the two were doing a clever end run around her. She had agreed to be open-minded about Andy's plea to finish at El Camino instead of transferring to Houston for senior year...but she didn't expect meeting Eric's parents would be enough to convince her to change her decision.

In the driveway, Andy climbed in the back seat of Eric's clunker and greeted Eric and three other guys. All of them would be seniors when school resumed, and Andy felt privileged to be included in their elite group.

He already felt the aura of "cool-ness" draped around his shoulders like a king's cape of jewel-encrusted velvet.

Eric zipped out of the driveway while telling an off-color joke he'd seen in his email that morning.

Andy saw a car coming. "Look out!"

Eric braked, and all the boys laughed in relief at the near miss.

Late that afternoon, Eric and his family poured out of a dusty sport wagon at the curb, bearing foil-covered casseroles. Fast food litter spilled out of the doors with them.

Andy hurried out of the house to greet them, saw the mess at the curb, picked it up and tossed it on the floor of the back seat.

"Sorry we're late," Eric said. He indicated his younger sister, age fifteen. "Cara kept changing her outfit and doing her hair different ways."

Cara socked his arm and hissed, "Don't tell him that!" She beamed at Andy. "Hey there, Andy. Thanks for inviting me. It's really so wonderful to see you."

He shrugged, clueless what her gushing meant. "Yeah, sure. No big deal."

The family consisted of the parents and three kids. Peter, ten years old, wore swim trunks, snorkel and fins, and carried a battered ice hockey stick. He raised the stick in the air. "Greetings, earthlings!" Chattering in an improvised alien language, he stalked around them, brandishing the stick.

Jemma came out the front door and lifted a hand in greeting. She wore slacks and sandals, and appeared to be a typical suburban mom, welcoming guests for a casual party.

Eric's mom, Sylvia, was overdressed for the barbecue, in a cocktail dress and stilettos. Her balding husband, Stanley, in rumpled shorts and a Hawaiian shirt, looked like he had just gotten up from a nap.

"I'm Andy's mother," Jemma said.

"I guessed that," Stanley said, chuckling as they shook hands.

"Won't you come in? My husband is already on the patio, cooking. We can have cold drinks out there."

"Say, my feet are killing me in these torture heels." Sylvia kicked off her shoes and tossed them in the car, going barefooted.

"Our boys have become such good friends lately," Jemma said, leading them toward the house, "it's time we all got to know each other better."

Andy sent her a pleading look, *Go easy on them!*

She returned a reassuring wink.

Peter whacked the shrubbery with his hockey stick. "Die, Klingons! Die, Romulans, die!"

Jemma tried to get his parents' attention but they swept into the house and followed Andy and Cara towards the kitchen.

Jemma called out to the boy, "Time to eat. Come inside."

He put the snorkel tube in his mouth and shuffled toward her. The flippers on his feet slapped the ground with each step. He breathed heavily and made experimental noises with the snorkel tube, all the while banging the hockey stick against everything in his path.

She snatched the stick and put it inside the house, in the foyer's brass umbrella stand.

He reached for the stick but she stopped him.

"It'll be safe here," she said firmly. "You can pick it up on the way out later."

As they walked through the foyer to the kitchen, Peter stopped at a portrait of a younger Andy with his arm around a Golden Retriever. He peered at the portrait through his snorkel mask, then took the breathing tube out of his mouth. "Eric didn't say you got a dog."

"My sister--Andy's Aunt Lulu--painted that for us about four years ago. We lost Joker last year."

"Didn't you try to find him?"

"I mean that he died, Peter. He got sick and couldn't keep on living. Joker was the best dog ever and we all still miss him a lot."

"How come you don't get another dog?"

"Maybe we will someday, but Joker's a hard act to follow. Do you have any pets?"

"Just a lizard. His name is Fred."

In the kitchen, Hart hurried to take the casseroles as Sylvia and Stanley stood hesitating by the gourmet cooking island.

Since the teens wore swimsuits under their shorts and t-shirts, they shed their outer garments and hurried out by the pool.

"Your wife said don't bring anything," Sylvia said to Hart, "but in my humble opinion it's not a barbecue without my secret ingredient cole slaw, and my special green beans with fried onion rings. I'll share my recipes if you want."

"Wonderful," Hart said, as always diplomatic.

Outside, as they finished eating a gourmet mixed grill at the umbrella-covered patio table, Jemma noticed that Cara shyly watched every move Andy made. She wondered if her son had any idea that the girl nursed an aching crush for him. From Andy's reaction, it was apparent he only saw Cara as his buddy's sister.

Well, Jemma thought idly, *all that will change in time--but there's no hurry.*

She knew the point of this get-together was to sway her opinion about Andy's living with Eric's family when school started, but even if Sylvia and Stanley scored a perfect ten on her checklist, she still wanted Andy in Houston so they could see each other more often.

Hart brought out a dessert tray and placed it next to the centerpiece of flowers and a sand castle ornament Andy had made as a child. There was a large bowl of assorted berries and a fresh lemon tart. "Help yourselves while I get the coffee."

"It looks awful fancy," Sydney said.

"*Tarte au Citron,*" Hart said.

Carla spoke up shyly, "That means lemon pie, doesn't it?"

Hart nodded. "But it sounds fancier in French."

She pointed to the fruit. "Strawberry is *fraise.* Did I say it right? I'm taking French next year and I want to get a head start."

Hart helped her with the pronunciation, and then named the other berries in French. Pointing to a separate dish of ripe red cherries, he said, "And cherry is *cerise.*" Pointing to a bowl of what looked like whipped cream, he added, "The *crème fraîche* is for dipping the strawberries and blackberries." With a smile, he left to get the coffee tray.

"Yum," Sylvia said while chewing a slice of the French tarte. "This is totally awesome." When Hart returned with the coffee, Sylvia appraised Jemma. "I need to take a page from your book, as they say, learn how to train my hubby to do all the work."

Jemma blinked. "Hart volunteers." As the idle conversation about desserts continued around her, Jemma recalled the first time she met Hart....

After breaking up with Mike upon graduating in Arizona, Jemma had moved to Los Angeles and earned her master's degree at UCLA as intended. She was in the midst of her Ph.D. studies when she attended a party hosted by her biochemistry professor.

As she crossed the crowded room to the buffet table, she noticed a man staring at her in fascination.

Blond, stocky and boyishly-goodlooking, the man was standing behind the table with the catering staff. He wore a chef hat and his name, she found out, was Hartley Powell.

Hart soon introduced Jemma to his world of sensual pleasures and epicurean delights. Satin sheets, massage oil, candle-lit nights in bed. Reading poetry out loud. French cuisine that delighted taste buds she had ignored for years. Her cafeteria-fed body awoke to Hart's culinary skills as if mesmerized.

The first time Hart came to her apartment, he shuddered visibly upon seeing the minimal decor of her Spartan lifestyle. In the kitchen, he nearly wept at the travesty, then began emptying cupboards of instant coffee and boxed cereals, and the freezer of frozen prepared meals.

Any food allergies? was his only question before leaving for the grocery store to restock and prepare a gourmet meal.

While he was gone, and then when he returned to get busy in the kitchen, Jemma worked at her computer. Later, she became aware that he held out a spoon for her to taste a fresh raspberry sauce.

Quickly, they established a routine. The only thing he asked was that she keep him apprised of her schedule.

At that time, Hart was *sous* chef at a Beverly Hills hotel, moonlighting as a caterer. He had a burning ambition to open his own French café. Short-term, he seemed content to spend time with Jemma when she was available. It didn't occur to her that he did much of anything when they were apart.

He'd appear with a cup of fresh-brewed coffee with wrapped squares of sugar in the saucer just as she finished printing a thesis, or let her sleep late when she'd been studying all night for an exam and then awaken her with homemade croissants and apple butter.

After they'd been together for six months, Jemma discovered she was pregnant, an accident she blamed on switching birth control methods without consistently using a backup. In a panic, she kept the news a secret while she ran down the list of choices: abortion, adoption, raising a child as a single mother.

Hart noticed her reflective mood and asked what was going on.

She told him, and admitted she had considered all the possibilities. Although she'd decided against terminating the pregnancy, she was not prepared to give up her baby for others to raise, and the idea of abandoning her dream of space travel was crushing her.

Hart was delighted by her news. Without hesitation, he proposed marriage and told her he was more than willing to take the traditional stay-at-home parent role while she continued studying for her doctorate.

He became happily obsessed with every aspect of her pregnancy, and also with moving together to a big house in the suburbs so their child—hopefully children, eventually—would enjoy all the advantages he'd lacked growing up in a single parent home in Seattle.

The only specific plan Jemma made for the coming birth of her first and, she decided privately, <u>only</u> child, were to line up a top-notch obstetrician in Beverly Hills.

But something happened to Jemma on the October evening when her son was born. The crimson sunset sent a warm glow into the birthing room as she looked in his eyes for the first time.

Her heart stretched and changed until it became a mother's heart, capable of great love, great sacrifice and great sorrow.

She recognized that her lifelong goal--commanding a space shuttle team-- was not incompatible with this new overarching purpose: to guide and protect Andy until he stood sturdily on his own feet.

Jemma surprised both Hart and herself with this shift in her ambition toward deeper meaning, because neither of them had expected her to embrace motherhood at all.

Although she never became a warm and fuzzy do-it-all soccer mom–she left the day-to-day raising of their son to Hart's capable hands–as Andy journeyed through each milestone, she shielded him from danger and prodded him to greatness with the ferocity of a lioness.

Later, when everything changed, she felt de-clawed.

On the patio, while the adults and teens chatted about Hart's restaurant and ideas for his ever-changing dessert menu, young Peter picked through the bowl of mixed berries with his fingers, ate the strawberry slices and put back other fruit he had licked but rejected.

Jemma and Hart noticed the boy's antics at the same time. She caught Hart's eye and they shared a grimace.

Andy saw his parents' interchange and took the bowl from Peter. He gestured to Eric and Cara. "Come on, let's go for a swim." He led his three guests to the pool and started a volleyball game in the water.

"You've got a great backyard," Sylvia said. "We don't have a pool. Say, maybe we should live here while you're in Texas. Andy could keep his old room. That'd be a win-win, huh?"

Jemma smiled, both polite and noncommittal, realizing she wouldn't have to be the one to play the heavy this time, because she was confident that Hart would never agree to this family's residing in their pristine home without constant supervision.

Stanley accepted a cup of coffee. "So, Jemma, what's it mean to be an astronaut-candidate? How do they decide who gets to blast off next? Need me to text my vote for you to American Space Idol?"

His wife guffawed appreciatively.

"That might help," Jemma said, "especially these days. Actually it's a similar process in many ways. I went through extensive interviews and testing, and then I advanced to the small group that's in training now to be astronauts." With a smile, she added, "But I won't be getting a recording deal out of it."

"She makes it sound easy," Hart said, "but I couldn't do it. They put them through a rigorous course of studying subjects I can't even pronounce, then flight training, then survival training and mission training and special training." He smiled at Jemma. "Really proud of you."

"Thanks," she said, appreciating his support.

Hart got up. "Don't let me cut this short, but I've got to get going to the bistro. You guys stay as long as you want, and I hope to see you again soon."

After Hart left, Jemma explained, "I know he wanted to visit longer, but he's negotiating with the Food Network for his own cooking show, and in between running the restaurant with his manager, he's perfecting the recipes he'll cook during his next interview."

"Man, I'm impressed," Stanley said.

"Your whole family is all go-go-go," Sylvia added.

"Yeah," Jemma said, "I guess we are."

When Andy ushered the kids into the house to change out of their wet suits, Jemma lingered outside with Sylvia and Stanley, who had a barrage of questions about how she came to be in the astronaut program.

"Have you always wanted to be an astronaut?" Sylvia asked.

"If you put my DNA under a strong microscope," Jemma said, "you'd see 'NASA' stamped on it."

"Really?" Sylvia asked, agog.

"She's kidding you, hon," Stanley said.

"Oh, I know that," Sylvia said.

Peter was the first to finish changing. He burst out of the house, gliding in his sneakers and swinging the hockey stick as if he was on ice, knocking into potted plants.

"Careful of the flowers!" Jemma called out.

Andy, Cara and Eric joined them on the pool deck.

Peter changed his game from imaginary ice hockey to soldiering, holding the hockey stick over his shoulder like a rifle. He marched back and forth, then turned a chair around and sat with his back to the table, heedless of the long stick over his shoulder. He knocked the floral centerpiece askew and sent the homemade sand castle ornament flying.

Andy cried out. He leaped to catch the sand castle, but missed.

When the castle ornament broke, a buffalo nickel rolled out.

Andy picked it up and looked at the Indian head, then on the reverse side, an American buffalo.

Jemma gathered the sand castle pieces and looked at the bottom portion that read: "Happy Mother's Day! love, Andy." She put the pieces in an empty bowl.

"I'm awful sorry," Sylvia said. "Let me take that home and glue it for you."

"It's beyond repair, but thanks for the offer. Andy made it for me when he was about Peter's age. He still loves building sand castles at the beach. For a while we thought he might want to be an architect."

"Everybody knows you want me to be a doctor," Andy said.

"You want it too, don't you?" Jemma took the buffalo nickel, saw a hole bored in it to wear on a necklace, and saw the letter "Q" scratched on the buffalo. "My grandfather gave me this years ago. What was it doing inside the sand castle?"

"I forgot all about it," Andy said. "Now I remember. I hid it, like a time capsule."

"What's the 'Q' for?" Stanley asked.

"My grandfather's name was Qaletaqa," Jemma said.

"That's an unusual name," Sylvia said.

"It's Hopi," Jemma explained. "The name means 'guardian of the people.' He's been gone since I was about eleven or twelve, but I recall his stories about growing up on a reservation."

"We're going to visit the reservation this summer," Andy said, giving Jemma a hopeful look.

"If possible. If not, then the winter holidays, okay?" She handed the nickel to him. "Why don't you wear it for luck?"

Andy and Eric went into the house with the nickel.

"Pick up a gold chain for it," Eric said, flashing his shoplifted diver's watch for emphasis.

"Oh, I'll use a string or something," Andy said, his cheeks flaming because he couldn't force himself to be as nonchalant and cool as Eric.

Eric scoffed. "My way is faster than saving your allowance for stuff you want."

Andy hesitated and glanced back at his parents. "My folks would kill me."

"They'll never know. Seriously. Parents are idiots. Next time I see you, you better have something to show me. And make it something good. Not a candy bar. Something expensive."

At the mall, Andy browsed a toy store, his nerves on edge. He wore shorts, and a lightweight vest with deep pockets. He glanced around casually, then slipped a handheld GPS unit out of its bubble pack and into his vest pocket.

The store manager watched him covertly in a surveillance mirror hung near the ceiling.

Unaware, Andy grabbed a couple of board games at random and hurried to the checkout, his hands shaking. He paid cash for the games, not noticing one was a Barbie adventure game and the other was for kids under five.

The GPS seemed to burn a hole in his pocket.

As he passed through the store exit to the mall, the manager's hand clapped him on the shoulder.

Sitting at the kitchen table, Jemma painstakingly glued the sand castle ornament together, frustrated that small pieces were missing. They must have flown off onto the deck and been overlooked. She went outside to search, but had no luck.

The deck was the same sandy color as the ornament, and if any bits were on the ground, they had blended with their surroundings. She picked up one promising piece, but it turned out to be a clod of dirt. Tossing it aside, she remembered something, and pushed aside an overgrown plant to reveal the corner of the deck.

There in the concrete were three handprints and a pawprint, made when the deck was poured years earlier. A name was etched below each print: "Jemma," "Andy," "Hart" and "Joker."

She smiled, remembering that day. Andy was five, and Joker was a rollicking puppy. Hart's parents had visited for a week that summer, and the family took them to many of the popular tourist destinations in the L.A. area. Among other spots, they visited the Chinese Theatre in Hollywood and had fun seeing the celebrity footprints and handprints set in concrete. Andy clamored to do the same, and since they already planned to replace the cracked and stained backyard patio with a new one, it was easy to fulfill his special wish.

Now, sitting back on her heels, she fit her hand into her old handprint, then touched Andy's small print. She looked up at the big house, thinking fondly, *How could one boy fill all that space....*

She got up and took the poorly-mended sand castle ornament into her study. She put it on her desk, liking it anyway, because Andy had made it for her.

At the police station, a hand was still on Andy's shoulder, but this time it was his father's, giving a reassuring squeeze. They were alone in a small waiting room, the door closed.

Hart said gently, "First time?"

"Really stupid," Andy muttered, nodding.

"Hmm. Yeah, it was stupid when I did it, too, at about your age. With the same results. Don't worry about this. But make your first time the last, all right?"

Andy nodded again, this time in relief.

The door crashed open. Jemma stormed in and stopped in front of Andy. She bent, her face inches from his. "What the hell were you thinking! Know how bad this'll look on your college applications?"

Andy averted his eyes.

"I called an attorney," Hart said evenly, "and this incident won't be on any records. In a couple of weeks or so, we'll meet with a judge in chambers and settle the whole thing. The records will be sealed because of his age."

"Be glad it wasn't a more expensive item," Jemma said to Andy, "or you'd be facing felony charges."

Hart made a tamping down gesture. "Let's not lose our heads over this. The store is willing to be reasonable. The charge will be dropped to trespassing– being in the wrong place at the wrong time."

"I'll pay all the fines," Andy said. "And whatever the lawyer costs. I know this was dumb."

"Dumb? It was idiotic!" Jemma slammed a hand on the table. "This isn't how we raised you. I'm so disappointed in you I can barely speak."

"He's disappointed in himself already, Jemma." Hart looked at his watch. "I need to get back to work. Can you take him home without turning this into Armageddon?"

She stared at her husband. "You think this was a harmless prank?"

Andy slouched between them, studying the floor.

"I think he learned a valuable lesson in a hard way," Hart said, "and it needs to be kept in perspective."

"Hey, I didn't create this drama," Jemma said.

Hart looked at her a moment. "But you can choose whether or not to feed it."

Turning her back on Hart, Jemma looked at Andy. "You know what hurts the most? You told them you don't have a mother."

"I didn't want them to call you."

"But they found my ICE number on your cell, and this certainly qualifies for 'In Case of Emergency'."

"Don't tell Eric, okay?" Andy asked, not looking at her.

"That's what worries you the most?" Jemma was incredulous. "That your buddies will find out you went looting but got caught? What? You'll lose face?" She studied his lowered head. "Did Eric put you up to this?"

His shoulders hunched a little tighter.

"And this is the guy you want me to let you live with, during a critical year of your life, your final year of high school."

Hart got up. "Know what? I'll tell the restaurant I won't be back today. They'll have to manage without me. Andy, I'll drive you home, soon as they finish the paperwork."

Jemma shot Hart a narrowed look, but did not say anything.

As Hart and Jemma pulled their cars into the driveway, one after the other, Jemma used her remote to open the garage door and they parked inside the double-bay garage, side-by-side.

Andy leaped out of Hart's sedan and ran toward the door into the house. Jemma killed her engine and hurried after him.

"Just because they released you," she called out, "doesn't mean this is over."

Andy spun around. "What if NASA finds out you've got a criminal for a son? This isn't about you, Mother. This time it's about me."

"I expect better from you."

"Know why I don't want to move to Houston? To get away from you and all your rules!" He stormed into the house with Jemma on his heels, entering from the laundry room into the kitchen.

The alarm panel was beeping: intruder alert. She hastily disarmed the system and turned to follow Andy.

Hart grabbed her arm, letting Andy get ahead. The boy sped out of sight and was heard racing up the stairs to his room. "Lighten up, Jemma. He feels bad enough without you making it into a federal case."

He strode into the kitchen and got a cold bottle of water from the fridge.

Jemma crossed the room to join him at the island. She shoved a bar stool aside even though it wasn't in her way. "Hartley. Our son was just arrested and fingerprinted."

"Which happens all the time, even in the best of families. He broke the law, and he's remorseful. I bet every kid tries shoplifting at least once, or taking money from their mom's wallet. It's human nature to push the limits or do something dumb you know isn't the right thing but it feels like a shortcut to something else you want. Don't make him out to be a hardened delinquent. He learned his lesson."

"I don't believe this. You act like he got his nipples pierced. Not our preference, but no big deal in the long run and he can always button his shirt up." She looked at him a long moment. "I won't applaud everything Andy does just because I love him."

"You're the one with the whip hand, pushing him to be number one, year after year. A lot of pressure. Give him some freedom to be himself. That's all anyone wants."

Still furious, she spun away and hurried back into the laundry room. She grabbed a pair of old running shoes from the floor, changed into them, opened the garage door and then took off running, hiking up her pencil skirt so her legs had freedom of movement.

As she ran for several blocks, she let the anger and frustration slide off her shoulders like an old worn-out cloak, and allowed her reasoning mind to examine the facts logically and fairly.

Her breathing slowed its rapid hammering, and rational thinking prevailed.

Coming to a decision, she turned toward home, her sweat-soaked blouse and skirt clinging to her skin.

After a quick shower, Jemma changed into shorts and a cotton shirt, then went into the master bedroom's walk-in closet and rummaged through an old storage box filled with mementos.

She came across a snapshot taken with Mike McLeod at college graduation. She put it back in the box and found an earlier one at age sixteen in front of a Cessna 172 holding her pilot's certificate, flanked by her instructor and Mike. This photo was a framed enlargement. An inscription read: "Hot Wings! You fly me to the moon. Love always, Mike."

She kept the picture out and found what she was seeking: a small enameled jewelry box. Inside it, among a few pieces of heirloom jewelry she never wore, she located a gold square-shaped charm awarded to her by the most prestigious undergraduate academic honor society. It was her Phi Beta Kappa key.

After polishing the charm, she went down the hall to Andy's bedroom and rapped lightly on the half-open door. "May I come in?"

Andy sat at his desk, engrossed in a poker game on his laptop. When he heard her voice, he glanced up warily, but nodded.

She sat on the edge of the bed. "I'm sorry I blew up at you. I was shocked, and let my emotions rule my behavior."

"That's okay."

"I'd be a shoddy mother if I didn't offer guidance when you head down the wrong path. But I won't bring it up again, as long as we're clear that it won't happen again."

"Agreed. And I am sorry. I feel shitty about it."

"That's a good sign. It means you still have a conscience." She held out the Phi Beta Kappa key. "You'll be driving soon. Thought you might like this for your key chain."

"You never even let me touch this before."

"I know you've got it in you to excel at academics like I did. That's why I couldn't believe you'd sabotage yourself. Don't throw away your potential, Andy."

He accepted the peace offering.

She showed him the photo of herself with the Cessna. "Maybe you'd like to take flying lessons in Houston. You've always enjoyed it when I take you up."

"But you hardly ever go flying. I figured you didn't like it anymore."

"I've been preoccupied with training, but we'll go again soon. When we're in Houston, I'll be busy at the Space Center, but I'll definitely make time for special outings with you."

He looked at her. "So...living with Eric is out?"

"It's pretty obvious he put you up to that stunt."

"I've got a mind of my own."

"And I expect you to use it from now on."

He read the inscription on the photo. "Who's Mike?"

"We were engaged a long time ago. I have no idea what he's up to these days. We didn't keep in touch."

"But you must have been in love with him, if you were going to get married."

"I met your dad a couple years later, and now we've got this great family and a fabulous life that we're going to take really good care of. Right?" She got up. "The treadmill is broken again. Could I run with you tomorrow? Got to keep fit for NASA."

"Yeah, sure, Mom."

That night, lying next to Hart in their king bed, the gulf between them as wide as if they slept in twin beds a mile apart, Jemma asked softly, "You asleep?"

Hart did not reply. His back was to her, and she couldn't see that his eyes were wide open as he feigned startled drowsiness. "Hmm, what?"

"I'm sorry for my heated words earlier. I know you don't approve what Andy did any more than I do. Lost my cool. Hart, I've been thinking a lot lately...about us. Let's make a fresh start when we move to Houston. Leave the past behind.... I'd like a promise from you that you'll make a commitment, too, to make things different between us. We both need to change, start caring more about each other's lives. Recreate the intimacy we've neglected. I want this to work.... I'm willing to do what it takes. Are you, Hart?"

His breathing was slow and even.

Feeling foolish and stupid, she turned away, but not to sleep. Restless, she couldn't seem to stop her mind from going over and over what Andy had done and why this had happened.

At least one thing was certain in her mind: Andy wasn't going to stay with Eric's family for his senior year of high school.

Chapter 4

During the night, the weather changed. A hot dry wind swept in from the desert, as it often does throughout the year, and sped across Los Angeles in a headlong dash to the sea.

The sound of brass chimes pealing madly outside her window awoke Marybeth from a vivid dream. She reached for her dream journal and hurried into the closet to scribble by flashlight before the details faded.

In the dream, she was on a roller coaster ride, but instead of sitting erect on the typical hard molded seats with a safety bar, riders lounged on massive couches, at ease and unconcerned by the hair-raising turns and plummets. One woman gave herself a manicure, while another slept heavily, drool seeping from her open mouth. But Marybeth, alone and rigidly upright in the center of a couch, couldn't stop screaming. Her fingernails dug into her thighs. Overwhelmed by terror, she called out to Naomi for help.

The amusement park vanished. In the dreamscape, all was still, as if that dream abruptly ended and a new one began. A soothing golden jade light enveloped her.

Naomi's voice said clearly in her ear, "Neaten up your bookcase, Bunny."

When she finished jotting the notes, Marybeth sat a moment longer, wondering what the cryptic message meant. Cabot had unpacked her book boxes after they moved in, tired of tripping over them, and she knew the books were already neatly shelved.

Neaten up your bookcase, Bunny.

Tiptoeing, she left the closet, and with a nervous glance toward the bed where Cabot snored like a buzz saw, she sped to the living room. With the flashlight beam, she scanned the shelves, orderly and straight, filled with her collections of fiction, travel guides and books on film and acting.

As a child, Marybeth was her grandmother's favorite, in part because she was so amiable and kind. No matter how often her parents' flaws cropped up in her life, and their offhanded emotional neglect of Marybeth, the girl remained sweet and soft-spoken, always hoping to earn the love and affection it seemed others deliberately withheld. Marybeth's love for all creatures, her gentleness and her unconscious habit of wrinkling her nose while concentrating had earned her the family nickname of "Bunny."

Her nose wrinkled now as she puzzled over Naomi's message and then finally dismissed it as the meaningless product of her dream.

The overhead light snapped on.

She turned, startled.

Cabot stood in the doorway, scowling like an angry father. "What the hell you doing now, Marybeth?"

"I–"

He took the flashlight from her, flipped it off and handed it back as if he'd just disarmed a grenade. "What's all this? An acting exercise to pretend you're a burglar?"

"No, I...I heard a noise and wanted to be sure everything was all right."

Outside, wind whipped through the trees. A branch cracked and fell to the street. Marybeth jumped.

"A tree branch," he said scornfully. "Come back to bed. I'd like to get some sleep, if you don't mind. Must be nice to have the kind of schedule that lets you roam the house in the middle of the night, knowing you can sleep in till noon if you feel like it."

"Be right there." She hesitated, knowing he'd demand a reason for the delay. "I'll drink a glass of warm milk to help me sleep."

"You do that." He turned toward the bedroom and strode off.

She looked at him a moment, infuriated by the way he talked to her, but terrified to talk back, knowing his resulting fury would be too strong for her to handle, and might even destroy her. She silently shrieked at his impassive back, *Who the hell do you think you are!*

But she stayed silent.

She started to leave, planning to take a sip of milk from the carton, just in case Cabot checked her breath, but an inner impulse prompted her to take another quick look at the bookshelves, wishing for proof that Naomi finally sent a message, albeit a strange one.

Neaten up your bookcase, Bunny.

After a moment, Marybeth noticed something, and she smiled to herself. The books did indeed require "neatening"--because they were not in the order she habitually kept them.

Cabot had placed them on the shelves according to size, but she always grouped them by category.

With a nervous glance down the hall to the master bedroom, she turned off the room's light and switched the flashlight on again. She gingerly re-ordered a few books, afraid to make any noise.

First she put all the unused travel guides--those symbols of her yearning to get away and see a new world--on a shelf together, and then grouped some of her books on acting methodology.

Yawning, disappointed there seemed no purpose for this task, she decided to finish the task another time.

As she started to leave, a small book fell from a top shelf and landed at her feet.

She was positive she had not knocked it down. In fact, she had not even touched the bookcase.

Curious, she picked it up. The book was "A Year in Provence" and when she opened it, there was an envelope inside. Even without using the flashlight, she knew that her name was handwritten on it in Naomi's colorful attempt at calligraphy.

Remembering this book was her last gift from Naomi, she opened the birthday card and read the note written in purple ink: "Joyeux anniversaire, ma cousine! Save this to read on the plane. Don't ask Cabot if you can go to France with me. TELL him you're going!!! We'll write our own bestselling memoir and call it 'Our Month in Provence' —with vegetarian recipes (you'll see what I mean when you read this book!). Love ya, Naomi. P.S. Ask me something in French— I'm taking an immersion course and you should too!!!!"

Tears of regret sprang to Marybeth's eyes. They'd never studied French together. Never planned their itinerary for Paris and Nice, or bought their tickets. Never wrote a book together.

Marybeth clutched the book like a lifesaver. She sobbed soundlessly, a useful skill acquired from a lifetime of practice, then switched off her flashlight, wiped her eyes, dashed to the kitchen, took a swill of milk from the carton-- cringing when her lips touched a dried milky crust on the spout--and then returned to bed to sleep a few hours with the book tucked beneath her pillow.

As she fell asleep, Marybeth prayed for another dream from Naomi.

Mid-morning, Jemma and her son Andy ran in the hills near their home in the San Fernando Valley. Andy wore the buffalo nickel on a silver chain she had just given him.

The sky was the smog-free blue that revealed itself to Angelenos when Santa Ana winds gallop across the sprawling metropolis. Telltale signs were all around. Broken branches dangled from trees or lay on the ground below a trunk's fresh scar. Torn newspapers and junk mail ads littered the streets. Parked cars were filmed with a fine layer of dust and yellow pollen.

Jemma glanced sideways at Andy and asked him quietly, "Why did you do it?"

He shot her look of panicked exasperation.

"Why buy those two board games, if you weren't going to pay for–"

"You said we wouldn't discuss this, Mom!"

"But I saw the shopping bag and receipt you left in Dad's car. I want to know how your mind works, Andy. Obviously you didn't pick those two games because you wanted them for yourself–"

"Can't we drop this?"

"And if you needed more money, all you had to do was ask. I'll call the credit card company today and set you up as an authorized user on my Visa."

"You don't get it!"

"I'm trying to," she said. "I really am."

He lengthened his stride and pulled ahead.

Marybeth emerged from the built-in sauna that was part of the master bedroom suite, then showered and styled her newly colored hair. Shiny scarlet curls tumbled to her shoulders, a bold change from her usual straight flaxen blonde hair.

She smiled, liking the sensation of freedom from herself. At a glance, she looked radiant, deflecting the discovery that her smile did not reach her perpetually sad eyes.

After dressing in snug designer jeans, strappy stilettos and a sheer blue blouse over a nude camisole, she put the final touches on her makeup.

She was on schedule, and feeling confident and pleased with herself. In five minutes, she'd leave for an audition, trying out for the female lead, Cerise, in a time travel movie called "Seven Funerals."

She was excited to meet the writer/director and make a good impression on him, and with this intention, she pushed aside reminders of other failed auditions. *Think positive!* her former therapist had often admonished her. And so, clutching a positive attitude as if holding the key to success, she put on another slick of lipgloss and turned to leave.

When Jemma caught up with Andy, she started to say something more about his arrest, but he held a finger to his lips and pointed out a cottontail rabbit munching on a neighbor's verdant lawn.

They quietly approached on the street. However, sensing them, the bunny stood on its hind legs and froze in place, as if lack of motion rendered it invisible. As they got nearer, invading its comfort zone, the rabbit bolted into a nearby hedge with a flash of its plump white cottontail.

"Not always that easy to hide," Andy commented, his voice sounding bitter.

Jemma gave him a searching look.

The breeze stirred copper chimes hung in a tree, creating a sound as clear and pure as church bells.

Jemma and her son ran at a steady pace--side-by-side in silence--each absorbed by troubled thoughts, their mouths tight with unexpressed resentments.

Marybeth's garage door swung open, operated from inside the garage by remote control. Hurrying out of the house from the kitchen, she slipped into her white convertible, eased the door shut and turned on the engine, praying for the noise of a gardener's blower up the street to cover the noise, and began slowly backing out of the driveway as if a contrived stealth mode would make her invisible.

She didn't raise the convertible top even though it meant her hair would be windblown. There wasn't time. She needed to get away before Cabot pulled one of his delaying tactics, and made her late.

She reached up to press the button that would shut the garage door, but her fingers froze. *Too late.*

The kitchen door banged open.

Cabot hurried out with the parrot on his shoulder. He ran into the driveway and thumped the car hood to get her attention. "I was still talking to you, Marybeth!"

She braked, and called out to him with careful politeness, as if unaware he'd been trying to get her to stop in the kitchen before her mad dash to freedom. Instead of asking him to finish what he'd been saying when she hurried out, she tried to distract him. "Need anything while I'm out?"

"I called your dentist."

Her eyes shifted slightly, but she kept smiling.

Cabot shook his head in disbelief. "Your appointment isn't today. It's next week. As you very well know. Where you headed now, Marybeth? Another freaking audition?"

Sensing she'd be a fool to fib again, she nodded. "Please don't make me late."

He ambled closer, suddenly moving in an approximation of slow motion, a complete switch from his flying leap moments ago. "How am I the one doing that, Marybeth? I'm not the one dashing in and out at all hours, claiming errands, faking appointments with dentists."

"I do have errands. For the house."

"I don't even know where you are half the time. My own wife. It's got to stop, Marybeth." He looked at her a moment. "Another new outfit? You never wear the clothes I pick out for you. Why don't you wear that green striped dress I–"

"Because it's ugly! Cheap! Doesn't even have a proper hem. They just stitched the bottom edge on a machine. Looks like something an old farm wife would wear to milk the cows."

In the stunned silence, she barely breathed, waiting for his explosion.

He shook his head slowly and sighed beneath his burden. "I've been patient with you, Marybeth." His eyes were moist, as if his spirit had been broken by her words. "I've tried my best to understand. You know, it has been very hard for me too."

"I know," she whispered.

"And we agreed this house would be a fresh start for us. But I'm the one doing all the work around here."

That's not true!

Swallowing her words didn't make the fury go away. Enraged, she rammed the brake pedal to the floor, fighting a sudden impulse to throw the gear into Drive, stomp the accelerator and knock Cabot down like she was driving a steamroller. Then she could be on her way to the audition without restrictions.

"Pick a color and paint the damned bedroom," he said flatly. "How many weeks does it take to decide the color you want? We can't get the new carpet installed until the walls are done. Is the logical sequence of events that difficult to understand?"

"Can't this wait?"

"I'm tired of all the waiting I do for you."

"I'm sorry. Dear." She used the dulcet tone that sometimes, not always but sometimes, managed to ameliorate his anger. "I'll pick a paint color this afternoon as soon as I–"

"You spend too much time going to acting classes and reading scripts and auditioning for parts you'll never get."

Fuming inwardly at the delay, she sneaked a peek at the car's clock.

He saw the movement of her eyes. "You should have weaseled your way out of the house earlier if you were so afraid of spending five precious minutes talking to your husband."

"I...I told you I was going."

"I give and give and give, Marybeth. And all you do is take."

"No, that's not true–"

"I don't ask much."

"I'm doing my best, Cabot." She put on her sunglasses, hoping he'd take it as a signal to allow her departure. She lifted a hand in farewell.

"I don't understand how you can spend so much time and energy on something that never pays off. You know they'll reject you again." He stroked his parrot. "I hate to see you get hurt."

Bile rose in her throat. She felt the urge to vomit but managed a careless laugh. "Well! Maybe today will be my lucky day."

He looked at her a long moment. "All right. But be careful. And come right home."

She started to nod, but lifted her chin, almost defiant. "Stop telling me to be careful. You caution me every single time I leave the house, as if the world is such a scary place I'd better stay home under your thumb."

"I don't know what's gotten into you, Marybeth. Maybe I should go to your next therapy session with you and talk all this over with your doctor. See what he can do to finally fix your crazy thinking."

"I've got to go." She took her foot off the brake and eased backwards out of the driveway, her hands trembling on the steering wheel. "Bye!"

"If it was me," he called out as she slowly reversed out of the driveway, "I'd have given up long ago and gotten a real job. I guess we're different that way. I expect a paycheck or some form of compensation when I work. But...I guess everybody deserves a hobby."

The words Naomi wrote on her birthday card sang in Marybeth's head. Emboldened, she called out, "I'm not asking permission to go to the audition, Cabot. I'm telling you that I'm going!"

He turned on his heel, stomped into the house, and slammed the kitchen door behind him.

Her pounding heart drowned out the throaty purr of the car engine. Trembling all over, Marybeth braked the car. She closed her eyes, took a measured deep breath and shakily exhaled, then straightened.

She stabbed the garage remote button like a detonator, and peeled out.

Her cell rang. Jolted, she recognized the Caller ID and answered at once, using hands-free calling. "Rodney? Hi. I know, I'm sorry I'm running a little late. I'm on my way but traffic on the 101 is a disaster. Stall Mike for me? I really want to read for this part. I know I'm right for it. Please give me a few extra minutes to get there?"

After he agreed and they ended the call, she glanced at the clock, and blinked away tears of frustration.

Living on a cul-de-sac meant she had only one way out of her street, and so she headed that way, cutting dangerously close to a parked car. At the mouth of the cul-de-sac, she usually turned left to go to the grocery store and other errands, but today she took a right at the corner and began winding down the hill in the direction of the main boulevard that led to the freeway onramp.

Andy and Jemma approached a winding street that led down to the one they'd take to go up again and homeward.

They had a panoramic view of the broad San Fernando Valley, looking eastward, but Jemma's thoughts were not on the view. She studied Andy as they ran, knowing she wouldn't be satisfied until she had an answer to the question that had kept her tossing and turning all last night. "Andy? Are you doing drugs?"

Stunned, he made a harsh noise of disbelief.

"I promise I won't get mad," she said. "Just tell me the truth. We'll get help for you."

He blew out a grunt, frustrated he couldn't get through to her. "But I don't need help."

68

"Eric is a bad influence on you. I don't want you to see him again."

"Shit, Mom! You're a total control freak." Andy sped off.

"No, Andy. Wait!"

Without looking back, he yelled, "You don't get me at all!"

She stopped, stymied.

He ran around a curve, and was out of sight.

Knowing she'd handled this badly, Jemma trotted after him.

Rounding the curve, she saw Andy running downhill, his feet skimming the ground like pebbles skipping over water.

As she hurried after him, Jemma noticed a white convertible coming down another street, heading for the same 3-way intersection as Andy.

The driver's flame red hair whipped like a banner in the Santa Ana wind. The sun shone on the waxed metal of the arctic white car.

From her vantage point higher up the hill, Jemma felt a rising sense of alarm at the somewhat erratic way the driver negotiated the series of quick curves.

Jemma looked at Andy, running steadily. "Stop, Andy," she yelled. "Stop!"

The capricious wind tossed the words back over her shoulder.

In the distance a siren shrieked its way to nearby West Hills Hospital.

Gusts of wind whipped Marybeth's red curls. With an impatient gesture, she shoved her sunglasses back like a headband to secure the tangled mass, knowing she should put the top up to protect her hairdo, but hating to take the time to stop and do it.

She had to get to the audition and prove everyone wrong about her acting talent.

She had to, or she'd never believe in herself again.

Glare blinded her eyes as she took the curve, not speeding, but not slowing down.

She had to keep swerving the wheel to avoid torn branches that had been hurled haphazardly into the street by the hot wind.

New to the neighborhood, she was oblivious to the upcoming stop sign hidden today by a large half-broken branch that dangled from an overgrown California pepper tree near the curb.

The sights and sounds of suburban life snatched at Jemma as if to distract her attention. Chimes hung from tree branches and balconies rang out like alarms, with a clamor and a clang as they spun.

A girl pedaled her bike uphill, grimly determined not to get off and push it. She called out a half-hearted greeting but Jemma ignored her.

In a shuttered house, a telephone shrilled.

A gardener loaded his truck with lawnmower and rake. Giving her a friendly nod, he backed out of the driveway.

Jemma detoured into the street and ran around him.

With a squeal of bald tires, the dilapidated truck turned a corner, leaving behind mingled odors of gas fumes and cut grass.

The distance between Jemma and Andy seemed to stretch as if Andy stood on a stationary platform and the horizon retreated, taking him further and further from her.

How will I ever catch up?

A memory replayed instantly, and she was...

Chasing little Andy in their backyard. He shrieked in delight as she pounced on him. She scooped him into her arms and showered kisses on his chubby cheeks. He clung to her neck, his smile so dear her heart tripped with joy as she hugged him close and inhaled his little boy aroma of musty dirt and baby sweat and Ivory soap.

Now, from the eaves of a large house, glass chimes giggled and danced in the wind, and then whirled crazily in the rising wind and crashed to the flagstone path below.

In a gated yard, a neighbor's large dog barked.

Jemma hurried on.

Behind a garden wall at the corner house, unseen bamboo chimes clattered a coded warning.

The white convertible roared wickedly towards Andy.

Frantic to get her son's attention, Jemma cupped her hands around her mouth and screamed his name into the wind.

As he dashed away from his mother, Andy forced himself to breathe more calmly, to get into his natural rhythm of running. Lately, Andy'd been intrigued by a recurring dream that all the guys at school were gathered around, talking about him, even praising him and saying they were glad they could call him a friend. It was strange, but it served to bolster his commitment to infiltrate Eric's group. The dream energized him to push forward with his plan for senior year to be totally cool. For a moment, he even forgot about his shame at getting caught shoplifting, and the total upheaval with his parents.

He wanted to discover his own inner drive to match or exceed his parents' ambition in their own lives. He knew they wanted the best for him. He scowled, ashamed that he had let them down, let himself down.

He'd seek, he'd find what he wanted to do that would make a big impact, but, seriously, in the meantime, wasn't he entitled to some fun?

He rehashed the argument with his mother, and felt his annoyance flare. She'd really be pissed when she realized what he had in mind, that he was going to find a way to not move to Houston even if he had to run away. He was going to put aside conquering the world for now and focus on enjoying senior year of high school. And his new friend Eric, despite his mother's anger over what she saw as an unsuitable friendship, was going to open the door to that coveted experience.

Thinking how cool it was going to be to swagger into a classroom and take any seat he wanted, even next to one of the most popular senior girls, Andy ran toward the 3-way intersection and leapt off the curb to cross to the other side just as...

Marybeth's car hurtled past the stop sign on the short arm of the T-intersection.

Watching from above, from up the hill, there was nothing Andy's mother could do.

Events that Tuesday were intricate folds in the fabric of time, each moment seamed invisibly to the next.

Jemma kept running, determined to avert an accident. The heat of the day was cloying, as if suddenly humid and tropical and dense. It felt she was having to push through the waves of heat, like a mirage shimmering up from the freeway when driving in the desert. She tried to go faster but her legs were exhausted and leaden.

She waved her arms wildly and gasped out another warning. "Andy! Look out! MOVE!" Her words sped away behind her like a kite tail. The words didn't, they couldn't, reach Andy's ears.

He was lost in thought, heedless of his surroundings.

The white convertible was closer to Andy than Jemma was.

And the immutable laws of physics thwarted her efforts to reach him or gain his attention in time.

Squinting into the sun, Marybeth abruptly noticed the running teenager bound off the curb to cross the street. She swerved, then overcorrected her steering.

The car spun, fishtailing.

The scene on the safe suburban street played out as if it was following an impeccably choreographed script.

The gleaming grille of the car struck Andy and flung him like a ragdoll against a nearby garden wall. The back of Andy's head hit the stone wall, and he sagged to the sidewalk.

The thud of the impact reverberated in Jemma's heart.

As he fell, Andy's fingers caught on his necklace. The broken chain and its buffalo nickel clattered to the ground.

A shower of crimson petals rained on Andy's face from the bougainvillea cascading overhead.

Panting, Jemma reached her son just as Marybeth gained control of her car and stopped at an angle in the middle of the street.

Marybeth turned off the ignition and leapt from the car, horrified. She cried out, a soft keening lament.

Jemma glanced at the red-haired young woman. "Call 9-1-1!"

Marybeth fumbled in the car to find her phone, locating it where it had fallen on the passenger floor, and phoned for help.

Jemma crouched on the sidewalk. "Andy? Andy!"

Blood trickled down the stone wall.

She searched for a pulse. Forcing herself to speak calmly and clearly, she repeated her son's name.

His eyelashes moved.

Did they move? Or did I imagine it? Was it the wind?

There were no neighbors out jogging or dog walking. No cars to flag down for assistance.

Where are all those people Andy waves to whenever we go out? Where are they now, when we need help?

"Say something, Andy. Please. It's Mom. Talk to me."

He didn't respond.

She stripped off her t-shirt down to the sports-bra beneath and rolled the shirt into a soft compress to put under her son's bloody head.

She knelt over him.

She checked Andy's mouth for obstructions and then began pushing down repeatedly on his chest to mimic a steady heartbeat. She counted carefully, silently, giving thirty chest compressions for every two rescue breaths, grateful she knew the latest procedure to follow, although she'd only practiced on plastic dummies.

All the while, her thoughts tumbled at warp speed.

Andy. Her Andy. This was the son she had long ago declared she would die for, if it ever came to that, whom she'd shield from bullets or marauders.

This priceless son...this boy who was life's best gift to her...he was... he was...No!

He's dying.

With that realization, Jemma's heart cracked, shifted and recombined, forever altered.

To Jemma, waiting for the paramedics, it seemed that time stretched as if made of elastic. Everything took longer than it should, longer than was possible, despite only seconds of real time passing.

Without stopping CPR, Jemma glanced over at the red-haired driver. The woman stood like a mannequin outside her car, frozen in the middle of the street. Commuters would be coming home soon and need to pass.

Odd how such a practical thought could intrude itself, but Jemma was a logical, goal-oriented perfectionist.

"Call 9-1-1 again!" she yelled out. "Move your car to the curb! Then come over here and dial my husband on my phone."

Marybeth gave a small nod, as if grateful for instructions.

This must be a scene from someone else's life, Jemma thought as she continued the chest compressions, and surely not her own, which had been going so well. Overall. Hadn't it?

She and Hart would repair their marriage. Wouldn't they? The quarrels with Andy about Houston, about the shoplifting episode, those could be mended, too. Of course they could.

Oh, Andy! Out of all the mismatched relationships in her life, why was the one best thing fading beneath her normally capable hands?

After Marybeth dialed Hart's bistro, Jemma snatched the phone and hunched it against her ear so she could continue CPR. She explained the situation, gave their location and told him an ambulance was already on the way.

In the meantime, she would continue CPR and Hart would pray for a miracle.

As she tried to revive Andy, she thought how strange it was that even in a time of stress your mind could splinter into separate chambers, each with its own hamster running in a wire wheel, spinning faster and faster.

As she breathed into her son's mouth, she thought, using a term of endearment she'd coined when her son was very small, *Andy, my dearling, I love you.*

She searched his face for signs of life. She pressed her fingers against his neck and felt heat pulsing. Blood throbbed in her ears, but was it hers or his? Their lives were co-mingled, mother and child.

A fact crashed into her awareness: Her fingers might not be fast enough, her thrusts powerful enough, her breath clever enough to draw back a life that was ebbing.

Her agony became a camera filter through which she observed the next minutes in a blur of sights and sounds. Through it all she pictured her son's face, the face she'd loved from the moment he was born, the face that lit up with joy, the eyes that sparkled with mirth and intelligence. How could he be leaving?

Barely sixteen years together was not nearly enough.

In her line of sight, Jemma noticed the broken chain of his necklace lying on the sidewalk. Nearby was the old buffalo nickel that her grandfather had given her so many years ago.

She kept up the rhythmic CPR motions, seeking a response.

Jemma heard the approaching siren, but only when the flashing lights were upon her did she feel a spark of hope.

She willed her son to hold on, told him silently that he'd be fine in a few minutes, and they would laugh in relief about this day in years to come, this day when he'd had such a close brush with death, but they had emerged the victors.

There was so much she had never said before, that she had thought but not verbalized. Now she said simply, "I love you, Andy."

As the paramedics put an oxygen mask over Andy's face, she gripped her boy's hand tightly. Always before, unlike now, there had been the quick warm response of an answering squeeze.

Other hands moved her aside so they could give medical care to her son.

As if in a bad dream, she heard crisp orders barked into radios, an urgent report given on what the emergency team found at the scene. A request for immediate backup and police support and a tow truck.

It seemed she was observing a movie being made. It was common enough in Los Angeles to come across a scene being filmed. But where were the long white trucks you always saw on location? Where were the cameras, the strobe lights, the other actors?

Without moving far from her assigned mark, she shifted to keep Andy in sight.

She watched anxiously. Was he responding at last? Was he going to live?

She hated being this powerless.

Peripherally, she saw Hart's car pull up to the curb. He raced to see their son. She heard Hart's cry of shock, his quick questions of the paramedics, and their unsatisfactory replies.

He joined Jemma. They watched the paramedics work briskly and impersonally at their task of reclaiming a life, if possible.

It was still light, but to Jemma, darkness crept in, and with it a deep coldness that seeped into her bones. Feeling she would never be warm again, she rubbed her bare arms.

She reached out with a hesitant hand, wanting to touch her son, caress his cheek, smooth his hair. But she wasn't allowed near him.

A gathering crowd of onlookers drew apart when a police car pulled up. The officer in charge directed events. A tow truck came to impound the driver's vehicle.

The sky was red with the glow of tail lights and emergency flashers.

Jemma idly recalled an old saying from when she and Mike used to go sailing on Apache Lake, outside Phoenix: *Red sky at night, sailors delight....*

This was no delight.

Hart grasped Jemma's hand.

In her mind, in her heart, Jemma spoke to Andy, sending urgent messages of devotion and entreaty. *Please, Andy. Breathe!*

Sounds filtered towards Jemma as if she was underwater.

During their school days in Phoenix, she and Mike would play games in his backyard swimming pool. They took a deep breath, ducked underwater, and then opened their eyes and spoke, carefully enunciating a message for the other to decipher. When they ran out of air, they'd surface, gasping, and compare what was said and what was heard. Mike said: *I asked if you want a cherry Popsicle at my house.* She said: *No, you said 'It's very icky to eat a mouse!'*

Now she wanted to misunderstand what the paramedics were saying about massive head trauma.

People stopped to watch, filled with curiosity and horror...and open relief that the accident had not touched them personally.

It was the time of day to come home after summer school or sports or errands or work. The time of day for families to gather and share what happened during the day. The time for greeting and hugging each other.

A familiar voice called out, "Mrs. P.?"

She looked up and saw Eric. All her rage spewed. "This is your fault!"

Confused, Eric stopped his bicycle and got off. "What do you mean?"

Hart shook his head and made a small gesture to dismiss Jemma's accusation. He pointed to Andy, and the paramedics.

Eric's face registered shock. "He'll be okay, won't he?" He dropped his bike and hurried to them.

Jemma noticed a woman taking photos of Andy with her cell phone.

Glancing around, she saw others doing the same. Some were moving their phone in a slow arc, clearly making videos. She screamed out, "Have you no decency!"

Eric moved through the crowd, holding a hand over camera lenses in passing. He stopped in front of two guys in their twenties who were gloating to each other about being the first to upload their video to YouTube and go viral.

Eric stopped in front of them, glowering, using his full breadth and width and the physical strength of a football fullback to intimidate the two smaller men.

One of them dared a snarky response. "What?"

Eric's fingers curled into fists. He breathed roughly, as if trying to control his temper from exploding into violence. With a jerk of his head to indicate Andy, Eric said, "Go home and be grateful it's nobody you know."

Eric joined Andy's parents and stood behind them like a bulwark, protecting them from idle questions and curious glances.

A paramedic looked up at Jemma and Hart with a grim message on his face.

Jemma bellowed one long "No!" of disbelief, protest and refusal, as if the force of her will could push away reality.

She rushed to take Andy in her arms.

It seemed to Jemma that a man's voice spoke directly in to her ear, saying "Don't worry, he'll be all right--he'll be with me." She glanced up, but there was no man near her. The voice felt familiar to her, but she brushed off the experience and concentrated on kissing Andy's forehead and whispering words of love to him.

Hart sank to his knees on the other side of Andy, stroked his son's face, and broke down in ragged tears. He reached a hand out to Jemma and clasped her shoulder, as if needing to complete the connection between the three of them for one last time.

Behind them, the sidewalk by the garden wall was empty except for Jemma's bloodied shirt that she'd pillowed under Andy's injured head.

The buffalo nickel and its silver chain were gone.

Inside Simon Tarzyn's production office, Mike looked at the list in front of him. Only one actress was a "no show" for today's casting call.

Mike had narrowed his choice for "Cerise" to three young women who had auditioned, but he wanted to see this last one as well. He held her headshot, still liking her look and that sweet vulnerability in her soulful gaze.

He called out to Rodney, who was busy packing their files. "You ever reach Marybeth Lacroix?"

Rodney shrugged. "Ages ago. Said she was on the freeway and would be here soon."

They shared a skeptical look.

Mike tossed Marybeth's headshot aside and picked up his short list. "I guess we'll go ahead and call back these three, and then I'll make a decision."

Rodney nodded.

Mike glanced again at Marybeth's photo, disappointed. He got up. "Can't wait for someone who doesn't even care enough to show up on time."

Chapter 5

Andy stood up. He grabbed the buffalo nickel and its broken chain from the sidewalk. As he strolled away, heedless of his parents, the gawking crowd and the ambulance lights, he noticed the chain had somehow mended itself.

Not questioning the phenomenon, he strung the nickel on the now mended chain and fastened it around his neck.

Up ahead, he noticed a small group of people beneath a bright street light, beckoning.

"Come on, Andy," an older man's friendly voice called out. "This way. We're here to welcome you."

Andy ignored him, his mind still clouded by anger and resentments over the recent argument with his mother. He passed the strangers and kept walking.

The light and the group were suddenly just ahead of him.

This happened repeatedly, no matter which direction he took to evade them: they were always in front, encouraging him to come join them. But he didn't know who they were or what they wanted.

He scowled. "Stop bugging me!"

"You really should come with us," a woman in her thirties called to him in a kind tone. She spoke with an Italian accent and wore clothes from the 1940s.

"More rules?" Andy asked, scoffing. "No thanks."

"But, Andy, you have to!" The older man took a step toward him.

The Italian woman held out a staying hand to the man.

"He can't refuse his own Life Review," the man insisted to her. "No one can. Everyone has to do a spiritual examination and evaluation."

"But he can come to the decision on his own," she said, "even if the journey takes a circuitous path...I have an idea that might help."

As others in the group watched with interest, the woman looked beyond the bright light, gave a low whistle, leaned lower and made a beckoning gesture as if to a child.

Not paying attention to them, Andy kicked at a rock in the street, deciding which way to go next.

As he turned away from the light, a figure came around from behind the group of people and loped toward him on four legs.

"Joker?" Andy grinned. "Hey, come here, boy!" He crouched and held his arms wide for his dog.

The Golden Retriever flung himself into Andy's embrace. Andy hugged him tight, accepting readily that the dog which had died of old age was now young and in his prime, pale golden blond and frisky.

Joker licked Andy's face.

"Gimme four!" Andy held up his hand for a high-five. The dog held out a paw, as Andy had taught him years earlier. "Always said you were the smartest dog. Want to go for a run?"

"Andy," the older man interjected, "stop playing with your dog and pay attention to me. You cannot escape this. Everyone has to do it. No exceptions."

The woman looked at the man in exasperation. "Stop nagging him!"

"There's a reason we have rules," the older man said to Andy as if she hadn't spoken. "Nobody is so special they get to flaunt them. Bring your dog if you want, but you must come with us."

"Oh yeah?" Andy glanced around, seeking another way to go.

A new path opened up into a wooded area that hadn't been there moments earlier. He set off at a trot, with Joker at his left side, the way they used to go jogging together. Over his shoulder, he called out to the older man, "Make me!"

Within moments, he and his dog were in the woods, running easily on a smooth path.

Behind Andy, the Italian woman held the group back from following. "Let him be," Gabriella said. "He will come to us in his own way."

"I'm not so sure about that," the older man said. "He's so stubborn. I don't want to have anything to do with his case. Go ahead and handle it yourself, Gabriella, if you're so eager to prove yourself to Qaletaqa. I know you're going for the gold," he added, with a glance at her silver armband.

Andy ran for a long time, tirelessly.

"Hey, Joker, how about a run on the beach like we used to?"

The path curved, and the wooded area opened onto a sandy beach, with gentle turquoise waves rolling into shore.

After playing Frisbee on the beach with his dog, Andy decided to build a sand castle. The beach was empty, not even a stray piece of litter or coffee cup in sight. Nothing he could use but his hands. But as he turned, he saw a bucket filled with scoops and different shaped containers that he could use for digging and molding the different parts of a castle.

He began creating an elaborate castle structure with a large moat, the biggest castle he'd ever made, concentrating on each detail, seeing only what he wanted to be aware of, and finding new tools just as he needed them. When he had the desire to add flags to the towers and a drawbridge over the moat, the materials he needed were immediately at hand.

After a while, he indicated the completed masterpiece to Joker with a dramatic gesture. "Done!"

He strolled along the shore, picking up seashells and tossing them into the water, enjoying the quiet, but feeling there was something he should be doing.

He stopped, and looked at his dog for a long moment, then realized the answer. "I know! Mom said we could go to the Hopi Reservation this summer. Let's get there first. Surprise her."

He set off at a run, his dog by his side, and as he neared the parking lot he passed two surfers heading toward the water with their longboards. "Hi there!" he called out.

The surfers acted as if they didn't hear him.

Andy laughed, not caring. "Hey, you guys know the way to Arizona?" He pretended they answered him. "Oh, go east. Thanks, got it." He looked at Joker and said solemnly, "We go east."

Running eastward, within moments Andy was at the Colorado River, nearly two hundred and fifty miles away from where he'd started at the Pacific shore.

Continuing along the river, he came to a wide bridge and saw a group of teen boys bungee jumping.

One of the boys, wearing khaki shorts, called out to him. "Want to be next?"

"Oh, uh, no thanks," Andy said. Not knowing the boy's name, he added, "You go ahead, Khaki."

"Let me guess," a boy in a striped shirt said. "Your parents don't allow this. Too dangerous, right?" Stripes sneered at him, mocking.

Andy watched in envy as the boys took turns jumping from the bridge and shrieking as they bounced at the end of the bungee, mere inches from the water surface.

"Hey, watch me," Khaki yelled. He changed the length of his bungee cord.

"Ooh, going for the bottom again?" Stripes asked.

Khaki nodded, tested the knot on his harness and leapt off the bridge head first. He dove deep into the river. As the boys waited, watching, the moments ticked away.

"He'll drown!" Andy kicked off his shoes and poised to dive in.

Khaki resurfaced and catapulted up and out of the water, swinging back and forth under the bridge, holding the bungee cord like a vine and yelling like Tarzan.

Andy felt confused, but he joined in the laughter.

"Your turn," a boy wearing a blue t-shirt said, holding out a harness to Andy. "Go on," Blue urged, "take it."

When Andy shook his head, Stripes said, "Come on, don't be a wuss. You see your folks anywhere around here? They'll never know."

A couple of boys began clucking like a chicken.

Andy felt uncomfortable, and embarrassed. He hastily buckled into the harness and let Khaki hook up the bungee cord.

"Don't we need to test it?" Andy tugged the connectors. "Make sure it's safe?"

The boys exploded in laughter.

"A newbie." Khaki indicated the water. "Go on, kid. Stop worrying so much." He patted Joker on the head. "I'll watch your dog." He shoved Andy off the bridge.

Startled, Andy kicked and screamed, and clawed to grab hold of something. But as he swung out over the water, held only by the springy cord, he laughed out loud, loving the freedom.

"No rules!" Andy yelled, his voice echoing under the bridge. "NO MORE RULES!!!"

The boys applauded.

When his turn was over, Andy begged for another. He stayed with the boys, jumping and diving, while his dog Joker waited patiently on the bridge.

The other boys played tirelessly and without breaks, but after a time Andy grew bored with the sameness of the activity. "I better get going."

"Important date?" Khaki asked.

The others chuckled knowingly.

"Wait," Blue said to Andy. He unbuckled his own harness and let it fall. "I'll go with you."

"You can't," Stripes said. "You have to stay because you've been here the longest."

"But," Blue said, as if realizing the truth, "that doesn't have anything to do with why I have to go."

The other boys tried to convince Blue and Andy to stay with them, but Andy whistled to his dog and the three crossed the bridge toward Arizona.

Seeing they were serious about leaving, Khaki called out, "Who needs you, anyway! Good riddance!"

Andy glanced back.

"Don't pay attention," Blue said. "I used to say that stuff, too. They don't know how to leave, so they don't want us to."

Andy shrugged, not understanding but not curious to find out more. "Where is your family camped?"

Blue frowned.

Andy looked around vaguely. "We both must be camped near here, right? I didn't take a bus to get to this bridge and I don't even see a bicycle–" He broke off, noticing two bicycles lying in the street. "Oh. There they are. I guess we rode in. Together."

"Yeah," Blue said, accepting the easy explanation, "I guess we did."

In silence, the two boys pedaled away from the river on a blacktop road and passed a sign that welcomed them to Arizona, the Grand Canyon state.

Joker trotted effortlessly at Andy's side.

"Where you two headed?" Blue asked.

"Hopi Reservation."

"You an Indian?"

"My mother's grandfather grew up on the reservation. She's taking me to see it."

"Where is she?"

"She's meeting me there," Andy said.

"Yeah, right."

Andy flared up. "She is! She promised. I have to get there."

"You even know where you're going?"

Andy looked at him blankly, unsure how to answer, but feeling the question could be important. "Somewhere around the Grand Canyon. I think."

"Don't you have directions? A map?"

Patting his pockets, Andy found a folded map and stopped to study it.

Blue stopped his bike and grabbed the map. "Hopi Reservation. Founded in the year 1150. One and a half million acres. Shit, that's big. Looks like it's about four hundred miles from here, in the northeast corner of the state."

"We better get started now."

Blue balled up the map and tossed it at him. "I don't feel like going that way. See ya." Blue wheeled away.

Andy folded the map, and kept pedaling north.

After a short while, Andy reached the south rim of the Grand Canyon and stopped, uncertain. He sensed that there was something he was supposed to be doing, but he saw others camping, found an empty tent and lay down to rest, with his dog curled at his feet.

Later, he got up, not questioning why it was everlasting day, and began walking, the bicycle forgotten.

A couple of teen girls, one blonde and one brunette, strolled up and stopped him. "Hey, cutie. We're going hang-gliding. Why don't you come with us?"

He didn't have a good excuse not to, so he went with them. The girls introduced him to a party of several dozen hang-gliders, mostly in their teens and twenties, but a few were older.

"I've always wanted to do this," he admitted, as the blonde girl showed him the harness and demonstrated how to hold onto the triangular frame of the glider to steer it.

"Why don't we go tandem?" she suggested. "I'll steer."

"Okay, cool." After wheeling the glider to the edge of the canyon cliff top, they buckled into their harnesses.

"Ready?"

"Wait!" Andy grabbed her shoulder. "We need helmets. And parachutes."

She gave him a scornful look and pushed off.

As they soared high above the carved rocks of the Grand Canyon, gliding like eagles far above the sparkling river below, Andy laughed at himself. "Helmets? Geez, I'm a doofus. No regulations for me!" He let out a whoop.

The blonde turned her head and grinned at him.

They flew again and again, never needing to wait for a hang-glider to be free, because no matter how many people arrived or left, there were exactly the right number of hang-gliders for fliers, and each flight was completed without incident.

"We're all going dancing later," the blonde told him, putting an arm around Andy's waist as they walked away from the hang-glider. "Be my date? It'll be nighttime. Special. Wait till you see all the stars."

"Sure. Why not?"

Later at the dance, in the smoky darkness, the blonde grabbed two beers from an ice chest and handed one to Andy.

"No thanks. I'll take a Pepsi or something."

"You've got to be kidding me!" The blonde looked at him and then shrieked a string of curse words.

The brunette joined them. "What's going on?"

Her friend said, "I picked up an infant. He's not even old enough to drink."

Andy flushed. "Yeah, of course I am!" He grabbed the beer, guzzled it, grabbed another and angrily drank it.

"That's more like it. Let's dance," the blonde said. She stripped off his shirt and kissed him.

He snatched the shirt from her and swung it over his head as they danced. The music got louder and wilder. He looked at the band playing on a makeshift stage.

"You know how to play an instrument?" his date asked.

"I've been learning piano, mostly on my own with easy arrangements. But I always wanted to play guitar."

"So what's stopping you?"

"Yeah. What's stopping me?" Andy leaped on stage and borrowed a bass guitar from one of the players. The female lead singer smiled at him and nodded her okay.

Andy began playing, surprising himself that he sounded pretty good.

The blonde and her friends gathered closer and swayed to the music. After the set ended, Andy put the guitar down, crossed to the cooler and got another beer, only vaguely wondering why he didn't feel any effect from it even though he was not used to drinking alcohol.

"Hey," the blonde whispered in his ear, pressing against him, "let's get naked."

He looked at her and noticed that many couples were taking their clothes off and having sex. He started to consent, but vaguely remembered he had a different agenda. "I need to get going. Maybe next time I pass this way."

She shrugged and approached the next guy, "Hey, let's get naked."

Andy walked away from them, leaving the music and the party behind.

As he reached the highway, Joker fell in step.

Andy glanced down at him, abashed that he'd forgotten all about his dog since meeting the blonde. He patted Joker's head. "You're my favorite blond. Sorry about that."

They walked. Andy didn't know for how long. He wasn't tired. "Say, Joker, how long you think it'll take to go four hundred miles?" Andy looked up at the stars, as if he'd find an answer there. Thinking of the Hopi Reservation, he reached the outskirts of a village called Walpi at early sunrise. He saw an elderly white-haired man hunched outside a small wood frame house, peering in a window.

"Hey," Andy called out, hurrying closer, "what the heck are you doing?"

"Waiting for my wife," the man said.

"I thought maybe you were a burglar or something."

"What would you do if I was?"

"Uh, chase you away, I guess. Call the cops."

The man looked at him in amusement. "Want to wait with me?"

"I guess so."

The man settled under a nearby cottonwood tree and picked up the wood carving he was working on.

"What's that?" Andy asked as the man began whittling.

"A Kachina doll."

Andy reached out to touch it, but the man held it out of reach. "Don't."

"Are you a Hopi Indian?" Andy asked.

The man nodded. "Didn't you intend to reach a Hopi village?"

"Yeah."

"Then why would you be surprised to find a Hopi here?"

Andy shrugged.

"Not much for banter, are you?" the man asked. "That's all right. Tell me what you know about Hopi. I need to laugh."

"You don't have to make fun of me! I didn't hurt anybody."

"Hey, young fella, don't get heated up over harmless teasing."

"My mother is meeting me here."

"She is? What's her name?"

Andy looked at him. "Don't you know?"

"I think the question should be turned around," the old man said gently. "Don't <u>you</u> know?"

"She flies a Cessna. It's not her plane but she's in a flying club at Van Nuys airport and sometimes we go on trips like out to the desert or this one time we flew to San Francisco and then we all rode a cable car."

"So she's a pilot. What else does she do?"

"I don't talk to strangers."

"Good. I was enjoying the quiet until you burst into my space."

"I didn't. I was just walking with my dog."

"Where you from?"

"L.A."

"And you were just out for a stroll?" The old man chuckled, and bent his head to his carving, hiding his mirth.

Andy patted Joker, and addressed his dog. "Don't mind this old man. He's probably got Alzheimer's disease or something." He turned back to the Hopi. "How much longer will your wife be?"

The man shrugged. "Not much longer. I have been waiting for her for twelve years but now she is almost ready."

"And then where are you going?"

"You can come with us, if you want. Looks like you're a lone traveler and that's not always safe."

"I'm doing okay on my own."

The Hopi patiently finished his carving. "I need to paint it."

"Who's the doll for? Your granddaughter?"

"It's not a toy. We use Kachinas as gifts during a ceremonial dance, from the men to the women. The dolls are passed down to the girls in the tribe. Each doll represents the spirit of a deity, or an animal or one of our deceased ancestors. Kachinas are not just for tourists to buy. They are part of our heritage. We use them to remember who we are."

"Okay. I get it."

"You come to a Hopi village, but you don't know anything about us."

"Um, my mother's grandfather was Hopi. He lived here. Maybe not this village, but on this reservation."

"There aren't very many of us here anymore. Do you know his name? Maybe I have heard of him."

Andy touched the buffalo nickel. "His name is Q something."

He shook his head, knowing that he had heard the name before and should be able to remember it. His mind felt foggy.

The man glanced toward the house, and stood up, his face breaking into an eager smile.

Curious, Andy stood up, too, and watched as a woman emerged from a wall in the house and approached the man. "Is that your wife?"

Nodding, the Hopi left Andy and took the woman's hand in his. As the two embraced, their appearances changed to more vibrant and youthful vigor until they seemed to be thirty years younger in age, stopping their appearance at a comfortable middle age as if they'd discussed this before. They spent a few moments talking quietly.

The man turned to Andy. "Coming with us? We'll show you the way."

Andy stared at them, baffled. "I don't need to go with you. You go on. I'll see you around."

"But where are you going?" the woman asked. "You shouldn't be alone."

"Some guys I met bungee jumping said they're going to Vegas," Andy said, improvising. There was no way he was going to get stuck with a dull married couple who'd spoil his fun with a lot of do's and don'ts. "I promised to meet them."

"What about the promise to your mother?" the Hopi man asked. "To meet here?"

"I got that wrong. I forgot she changed it to Las Vegas."

The man and woman talked in whispers.

"He doesn't know he's dead, does he?" she asked.

The man shook his head. "I think you're right. But he seems like a good boy."

"Why did he come here?"

"Says he's got a Hopi great-grandfather."

"Well, dear, did he say who the man was?"

"He can't recall the name. It begins with a Q."

She looked thoughtful a moment. "Possibly Qaletaqa? Maybe we should pass the word along to watch for the boy."

"And maybe we shouldn't meddle. He'll be all right. He'll find his way."

The woman turned to Andy. "It's a long way for a boy traveling by himself." When Andy shrugged, she conferred in whispers with her husband.

Andy remembered the two bicycles on the bridge earlier. He smiled slowly, then concentrated on visualizing the Ferrari poster on the wall over his bed at home.

He looked up the street and saw a yellow Ferrari waiting for him, its engine purring.

The woman approached Andy with her hand out to him. "You said you're going to Las Vegas. How are you going to get there?"

"Don't worry about me." Andy grinned. "I'll drive."

Chapter 6

J emma stood in the open doorway of Andy's bedroom. If she could only figure out a way to move that heavy aquarium tank of his, she'd put it in another room so she could tend the fish elsewhere and wouldn't have to come in here at all.

She steeled her resolve then walked briskly to the coral tank, turned off the water filter and fed the fish. Knowing she had to wait for them to eat the flakes before she turned the filter back on, she stared sightlessly at the darting fish, counting out loud to one hundred. Algae was building up on the inner glass and she felt guilty for not taking time to clean it, to let the fish "see out" the way Andy always explained it.

The impact of Andy's accident was far-reaching. Jemma's control of her own world had slipped off its axis. All her life, she'd been able to hide her emotions, even deep pain, and maintain a calm surface, as placid as a mountain lake in summer. But now she exploded in anger at Hart for even a mild comment about the weather or a question about what she wanted to eat for dinner.

She couldn't seem to stop the endless cycle of thoughts begging frantically for answers that did not exist in logic: *How can I reverse this? How can I turn back time and have another chance with Andy? How can I wake up to the relief that* *his death was just a dreadful nightmare? What do I have to <u>do</u> to make things different? Where do I find a new reality where Andy is still alive?*

Jemma watched the fish, barely heeding her stream of consciousness because it was now a familiar refrain that hardly intruded on the counting.

One hundred.

She flipped the filter switch back on, turned on her heel and, as if she wore blinders, steadfastly looked at nothing in the room except the doorway as she headed to it.

The house phone rang. Hart's muffled voice came up from the kitchen, answering it.

She kept walking, and left the room.

Hart came up the stairs and met her at the top.

Still ashen from the effort it took to not collapse onto Andy's bed and hug his pillow for the rest of her life, Jemma woodenly bypassed Hart and started going down to her study.

He reached out a hand to stop her. "Will you help me pick things out?" He nodded toward Andy's room and held up the empty Nordstrom shopping bag he'd brought upstairs.

As if coming awake from a deep sleep, she looked at him. "Pick what things?"

"That was the funeral home."

She remembered hearing the phone ring.

He studied the shopping bag, avoiding her eyes. "They wanted to remind us to bring...to bring a...an outfit when we come this afternoon to choose a casket."

Jemma stared at him.

"Please, Jemma." He looked at her beseechingly. "I can't go through this discussion again."

"But I don't want strangers rubbernecking our son, lying in a coffin, unprotected."

"You don't have to help. I'll take care of this." Hart went into Andy's room and opened the closet.

Jemma stood for a moment, frozen, then came to life and raced to grab the pair of dress shoes in Hart's hand. She flung them back in the closet. "What the hell do you think he needs shoes for!"

Hart ran a hand across his forehead. "Yeah, you're right. Okay, a suit. He has one from my father's funeral last year. I hope he didn't outgrow it."

"Would you listen to yourself, Hart? It doesn't matter if it fits! They'll slit it up the back, they'll cut the seams, they'll do whatever it takes to make this dog and pony show work."

"Jemma. I would prefer if you leave the room now."

"You think his mother doesn't deserve a say in how the goddamned funeral is handled? He doesn't need special clothes. There isn't going to be a viewing. We aren't going to sit around staring at the empty husk and pretend that Andy is watching over us, wearing wings and a halo."

Hart sighed heavily. "I don't know why you have to make this even harder than it is."

"Harder? How am I doing that? I'm being practical. One of us needs to be."

He turned toward the dresser drawers and haphazardly put underwear, socks, t-shirt and a folded dress shirt into the shopping bag. At the closet, he shoved hangers aside until he found the suit he'd remembered, and grabbed it off the rod.

She watched in silence for a moment. "What I want doesn't matter to you, does it?"

"This isn't something I'm enjoying, Jemma. No parent would ask for this. But someone has to do it. You talk about being practical, but how is it practical to stand here arguing? And since you refuse, I'm taking care of what needs to be done. That's all. Don't make it harder. Just don't."

"You blame me for the accident."

He looked at her. "What else can I say to convince you otherwise? You've got that stuck in your mind and nothing I say will get it unstuck. Maybe you like having it there so you can gnaw on it like a bone and suck every bit of guilt marrow out of it. So go ahead. Blame yourself if it makes you feel important."

She slapped his face. "There is nothing I wouldn't do to reverse what happened. But I wasn't driving that car."

"Might as well have been." He idly rubbed the cheek she'd slapped, more for something to do than to ease any pain. "The way you keep going over the details of fighting with him and accusing him of taking drugs and then he ran off to escape you and then you chased after him, and you yelled his name again and again but it was too windy, the wind was in your face and he couldn't hear you and you have convinced yourself he deliberately ran into an oncoming car to get away from you."

"Well." She drew back, stunned. "That's quite a summary. And it certainly is revealing of the way you view it. I never said he deliberately did this. That's your sick interpretation, Hartley. I'm sorry I thought it was safe to confide my deepest fears and thoughts in a vulnerable moment. I should have known to keep my mouth shut in this marriage."

"Oh, for crying out loud, Jemma! Must we do this? Does it have to be about you and me making each other crazy instead of comforting each other?" He looked at her a long moment. "Does it have to be this way with us?"

"I don't know, Hart," she whispered. She was hurting so badly that she might as well have drunk acid. The grief was eating her up from the inside out.

She looked at him and realized that Hart had drunk from the same vial and his pain was probably the equal of hers.

"Hart...I'm sorry...I am." She gently touched his cheek. "I'm being a bitch. A super bitch."

He nodded wryly in agreement, with a tiny smile to show he was willing to reach a place of forgiveness.

"You deserve the kind of wife who'd put her soft loving arms around you and whisper words of kindness and comfort and peace." She felt deflated by her outbursts, like a descended hot air balloon now sprawled limp and lifeless on the ground. "I can't seem to find that woman inside me. I sense she's deep in hiding...if she even exists."

"She's in there, Jemma. I've met her before. Maybe you could invite her to come out? Tell her I won't bite?"

She held her sides, hugging herself tightly as if she could anchor her beating heart inside her body and keep it from imploding with the rage she felt over Andy's death.

"We'll hold the wake with a closed coffin." He hung up the suit at random in the closet and put the shopping bag on the closet floor. "Like you want."

She looked at his face, and saw his deep sorrow. She took the suit hanger and bag. "Put these in the car, Hart. My car. I'll drive. My anger keeps me alert, and I think you're about to curl up and escape in sleep."

They both smiled half-heartedly at her attempt at a joke.

"We'll go do this thing together," she said. "And I'll be supportive of your wishes. I know it's important for you to let people see that it's really Andy in the coffin...and not some terrible mistake, where they can't put all this to rest because they think not seeing the body, not seeing his face, means he's not really dead. I get it. I do. I really do. So, okay, we'll do it that way. But I don't have to look. I won't. I'll stare at the candles...or the flowers or whatever. And then later we'll do the dispersement at sea. Another day. Not the same day."

He nodded, but didn't reach for the clothes. His face crumpled, like he was about to cry.

She stroked his arm, like she would Andy when he was home from school sick with the flu. "Why don't you go lie down for a half hour? I'll put all the things they need in the car. I'll get you up when it's time to go. And we'll get this over with. One thing at a time, without thinking too much about it. One foot in front of the other, right? You can handle that, can't you?"

"Yeah. Yeah, I can do that." He started for the door, hesitated, then stumbled to Andy's bed where he crawled beneath the sheets and closed his eyes. Tears trickled from beneath his lashes.

Jemma looked at him a moment, wishing for the right words to say but feeling a terrible void as if this man was someone she didn't know and yet she was being called on to understand his thoughts and dreams and needs.

She smoothed a lock of blond hair off his forehead, then tiptoed out with the burial clothes in her arms.

They drove to the funeral home in silence, and Jemma zoomed into a guest parking space in front of the office. A sign pointed left for the chapel, but they walked straight and opened a wide heavy door marked with a small bronze sign that read "Office." Upon entering the elegant reception area, they were greeted soberly by a young woman dressed in a white shirt and black skirt. Her swift glance took in the bag of clothes.

"We're the Powells," Jemma said. "Melissa is expecting us."

"I'll let her know you're here. Please take a seat." The young woman turned away and spoke softly into the phone at her desk.

Hart sat stiffly on the edge of a chair, looking at his clasped hands.

Jemma, too restless to join him, wandered the room looking at the vases of fresh flowers, the innocuous landscape prints framed on the walls, the boxes of tissues placed strategically.

Classical music played from speakers hidden throughout the long room. Chairs were grouped near potted palms. Shaded lamps emitted glare-free lighting.

An older couple sat in a corner, staring away from each other, their shoulders slumped, their faces numb.

Jemma avoided their eyes, realizing she didn't want to invite a conversation. She did not want to know why they were here, whether it was for future planning for themselves, for immediate needs for a family member, or if they were waiting for a ceremony to start in the chapel.

She glanced at the exit door, wanting to bolt. She breathed slowly, forcing herself to remain and see the task through to completion.

"Mr. and Mrs. Powell?" Another young woman, a darker clone of the receptionist, approached them, her sensible pumps soundless on the thick, moss-green carpeting. "I'm Melissa. Will you come this way?"

Hart stood up, startled by her voice as if from a reverie. "Where–?"

"Just to my office," she said, soothing his unspoken fears of what was to come next.

They followed Melissa down a carpeted hallway with occasional half-moon tables holding a vase of flowers and the ever-present boxes of tissues.

She led them past a series of closed and unmarked doors into a quiet office where she ushered them to upholstered chairs at a round table. On the table was a large glossy binder, with the name of the funeral home on the cover, and the slogan "We care" emblazoned on it.

Jemma glanced at it. Her eyebrow arched. "That's comforting to know."

"Pardon me?" Melissa asked.

Hart shot Jemma a look, begging her silently to take it easy.

Jemma sat and pulled the binder to her.

Reaching out, Melissa took it and placed it in front of herself. "Let's not get ahead of ourselves. I'd like first to discuss what kind of ceremony you envision for your son."

"First?" Jemma asked politely. "Okay, first would be high school graduation. Then college. Maybe graduate school as well. A celebration of a big promotion at work. And then a wedding. Babies, he always loved being around kids. So then of course we have all those milestones as well, kindergarten graduation, birthdays, high school, college, wedding. You know, the typical cycle. That's how I 'envision' ceremonies for my son."

"Jemma–" Hart whispered in agony.

"I understand." Melissa smiled gently at both of them. "I know this must be very hard for you."

"Have you lost a child?" Jemma asked.

"No, actually I have not, and I don't presume to know exactly what you are feeling."

"Good. Don't try. You'll never get it right."

"Maybe we should get started." Hart looked at Melissa in desperation.

Melissa addressed him. "On the phone, we discussed having the wake here at the chapel, and then next week, the funeral service itself, again in the chapel, followed by interment on our grounds." She waved delicately toward the window.

Through the sheer curtains could be seen the parking area and beyond that the cemetery with its rolling green lawn and countless headstones set flush to the ground.

Hart nodded mutely as if hypnotized by her gesture.

"We have a variety of options to review," Melissa continued, "and I'd be happy to answer any of your questions as we go through them. Will that be satisfactory?"

Again Hart nodded.

Jemma stared out the window, picturing a burial in the cemetery. "I don't want burial in a casket."

"Jemma." Hart touched her arm.

"Cremation is an option that many of our clients choose," Melissa said. "You can decide whether to inter the urn, take it with you to display in your home as a permanent memorial, or disperse the cremains in some other fashion."

"Scatter the ashes. At sea." Jemma looked at Hart. "It's what we just discussed in Andy's room. Remember?"

Melissa nodded politely as if she'd been part of that discussion, and opened the binder. As she went over the options and prices, Jemma tuned out, letting Hart ask any questions he found necessary to raise.

Jemma became aware that Melissa had shut the binder and shifted to a new topic.

102

"And so before we proceed any further," Melissa said, "we need either or both of you to identify the body. Or if you prefer, you can give me a driver's license—"

Jemma cut in, "He didn't have one yet."

"—or other photo I.D.," Melissa finished smoothly.

"I..." Hart's face lost color. "I wasn't expecting this part, I guess." He began crying silently.

"Wait here, Hart." Jemma got up and looked at Melissa.

As the two women returned toward the reception area but kept going further down another hallway, Jemma said, "You probably think I'm difficult to get along with."

"Not at all. Actually, I've had people throw things at me, in their grief over losing someone they love. I try to think how I would react, and I don't take it personally."

"That's truly amazing. Both awesome and admirable." Jemma could tell that her sarcasm had gone right over the girl's head.

Inside a small antiseptic room, brightly lit by a ceiling fixture, Jemma identified her son's body. She knew it would not be easy to see him again, lifeless, and forced her scientific mind to verify this physical body was correctly labeled.

"I'm sorry," Melissa said, opening the door for Jemma to leave. "We try to make the whole process as painless as we can."

"Why?"

"Excuse me?"

"Why bother? Pain forces you to realize what happened."

Jemma walked briskly, heading back toward Melissa's office.

Melissa trotted after her. "If you'd like, we could look in here for a moment before rejoining your husband. You might want to spare him the decision about the casket. You'll need one for the wake."

Stopping, Jemma waited impatiently for Melissa to open another door. They went in. It was a wide room, with four caskets in it. One was occupied. Jemma's eyes widened, not expecting this. She noticed that the occupant, a gray-haired woman, had a face that was distinctly green-tinged.

Melissa turned to a display and began pointing out the various features of brass handles, mahogany versus oak cabinetry, and silk versus satin pillow lining.

"Save your canned speech." Jemma walked out.

In Melissa's office, Jemma grabbed her purse. "Get up, Hart. We're not doing this to Andy."

Melissa hurried in. "I'm sorry about that. She was not supposed to still be in there. There was a delay in her service due to her husband being hospitalized for a stroke. She's actually due for a touch-up."

"Who?" Hart asked.

"Let's go," Jemma said to him firmly.

"But...we haven't settled on the arrangements–" Hart protested.

Jemma grabbed the legal pad next to Melissa's presentation binder, and wrote on it. "Oak casket. White lilies. Open coffin for the rosary or wake or whatever you call it for this Saturday noon. Then private cremation, and I'll pick up the ashes next week."

Hart looked at her in confusion. "What–?"

"We'll take a boat out and scatter them at sea. He'd like that better than all this bullshit."

"Please, Mrs. Powell," Melissa said, "lower your voice. We have other clients here."

"Clients? Your clients are cadavers. The rest of us are suckers caught up in a system that makes a whole lot of money out of the business of grief."

"If you'd rather see our economy caskets," Melissa said, "I think I have some photos around here someplace. Yes, I'm sure I have a binder in my credenza. We don't keep actual samples on hand because, frankly, the clientele we have in this area are not interested in price cutting to that extent."

"You think it's about the money?"

"Perhaps it is. I'm trying to service your needs, Mrs. Powell. And so, if it's about the price, I can talk to our director about offering you a special payment plan–"

"I don't give a shit about the money," Jemma said. "But as long as we're paying this much, I'd rather give it to the scholarship fund we're starting in our son's name."

"The...what?" Hart asked, bewildered.

"Oh, Hartley, for fuck's sake stop saying 'what' like you're feeble-minded. Get up! We're done here." Jemma scribbled a fax number on the legal pad. "Send me the work order, Melissa. I'll sign it and fax it back to you with a credit card number."

Jemma left, not waiting for Hart to figure out he needed to move faster to keep up. Behind her, she heard Hart apologize profusely to Melissa for his wife's behavior and language.

The last thing Jemma could hear before she was out of earshot was Melissa saying in an unflappable monotone, "I understand completely, sir. And I am so very sorry for your loss. All of us here wish to make this process easier for you. We care."

Standing outside her car, Jemma waited for Hart, suspecting he was delayed by kowtowing to the entire staff, and perhaps even that green-faced lady in the casket showroom.

She stared across the private driveway at the unnaturally green cemetery, so quiet and still. From the distance, freeway traffic barely intruded its dull echoes of combustion engines and a thousand susurrating tires on the 101. A scattering of birds flew overhead. She thought maybe they were mockingbirds. Or maybe not.

What difference does it make?

A gardener started up a leaf blower nearby on the grounds. She smelled the gas fumes coming her way and idly wondered why the gardener didn't bother with at least a cotton mask over his nose and mouth. Or an oxygen tank on his back. Maybe he thought he was invincible, or maybe he didn't care if he died young.

Andy died young, younger than that gardener.

She felt exhausted, her eyes sticky with fatigue.

Hart emerged, blinking in the bright midday sun.

She unlocked the car with the key fob. He silently slumped in on the passenger side, and she slid behind the wheel. As she started the engine, she shot an inquisitive look at her husband. "Aren't you going to read me the riot act, Hartley? Warn me I'd better not act that way at the service on Saturday? That I'd better shape up?"

He looked at her a moment, his eyes red-rimmed. "Would...would it do any good?"

She put the car in gear and backed out. "Probably not." She glanced at him. "In case you can't tell, I'm totally pissed. No way I'm going to bottle it up just to be light and polite."

Chapter 7

In the aftermath of the accident, Marybeth felt completely alone and utterly worthless. No matter how many times she explained the events of that day to her husband, he asked yet another question that she'd already covered. And yet, by the way he rephrased it and hurled it at her, he made it seem as if he was bringing up a new issue that she was compelled to address.

It seemed to her that he fancied himself the District Attorney in a headline-worthy case, and she was under his magnified scrutiny.

Although he claimed to be on her side, to be offering loving support in this difficult time, Cabot commented sadly that she should have stopped that day, like all the other drivers around here would at that T-intersection.

"But I didn't realize there was a stop sign." She wondered why he couldn't understand this simple fact which she had pointed out more than once. "I usually take the back way to the store. I don't go out to the freeway that often and I haven't memorized all the streets in the short time we've lived here."

He accused her of using a flippant tone with him.

After she mollified him, he asked how it was that she didn't see the sign, even if she didn't recall that it was there.

"The wind broke a tree branch and the dangling branch hid the sign." She knew better than to remind him how many times she'd already said this, so she kept her explanation neutral as if telling him for the first time. "The police officer even took photos of it, showing that all I could possibly see from my angle was the leafy tree and all its big branches."

He badgered her about being on the phone, or checking her makeup, or changing the radio station, or putting in a CD, or drinking from her ever-present bottle of water instead of watching the road.

To each accusation, she tried to sound strong and sure of herself, but she was weakening under his assault. His methods were working, the same way a terrorist erodes your confidence in everyday routines and safety, and she now felt muddled about her role in the accident.

She was already immersed in a deep sense of grief over that boy losing his life because her car had hit him, and Cabot's studied attack on her, bringing up different scenarios as if they were true, made her question herself incessantly.

Had she been looking in the mirror, checking her lipstick instead of paying attention to her driving? *Had* she been fretting about her hair blowing in the wind? *Had* she been glancing down at the radio? Or the sticky note she'd written her directions on?

She clung to one indisputable fact: she *knew* she hadn't been on the phone, and that reality was verified by the police, who examined her record of calls.

"You realize the attorney will be expensive," Cabot said. "Even a civil case doesn't come cheap."

"I know, Cabot. I'm sorry."

"And this is going to wreak havoc on our car insurance rate!"

"I wish I could make it all go away," she said.

What she meant was that since she couldn't wish away the reality of the fatal accident, she wished that at least Cabot would go away.

Living with Cabot had grown to be a worse situation than living in solitude, which was the state he had rescued her from when they'd first met two years earlier at an investment seminar he was giving in Palm Springs.

The idea that she could simply open the door and leave was not something that occurred to Marybeth.

She felt trapped in this marriage, and helpless to change her life.

Marybeth napped fitfully on the living room couch, having been awake most of the night with tortured thoughts and now, mid-day, desperate for sleep.

Even more, she was desperate to escape Cabot's scathing looks, if only for an hour of oblivion.

She sank deeper into the soft cushions, and then dreamed that she was at a big event where she was in line for the ladies restroom, but the line was over two blocks long, and stretched outside the building.

She turned away and suddenly was standing in deep snow, shivering in a thin floral dress and sandals.

Naomi appeared at her side, laughing, and handed her a big red parka and warm boots. "Trust me to bring a spare set. Didn't you realize the high desert would be cold this time of year? You don't have enough sense to take care of yourself."

"I feel better, now that you're here."

"Hey, look." Naomi pointed. "They're stuffing strawberries over there. Let's go help them!"

Marybeth looked at her, excited. "I've never stuffed strawberries before."

Naomi held out a hand. "Don't worry, Bunny. I'll teach you. And we'll eat all we want."

The dream shifted, and they walked together into a peaceful garden where deer bent to drink at a sparkling stream and wild rabbits peered at them from the safety of tall grasses.

Marybeth smiled and took Naomi's hand.

Marybeth closed her journal and placed a protective hand over it.

Cabot let his outstretched hand fall to his side. "I only wanted a look, Marybeth. To get an idea of your state of mind, since you won't confide in me."

"You make it sound like I'm being stubborn. I have the right to privacy."

"Remember the days when you would read your journal entries to me every night while I rubbed your feet with that peppermint-scented cream you liked so much? It was expensive, that spa cream. But I didn't mind indulging you, buying tube after tube at that fancy organic store you think is so special."

"It wasn't that long ago. I remember."

"Now–" he glanced at the journal– "you act like I'm the enemy agent."

"Just my private little silly thoughts, Cabot. That's all. The therapist said I should--"

"Interesting about that therapist, isn't it?" He didn't raise his voice and yet there was a new darker note in the timbre that made her cringe.

"What do you mean?" She tried to meet his eyes but faked a stray eyelash or clump of mascara and looked down, pulling at her lashes gently between thumb and index finger as if trying to release an irritant.

"I reconciled our checking account this morning, and looked at some of the items online."

"Oh?"

"I think you know exactly what I mean."

She pretended to think. "Oh, you mean–why are the checks to the therapist made out to cash?"

He waited.

"They asked me to do it that way. Know what I think?" Her mind raced, desperate to cover her tracks. "I think they're trying to avoid income tax by not declaring all the money they get from patients."

"Strange that when I viewed the back of each check written by you, they were all endorsed by you."

"That's right." She looked him in the eye. "I cashed the checks for them at the bank and then gave them the money. I thought you'd appreciate having a record, that's why I wrote the checks in the first place instead of using the ATM."

Actually, she was always afraid to withdraw more than twenty dollars at a time from the ATM because Cabot would question her need for cash. Knowing that cancelled checks were not mailed to them with their monthly statements, she'd felt safe writing a check for each supposed therapy session, but then cashing it herself to have funds for aiding the homeless. She hadn't anticipated that he would take the time to go online and view the bank's digital record of cancelled checks.

She worried now what she had done to make him suspicious enough to investigate.

"Then that explains it." He made an expansive gesture, as if giving her his blessing.

She smiled, but not too broadly, careful not to show her relief.

"Let's get something to eat. I'll take you out. Get you out of the house. A change of scene will do you good."

Marybeth shook her head slightly, making sure it wouldn't look like a mutinous declaration, but only a simple, polite refusal that anyone might offer. "I'm not that all hungry."

"You have to keep up your strength. You're too thin as it is. Come on." His tone grew soft, purring coaxing as he tilted her chin up with his fingertip. "Fix your hair and makeup. Put on something pretty so I won't be embarrassed to be seen with you, and I'll take you out."

Cabot chose a romantic Italian restaurant, dimly lit. A silver-haired pianist played a soft medley of Dean Martin and Frank Sinatra hits in one corner while bantering with customers as they entered. Marybeth stood in the doorway, glancing around in dismay.

"I knew you didn't want some noisy burger joint or coffee shop." Cabot held up two fingers for the *maitre d'* to seat them. "You can't even hear yourself think in those places."

That kind of place was exactly what Marybeth had wanted, and hoped for. Someplace loud where she could pretend not to hear Cabot. Conversation would've been easier to fake with a lot of pretending she didn't quite catch what he said, and would he repeat it please. Those interchanges were easier to handle because she could stretch a single comment or trivial question to last nearly the whole evening, and thus evade his usual grilling.

Since the accident, since he'd increased his probing, Marybeth felt like she was on the hot seat permanently. She recalled seeing a film about someone in the resistance being questioned in one of the Communist countries during the Cold War, and the person didn't realize that each time they gripped the seat of their chair for strength, the sweat on their palms was being measured by a device in the chair pad, and their pulse was being analyzed to prove their nervousness meant they were lying.

That's what it boiled down to, she realized, watching Cabot eat in big bites, half the food sliding off his fork and landing on the plate or the white tablecloth. He was the interrogator and this was a power play in which he was determined to prove that she was lying about the accident and her part in it. For reasons of his own, he was going to prove that she was not an innocent participant in a deadly accident, but rather the perpetrator of a killing.

She put her fork down, her appetite gone.

"You're not eating," Cabot said, chewing. He tore a hunk of bread from the fresh loaf the waitress brought to their table, seeing the first one had been eaten. He used the bread to sop up the sauce on his plate, and then ate it, leaning over his plate so that bits of soggy crumbs fell from his mouth, disgusting her.

She made a pretense of eating, enough to get his attention off her. "It's so good. Thank you for bringing me here."

"Yeah. Knew you'd like it if you gave it a chance. Put some meat on your bones. You need to gain five pounds. At least. You're so damned skinny, you think you have to look like one of those stick-thin Hollywood actresses. I hope you see the futility of going to auditions. After all, look what it leads to," he added blandly, eyeing her over his wine glass as he took a long swallow.

Marybeth lifted her glass of water and took a sip, wishing hard for the right words to say so she could gain equilibrium, and yet unable to locate them on her tongue.

Later, in the car on the way home, Cabot, like a dog with a bone, brought up the subject of Marybeth's journal. "What do you write about all the time?"

"Just stuff."

"I can see from your face that you won't confide in me. So remind me what you used to write. You'd sit for hours with your precious notebook, oblivious to everything. I'd try to get you interested in going out to eat or going to a movie, and all you wanted to do was to sit in a corner, curled up with a pen and pad." He chuckled.

"You make me sound like a spoiled child who wouldn't listen."

He shrugged, affirming the description.

"I wrote...I wrote that you were such an incredible listener, and I felt so safe telling you everything. Absolutely everything."

As she spoke, she marveled that she had not only written long pages on that theme in their early days together, but had believed them completely. How had she been so deluded?

She knew things had truly been different between them then, and she had felt secure with him, or she never would have married this man.

"But something happened?" He glanced toward her briefly, his tone carelessly interested before he turned his attention back to the traffic.

That seeming disinterest in her response triggered her in a way that his usual needling did not. "Yes!" she blurted. "You began treating me differently.

Always scolding and correcting me, pointing out everything I do wrong until I can barely breathe without fearing that you'll say I didn't inhale the right way!"

"No, Marybeth," he said gently. "You withdrew from me. You became secretive. You pulled away, and no matter how hard I tried to love you back into our special little world, you resisted with all your might." His eyes brimmed with tears. "All I ever wanted with you was intimacy, but you are so cold, Marybeth. So very cold and standoffish. Everyone says so, but I defend you to them, and I explain that you are just not yourself because of some hard times. But I don't know how much more I can take of this."

She knew in her heart that she was not at all cold or standoffish. She was friendly and loving and warm. But she couldn't think how to explain herself in words he would comprehend. He never seemed to understand when she defended herself, and it just led to more frustration.

Now, since she didn't know what to say, she said nothing.

He took a hand off the wheel, reached over and grabbed her crotch. "In the mood, baby, after this nice dinner?"

"Oh, of course, Cabot. Dear." Marybeth grew icy inside, knowing it would be better to please him for a few minutes in bed than to have his wrath swell and grow if she rejected his advances.

That night, after being in bed with Cabot, pretending she was acting out a scene for an R-rated feature film, Marybeth took a shower with water as hot as she could tolerate, disgusted with herself and feeling unclean. But she knew that appeasing his needs would buy her peace for about a week, during which time Cabot would strut like a rooster, confident he'd impregnated her.

When he saw the inevitable negative test, he'd blame her, but she didn't dare tell him she'd begun using birth control secretly. She didn't want to have a baby with him, and in fact realized one day that the real reason he married her was that he thought her youth equated fertility. He wanted a son, and since the child she gave birth to last year had been a girl, she knew their loss wasn't the reason for his interest in another baby: it was that son he wanted, to carry on his name, to live out the dreams Cabot had failed to achieve in his own life.

She lay awake a long time, loathing herself for staying in this marriage. Finally, she fell asleep. And she dreamed.

In the dream, she was in a crowded restaurant complex. All the rooms were industrial gray with exposed beams and wiring. People talked loudly all around her, but she was alone, and felt they were hostile to her.

She was trying to find the correct stairs to go down, but kept finding flights that only went up. Finally she found the right staircase according to the note in her hand–but it was a drop-down fire escape ladder centered over an immense table where business people were holding a meeting.

Trying to get someone's attention, she tugged at one man's suit sleeve. He looked at her as if looking through her, then turned back to the meeting and used a flip chart to continue his presentation even though he was now alone at the table. All the others had gotten up and drifted off.

Marybeth pointed this out to him, and tried to climb on the table to access the fire escape, but he pushed her away.

Giving up, she hurried off, caught up in the mass of people shoving and jostling each other. One woman staggering toward her, pinch-faced and weary, wore a print dress and cradled her pregnant belly, protecting it from random elbow punches. Marybeth stopped, staring at the woman, both of them penned in by bodies.

She saw that something was wrong about the woman's pregnancy. It wasn't a nice round belly but scrawny and flabby like someone had tied a half-empty sack of flour under the woman's dress.

The woman glared at her, muttered something incomprehensible and shoved a man's back, trying to pass him. Marybeth tried to help the woman, but the woman turned on her in a fury, scratched Marybeth's face and shoved her aside.

Waking, Marybeth lay in bed, helpless to stop her tears.

She glanced at Cabot, snoring as loud as a jet engine on the other side of the bed. As quietly as possible, fearing he'd awake if she jostled the mattress, she slipped out of bed and went into the kitchen to start his breakfast.

Moments later, Cabot startled her by coming up behind her as she cooked French toast, barefooted and in her nightgown. He thrust her slippers in her face. "How could you stand to walk on that goddamned bedroom carpet, Marybeth? It's disgusting! Go wash your feet and put these on." He reached across her and turned off the stove flame. "Go on."

She took the slippers and raced out.

"If you could condescend to paint the damned bedroom," he called out after her, "we could get the freaking carpet installed and you could go barefoot all you want!"

She went to the paint store that day, and then painted the bedroom so that the new carpet could be installed. She chose a soft taupe, liking the neutral tone.

Even though Cabot had insisted she choose the color, as she painted the walls and he stood in the doorway watching, she could tell from the curl of his lip that he did not approve.

Too bad, she decided. *He'll have to live with it, or paint it something else himself.*

She almost giggled to herself, picturing his face if he could read her thoughts.

But rushing in on the heels of the giggle was the memory of hitting that boy with her car, and the sound of the thud, and the horror of realizing he was fatally injured. Killed by her. There was no room for laughter in her heart and she wondered if there ever would be again.

After cleaning up the paint mess, she stripped and took a hot shower. Her arm and neck muscles were sore from all the stretching, and she knew that a sauna would be more relaxing and water-conservation-friendly than this, so she turned off the water, got out, and then heated up the sauna room.

She wrapped a towel turban around her hair and secured a bath towel around her torso. She filled the special wood-handled plastic pitcher with water and took it into the sauna room with her so she could pour water on the box of lava rocks in one corner and increase the heat as desired.

Marybeth set the wall timer for twenty minutes and it began ticking down. She thumbed the rheostat switched down, to dim the overhead light, and sat back on the slatted wood bench, enjoying the solitude.

It occurred to her that she might be able to sweat away her guilty feelings, purge her shame and self-hatred. When the timer dinged, she set it for another twenty minutes. At the end of the second twenty-minute session, she still felt terrible, and so she reset the timer.

As she poured water onto the lava rocks, she whispered a Bible verse she'd read earlier that day, seeking comfort in her grandmother's copy of the ancient texts but instead finding condemnation,

"But the wicked shall perish...Into smoke shall they consume away." During this, steam billowed from the rocks and she visualized her wickedness being consumed.

The door banged open.

Cabot stood backlit in the doorway. "I've been looking everywhere--!" He spun the timer off. It dinged loudly in the sudden silence. He pushed the rheostat switch up to glaring brightness.

Marybeth squinted, and huddled in the corner of her bench.

"Didn't you hear me calling you?"

She shrugged. She wasn't sure now, but began to suspect that she had heard his voice calling her name and had pushed it out of her reality the way she wanted to push him off a cliff.

Feeling bold, she held out the empty water pitcher to be filled. "And reset the timer."

He observed her weak, overheated condition. "How long have you been in here?"

Apparently realizing she didn't know for sure, he helped her up and to the bed. She had shoved the bed into the center of the room so she could paint around it, and now she felt like she was floating on an untethered island or on a cloud. He flung open the windows.

"Didn't you know you have to air out a room when you paint? The fumes are disgusting in here. If it doesn't clear by bedtime, I'm going to a hotel."

"Yeah, good idea," she mumbled.

He went to the bathroom and hurried back with a tumbler of water that he insisted she drink. "You're probably dehydrated. What was that stunt supposed to prove? You going to cop an insanity plea or something? Claim you were out of your mind when you were driving, and beg the judge to take pity on you?"

She stared up at the ceiling.

She stabbed a fist against her chest. "Their sword shall enter into their own heart."

"What the hell are you talking about?" Cabot looked at her in dismay, then noticed her Bible open on the bedside table. He saw she'd been reading the Psalms. He shut it away in a drawer. "Marybeth, a good marriage is based on love and respect, and I don't feel much of either from you. Haven't in a long time. Are you listening to me? Do you hear me?"

She slanted a look at him. "I hear you. I do hear you, Cabot, because all you do is talk, talk, talk night and day."

"I'm going to forget you said that, Marybeth, because I know you're not in your right mind. But you're so combative, it's hard to know what to say. Feel like I'm walking on eggshells around you all the time." He turned to go, then turned back with a bereft sadness in his eyes. "Food for thought, Marybeth, that's all I'm saying. Food for thought."

Chapter 8

A yellow Ferrari sped down the brightly lit midnight streets of Las Vegas, Andy at the wheel. He glanced around, surprised to see that not only were the streets empty of cars but there weren't any people going in and out of the casinos, hotels and restaurants.

"Where is everybody?" he asked Joker, sitting beside him in the passenger seat.

Joker remained silent.

Andy pulled into the entry of the Treasure Island Hotel on the Strip and left his car for the valet service, assuming the attendants on duty must be parking other cars and would return shortly. It didn't occur to him to worry about leaving the key in such an expensive car and simply walking away from it.

He found Joker a cool spot in the shade. A large bowl of water was already there. "Wait here," he told his dog. "Be right back."

Glancing down at his shorts and sneakers it, occurred to him that he should be dressed more nicely for his first visit to a casino. As he approached the reflective glass doors, he admired how sharp he looked in designer jeans, boots, a crisp shirt and a casual jacket over his shoulders, just like in a magazine ad he'd seen recently. He didn't question the abrupt change in his appearance.

He ambled into the hotel lobby. The Wheel of Fortune lit up as if beckoning him to come closer. Chips awaited him on the table. He put them all on a bet and waited for the dealer to spin. Since no one was there, nothing happened. He spun the wheel, and won. Chips appeared at the dealer's side of the table, so he scooped up his winnings, laughing. "Pirate's booty! Avast, me hearties. No jackanapes allowed here!"

He moved on to the roulette table and then a craps game. He won easily no matter what he did, but it wasn't much fun since there was no challenge or risk.

Then he sat at a high stakes poker game in a private room, dealt his own cards and began playing, imitating the games he'd played countless times on his computer.

"How's all this working for you?" a male voice asked behind him. "Having a good time?"

Andy shrugged without turning.

"I hear you've been looking for me," the man said.

"Not looking for anyone," Andy replied, intent on winning the game.

"Look at me, Andrew."

Confused by the commanding voice, Andy swiveled around.

He saw a smiling Native American man in his mid-thirties, dressed casually in jeans and a sleeveless shirt but wearing a wide armband on his muscular left arm. Andy stared at the armband, dazzled by the brilliant white light it emitted. He scowled, and looked away, feigning disinterest. "Do I know you?"

The man straddled a chair and continued smiling at Andy. "I think you do." He nodded toward the buffalo nickel Andy wore on a chain.

Andy touched the buffalo nickel. Understanding flooded him. "This is yours. You're...my great-grandfather?"

"'Q something,'" Qaletaqa teased. "Isn't that what you told them my name is?"

"Qaletaqa." Andy looked at him closely. "But you're not an old man. And what are you doing in my dream?"

With a laugh, Qaletaqa stood up. "Come with me, Andrew."

"Where are we going?" Andy asked as they crossed the casino.

"Have you been through orientation yet?"

"You mean those people with the bright light? Nope. And you're not going to be able to talk me into it, so safe your breath."

"Then let me show you something."

Qaletaqa took Andy to the top of the Stratosphere Tower, at the northern end of the Vegas Strip. "It's the tallest observation tower in the United States."

"Wow." Andy looked around at the city lights. "What a great view!"

"Now look up." Qaletaqa gestured at the sky, and they instantly traveled together away from Earth on a route that took them past the International Space Station.

"I never realized how huge it is," Andy cried. "No wonder my mom wanted to go there. I guess I never got how important it is to her, to be an astronaut."

"But now you understand?"

Andy nodded.

"There's a bigger plan than one woman going into space because she's always wanted to," Qaletaqa said. "Many 'want' a trip into space. Few get to go. Did you know that your death has the potential of disrupting a plan that was set in motion many years ago?"

"My...? What're you talking about? I'm not dead. I'm just dreaming. Or...or something."

"Alive, you use physical senses, but after death you must rely on your inner sensory perception. Can you notice the difference? Have you been hungry lately? Or tired?"

Andy tried to think, but it was confusing.

Leaving Vegas far behind, Qaletaqa took the boy through a star-forming region of massive pillars and cones. "These are incubators for new stars. I never tire of this view, Andrew. The universe we live in, the energy around us is spectacular, isn't it?"

"This is the coolest dream I ever had. It feels so real!"

Swirling dust particles reflected the blue light of older stars. Golden galaxies burst like fireworks.

"Change is the one constant in the universe," Qaletaqa said. "Birth. Death. Rebirth."

They circled a giant pillar-shaped nebula where a new star was forming at its tip. Andy watched in awe, fascinated.

"Do you remember me yet," Qaletaqa asked him, "from long ago?"

"I...I'm not sure. Maybe." Andy felt that his thoughts were not connecting sharply. It seemed like he was moving in a fog, and there were too many things he didn't understand.

Andy and Qaletaqa were back on Earth in daytime, walking along the inside of a railroad track in a desolate area of sagebrush, jackrabbits and lizards. The air filled with the rumble of an approaching train. Andy looked at his side and realized Joker had joined him again.

"I thought I left you in the car in Vegas. Where do you go, anyway?"

Qaletaqa smiled. "He can't answer you. He waits in safe places when you get so distracted that you forget about him. No harm can come to him."

"Well, that's good, anyway." Andy stopped.

"Something troubling you?"

They looked at each other a long while.

Andy began slowly nodding as he gained clarity, and understood that he had died in an accident, and was now experiencing his existence at a different vibration.

With the realization that he was dead came the ability to sense other things as well. "It's my mom. She misses me. It's my fault she's grieving. I should let

122

her know it didn't hurt to die, and we're both safe." He put a hand on Joker's neck.

"Good work, Andrew. People who die suddenly often have a transition period where they don't understand what has happened, but you have moved swiftly. Come with me." Qaletaqa held out a hand.

"Where are we going?"

"The journey home is not as long as you might expect."

Andy frowned. "Home?"

The train rumbled past, leaving behind an empty track.

Two young boys shrieked their way down the stairs of the Powell residence, and tumbled into the kitchen, bouncing into Hart as he cooked dinner at the island. "Hey, careful," he said lightly, "or you'll end up with fresh mango salsa all over you and we'll have to scrape our chips on your arms instead of dipping them into a bowl."

The boys giggled and grabbed from the basket of home-made tortilla chips he offered.

Jemma's younger sister, Lulu, hurried in on their heels. "I'm so sorry, Hart. I was helping Jemma fix up the guest room and the boys got tired of being good. Never does last long. Are you sure it wouldn't be better for us to go to a hotel?" While talking, she wrestled her sons into seats at the kitchen table and gave them crayons and coloring books.

"Of course you'll stay here," he said. "It's good for us to have you in the house."

She poured them both a glass of wine. "This is so shitty, isn't it?" she said softly, patting his back. "Holding up okay? Wait, sorry, I know that's a dumb question. But it's the only thing I could think of."

He nodded. "I know. And 'No, not really' would be the answer to that. I'm trying not to think too much."

Lulu pulled her waist-length straight black hair into a ponytail, and began chopping vegetables on the cutting board. She had flown in from Phoenix with Matt and Todd, ages seven and five, feeling it would be too chaotic to expect her parents to watch them, and not wanting to ask a favor of her ex-husband who had recently remarried. Lulu and Jemma's parents would arrive in time for the funeral, but meanwhile Lulu felt that she could be of assistance with the details leading up to it.

"I hope you won't mind being a buffer zone," Hart said abruptly, turning away to slide a casserole of cheese enchiladas into the oven.

She looked at him sharply. "I know how my sister can be, and I don't mind taking the heat." She smiled at him. "Be sure to let me know if there's anything I can do that would be of real help to you. I keep asking her and she says she's got it all under control. Knowing her, that means at some point soon she's going to snap."

"Already did." Hart crossed to the table with the basket of chips and a bowl of fresh guacamole. "Hey, boys, here's something to get started on."

Lulu appraised Hart. She was an artist, and accustomed to noticing the finer points that others might miss. "You're good with kids, aren't you? This is such a damned shame. Andy was such a special guy. I can't get over it, that he's gone."

Hart nodded. "A big thing you can help with is keeping us busy and active the next few days. I'd like to avoid down time where we stare at each other and try not to talk about Andy."

"So you're able to take some time off from the bistro?"

"My manager will run things, and I'll be in touch. We'll limp along until I can convince myself that's what I should be doing. Right now, I can't think about work, but everybody I talk to tells me it helps. Gives you something to focus on, to keep distracted. I guess I'll find my own way. Never thought I'd have to...." He choked, and left the room quickly.

With a sigh of sympathy, Lulu took over the meal preparation, glancing at her sons now and then and feeling overwhelmed with gratitude for their safety and health.

Jemma searched the DVD collection in the family room and gathered some kids' movies she thought her young nephews might enjoy. Touching each box brought memories of watching with Andy, sharing a bowl of popcorn, seated on the long couch with Hart on the other side of their son. Always, Andy in between them, his love keeping them together.

She stood up briskly and went into the kitchen to join the others, knowing she should eat, knowing she should keep up a semblance of normalcy.

Hearing the kids laugh, her steps slowed, but she forced herself to go in and eat dinner.

"Hey, Lulu," she said, entering the kitchen. "I don't think I thanked you yet for coming, but...well, thanks. I do appreciate this." She held up the movies. "Thought we could watch something after we eat."

"Great idea!" Lulu took the DVDs and set them aside. "Go to bed early if you'd prefer. I'll keep the boys' noise down to a low roar."

"That's okay. Where's Hart?"

"He'll be right back."

"Oh. Yeah, I see. I guess we'll both vanish now and then, to find something to hold onto, something...." She trailed off, forgetting what she was going to say.

Hart came in and took the enchiladas out of the oven. "Let's eat!" he called out, overly jovial, his voice thick from crying.

During dinner, both Hart and Jemma studiously avoided looking at the chair in between them where Andy normally sat. Todd was perched there, chatting about the plane ride from Arizona and not seeming to understand what was going on and why his mother kept telling him to pipe down.

"But I don't want to pipe down," Todd said. "Why do I have to? This is my indoor voice."

Lulu got up. "How about those movies Aunt Jemma found for us to watch? Anyone want popcorn? I saw some in the pantry and I'll fix it."

"Why don't you get the boys settled and start a movie?" Jemma suggested to Hart. "My sister and I will clear up in here and join you."

When Jemma and Lulu were alone, Lulu said, "I brought along an old bottle of Valium from when I was freaking out going through my divorce." She took the bottle out of her pocket and pressed it in Jemma's hand.

Jemma set it on the counter. "No thanks." She began loading the dishwasher.

"Stop being so hard-headed, Jemma. Everybody needs a sedative now and then, to help them through the rough spots."

"What happens when I run out or when the drug wears off? The only thing is that the people I'm annoying will be safely out of my radar range and won't have to hear me rant about the accident and what Andy's death means to me. My feelings won't magically go away because I pop a pill. Maybe I can put it off, but not forever. I'd rather keep my mind clear. I can do that much for his memory."

"I didn't mean anything bad by it."

"Yeah, I know you didn't. We just don't see things the same way. Go on in the family room. I'll finish up and be there in a few minutes."

"At least let me put the leftovers away."

"If it'll make you feel better."

Lulu grinned. "You know I'm a people-pleaser at heart and I'd rather be helping out than sitting on my butt being waited on."

"I'm glad you came. Did I say that already? I think maybe I'm repeating myself."

Lulu covered the serving dishes and put away food. "I'm going to throw a load of wash in for you. No worries."

Jemma smiled at her, grateful for the help.

In the laundry room, Lulu sorted laundry piled high in the basket, and started a load in the washer. Humming to herself, glad to be busy, she tidied the friendly clutter against one wall where running shoes, winter boots, tote bags and cleaning supplies fought for space. She put the tote bags up in a cupboard, and then noticed a backpack on the floor, in a corner by the door to the garage.

Opening it, she saw it was Andy's. She ruffled through the contents to be sure there wasn't anything important that she should take out for his parents to see. But there were only odds and ends. A new can of tennis balls. A couple of energy bars. A bottle of water. A glossy gift catalog folded open to a display of lava lamps for sale. The green lamp was circled with a pen, and she assumed it was something the boy had wanted to order.

"Oh, no," she said to herself, holding the backpack, overcome by sadness and feeling impotent to change anything for her sister.

There was no way she was going to burst into the kitchen with it and ask Jemma where to put it. She decided it couldn't hurt to tuck the backpack away and let Jemma or Hart come across it some other day, when they were stronger.

She shoved the backpack onto a high shelf in a cupboard and firmly shut the door on it.

Marybeth sat in the living room in her favorite wingback chair, looking out the front window. Her journal was open in her lap, but she merely tapped the pen idly on the fresh page, not feeling like writing.

She saw a homeless man shuffle around the cul-de-sac and stop to pick up a piece of fast food litter. When she saw him lick the paper, Marybeth leapt up, slid the journal under the chair cushion and hurried into the kitchen, filled with purpose.

She was cutting a thick sandwich when Cabot walked in.

"Hungry?" he asked. "We just ate."

"Oh, yeah," she muttered. "Um, I remember you said I'm too skinny." She wrapped the sandwich in a paper towel and headed for the back door, which led to a side yard and the gate to the street.

"Going somewhere?"

"I'm...going to take a little walk."

He blocked her from opening the door. "Want some company?"

She grew annoyed with herself for the game-playing. "If you must know, I saw a homeless guy outside and I made this for him. So, if you'll excuse me, I'm going to give him a sandwich because he looks hungry."

Startled, Cabot drew aside and let her turn the door knob. As she walked out, he called after her, "He's not going to take it from you. All those guys are mental cases and they don't want charity."

For a brief moment, she hesitated, and started to go back into the kitchen, but instead she began running, and didn't stop until she was in front of the homeless man. She thrust out the paper towel. "It's for you. A sandwich."

The man scowled. "What am I going to do with that?"

"Please don't drop it in the street," she begged, suddenly desparate to get through to him. "Please! My husband is watching. I know he is. And he'll never let me live it down if you don't start eating the goddamned sandwich. So just eat it! If you have any shred of human decency, at least pretend to eat it, and then you can walk away and never have to see me again."

The man began eating, without peeling away the paper towel. As he wandered off toward the street's only outlet, he muttered, "You meet all kinds these days. Loonies on the street everywhere I go. Poor little thing. Sweet little thing. Crazy loony, mixed up girl."

She watched him walk away eating, talking to himself, but still holding the sandwich. Thank God he didn't toss it aside.

Her heart raced, jolted by the knowledge that she could now stroll back in the house with her head held high for the first time in what seemed like months, knowing that for some reason, what she had just done had been one of the bravest acts of her entire twenty-three years on Earth.

It felt good.

It felt freeing.

It felt like a new beginning.

Standing in the stairwell with her sister Lulu, Jemma looked at the photos. Most were of Andy, growing up. Some pictures were of Hart or Jemma when they were younger, long before they met.

There was one of Jemma visiting her grandfather on the Hopi reservation when she was ten, and another with Lulu in the photo as well, holding his other hand.

"Remember that trip?" she asked Lulu. "You were pretty young, about seven I guess."

"I think I remember seeing the pictures more than I actually recall the trip itself," Lulu said. "Know what I mean?"

"Yeah, I do. Your memory gets tricked when others talk about the trip like you should recall being there."

Lulu peered closer at the photo with her in it, and saw a boy's arm at Jemma's left side.

"Who's that?"

"Who?"

"There's a boy standing there, with you. Camera cut him out of the picture."

Jemma thought a moment, then her face cleared. "Mike went on that trip with us."

"You've known him forever, haven't you?"

"I haven't seen him in years, Lulu. We were neighbors, and took him along on a trip to the reservation. I remember now that he was very envious when

Grandpa gave me a buffalo nickel to wear on a piece of rawhide around my neck."

"I don't remember that. Do you still have it?"

Jemma shook her head, not wanting to get into the whole story of how the necklace came to be lost on the day of Andy's accident.

She looked at a picture of Andy's first birthday and gently touched his face. "This boy's been gone a long time. Replaced by a two-year-old." She pointed to a photo where Andy was posed with his parents on either side of him, all three behind a big cake with a number two candle on it. "That one by another boy. And another." She indicated the various photos taken year after year as Andy grew up. "But they're all gone now.... No sixteen-year-old in the wings, waiting to slip into the spotlight and call me Mom."

"Oh, Jemma, I wish I had magical words to help you feel better. I feel so helpless to say the right thing."

"I don't think there are any right words. But thank you." Jemma grasped her sister's hand. "It means so much, having you here. I thought I didn't want you to come, and I know I wasn't very welcoming–"

"I understand. This is so difficult."

Andy and Qaletaqa reached Union Station in downtown Los Angeles. Joker was still at Andy's side. The station's floor plan was a cross, as in a cathedral, and the style of the old building combined Spanish Colonial Revival and Art Deco.

Passengers streamed through the lobby.

"How come I can see all the people?" Andy asked. "Everywhere else I've been, I hardly saw anybody at all. Even Las Vegas was empty."

"Your awareness is growing. You are willing to see more, so your frequency rises and a broader array becomes visible to you."

"Are we here for a special reason? I mean, is a train station how people get to heaven?"

"Many people find it comforting to gather after death at places like airports, bus and train stations, or ship docks. The idea of going on a journey is one that resonates as being familiar."

"Symbols and metaphors, right? Okay, so now I'm going on a trip?" Andy noticed that a black armband was on his own left arm, while Qaletaqa still wore the heavy gold metal band. "When do I get something fancier, like yours?"

Amused, Qaletaqa said, "One thing at a time, Andrew. You have to earn each advancement by raising your consciousness. You don't elevate yourself by merely wishing for it. You have to do the actual work of evolving past your fears and limiting beliefs."

Looking around, Andy saw dozens of after-life people, all identified by the same black armbands, passing among humans who remained oblivious to their presence. Here and there, he noticed guides wearing silver armbands who gathered the others into smaller groups.

"I want you to meet someone," Qaletaqa said.

Gabriella stepped forward, smiling at Andy. She wore a silver armband. Her dress was black and white polka dot with a dainty wing monogram on the breast pocket. Her long brunette pageboy was held back with combs in a style from the 1940s. A tiny white hat tilted forward over her wide-set dark eyes.

Joker hurried to greet her and she patted him fondly.

"I know you." Andy hesitated, trying to remember where he had seen her before.

"We met only briefly." Gabriella's Italian accent was soft and melodious.

"Hey, I've heard your voice before!" He paused, frowning, sensing he'd heard it many times. But the memory was vague, hazy. He grabbed at the most recent memory of her voice. "You're the one who was under the street light and kept trying to get that older guy to stop bothering me."

She nodded. "I'd like to show you around, Andrew, but that will have to wait for a short while. In the meantime, I have an orientation group to welcome, and you can come with me."

Qaletaqa melted into the crowd.

Gabriella gathered a group of new arrivals, all wearing black armbands. "Do not worry if you are still confused and have forgotten who you really are. We will help you reconnect with your history."

In her darkened bedroom, Jemma sat up abruptly, wide awake, but remembering a snippet of the strange dream she just had.

"Reconnect with your history? What--?"

Chapter 9

Feeling like an automaton, Jemma greeted guests as they arrived at the chapel for the wake, her back turned to the open coffin in the front of the chapel where Hart sat in pews with other family members including her parents.

They had combined the wake with the memorial service, and would scatter the ashes in three days with a smaller party in attendance. Jemma had explained to Hart that people would be grateful to not have their schedules disrupted by too many events, even though no one would ever admit that out loud because, in her experience, whatever was the most practical in life often sounded unfeeling.

On a large wall-mounted television monitor, a slide show played along with soft classical music. Hart had put together the collection of photos from their albums and the staircase gallery, showing Andy growing up and all the things he had been interested in from sports and tropical fish to poker games and scholastics.

"Thank you so much for coming," Jemma repeated, accepting condolences. She ran on auto-pilot, ignoring questions, giving the same welcome to everyone.

If asked to tell who had come in the door in the last ten minutes, she'd be hard pressed to create a list. But this coping mechanism allowed her to stay upright, and give a semblance of being in control.

"Oh, you're just being so brave, Jemma." Sylvia Blum grabbed Jemma's hands in hers as Eric's family entered. "I'd fall apart if anything happened to one of my kids. But look at you, dry-eyed and full of strength, taking it all in stride."

"Thank you for coming." Jemma knew this woman would never comprehend the depth of grief that had ripped Jemma's dreams apart. *Taking it in stride? What does this idiot know about me and what I'm feeling?*

Sylvia called out to her oldest child, "Eric—bring that gift for Mr. and Mrs. Powell over here, hon."

Jemma realized that "Mrs. Powell" sounded almost foreign to her. She'd grown used to be calling "Dr. Malotki" by everyone at NASA, in the science community and in other country's space programs.

All these years in her marriage to Hart, she'd been living two lives: the one in her world of science, and the one at home with her husband, son and family friends. Vaguely, she realized that those two worlds were now demanding a decision from her and would no longer tolerate peaceful co-existence.

She glanced away, and noticed that although young Peter had left his hockey stick at home today, he was busy stuffing his pockets with hard candies from a basket on the table. Oddly, instead of annoying her, the sight brought a small smile to her lips. She was reminded of Christmas the year Andy was six, when he'd presented holiday guests with his own homemade dessert to rival Hart's cherries flambé. Andy had crushed a fistful of candy canes taken from the tree and stirred the bits into softened vanilla ice cream, spooned it into a Santa-shaped cake pan, decorated the top with chocolate sprinkles and then put the pan in the freezer…creating a frozen treat they'd all enjoyed.

Eric broke into her thoughts, mumbling, "This is for you, Mrs. P.," while thrusting out an eighteen-inch square flat box wrapped in black tissue.

Taking the package, Jemma noticed red stains on Eric's hands, but he shoved his hands in his pockets and she thought no more about it. She noticed that Eric wore a black armband, the thin fabric rent to symbolize his grief. She smiled again, thinly, appreciating his gesture of bereavement.

"It's from all of us." Eric's dad, Stanley, indicated the box. "We're sick about this, Jemma. Such a shock. Excuse me while I go give our sympathy to your husband, too." He walked up the aisle towards Hart.

Cara sobbed openly and between the tears, whispered to Jemma that she had picked out the gift.

"Open it later, Jemma, when you get home," Sylvia said. "But I'll tell you what it is, in case you're wondering why it's kind of heavy. It's a memorial stone, well, it's made out of resin really, or you couldn't even pick it up, to put in your garden, and it says on it—Wait, I wrote it down." She fumbled in her purse and read from a scrawled note. "It says, 'If tears could build a stairway, and memories a lane, I'd walk right up to heaven and bring you home again.' I think that's very touching, don't you? I ordered it from a catalog. Even paid extra for overnight shipping."

"Thank you. Very thoughtful." Jemma set the gift down on a long table, among the many cards and flowers people were bringing.

The chapel was nearly full, and yet more were coming in the door. She turned to greet them, but then noticed that Eric was moving off with his family. Ignoring the newcomers, she reached out to touch his arm, the one with the black armband on his shirtsleeve. "Could I talk to you a moment, Eric? In private."

He followed her reluctantly into a small empty room adjacent to the chapel.

She shut the door quietly. "My husband tells me that I shouted at you that day. At the scene of the accident. That I blamed you for it." She looked at him but he wouldn't meet her eyes.

"Yeah," he mumbled.

"I'm sorry, Eric. You shouldn't have to carry that burden of guilt so let me remove it. People think that because I'm a scientist, somehow I am one-dimensional and incapable of speaking in the heat of emotion and anger. As if I'm incapable of being even...illogical...at times."

"You mean like Mr. Spock. That's okay." He glanced toward the door, clearly wanting to escape.

"But do you know why I said it?"

"No, not really."

"Let me tell you something about Andy that he specifically asked me to never tell you."

Eric looked at her, his curiosity piqued.

"The day before...before the accident," she said, "Andy got picked up for shoplifting."

Eric gasped.

"Interesting. That was my reaction too, and there was something odd about the way he begged me not to let you–specifically you, Eric–know about the arrest. It prompted me to ask him if you had put him up to it. Maybe on a dare, or telling him it would help him fit in with the more popular kids. I love my son, and I know he didn't think he was very cool. But he was. He was great. Fantastic and amazing...." She wiped her eyes. "Anyway--"

"I didn't mean for all that to happen." Eric's cheeks flamed.

"–I couldn't get over it, that my son who was such a smart kid and had such a bright future would do something that self-destructive. Sabotage himself like that."

"Oh, shit, I'm so sorry, Mrs. Powell–"

"And so, when Andy and I were out running the next day, I couldn't let go of it. I tried, but it kept eating at me. I had told him we wouldn't talk about it again if he promised never to do anything like that again. But I couldn't stop searching for answers. I accused him of being on drugs."

"Andy? No way–"

"I was desperate to get at the 'why'—I wanted...no, I *needed*...to understand! How could I help him if I didn't know what was going on in his life?" She looked at Eric. "I'll get to the point and let you get back to your family. You ever heard the phrase 'scared straight'?"

"Well, yeah, I guess so. I think in a movie."

"I don't want to know the details of your life, Eric. I really don't. I've got enough on my mind right now, including the fact that the last thing my son heard from me was an accusation—and he ran off to avoid having to talk to me a single minute longer. That's when he was killed."

"So that's why you blame me? Kind of like indirectly?"

"If there's anything that can come out of this that is positive, let it be a turning point for you. Andy told me you're good at math but you're convinced you're a poor student."

"I never got good grades, never will."

"With that attitude, you won't. It's called a self-fulfilling prophecy. See what you can learn from all this, Eric, and don't ruin your life." Without waiting for his reaction or response, she opened the door and rejoined the crowd in the chapel.

Walking firmly toward the front pew, passing people with outstretched hands wanting to talk to her, she sat next to Hart and grabbed his hand. When the service began, as she had told him she'd do, Jemma stared at the vases of flowers and not at the open coffin a few feet away.

Andy sat outside the Griffith Observatory, one of his favorite places to visit when he was a kid. He loved the Planetarium, and the Foucault pendulum. He knew that Griffith Park as a whole was a popular destination since there was so much to do and see including hiking, golfing, picnicking and horseback riding.

The park covered more than four thousand acres, and had ten million visitors a year. There were nature trails, amusement rides such as the children's train or the old merry-go-round with its distinctive red and white striped canopy, and the world-famous Los Angeles Zoo. Griffith Park was the largest municipal park and wilderness area in the United States.

The land had been donated to the city early in the twentieth century by an eccentric millionaire, Colonel Griffith J. Griffith who wanted the area designated for people to enjoy, including the vista from its tallest point, Mount Hollywood, which became the top of a popular hiking trail, giving 360-degree views of the entire Los Angeles area.

There were separate overnight camps for groups of boys and girls such as scout troops. A southwestern museum, the Autry Museum of Western Heritage, named for cowboy film legend Gene Autry, resided in a corner of the park, and elsewhere were an outdoor Greek Theater where concert artists performed, and a train exhibit called Travel Town with scaled-down steamer train rides and birthday party facilities.

Because of its open spaces, abundant trees and wilderness hillsides, the park had long been a companionable place for spirits to gather, whether they had died in Los Angeles or not. Some came for celebrity sightings, and were welcomed with a *laissez-faire* attitude. As long as you didn't cause trouble, or interfere with the work being done, you could stay as long as you wished.

The Griffith Observatory was also part of the parklands, but houses had been built on land between it and the rest of the park so it was a separate trip.

Unless you could travel there by thought, as Andy had. Now, he sat on the steps and rested his chin in his hand, mulling over what he should do next.

He noticed some teenagers walking by, and heard the words "Acapulco" and "spring break." Hurrying to catch up with them, he called out, "Hey, what did you just say about going to Mexico for spring break? Isn't it kind of early for that?"

One of the guys laughed, and Andy recognized Khaki from bungee jumping. "Hey, yourself, kid," Khaki said. "Spring break is year 'round now. Get with the program or get left behind. Girls in bikinis. All the beer and sex you could ever dream of. You going to stand there gaping like a nerd, or are you coming with us?"

I'm a nerd with a capital N.

Andy shrank at the memory of admitting to Eric that he'd never be cool. And yet, here was an opportunity he could accept, if he wanted to. Couldn't he?

"I'm not a nerd!" Andy eagerly joined them, thrilled to be invited.

If, instead of dashing off to Acapulco for fun in the sun with Khaki and his other new buddies, Andy had gone up the outside stairs and around to the Observatory's overlook platform, with its coin-operated telescopes and tourists taking photos of the city below, he would've encountered Gabriella and Qaletaqa, arguing about what in heaven's name to do with him.

"But he still won't do his Life Review," Gabriella cried out in frustration. "I cannot work with someone who has that attitude. You're not being fair, saddling me with him."

"Three people blame themselves for his accident. Each played a part in it, and now each one has a chance to grow and learn from the experience."

"You expect me to facilitate this?"

"How long did you work with the Invisibles team?"

"I have the sensation that you know precisely how long."

He nodded, admitting the truth in that. "Over the course of many years between the two World Wars. Because of the sessions or séances you and the other team members initiated with those existing on the physical plane, they wrote enlightening books–"

"*Our Unseen Guest, The Betty Book* and many others then and since."

"–that opened a window onto the reality of an unobstructed soul, an unobstructed universe. Teaching humans how to enter a higher state of spiritual consciousness."

"I was proud to be a small part of it and participate in the sessions, communicating our ideas to our contacts like 'Joan' and Betty. When the team declined to be identified, in order to keep the focus on the principles we wished to teach and not our own personalities, the humans named us the Invisibles. We were eager to break through the barriers of limited thinking and teach the truth about eternal life, and thus bring comfort and awareness to those still living."

"Did everyone on your team—either living or in this dimension--always display the perfect attitude?"

"Sometimes people are impatient." She slowly smiled. "Don't say it. I know my worst flaw and I am still working on it."

"I want you to enlist Andy on your Dream Spinners team."

"Andrew thinks he should be able to play all day. Can't you put him on someone else's team?"

"Promise that you will give him a chance."

"I know why you are promoting him. You are not fooling me."

"I did not expect to, Gabriella." He looked out at the city.

"Am I supposed to give my usual pitch? Tell him to understand only a few qualify to be a Dream Spinner and he'll be part of a great movement to awaken humanity?"

He chuckled. "Be sure to explain the spiritual awakening of humankind is gathering momentum and we will help it reach the tipping point. From there, we will be able to help it grow rapidly, so that even children are taught at a young age how to find their purpose for living and not waste their time on earth getting by with the minimum awareness."

"I trust that you know best. And I also trust that you have an additional motive."

"Let me explain my theory," Qaletaqa said. "She's so full of guilt and remorse that when she reaches the point of believing the messages are from her son, she'll listen. And then she'll take action."

"Her NASA project is that important to you? Won't someone else do it, if she doesn't?"

140

"You, of all people, should recall how devastating that attitude has been throughout human history."

"You're right," she said.

"Not only will her project redress a grave wrong, but even more, it will inspire the women of the world to stretch and unfold their wings, and see what they are capable of doing." He looked at her, as if waiting for her to leap to the next logical statement.

"Naomi? No. I wouldn't count on her if I were you."

"What's happened?"

"Didn't you know? She went back in the Gray Zone. Again."

Qaletaqa grew thoughtful. "Maybe she will listen to Andrew. Allow him to visit her, but let him believe it is his own idea, or he will resist. Do it with caution, and know that if he finds out, he will resent being manipulated, even though it is for the greater good. He will not be able to sense yet that it could help his mother indirectly."

"I'll find a way." Gabriella nodded. "Naomi just might listen to him. She's already heard everything I have to say on the subject, and a new voice might get through to her where I have failed."

"As long as you are exploring ways to help her, you have not failed. You haven't found what works yet. I have every confidence that you will succeed with her."

Joker nudged Gabriella's hand. To Qaletaqa she admitted, feeling exasperated, "I thought if I allowed his dog to join him, that Andy would keep Joker in his sight at all times–"

"And you'd be able to keep Andy in yours?"

She smiled, busted. "It was worth a try. I wonder where he got to this time?"

"Think where the boys like Khaki go. He's probably with him. Khaki wouldn't have been able to resist a new arrival to play with in his Never-Never-Land idea of heaven."

"I'll track him down." She laughed. "After all, how far could the boy get? I only have the whole known universe to search."

The morning of Andy's memorial service, Cabot went outside to get the weekly community newspaper from the driveway and opened it to see a front page photo of Andy Powell, with details about the accident. As he turned to go back in the house, he was startled to see that someone had paid them a visit during the night.

He hustled inside. "Marybeth!" he hollered down the hall. "Come here! I need to show you something."

She came out of the bedroom, tying her robe, her long hair tousled from sleep. "What is it, Cabot? You sound so upset."

"Come out front."

"Can't I get dressed first?"

He took her by the elbow and propelled her to the front door and then down the path to the sidewalk. "Look," he said, turning her to face the house.

She paled. "Oh my God..."

With red spray paint, someone had written "Killer" in large bold letters, in five different places on the house and garage door.

Trembling, she hurried to the hose, turned it on, and then sprayed water over the graffiti, but nothing happened.

"You can't wash it off, Marybeth." He looked at her. "It's spray paint. I paid a lot of money to have this house exterior painted because you said you couldn't do it."

"I get dizzy on tall ladders," she whispered. "And it's so hot to work outside. Triple digits every day."

"Didn't you grow up in the desert? You're the one who wanted to move here. Everyone knows the Valley gets scorching hot."

Quietly, she said, "I wanted to move to Hollywood...it's not as hot there, only gets hot in July, August. People don't even use air conditioners that much."

"But the home prices are a hell of a lot higher. Could you be reasonable for one minute, princess?" He waved the folded newspaper at the graffiti. "What are you going to do about it? I don't want the whole neighborhood to come out and see this!"

"Maybe there's something at the paint store, a graffiti remover I could get." Tears filled her eyes as she looked helplessly at the house. "Who could have done this?"

He looked at her appraisingly and then asked very gently, "Did you?"

"What? No! I didn't. I swear I didn't." She held out her hands. "Look. I'd have red paint on me if I did this."

"You could've worn gloves."

"Go look in the trash. If I did this, you'll find the gloves and the paint cans."

"You could have thrown it all away in a neighbor's bin."

"I'd know if I had done this," she said, "and I am positive I did not."

"Maybe you were sleepwalking. You've been so agitated lately."

Marybeth felt an hysterical laugh bubbling up. How could she be trapped in this ridiculous conversation? She thought of Naomi, who had never been at a loss for a quick retort. She'd know what to say to Cabot. She wouldn't be cowed by the strutting peacock Marybeth had married.

With an inward sigh, Marybeth shot a resentful look at her husband.

"I've never sleepwalked in my entire life." She put the hose away, then turned to him, abruptly furious, and tired of always stuffing her feelings. "Why are you gaslighting me, Cabot?"

"What the hell does that mean?"

"You're trying to make me think I'm crazy. That I got up in the night and put on gloves and got out a ladder and spray-painted the house with...with that word." She felt like screaming, but did not, knowing it would send him over the top with rage.

"You wouldn't remember if you were—"

"Sleepwalking? It would have to be pre-meditated because we haven't bought red spray paint, or any color for that matter. Even if the previous people left an old can in the garage, it wouldn't have been enough to do all that. This probably took a few cans. I would've had to buy it in advance."

"Well?" He looked at her steadily.

"You know I didn't."

He held up the newspaper's front page for her to see. "Look, Marybeth. You're finally famous! Maybe we should leave the graffiti up and charge people to see the house where you live. Get our address in one of those souvenir Map of the Stars Homes that tourists buy. Come and see where the boy's killer lives."

"Please stop talking that way, Cabot. Just—"

"Enjoy your little victory, Marybeth. Insanity plea might help with that civil suit. Enjoy this triumph while it lasts."

Mike McLeod opened his garage door and put his golf clubs in the trunk of his car. Noticing the newspapers in the driveway, he picked up the *Los Angeles Times* and tossed it in the car, planning to read it when he stopped for coffee after an hour or so at the driving range.

The weekly community paper was at the edge of the lawn and had been soaked by an automatic sprinkler. It was too sodden to read and he didn't bother unfolding it.

He took it to the side yard and tossed it in the recycle bin.

Marybeth waited impatiently for the paint store to open, and as soon as the male clerk unlocked the door, she rushed in. "Somebody put graffiti on my house with red spray paint. I need something to take it off."

144

He helped her pick out the supplies she needed, and then while the clerk scanned the items in Marybeth's basket, she spotted a display rack of hand tools that included scissors.

She approached it, glancing over her shoulder because she had the eerie sensation that Cabot was watching her, and hastily selected a pair.

Marybeth felt a terrible sense of failure about every aspect of her life. Why hadn't she been able to make her marriage succeed? Why hadn't she done better with her acting career? Why, why, why... The question always circled back to Why didn't my parents want me? Why did Naomi have to die? Why did Stephanie...

Abruptly, Marybeth cleared her throat. "Add this to my order," she said to the clerk.

The clerk didn't hear her over the music playing from his iPod speakers, but saw the scissors being shoved toward him across the counter, and so he rang them up.

Hoisting the ladder, Cabot helped Marybeth with the places she could not reach, as they covered the offensive word with primer, and later a fresh coat of paint just in those areas, blending the edges of the fresh coat to match the rest of the house, which fortunately was new enough that the patches didn't show.

"Know how much time I've lost because of this?" Cabot growled. "Time I would've used for better things like fixing up the house for you and making money so you can keep on shopping and going to auditions."

Marybeth brushed a lock of hair out of her face, wishing she hadn't needed to ask Cabot for help. "It won't take much longer."

"I don't just mean this." He gestured to indicate their graffiti removal project. "That accident destroyed more than one life. It's ripped a hole in this marriage. It's one thing after another with you, Marybeth. You're such a drama queen, you can't stand it if you don't have some big ordeal going on, so you go out and create one. I haven't been able to do much of anything except clean up the wreckage you cause. And this is just a small part of it."

Her mind was reeling with all the lies he spoke with such confidence as if saying them out loud made them true. "I'd give you back all the hours, Cabot, if I knew how to do that. I'd take the time out of my own life's allotment and give you every single minute you've wasted on me."

He looked at her for such a long time that she began sweating, nervous about what he might say in response to her sudden boldness.

"I don't appreciate your sarcasm." He sighed. "I try so hard to help you. You're my wife, for better or for worse, and you seem determined to make it all worse. I don't get you, Marybeth. I try. But I just don't get you."

She fell silent, knowing it was useless to explain herself any more than she already had during the past two years.

It would be equally futile to protest that, although he claimed it, Cabot didn't try at all to comprehend her and her dreams. Not. At. All.

In the guest bathroom, Marybeth took out the scissors she'd purchased at the paint store. She spread open the empty plastic shopping bag in the sink.

Looking at herself in the mirror, she couldn't help wondering why she had begun feeling more optimistic about her life after the simple act of giving a homemade sandwich to a homeless man. It was seemingly inconsequential and ordinary, and yet the repercussions to her self-image had begun rippling pleasantly.

Still, realizing that she'd never feel better until she was punished outwardly for what she'd done, killing that boy, she grabbed a hank of her lustrous thick long hair, took a deep steadying breath, and snipped it off near her scalp.

She stared at what she'd done. The bald patch. The hank of hair still in her hand.

It was irrevocable.

With a gasp, she let the scissors fall from her hand. They landed in the sink with a clatter.

She began thinking wildly of how she could hide that hole in her hair. A wig? A scarf? Glue or tape it back on like an artificial hair switch? Maybe a combover, like balding men used to disguise a thinning spot...in an effort that fooled no one?

Her heart raced in full panic as she stared at the long clump of hair gripped in her left hand.

Then she thought of Cabot and all the things he kept saying to her.

She thought of how miserable she was, living this way, always on edge, always trying to please and yet failing abysmally no matter what she did, what she said, how much she kowtowed to appease the angry Cabot god in the volcano.

Her hands trembling, she stuffed the shorn hair into the plastic bag. Her mind raced, inventing and discarding one excuse after another. What on earth would she tell him to explain this? How would she get herself out of this latest mess?

Keep cutting! Quick! Cut it all off!

A grin slowly spread on her lips.

Cabot loved her long hair.

Just do it!

When they were first together, he would watch her brushing her long blonde hair, and then he'd take the brush gently from her hand and spend an hour or more brushing her hair silently while they watched television. She'd felt pampered.

And later, when she was pregnant, he'd sit on the couch and have her sit cross-legged on the floor between his legs, with her back leaning against the couch. He cradled her head in his lap, and brushed her hair, making her feel loved and cherished.

Thinking of what Cabot said about letting people parade past their house to witness the word "killer" on it, she saw him with new eyes.

She saw how hostile he was to her.

Not just once in a while, in a bad mood that a different sort of husband would apologize for and make sincere amends for, but as a constant way of treating her, of controlling her, of keeping her under his thumb.

And yet, to her confusion, in public he fawned over her, he bragged about her, he told everyone how wonderful she was. She fell for it every time, believing (hoping) that public man must be the real Cabot, not the man she lived with behind closed doors.

When she was away from Cabot, in another part of the house, or at the grocery store alone, escaping his vicinity after one of his taunts or outbursts had been followed by his claim that she had "started something" and was fully to blame for any marital discord, Marybeth couldn't help wondering if he was right.

Most of the time, even when Cabot wasn't around, she had a sick feeling in her stomach that there was something intrinsically wrong with her that she couldn't have a happy marriage. Nothing made sense when she was around her husband. Their conversations were upside down and backwards, and yet he'd look her right in the eye and accuse her of inventing stories to make him crazy. He told her that if anyone was the victim in this marriage, it was he.

It never helped to think about the therapist who had told her she expected too much from a marriage, or that her depression could be treated with a popular medication (with additional prescriptions to offset the side effects of the first one) and then all would be well. The very thought of relying on an antidepressant to cope with life was depressing in itself.

But now, reflecting on her marriage and forcing herself not to slide into a haze of denial, Cabot's true colors seemed apparent to her for the very first time.

Usually she questioned herself, and let his claims of love and devotion and only wanting the best for her override what she thought she knew.

Usually, instead of trusting her own experiences, she let him define her reality by his terms.

Usually, she let herself slip back into a fog of pretending everything would get better soon, because it was less painful than facing the truth of her marriage. That merciful haze started to drift over her, as the anticipation of his reaction already had a whole script running in her mind. He'd say *What were you thinking!* and she'd say *I'm sorry, Cabot. I wasn't thinking at all, I guess* and he'd give her a long patient look, shaking his head as if exasperated with his difficult wife before asking *Did you get my shirts from the cleaners?*

But now, in this moment of looking at herself in the mirror, of really *seeing* herself, Marybeth knew she could not, would not be such a willing accomplice anymore. She wasn't going to tie herself into knots, agonizing over Cabot's reaction to her, and relegating her pitiful responses to the merciful release of pretending things would get better soon.

No more being a human pretzel, trying to appease, trying to please.

In a moment of sudden clarity, she realized their entire marriage was based on a mutual need that neither admitted or recognized openly: the need to have someone else to focus on so they didn't have to look within and heal what was wounded inside. More complex than a simple love-hate relationship that could be clearly defined. And yet was it really complex? Wasn't it very simply a matter of clinging to the dissension because it gave them something to talk about? And without it, they'd be in silence. Nothing in common. Nothing they shared other than superficial matters regarding the house and garden.

I'm done.

She looked her reflection square in the eye.

This time I mean it.

I quit!

Not one day more.

She ran her hands over her head, still stunned by what she'd done, but already feeling freer.

She acknowledged an inner prompting to admit that's precisely why she'd chosen this method of self-destruction. Her hair would grow back, and with it, she prayed, her fledgling self-esteem.

He's going to freak out.

Usually, that thought would send her into flight, scrambling into her full battle gear, campaign tactics at the ready to ameliorate his anger, to appease and assuage him before he could blow up at her, before he could escalate this ongoing war of terrorism against her.

But now, instead of bracing herself for an onslaught, she felt a tiny giggle escape her heart, followed by more giggles bubbling up and dancing in front of her as if they came from a long-ignored child demanding to be heard, demanding to be loved.

Marybeth calmly picked up the scissors and then ruthlessly clipped and cut and trimmed...until all of her long thick hair was in the plastic bag.

Studying the final shocking results of her nearly-bald head, she knew Cabot would be totally furious, beyond all reasoning.

I quit.

Chapter 10

In Marybeth's backyard, the gazebo smelled of fresh paint and new lumber. After completing the project, Cabot had set up a black wrought iron patio table and chairs in the center of the gazebo, and then added bright cushions and a blooming potted plant. The gazebo made a dramatic difference in the yard even though there was still so much other work remaining on the list of renovations.

She passed through the kitchen and went outside, not bothering to acknowledge Cabot's presence at the counter where he was fixing himself a snack. Somehow, chopping off her hair had not provided the release from pain she had hoped for. It wasn't a sufficient punishment. She still felt deadened by remorse about the accident. Even Cabot's startled reaction to what she'd done to her hair and not proved satisfying. She didn't know what else to do, how else to move on from the deep sense of grief she felt about every aspect of her life.

Cabot watched from the kitchen window as Marybeth wandered into the gazebo, curled up in a chair and lay her head on the glass-topped table. From this angle, it looked like a young boy had found refuge there, with that dejected posture and ragged, boyish haircut that was already showing blonde roots. Minutes passed, and she didn't move. He couldn't tell if she was crying again or not.

Coming to a decision, he turned away and picked up the phone, dialing from an address book Marybeth kept in a kitchen drawer. After several rings, Marybeth's older cousin Yolanda answered with an Hispanic accent.

"It's Cabot. Think you and Tom could drive up and spend a couple days with us?"

"How's she doing?" Yolanda asked. "Poor Bunny."

"You know how she gets. I told her to talk it over with her therapist, but she said he wouldn't be able to help. She won't leave the house. I'm worried about her. I've been as supportive as any husband could be, and she hasn't snapped out of it."

"You're her champion, Cabot. Thank God she has you."

"I hate to be the one to tell you this–"

"What? Oh please, not more bad news–"

"Not that. But she did get hold of a pair of scissors."

Yolanda's alarm came over the phone. "What happened!"

"She hacked off all her hair. Did you know she'd dyed it red recently?"

"Her beautiful blonde hair? Why would she do such a thing? I don't understand that girl."

"Neither do I." He allowed a pained silence to linger before continuing. "Now she looks like some kind of punk. When I asked her what made her cut her hair, she looked at me and said I could figure it out if I thought about it. Whatever the hell that means."

"Did you lock up the scissors, in case she gets the idea to–"

"It's a suicide watch here. Has been for more months than I'd care to count. Know how stressful that is, watching her constantly for signs of instability? I already keep all the kitchen knives in a drawer with a padlock on it and I bought both of us electric shavers after…Well, after last year. But how can I be her guardian angel every minute of the day and night? I have to allow her privacy, let her lead the semblance of a normal life."

Yolanda sighed into the phone. "I suppose even a manicure set can be a deadly weapon."

"She's not a prisoner. I'm at my wit's end. It's not normal, Yolanda. A wife should be able to have a bread knife in her hand and not have her husband worry what damage she'll attempt on herself."

Yolanda was silent a moment. "I'm hosting a rabbit rescue adoption this weekend, but I'll call the other volunteers and see if someone will switch their schedule with me. Tom has a doctor appointment tomorrow, so we'll get there day after tomorrow, about ten in the morning. Count on it. And tell her to answer my emails. I've written so many times since you told me about the accident and she never replies."

At the south end of the Acapulco bay, on the curving beach near the luxury high-rise hotels, Andy sat at an umbrella table, drinking *pina coladas* with Khaki and five sexy girls in bikinis, just as Khaki had promised.

Andy wore cutoff jeans, sandals and a Mexican shirt, unbuttoned.

Others in their "spring break" party played volleyball on the sand or splashed in the surf, careless and carefree. Wandering vendors offered souvenirs, newspapers and massages.

Lucinda was an exotic brunette with luscious curves spilling out of a tiny red bikini. She looked across the table at Andy, and said in a London accent, "He simply couldn't handle it."

"Am I supposed to know who and what you're talking about?"

Khaki chuckled and leaned in. "Go with the flow, Andy. You'll catch on."

"That evening—I'll never forget this—my mum went out of the flat," Lucinda said. "Usually she stayed in every evening, tired from running her shop in Notting Hill, but I wanted Rocky Road for dessert. She always indulged me. We didn't have any, but I couldn't stop wanting it. I had just applied an expensive hair conditioner and so my mum volunteered to run to the corner for the ice cream."

"And, uh," Andy said, trying to go with the flow but not seeing its direction yet, "the guy at the store couldn't handle the order?"

She stared at him blankly. "My boyfriend was insanely jealous. I broke up with him because I was tired of his scenes wherever we went. But then he came to the door when my mum was out buying ice cream, and he was crying. He begged me to let him in so he could give me flowers and apologize."

"And you opened the freaking door?" Andy asked. "Are you nuts?"

"I jilted him. He must have been watching the building and knew I was alone. I let him in. He stabbed me. Eight times. I counted them. Eight. He brought the knife with him, and took it away when he ran out. I bled to death on the kitchen floor. My mother came home with the ice cream, and she found me. It was awful. Really ghastly. Then he vanished. They never found him to bring him to justice. I think he left the country. My problem has always been that I'm too kind-hearted."

"You've got to be kidding me," Andy muttered. "You rattle off that script like it's for a soap opera, not something that actually happened to you that was tragic."

"Leave her alone," Khaki protested. "Go on, Lucinda."

"You see, he simply couldn't handle it."

"She's starting up again at the beginning." Andy was bewildered that Khaki couldn't see that.

The other girls at the table began telling their own stories of how they died, each one trying to out-shout the other, until the clamor was unbelievable.

Andy put his fingers between his lips and whistled shrilly.

They stopped talking and stared at him.

"One at a time, ladies. One at a time." Andy pointed to a girl in a coral bikini. "You're up next. Don't spare any details."

Khaki applauded, and then ordered another round of drinks from a passing waiter.

As the girls continued with their tales of woe, Andy grew bored. At first it had been exciting to arrive in Acapulco, to order as many cocktails as he wanted, and to kiss whatever girl was at hand, but he already found this empty lifestyle tedious. And why did they all want to talk on and on about how they died? He hadn't even bothered mentioning what happened to him. It lasted such a brief amount of time, why belabor the issue?

He glanced up from his musings to see Gabriella a few yards away. His dog Joker was at her side. He felt a twinge of jealousy that Joker had formed this friendship with someone else, but decided that was just friendliness on the dog's part and didn't mean disloyalty.

The Italian woman was dressed for Acapulco in a 1940s-style shorts outfit with a bare midriff top, high wedge espadrille sandals and a big floppy white hat. She wore bright silver globe shaped beads around her neck, and her silver armband was in place, as always.

Andy had the feeling those armbands everyone wore were a device to help newcomers see who would be more equipped to help with a question, rather than being marks of hierarchy. He wondered how long it would be before his black armband changed color, and what he might have to do to make that happen.

He found himself smiling at Gabriella, glad to see her. Recovering quickly, not wanting her to guess he was warming up to her, he called out, "Hey, Joker. Come here, boy!" When his dog sprang across the sand to his side, Andy tried to introduce the others at the table to his dog, but they were immersed in talking about how they died.

He realized they would keep on like this, possibly for eternity, but that he didn't have to. He got up to leave. "See you later, guys."

Gabriella nodded in approval, proud of him.

Khaki slanted him a look, but shrugged. "You'll come running back when you get bored with all the lessons people like Gabriella think you need to learn."

Andy looked at him, tempted to say this party is what was boring him, but he sensed that Khaki wouldn't comprehend.

Andy joined Gabriella. "Looking for me? Or is it some strange coincidence that you happen to be in this part of Acapulco the same time as me?"

She shrugged, amused.

"Cute outfit," he said. "But what's with all the changes? Every time I see you, you've got something new on, like you stepped out of an old movie like 'Casablanca' or one of those MGM musicals where everybody's always bursting into song and dancing around in an outfit nobody would wear on the street."

"Someone I met once, who should understand the power of metaphor, told me that I must be shallow and flighty since I am, as she put it, fixated on clothing." She raised an eyebrow, challenging him.

"Okay. The keyword is 'metaphor,' right?" Andy thought a moment, then smiled.

"You think you have an answer?"

"Those girls," he said, pointing back at the umbrella table, "don't really understand they are dead. They're caught up in some kind of fantasy thought world, where they float along, partying. And, ironically, talking about how they died. Other guys I've met are all about having a good time, playing at high risk sports but actually there's no risk, and not having to <u>think</u> at all." He looked at her. "I got into it for a bit. It was fun. But..."

"Yes, Andrew?"

"Not very satisfying."

"No, it's not, is it?" She smiled at him, as if he was earning her affection. "You are so right to say that people like those you've met lack perception they are dead. It's not that they refuse to accept death, they are unaware of the new dimension they inhabit. Would it surprise you to learn that the boy you call Khaki died over three hundred years ago as an old man, but got caught up in his fantasy of enjoying youth and hasn't let go of it yet."

"Wow. Okay, that's weird." Andy glanced back at Khaki, who lifted his *pina colada* in a silent mocking toast, guessing that he was the subject of their conversation.

Gabriella brought Andy's attention back to her. "We were talking about fashion?" She snapped her fingers and the sporty shorts outfit changed to a long flowing evening gown with a sequined parrot embroidered across one shoulder.

156

"Cool. Change can be fast, or slow. You show us that, by changing your clothes all the time. It's like a visual cue, to prompt people to leap to a new idea and a new understanding of their potential. We can stay stuck in the old outfit like Khaki, to continue the metaphor, Teacher," he added with a grin, "or push ourselves to grow and change."

They walked together along the shore. Joker dashed in and out of the waves, keeping up with them.

"What else are you thinking about, Andrew?"

"Remembering that when I was getting ready for a track meet, all I had to do was just *think* about putting on my running shoes, and immediately my whole body vibrated at a higher level. That's the word you'd use, isn't? Vibrate?"

She nodded. "We are all pure energy, vibrating at different frequencies. When we develop our consciousness, we can raise our frequency and be at a higher plane of understanding."

"Whenever I put on my running shoes, my focus gets narrower and concentrated. Other stuff doesn't matter anymore. It's like it doesn't even come into my line of sight. All I see is the path in front of me and I start running."

"What do you think I feel like doing when I dress like this?"

"Well, in that fancy dress, maybe you feel like going dancing. I hope you can find a partner, because I don't know how. My dad was going to teach me in time for the senior prom next spring." He smiled. "From what the past couple of days have been like for me, I'm guessing I'll catch on fast and dance like Fred Astaire if I want to."

She laughed.

"When I first met you," he said, "when you were under that streetlight, you were wearing a navy suit with padded shoulders and a white blouse with wide lapels. Your hair was pulled back and you wore pearl earrings and a pin that looked like angel wings."

"You noticed all that?"

"At the time I didn't, but I can picture you now. You looked very serious. I think that when you choose to wear a suit like that, you feel more businesslike and you transmit a message that people should listen up."

"You didn't exactly listen to me, did you? You ran off with Joker."

"But now we're here on a beautiful beach. If you want to go dancing, we could find a nice place."

"That will have to wait for another time, Andrew."

"We're here. It's supposed to be a full moon tonight. I'm not making a move on you, it just seems maybe we could enjoy dinner and dancing together."

"Your grandfather sent me."

"It's hard to think of him as my grandfather. Great-grandfather, actually. He only looks about ten or fifteen years older than me."

"All right, I'll say Qaletaqa from now on."

"What does he want?"

"I came to invite you to a funeral."

He scoffed. "A funeral? Whose?"

"Yours, Andrew."

"Oh." He looked at her. "Shit. Do I have to go?"

"Most people want to, out of love. Out of connections. Show up for their family and friends, be there to offer comfort and support. And, of course," she added with a teasing smile, "to see the turnout."

Andy's family, neighbors and friends boarded a rented yacht at Ventura Harbor. People on other boats watched the somberly dressed crowd with curiosity. Jemma had planned a small private ceremony, but Hart had overridden her decree and made welcome anyone who wanted to come. The boat's capacity was 100 and it was filling rapidly.

Spotting Eric in the crowd, Andy called out, "Hey, Eric!"

Gabriella touched his arm, silently reminding him.

"Oh yeah. Stupid. He can't hear me." He looked around.

Daisies wafted from above and drifted on the calm water. "Not yet, boys," a woman's voice called out softly. "Wait a little bit, okay? I'll tell you when."

"Hey, that's my Aunt Lulu," Andy cried. "I haven't seen her in ages. She must have Matt and Todd with her. I wonder who else is here."

As the boat left the pier and headed out into the Pacific Ocean on its special journey, Andy left Gabriella to explore the yacht. He saw that his dad's mother and older sister had come down from Washington state where they shared a small retirement house on a lake. There were assorted cousins and aunts and uncles on both sides of Andy's family tree. His mom's parents were there, and he was right about Lulu and her boys, but it felt strange to not be able to get them to notice him.

He realized everyone was very sad about his death. Finding Gabriella, he said, "Can't you let me tell them that I'm okay? That they don't have to cry because we'll all be together again someday?"

"I'm sorry, Andrew. That is not how we do things."

Frustrated, he turned away and mingled with the crowd as everyone began gathering for the ceremony.

Guests took stems of white flowers from baskets being passed by several of Andy's friends from school, including Eric and his sister Cara.

"Cara–" Andy reached out to touch her. "I'm sorry I didn't realize you liked me that way. I would've been nicer to you if I'd known. Maybe we could've gone to the movies together or something."

Gabriella appeared at his side. "It sounds like you are ready for your Life Review." She held out a hand to him.

"Here? Now?"

"It's the perfect place and time."

Suddenly nervous, Andy pointed to a wooden urn displayed on a table next to flowers. "Is that what I think it is?"

"Your earthly remains. Dust. Nothing you need."

The officiate for the ceremony spoke into a microphone, and several people came forward to offer eulogies they had not shared at the memorial service.

Andy watched as his parents each said a few words about him, and then picked up the scattering urn together. Hart slid back the top. Jemma saw the cremains, balked and stepped back. Guests leaned over the rail to bear witness as Hart scattered the ashes then gently dropped the biodegradable urn in the sea.

During this, Andy noticed that his mother closed her eyes.

At the sound of the splash, her breath caught. She held her sides, standing alone.

He saw that his dad welcomed all the hugs and offers of sympathy, and he sensed that Hart would come through this ordeal and manage to lead a good life.

But his mom's behavior worried him.

Guests began tossing flowers into the water. Some called out a quiet goodbye to Andy.

"But I'm HERE! I'm not gone. Stop saying goodbye. I'm right here with you!"

Gabriella slipped her arm around his waist. "Come with me, Andrew. Your Life Review will help you transition."

Glancing back at his funeral, he went with her to the top of the yacht. "Okay, so what now? Does my life flash before me like a video on high speed?"

"Be calm, Andrew. Be still. Open your soul fearlessly to this experience."

He nodded, and slowly relaxed, giving up his frustration over not being able to touch and talk to his parents and friends. He let all anxious thoughts float away like those daisies on the sea.

As he did so, Andy felt surrounded by a loving presence, one that accepted him completely and wanted only what was good for him. Relieved, he realized he was not about to be scolded or condemned, but rather helped to evaluate the progress he had made during his time spent on Earth as Andrew Powell.

He saw scenes from his life where he was interacting with others, and in each relationship he was able to recognize things he had done well and also the missed opportunities for more love. He saw the mistakes he'd made, such as taking that GPS unit from the store and arguing with his mother, but he felt awash with forgiveness for human failings.

"It's all about love," a voice said in his thoughts.

"I loved," Andy whispered, nodding, "but I could have loved more deeply. I made a difference, though. I made contributions to other peoples' lives. Mine wasn't a wasted life." After a moment of reflection, Andy looked at Gabriella, grateful she had urged him to accept his Life Review.

Aware that he was now vibrating at a higher frequency, Andy returned to the funeral. He saw his mother absently take the white rose her dad offered as he put an arm around her shoulder and murmured words of comfort.

"That's my grandpa," Andy explained to Gabriella. "He's Qaletaqa's son."

"I know," she said.

Jemma looked up.

Andy grew excited. "Hey, she's looking right at me, Gabriella!"

Gabriella let him believe it, knowing he'd soon find out it wasn't true.

Just beyond Andy was a huge vase of white lilies. Jemma dropped the white rose and pulled away from her father's embrace. Her mouth taut with rage, she stormed through Andy, grabbed the vase, pushed past startled guests, heaved the vase overboard and watched it sink.

Jemma said, vowing to herself, her voice barely audible, "I'll never forgive That Woman."

Andy looked at his mother, confused, then turned to his companion. "Gabriella?"

"We should go now, Andrew. I think it's for the best."

"Please let me help her. She's so bitter. I've never seen her like this."

"Your death shocked her. It's part of the human experience to lose the ones we love, and now it is her choice how she handles her grief. We have to allow her to find her own path."

"That can't be right. I'll find a way to help her."

Andy heard his name shouted from out on the water. Curious, he looked in that direction and spotted Khaki, Stripes, Blue and other boys scuba diving off a sleek mega-yacht that was over a hundred feet long.

"I brought your gear," Khaki called out. "Hurry up and join us. The diving is great today! And we're swimming with a whole school of dolphins. Totally cool, dude!"

Andy took a step toward the rail. He waved to the boy who had bicycled partway to the Hopi Reservation with him. "Hey, Blue. I thought you left."

"Khaki was right." Blue beckoned him. "This is way more fun. Hurry up and get your butt down here!"

Hesitating, Andy looked back at his mother. Even though he knew that she couldn't hear him, he asked, "Mom—what do you think I should do?"

He spent a moment remembering all the times she'd encouraged him to study when he was tempted to hang out at the mall or skateboard park with the other guys. *You have a great mind, Andy, and with it comes the joyful obligation to spend more time on things that might seem boring in the short term, but will pay off in rich rewards later. You can go out this evening for a couple of hours. I don't expect you to work like a machine. Life is supposed to be fun, too.*

The boys kept calling to him from the phantom yacht, urging him to hurry.

"Sorry, guys," Andy said. "I've got something else to do. See you around."

As soon as Khaki realized Andy meant what he said, the boys and the yacht vanished.

Andy wondered if they had been there at all or if he'd only imagined it. He turned back to Gabriella and waited.

She studied him a moment. "Does this mean you are ready to get serious?"

"Yes."

"Would you like to learn how to be a Dream Spinner?"

"What's that?"

"I tested your mother's receptivity and she was able to hear a short message from me."

Andy grew excited. "You mean I'll be able to send her messages?"

"I cannot guarantee she will recognize them as being from you."

"But she'll hear me?"

"There are many variables, Andrew. You'll learn more about it as we progress. Please be aware there is no guarantee she will pay attention to any of the messages we send in her unconscious time. You could shout for five years or five hundred and not be heard. But it is a method that sometimes works. Her living consciousness is more open to us in her sleeping state than in her waking state."

"Teach me how to do it!"

"All right then, Andrew." She beamed at him. "Come with me and we'll get started."

Chapter 11

Fifteen candles burned low, part of a tribute to Andy displayed on the piano in the living room. There were framed photographs, scrapbooks, photo albums, track trophies and sand castle contest ribbons.

Hart and Jemma greeted their guests and accepted condolences, gradually getting moved apart by the crowd until they stood at opposite ends of the room.

Many of the people had been on the yacht earlier, but neighbors dropped by now, as well, and people who had not wanted to, or had not been available to make the drive out to the harbor in Ventura.

The staff from Hart's bistro catered the reception, and Jemma had little to do that day but get dressed on time, get in the limo when told to do so, go on the yacht, get off the yacht, and now accept the sympathy pressed upon her.

She had never been a hugging, demonstrative sort of person, and all the arm patting and cheek stroking and shoulder squeezing made her feel like running from the next pair of outstretched arms.

"God wanted another angel." An older woman she'd never met gripped Jemma's arm and shook it for emphasis.

"God needed another rose in his garden." A neighbor patted her shoulder, then plucked a flower from a nearby vase and pressed it into Jemma's hand as if to drive the point home.

"Only the good die young," Stanley Blum told her, and others in the line picked it up as if from the air and repeated it.

Jemma nodded politely at each comment and murmured, "Thank you for coming."

Eric signed the guest book, tore a scrap from a back page and wrote a note. He tucked it into one of the picture frames on the piano, glanced around to locate Jemma, went up to her and waited until the people talking to her moved away to the buffet.

"Sorry I couldn't find his buffalo nickel, Mrs. P. Your husband asked me to look around at the...you know, where the accident was. I looked everywhere, even under all the bushes but it...wasn't there."

"I guess someone found it," she said dully, "and kept it."

He started crying. "He was my best friend. I miss him an awful lot."

She awkwardly patted his arm.

Snuffling, he moved off to go hang out with the other teenagers gathered in the family room where they stood in a circle, talking about Andy and what a great guy he'd been.

As Jemma looked around, she did not see a single person she felt close enough to confide her feelings in. Her sister was trying so hard not to show relief that her own boys were safe, and Jemma didn't want to add to Lulu's unwarranted guilt by sharing how bereft she felt now that Andy was gone. Her parents, and Hart's family, were so overwrought by the loss of their oldest grandchild that she didn't want to burden them with her grief. She felt their sorrow, and tried to help them cope.

It didn't seem right, either, to ask Hart to help handle her bereavement when he had his own pain to carry, and so, although Jemma had always a long list of acquaintances and work associates, now she was paying the price for her lack of a close confidante.

The only person with whom she felt anything close to that sort of bond was her friend at NASA, Fran Hastings, but Fran had not shown up at the funeral, despite her promise to attend. Jemma knew that Fran had a heart condition she tried to keep a secret so her job would not be in jeopardy, and now Jemma hoped that Fran was doing okay. Deciding to try to reach Fran by phone, Jemma excused herself from the group of guests encircling her and slipped off to the quiet of her study, in a downstairs corner of the house. Once inside, she eased the door shut and leaned against it.

Gabriella and Andy strolled through Griffith Park near the Old Zoo picnic area. There were a dozen empty steel cages in a long row, built against a steep hill. From Andy's viewpoint, the cages seemed to be filled with shadows and swirls of smoke in vaguely human shapes.

"Gabriella? Are those people in there? I mean, dead people like us?"

"You must not go in there, Andrew. We call it the Gray Zone. The ones who choose to stay in there are sad, lost souls. You are not advanced enough to help them."

He shot her a look of annoyance, his pride piqued.

"Each of us creates our own reality on Earth," Gabriella said, "and here in our dimension as well. If you think you'll die and go to heaven, then you end up in a realm that fits that vision, complete with cherubic angels, harps and halos. If you expect to be punished for your sins and transgressions, then your mind will create the reality of hell or limbo for yourself, and no one will be able to convince you that it's all in your own imagination."

"So they think it's a sentence or a judgment from higher up, and they stay stuck?" Andy thought a moment. "What about guys like Khaki and those girls in Acapulco? I got the feeling they were continuing their life, maybe doing different things they couldn't afford before, but basically thinking the same way they did when they were alive. Is that right?"

"You filter everything through what you believe about yourself and your reality—what you think is possible and impossible. If you have a lower awareness of the power of consciousness, then the entire 'after-life' becomes a game of seeking pleasure with like-minded souls. But then, as each individual opens to awareness, their experience broadens."

"Which explains my trip to Las Vegas where it seemed like a ghost town. I guess some part of me realized I was dead and so I didn't expect to see humans. I bet there were a lot of other ghosts--or whatever you call us–there, but I didn't notice them. Those other guys, Khaki and Blue and Lucinda and others I've met...could they go on like that forever?"

"If they so choose. But I can sense you are worried we allow it to happen when they clearly need guidance."

"Doesn't seem fair."

"It wouldn't be," Gabriella agreed. "We give them freedom to discover for themselves what they need to know, because that is more valuable than imposing ideas upon them. But we do not abandon them, ever. They are always surrounded by willing guides, waiting to help at the first sign their assistance would be welcome."

"Like you did with me." Andy chuckled. "So, that means some people choose to be teachers or guides in the after-life, right? And when a lost soul gets bored or tired of experiencing the same thing again and again–like bungee jumping day after day and then playing on a beach and then going to a nightclub–they reach out for help, they invite a higher awareness. Is that right?"

Andy glanced over at the Gray Zone. He saw a man with a silver armband emerge from within, escorting a woman who abruptly turned from foggy gray to full color and hugged her guide.

"You mean like her? She finally listened?"

Gabriella nodded. "At that instant of asking for help, someone is there to show the way to advance. All of us have the same joyful eternal nature of creating what has not existed before, of expanding in this incredible, unlimited field of infinite possibilities. But many people grow and evolve at a much slower pace than others, and there is no blame in that."

"I wish I'd studied this kind of stuff in school. I think it would make life a whole lot easier for everybody if they really understood the power of their own thoughts."

Jemma's study was well-organized, neat and orderly, and yet also inviting. On the desk was her laptop computer and printer. Walls were crowded with photos, some personal and others related to her career in science. The tall walnut bookcases held neatly shelved books about women in space, as well as NASA memorabilia. There were handmade gifts from Andy, and framed drawings. Two comfortable chairs offered sanctuary beneath the corner windows.

She called Fran's number on her cell, but it went straight to voice mail so she left a brief message.

Sounds of the waning reception drifted in. Jemma stood at the window, staring out into the dusk of late summer evening. The doorbell rang, and she heard high heels click toward the front door. Moments later, she heard Lulu answer the door and introduce herself. The visitor was Fran Hastings, and so Jemma was not surprised to hear a gentle tap at her door.

"Come in," she called out.

The door swung open a few inches and Lulu looked in. "Jem? It's Fran–"

Jemma nodded and Lulu held the door wider.

Fran bustled towards her, out of breath, and took Jemma's hands in her plump ones. "My heart aches for you, my dear."

Here, at last, was someone who understood her and would not launch into flowery speeches, promises of prayers, or excessive physical contact. Jemma indicated the chairs and they sat next to each other.

"I'll slap the next person who tells me God needed another angel," Jemma said.

Fran relayed messages of sympathy from various people at NASA. "I'm sorry I couldn't be here for the ceremony. I was tired after the flight and decided to sleep late instead of renting a car to drive out to the pier. I tried to leave a message on your phone but your mail box is full. How did it go?"

She shrugged and met Fran's gaze. "Just your typical funeral for a teenage boy, I guess. In a word: heartbreaking." She got up and paced. "I can't imagine how parents go through this and then keep on going, holding their grief day after day while looking normal on the outside."

"I know it's a trite thing to say, Jemma, but you do know that time will help. Don't be too hard on people for what they say. It's difficult to know the right words at a time like this." A bit sheepishly, Fran added, "When my David died I told the little kids 'Grandpa is in heaven.'"

"Nice thing to say. To children."

They looked at each other, two skeptics in accord.

"Sometimes I..." Jemma began, then fell silent.

"What?"

Jemma shrugged, ready to dismiss it, then confessed, "At the accident, there was a...well, a moment when I heard a man's voice say, 'Don't worry, he'll be all right--he'll be with me.' The voice seemed familiar."

"One of the paramedics?"

"More like someone from long ago, but of course you're right. One of the paramedics trying to offer comfort as they got ready to take Andy to West Hills. After all, when it's over, it's over. Sometimes I even think I see Andy or hear his voice, but I guess everyone goes through that stage."

"The imprint of memories is strong."

"Wish I could believe in all that other crap. Must be a comfort...."

Fran nods. Maybe it would be.

"You know, Fran, I used to briskly handle half a dozen things at the same time, almost ambidextrous in my attempt to do more than the average person. 'Multi-tasking' hardly described it. Now if I try to walk and talk at the same time, it's sensory overload. If I'm interrupted mid-sentence, I forget what I was saying."

"That happened to me when my husband died. You're distracted now. It's natural."

Jemma nodded. "Glad you're here now, because I...well, frankly I was feeling very alone." She tried to smile, but found the muscles necessary for it were unwilling.

Fran glanced around at the NASA memorabilia and shelves of books related to space travel. Her gaze stopped on a book about the Mercury 13 women, the first female astronauts back in the 1960s who never got a chance to fly in space.

"I told two of your favorite women about Andy," Fran said. "Jerrie Cobb and Wally Frank. Both of them send their sympathy and wanted me to tell you how sorry they are. Actually, it's a very long list, all the people who care about you and want to see you in the astronaut corps."

"Between us, Fran, I don't know about that anymore."

"Oh, that's not why I'm here," Fran said. "It came out sounding that way, but you know I'd never–" She stopped herself and admitted wryly, "Well, maybe I would. The space program has been my top priority for thirty years. I always wanted to be the type who'd qualify as an astronaut but I'm not smart enough and my heart has always been a little weak."

"I used to be afraid of wasting time, always feeling I didn't have enough of it to spare. Now I have such a surplus I feel overwhelmed each day, how to fill the long hours...."

Fran smiled gently. "I know from experience, work helps with that."

There was a long silence between them.

"Fran–"

"Yes?"

"I'm going to use that four-letter-word you claim you never expected to hear from me."

"It's too soon for a decision like that."

"I quit."

They sat in silence for a moment, both absorbing what that meant.

Finally, Fran asked, "How long did you work for your spot on the candidate list? Ten years? Longer than that, right? Since you were a schoolgirl, if memory serves. Remember when you brought your husband and son to the Space Center and gave them a tour? Remember what your son said to me when we met?"

Jemma's expression said that she remembered.

"He told me something like, 'You make sure they take care of my mom when she's up in a space shuttle, Mrs. Hastings, because sometimes she forgets to even eat.' He was worried that you get so intense about your work you neglect to take care of your own needs. And so I'm here. And I'm going to take care of you, Jemma. Maybe not physically--I know you have friends and family for that and I have to get back to Houston. But I'll be your cheering team, the way Andy was. And I'm not going to let you throw away a lifetime's work. He wanted you to be an astronaut. It was his dream too, for you. You know that, don't you?"

"Andy was thrilled. The only problem was about school--not wanting to move to Houston. It was never about NASA. Only about not leaving his friends."

Jemma heard voices in the foyer and Hart welcoming new guests and saying goodbye to others.

"I should let you get back to your reception," Fran said.

"Have lunch with me tomorrow? My mom and my sister want to get me out of the house, and I'd love for you to join us."

When Jemma rejoined the reception, she wished she had talked Fran into staying longer. Even though she knew everyone here, it felt like she was lost in a group of strangers.

Hart drank coffee with several guests, including his mother and sister. His mother leaned over and said something to him. He reluctantly rose and crossed to Jemma. "My mother wants to go to church in the morning. I'm supposed to ask if you'll join us." He shrugged helplessly.

"You know my opinion about religion," she said. "The answer to 'What comes next?' is 'Nothing.' This is all we get. There isn't any 'heaven' out there. Andy is gone. Chanting mumbo-jumbo and lighting candles in front of a statue won't bring him back. No matter how much we wish it would."

"That's not what she—"

Striding to the pianist, Jemma shoved his hands off the keys and slammed the lid. Confused, the hired piano player got up from the bench.

She saw Eric's note—"They're together now"--stuck in the frame of a photo showing a younger Andy hugging his dog Joker. She crumpled the note, then looked at the fifteen candles. She realized people were staring, but she didn't care.

"Jemma—" Hart said uncertainly, approaching.

She snuffed each flame between her fingers, enraged by her loss, inured to the pain. "Goodbye, everyone!" she called out. "Goodbye. Thank you for coming...Now please get out."

"I didn't know you even cared for Chinese food, Jemma," Mrs. Malotki said, looking around the restaurant her daughter had suggested for lunch.

"Andy liked this place," Jemma explained as the four women looked at their menus. "After Hart opened the French bistro, Andy was worried that if people saw us eating in someone else's restaurant, it would make them think his dad's place wasn't any good. But since Hart doesn't serve Chinese food, Andy decided it'd be okay to eat here."

"Oh, that's so cute," Lulu said.

Fran smiled. "He was a good kid."

"When did you meet him?" Lulu asked. "Oh, wait, I remember that trip. Jemma sent me NASA souvenirs for the boys."

"Andy was very proud of his mom," Fran said.

"It's a shame this had to happen now, of all times," Mrs. Malotki said.

"Why do you say it that way, Mom?" Jemma asked.

"Well, you certainly aren't going to want to go up into space now. It's far too dangerous anyway. That would be a real cruelty to Hart, taking such a risk."

"We've talked about the risk before, Mom. Please, let's not get into this. Let's enjoy this chance to have lunch together and talk about something else."

The waiter came and took their order.

As Jemma tried to steer a conversation toward discussing the weather, Fran quietly interjected, "What about correcting the history books, Jemma? What about getting Jerrie Cobb into space, or at least her proxy? What about–"

Jemma gave a mocking laugh and cut her off. "Setting things right for the Mercury Thirteen women?"

"Your words, not mine, dear. Take time off with your family. Then come back to the Space Center. When my husband died, I found that, even though it's a cliché, work did give me a purpose–" Fran faltered and tried to open her purse. She fumbled. Her color was off.

"What's wrong with her?" Lulu asked, alarmed.

"It's her heart." Jemma opened Fran's purse, found the vial of nitroglycerine and put a pill under Fran's tongue.

In a few moments, Fran recovered. "I'm so sorry, ladies. Maybe I should cut this short and go back to my hotel."

"I'm glad you're feeling better," Mrs. Malotki said, "but I must say, you have a lot of nerve trying to convince my daughter to go ahead with her crazy plan of being an astronaut."

Fran got up and faced Jemma. "Is it a crazy plan, Dr. Malotki? You're the one who convinced me that sometimes we have to go outside the box to get results."

"I said a lot of things, Fran. Someone else will do it if I don't."

Fran leaned in to hug Jemma and whispered, "You know damn well you're the only one who can do this. It's your destiny. Take some time off, then come back to us."

Jemma looked at her, but did not reply.

Cabot dug planting holes, sweating in the strong sun. He measured and spaced the holes evenly along each side of the straight path from the sidewalk to the front door. Five-gallon rosebushes waited in the driveway, having been delivered by a nursery.

Marybeth dragged a bag of soil amendment toward a hole. She wore gardening gloves and a hat to protect her face from sunburn.

"Hurry up," Cabot said. "I'm doing the hard work. Can't you at least keep up? You've only done two. Ten to go."

She nodded, well aware how many were left, and mixed soil amendment with loose soil in the bottom of the hole, then cut into a container to loosen the plant, set the bush carefully into the prepared hole and filled it in with more soil amendment.

Taking a break to stretch his back, Cabot admired one of the bushes she planted. "Look at all these buds! Dozens on each bush. They'll bloom the rest of the summer and on into fall. They'll probably go through several more budding cycles and we'll have roses at Christmas."

Marybeth tightened her lips into a smile. "They'll look nice."

"Nice? There you go with that snooty tone. You're pissed because you wanted white and I ordered pink."

"I just thought white would look more classic with a green-trimmed house, but I'm sure the pink will be beautiful."

"Feed and water them after you plant each one. I don't care if you have to stay up half the night to finish, you agreed to do the planting if I dug the holes."

"I know." She nodded and planted another, wincing when thorns scratched her bare arms.

He looked at her, sighing. "Oh, Jesus, can't you tell when I'm joking?" He began planting rosebushes. "You're so sensitive. I was just kidding, trying to get a laugh out of you. Why do you have to take everything I say so seriously?"

At the cul-de-sac's entry, someone on a bicycle watched Marybeth and Cabot from beneath the purple shadows of a jacaranda tree. When a car approached, the figure quickly rode away.

It was Andy's friend, Eric.

Andy watched Joker play with live dogs on the sloping grass. "Gabriella? How come the dogs can see Joker, but their humans can't see us?"

"The dogs are at a similar frequency. To Joker, there's not much difference between life and death, other than the obvious physical things like getting hungry. He knows how to experience a fullness of self, a delight of consciousness, no matter what dimension he's in."

"Makes me wish humans were more like that. But I guess there's no sense wishing things were different. I'm discovering that things are the way they are, and the easiest path is to go along with the new program."

"You have learned a lot." She smiled at him. "But don't start thinking you are perfect. Our real work is about to begin."

"Thanks for the encouragement!"

"Andrew, let's be serious a moment."

He nodded.

"Drowning. Poison. Severe injury. Fire. Car accident. Murder. Heart attack. Suicide. Old age. War. Gang shooting. Illness. What is the one single thing they all have in common?"

Joker ran up to Andy with a tennis ball in his mouth, and Andy began tossing the ball for him to fetch.

176

"They're all violent," Andy replied to Gabriella. "No, wait. You said illness and old age, and they aren't in that category. Unless you just mean they are all ways people can die?"

"I'm sure you could add to the list, but what they all have in common is they serve to separate the physical body and the immortal soul. The moment a person is born, he is headed toward death by some means. There is no avoiding it. Even Houdini could not escape it."

"If it's always been planned that being on Earth is a temporary visit," Andy said, "then what's the point? Why bother?"

"Having a physical experience gives so many opportunities to learn more about yourself, to develop and to grow spiritually. And to create more love and joy!"

"But why don't we get taught how to do that? So many people are unhappy and depressed and stressed out because they don't even know these basic concepts."

"That's one of the things we Dream Spinners are working to change."

After Jemma's and Hart's relatives left, the household routine drifted into a new normalcy. Lulu decided to stay an extra couple of days on her own, to help Jemma with thank you notes and anything else that might come up.

After putting another stack of stamped envelopes in the mailbox for pickup, she said to Jemma, "That's enough of duty for a while. I'm taking you out for a massage."

"I have to admit that sounds like a wonderful idea."

An hour later, Jemma and Lulu were seated in a dimly lit, serenely decorated waiting room, wearing nothing but terry robes and paper slippers, and sipping herbal tea. On the table in front of them were glass bowls with floating flower blossoms, and a small copper fountain. The sound of falling water was gently soothing, in harmony with the flute music coming from hidden speakers. A door opened and a young woman in a pastel green smock looked in on them expectantly, glancing from face to face.

"This is my treat, Jemma," Lulu said. "You go first."

By the time the massage reached the middle of Jemma's back, she was crying soundlessly and unable to stop the flow. The sympathetic masseuse, a woman who said her favorite aunt had died recently, had already warned Jemma that the massage might release emotions as well as tension, and had equipped her with a handful of tissues.

Now Jemma swiped at her eyes and nose and tried to give herself over to the simple pleasure of the massage and let her mind be still. Afterwards, Jemma returned to the waiting room, and gave Lulu a hug of thanks for the experience.

Lulu left to have her own massage. In Jemma's absence, someone had placed a pitcher of chilled water on the table along with small glasses. Slices of cucumbers floated in the water, flavoring it delicately. She poured a glassful.

When Lulu returned, she paid for their massages, took a gym membership application and handed it to Jemma. "You could join and pay month-to-month. Cancel anytime. But you'd get discounts on massages, and it's a great place for your workouts."

While Jemma relaxed in the spa section of the gym, Mike McLeod finished a yoga class in the glass-enclosed room used for instructor-led courses. He crossed the crowded gym floor, where all the weights, treadmills and exercise bicycles were arrayed, many in use now, to the locker room.

He showered and changed, mentally preparing for the upcoming meeting with his director of photography. They had a green light on "Seven Funerals" and were in the pre-production phase of finding locations, fine-tuning the script, finalizing the cast, and getting started on costumes.

The list was long, and as the film's director, Mike was involved in all stages of the project from script treatment to theater release date.

As the screenwriter, he'd been involved from the time he first conceived the story. It was a romance, inspired by his first love, a woman he'd never been able to forget, even though both of them had gone on to marry other people. Jemma was a memory that wouldn't go away.

He'd hoped writing the script would be a cathartic experience. But he was wrong in that. It seemed that lately his thoughts were filled with memories of her more than ever. In the parking lot, Mike tossed his gym bag in the trunk of his car and drove away.

Moments later, Jemma and Lulu emerged from the gym and walked to Jemma's car, talking idly about the beautiful summer day and how luxurious the massages had felt.

When Jemma got home, she felt so relaxed and tired, she went upstairs to nap. Hart had gone to his bistro, too restless to stay homebound another evening. Seeing that Hart would be busy, Lulu suggested that they have a girls' night, watch old movies and order pizza delivery. Lulu would be leaving the following day, and wanted a quiet evening with Jemma before going.

The sound of the doorbell woke Jemma and she hurried downstairs. Lulu was already there, paying for the pizza. "Let's eat while it's hot." Lulu shut the door. "I made a salad. All that's needed is you on the couch with your feet up."

In the family room, Lulu handed Jemma a paper plate with a big slice of pizza. "That's all the serving I'm doing. It's strictly grab-for-yourself from now on."

Jemma looked at her a long moment. "I couldn't have handled this without you."

"No problem." Lulu took a paper from her pocket. "I found this online and wanted to share it with you."

"What is it?"

"Here, I'll read it while we eat, then we can watch a movie." Lulu unfolded the page and read from it, "Appalachian cure for a grieving mother: Fill a mason jar with the smallest pebbles you can find. Each morning, take out the tiniest pebble, go outside and throw it as far as you can. When all the pebbles are gone, so will be your sorrow." She folded the paper and tucked it under a book on the table. "In case you want to read it again."

"I have a question," Jemma said.

"What's that?"

"Where will I find a mason jar that's big enough?"

Chapter 12

When the next weekend arrived, Yolanda and Tom entered the small house on the cul-de-sac, bringing in little gifts, magazines and candy for Marybeth.

"What did you bring me?" Cabot asked.

"Oh, I–" Yolanda began uncertainly.

"Just kidding." He laughed and embraced both of them in big, hearty hugs. "Come on in. I can't thank you enough for making the trip. It's so good to have you here."

Marybeth joined them in the living room. She was waif-like in her new shorn hair, and the ragged jeans she wore daily. With a desultory hello, she kissed Yolanda's cheek and murmured polite phrases about being glad they came to visit. "But what's the occasion? I thought you weren't coming until Cabot's trip to Cleveland?"

"Your darling husband thought we could help you by being here," Yolanda said.

Marybeth smiled dutifully. "My darling husband is so thoughtful, isn't he?"

Cabot shot her a narrowed look.

As soon as he had the chance, Cabot took Yolanda aside on a pretext of needing her help in the kitchen, leaving Tom and Marybeth to go out to the gazebo where he had refreshments waiting.

"I didn't tell her I found out about her latest deception, Yolanda, but when she refused to go see her therapist, I called him myself. To discuss what I can do to help. They barely remembered her name!"

"What? I thought she went two times a week for therapy."

"So did I. I don't know where the money went, but she quit going weeks ago, long before the accident. She would leave the house and tell me she was going for her session, then she'd be gone the right amount of time and show up here again. Turns out she was writing checks payable to cash and cashing them, but she told me they asked her to pay them under the table. She lied about the whole thing. Tell me that's not crazy, Yolanda. Tell me. I want to know how I can help her when she won't even cooperate."

"I'm so sorry you've got this to deal with," Yolanda said. "I didn't realize she'd gotten this bad."

"Can you talk to her? I've tried everything."

"Oh, I'm sure you have," Yolanda said. "I remember when you two met. I was so worried about her because she'd broken up with Robbie and kept crying over him, desperate to know if it was a mistake. He didn't want to move to Hollywood for her to live her dream, but it was too hard for her to keep living in Palm Springs and drive in for auditions."

"She led me to believe that he broke up with her."

"I'm sure it was her idea. I think you must have met her only about a month or so after that. I know it wasn't very long. Didn't you meet at a lecture you were giving?"

"She had a small inheritance from her grandmother–"

"My grandmother, too," Yolanda reminded him. "And I also got some money."

"--and wanted to invest it," Cabot continued as if she hadn't spoke, intent on relaying his melodrama, "so she attended an all-day seminar I was giving for novice investors. I took her out to dinner afterwards and frankly, Yolanda, I was smitten. I'd never met anyone as lovely and light-hearted. She was so sweet, I wanted to gobble her up." He laughed, remembering.

"You really wined and dined her, didn't you? And she's never been much of a drinker. I'm sorry we couldn't rush off to join you in Vegas. I'll never forget how excited she was when she called to say you two were getting married and you were going to live together in L.A."

Bitter lines framed his mouth. "She used me."

Yolanda said, reaching out to stroke his arm. "I'm sure you're wrong. It was a wonderful coincidence that you already lived where she wanted to be. Don't think badly of her. Please?"

"I'll hold onto my precious memories of the early days we had together that were so loving and special."

"Do that, and meanwhile, I'll have a good long talk with her and see if I can't help her get her priorities straight."

He nodded, letting out his breath in one thankful gasp. He gave her a long hug, squeezing her tight.

Later, Yolanda suggested to Marybeth that it was time for girl-talk and drew her younger cousin out of the gazebo to stroll around the backyard. "Look what a pretty garden you have now. This is wonderful. You two have worked so hard on this place, creating a home of your own. Nothing like the pictures you emailed me when you first moved in."

"It's all Cabot's work. I didn't really do anything. A little paint inside is all."

"I bet you've done more than that, dear," Yolanda chided gently. "You always diminish your contributions, but you can't fool me." Yolanda kept her arm around Marybeth and walked her through the garden, commenting cheerfully about everything they passed.

"You don't have to do this." Marybeth pulled away. "I know why you're here." She touched her ragged hair. "Yolanda, how can I live with the sin of murder on my soul?"

"Bunny! It was an accident! No one is accusing you of–"

"It doesn't matter what the judge decides. The tree branch covering the stop sign? So what? It was an intersection, even though it was only a three-way intersection, and I should have made a complete stop as a matter of common safety. I was thinking about getting to my audition, and look what my distraction did. A boy's life is gone. His family will never be the same. His friends. His future–"

Marybeth bent and picked a ripe beefsteak tomato. She squeezed the tomato until it burst. Red juice and tiny yellow seeds dripped over the scars on her wrists

Yolanda tossed the tomato aside and wiped Marybeth's skin with her fingers. "Stop it, honey," she said softly. "You're making yourself sick. Cabot's worried about you. That's why he called me."

"I guess I'm supposed to be grateful he didn't call my parents. Like they'd care."

Taking Marybeth's hand in hers, Yolanda gently stroked the slender fingers and talked soothingly about parents who didn't handle it well when a change-of-life baby appeared. "You've always had my love, Bunny. You know that. Let's not get sidetracked by childhood problems that are in the past, okay? It keeps them in the present with you. Try to let it go, and let go of the accident, too. It's in the past now, it can't hurt you unless you let it."

Marybeth glanced toward the house. "When I met Cabot, he was so kind and protective of me. He was serious. Mature. Fatherly, in a way. With Robbie, it always seemed we were two lost lambs, trying to hold each other up, hoping love would be enough. Then, with Cabot, he was so completely different from Robbie, that I latched on to the idea of him. Do you know what I mean?"

Yolanda nodded sympathetically.

"The idea that because he was older and he taught people about serious things like finance, I felt that meant he would be a steadying influence on me. But not just for what I could gain, I know that sounds selfish like I was looking for a protector or a rescuer. I could see his need for someone like me. And I knew that if I had him to take care of, and to care for me, that between the two of us we could somehow rescue me from all the confusion I was feeling." She glanced at Yolanda. "Don't you dare tell him that."

"I never tell him about our chats or our emails, Bunny. I make it clear you are so private you don't confide in me. Your secrets are safe. I actually told him you haven't been answering my emails at all."

Looking reassured, Marybeth went on, "It seemed like we wanted the same things, a home and family, and I thought the age difference wouldn't matter. But I think it does. He treats me like I'm his toy. A hobby."

"That's not true–"

"I feel like I'm suffocating. He watches me constantly. Hovers around me. More now than ever."

"He worries about you–"

Marybeth blew out an impatient sigh. "Never mind. No one understands. I don't know why so many bad things happen to me, again and again. Like when Naomi killed herself." She paced like a caged animal. "I had no idea she was contemplating suicide. But according to Cabot I was supposed to act like it didn't matter that my cousin who was like a little sister to me--my best friend-- my maid of honor--was gone. Cabot kept watching me and saying I needed to move on. 'Move on'? Where to! Nobody cared what I was going through when she died."

Yolanda frowned. "I loved Naomi like a daughter. Don't you dare act like I–" She caught herself. "Listen, Bunny, let's hold onto each other. We won't forget those we've lost, but we have to live in today–"

"Did you read that on a Hallmark card?...Okay. Sure. I'm sorry, Yolanda. I really am so grateful you came. It's wonderful to see you."

"Oh, honey, you've had such a hard time. You know, I was wondering about that therapist you go to. Don't you think it might help if you talk things over with him, about this accident you had? Get things straight in your mind?"

"I'm all right."

"I don't mean to push in where I'm not wanted, dear, but you can't handle this kind of thing alone. It's too big. And with your history, frankly–"

"You're afraid I'll get suicidal?"

Yolanda looked at her, silently agreeing. After a moment, she said, "Say, what about that support group you went to for a while last fall? The one that meets at the church near here? I could go with you so you won't feel so nervous about going in."

Jemma sat in the backyard hammock near the pool, staring blindly at the water as it rippled in the late afternoon breeze.

From inside the house, at an upstairs window in the master bedroom, Hart spotted Jemma. Moments later, he came out with a hardbound journal in his hand.

"Mind if I join you?" He dragged a lounge chair closer and sat. "I've been writing in the journal my staff gave me. They all chipped in to buy it, and said maybe I'd like to put down some of my memories of Andy while they're fresh."

"Did you expect them to go stale?"

He flinched.

"Sorry," she said. "I have an acid tongue and I take it out on you. I apologize."

"I know how hard this is on you, Jemma. Can you understand it's hard on me, too?"

"I know that." She got out of the hammock.

"I wanted to share something I just wrote. Will you let me read it to you?"

She started to refuse, but saw from his face that this was important to him, so she settled in a patio chair to listen.

He opened the journal and flipped through a few pages to the newest entry, then began reading. "Loss and life go hand in hand, but we turn a blind eye to loss until it is our own. We are not privileged to view all the unknowns. Sometimes we get a glimpse when a curtain parts in a candlelit window. We must see with the eye of faith. I believe we are on earth for a special experience but we've forgotten our spiritual origins. We seek answers from books and holy teachers but the truth lies deep within us if we are willing to be quiet and listen. During a time of grief, our aching hearts are open to messages. Little things, like a reassuring pat on the hand from someone who loves you. Today I felt my son Andy pat my hand."

Jemma gasped.

He looked up and hesitantly explained, as if braced for her to scoff. "It was amazing. I'll never forget the experience." He continued reading, "Imagine you are dining in a five-star restaurant. You savor each dish, and then you turn and say graciously to the hovering waiter: 'My compliments to the chef.' We understand that menus were planned, ingredients gathered and dishes prepared, all orchestrated behind the scenes by the master chef. For me, that chef is God, but you don't have to be religious to believe in a Master Creator."

"That's nice, Hart. Beautiful."

"There's more. Sorry, it's kind of long but I want to share it, if that's okay?"

"Sure. Of course."

"Some losses that we have are so minuscule we hardly notice them," he read. "Flakes of dead skin cells, stray hairs in a comb, the death of flowers on a vine or bees in the hive. Losses go on all around us, all day every single day, but the pain we feel about our own loss is in direct proportion to our emotional involvement. This means to me that my grief for Andy will be as deep as my love for him. It is a tribute, not a burden, to mourn my loss. When I learn how to let go of the pain and treasure the moments we had together, I will find peace in my heart, but I don't expect it to happen overnight."

"You're right about that," she interjected softly. She peered over at the journal and saw there was more writing. "I never realized you're such a good writer. Your cooking is an expression of your creativity, and so is this writing."

He continued reading, "Death severs time and labels the two pieces 'Before' and 'After.' All at once, every single event becomes something that happened Before Andy died, or After. Right now, there are sixteen years' worth of events on the Before side of the ledger, but gradually, the After side will get bigger and bigger and finally overtake the size of the Before. I think this transition period of adjustment is going to be hard, but since it's a 'transition' that means it will be temporary." He closed the journal.

"That was beautiful, Hart. I'm glad you found a way to write out your feelings and think things through."

"But?"

"I tried sitting with a notebook and pen and the only thing that happened is I started to write about the day of the accident and rage spilled into my hand so the tip of the pen tore through about ten pages." She shrugged, feeling bitter. "This was all my fault, and the feelings aren't going to go away by writing about them."

After Gabriella left to work with her latest orientation group, Andy wandered around the Old Zoo area and learned from the signs that it had been constructed in 1912 to house retired circus animals. In the mid 1960's the new zoo opened elsewhere in the park, and the old cages were no longer used.

To the average humans passing by with barely a curious glance at the small enclosures, inside the cages were dead leaves, a few candy wrappers, and ropy vines that hung down through the bars from the tree-shaded slope above.

But Andy knew this was the Gray Zone, filled with sad souls who had sentenced themselves to reside there.

188

He crossed the wide rolling lawn, past a creek rimmed with large boulders and picnic tables placed for park visitors. Exploring the cages, he bypassed the padlocked gates and climbed the slope behind them, then slipped down between bars, dropping to the floor below.

Inside, the Gray Zone was smoky and filled with swirling dark shadows. The bars between cages were gone, becoming a long corridor that twisted down and went beneath a large tree's thick old roots, tunneling down below into what he imagined must be hellish depths.

All around him were people of varying adult ages. Gabriella had explained that all children receive one-on-one transitional counseling to help them adjust and would never be left alone here. The ones here had chosen to be here, and resisted leaving no matter how many times they were told they had the power to do so.

He looked at the gray people, each so fully aligned with the shadows of negative thinking that they had lost all color and appeared gray in tone, head to toe. All of them wore gray armbands, and he took that to mean their awareness was at a lower level than his own. It made sense, when he considered it, and he remembered that Khaki and the others he'd met had also worn gray armbands rather than black. It seemed to indicate a "stuck" position.

The original zoo cages included a few with stone grottoes for lions or tigers. Where there were only twelve adjacent cages on the outside, in the Gray Zone the number counted in the hundreds, space being no limitation here. He walked around curiously. No one bothered him, and he began to feel that he must be invisible to them.

Andy pushed past people so shadowy he didn't see them until the last minute and then had to skirt them. His occasional "Excuse me," "Hello" and "Pardon me" got less cheery as he went along, and he stopped saying anything.

"Why bother?" he muttered to himself. "Everyone here ignores me." Although he no longer had physical senses, he was aware of a spiritual disconnect due to the thick atmosphere of despair and self-absorption. He equated it to a headache, so he rubbed his temples.

"Psst. Andy."

He turned quickly, but didn't see anyone.

"Over here," the girl's voice said.

He craned to see in the shadowy depths.

"In here, stupid."

He almost passed Naomi, but some sharp sense made him back up a few steps and peer again past the thick vines and heavy wisps of smoke, into the inner depths of a stone cave.

"Hi," he said. "Are you the one who called out to me?"

She didn't look up. Her voice was husky and low as she said, "Whatcha doin' in here, mama's boy? Better not get lost! There'll be hell to pay." She chuckled softly.

Andy stepped closer. "I'm here to help you. You don't have to stay this way, you know. I'll take you out of here."

"Somebody told you that?"

"Well, yeah. I mean, I figured it out after some things I heard, that people in here only think they need to stay, they're just, like punishing themselves or something. But you don't have to. You can be happy."

"I see. And you believe that?" She gave him a pitying look and withdrew further into her corner.

Naomi looked about twenty years old, slight of build, and her straggly gray hair was pulled in a ponytail with unkempt bangs sticking up like a haystack around her face. Her voice was so soft when she spoke that Andy wasn't sure if she had an accent that would betray her origins.

He didn't know why he felt drawn to her, but he had a growing conviction that it was important that he rescue her.

"I said–" he began.

"I heard you," came her laconic reply.

"Why are you here?"

"Waiting to get my own talk show," she shot back, "so I can be the one asking all the questions."

"Well, talk to me. What're you so afraid of?"

"Anything. Everything... Nothing."

"You don't have to stay stuck in this dimension," he said. "Take my hand. Come on, walk out with me."

"Oooh." She acted impressed. "That's all there is to it?"

"Seriously, why do you stay in here? It's disgusting!"

"Ever eat comfort food? Ice cream. Cake. Potato chips with onion dip. A big bowl of macaroni and cheese right out of the oven, the kind with buttered crumbs on top. Maybe it's not so good for you, but it feels soothing, like the home you still yearn for."

"But if you want safety, all you have to do is imagine a big mansion with tall iron gates and guards outside."

"Is that so?"

"Yeah, it's a matter of vibrations and frequency," he said. "Just raise your awareness and see your potential. Visualize what you want. I bet I could teach you."

"Oh my gawd," she drawled. "You read the Cliff Notes for Death 101 and now you're out to save someone. Listen, Andy, go earn your merit badge with some other charity case."

"I know about dream spinning," he said. "And if you're sad because you want to get a message to somebody who's still alive, I could help you."

"No free lunches, boy scout. Didn't anybody ever tell you that?"

He had a growing uneasiness that Gabriella had been right to warn him he'd be out of his depth in the Gray Zone. Remembering that the other girls he'd met enjoyed talking about their deaths, he asked, "How'd you die, anyway?"

She looked at him defiantly, and he saw that she was a very pretty girl, with a wide mouth, pert nose and beautifully arched eyebrows.

He waited and made a prompting gesture so she'd respond.

As if bored by the subject, she said after a long pause, "Killed myself."

"Suicide? That was stupid!" He regretted the comment, but it was too late.

She raked him with a long icy look. "It was an accident, asshole. Visiting hours are over. Beat it."

Jemma stood in the doorway of Andy's bedroom. After a moment's hesitation, she slowly entered and fed the tropical fish. She noticed the algae situation was at the point where she'd better do something about it risk losing fish. It was growing on the inside walls of the tank, and she knew if Andy were here, he would use the special magnetized scraper. She watched the fish feeding, and slowly ran the scraper along the glass by holding onto the magnet on her side of the tank.

Hart came in and indicated the fish food. "They say great minds think along the same track. Thanks for feeding them."

A bright blue tang--the one Andy called "Dory" because it was the same type of fish as the one in *Finding Nemo*--darted close to Jemma and seemed to look at her thoughtfully.

"Hi, Dory," she said.

Joining her at the coral tank, Hart silently watched the fish moving around. "I envy their simple life. Don't you?"

"I was thinking that maybe they handed out answers for things like this when they awarded prizes to kids with perfect attendance at Sunday School. And I'm the only one who doesn't have a clue because I played hooky. Hated going to church then. Still do. Too many hypocrites. Everybody claiming their God is the only one, and they've got the answers. If you don't believe the way I do, then that gives me the right to shove my religion down your throat until you agree with me, or else I'll kill you. That way I prove God's on my side. Maybe that's too harsh? You say that not everyone is like that? Oh well. Let's not get into it now. I don't want to argue."

"Please, Jemma. Could we have a real conversation? Andy's death is not going away and I think we should talk about our feelings. Share what we're going through."

She opened a desk drawer idly, and saw the Phi Beta Kappa key she had given him. Her breath caught. She picked it up and held it tight in her fingers, knowing he had been the last to touch it.

After putting the gold charm in her pocket, she turned on Andy's computer, brought up the folder of "recent documents," and looked at the list of files. Nothing of special interest but maybe she'd find something another time.

"I still have to copy any photos he had on there," Hart said, "and I'll be sure to save anything else that looks important." He sighed. "Actually, I'll never toss this out, in case there's something on it I missed. He used it a lot."

She started to turn off the laptop but noticed an icon labeled "Poetry."

"What's this?" she murmured, clicking on it. A document filled with poems opened. "He wrote poetry? Did you know about this?"

Hart nodded.

"How come I didn't?"

"He...he didn't want you to know."

"Why? I don't think anything bad about guys who write poetry."

"He was afraid you'd get mad."

"Mad?"

"That he was wasting time, instead of studying."

She slumped. "Was I that much of a taskmaster? I only wanted him to develop his talents and be the best that he could. I feel so sorry that he couldn't tell me about his poems."

"He was playing around with song writing, too, lately."

A wall calendar caught her eye, and she took it down from its hook. "Remember when we went shopping for his Christmas gifts last year, and you wanted to get this for his stocking?"

"But you wanted that one with the underwater scenes and coral reefs."

"And we ended up tossing a coin to decide."

He looked at her. "Why didn't we buy both of them? They were cheap enough. He could've put up two calendars. Seems so silly that we argued about it."

"The calendar is my enemy now. Do you feel that way too, Hart? Each passing day takes me further away from him. The sun rises and it sets and so ends another day without Andy in it." She put the calendar down.

"I've been thinking, Jemma," Hart began.

"I don't like the way that sounds. What's on your mind?"

"I got some info about grief support groups–"

"I won't go–"

"–And I'd like it if you'd go with me, at least to two or three sessions."

"Hart, please. Don't ask me to spill my guts in a roomful of strangers."

"Everyone I talked to who's been through this says the support groups are helpful. I'd like to give it a shot."

"Why don't you go on your own? It's not my thing, but that doesn't mean it can't be yours." She turned away and caught sight of Andy's rumpled bed. "Damn. I try so hard to come in, feed the fish and leave without looking at anything. But he's everywhere. In every inch of this house."

"Let's sell it."

She gaped.

He hurriedly explained, "I know we planned to rent it out while you're in the NASA program--"

"I'm not even sure what to do about that. About NASA."

"It's up to you, Jemma. I'll respect your final say in the matter. But—about the house?"

She looked at him. "Do you really want to sell?"

He shook his head. "What I want is for Andy to come dashing in the door and yell out 'what's for dinner'—but since that's clearly not going to happen, it's just too hard being here, where every corner, every square inch brings in a flood of memories."

"We could still rent it, like we planned."

Hart glanced around Andy's room. "I can't picture myself playing landlord to some family and having to drop by to fix a leaky toilet, only to see them laughing in our family room where we should be with our son."

Chapter 13

Jemma turned restlessly in her sleep, dreaming of escalators in a huge open air mall with cafes and shops on multiple levels.

She saw Andy in the crowd up ahead, but no matter what she did, he was always just ahead of her, but on a different level. She went up, and saw him going down on the escalator, so she raced to a down escalator, but in that short time he'd already gone up two levels.

Distressed, she glanced around. Thinking she saw him in the distance, she sped to catch up, but when she tapped the boy she'd chased on the shoulder and he turned to face her, it wasn't Andy.

She awoke abruptly and sat up in the dark. It was just past midnight. She forced a laugh. "Like some cliché in a badly written movie. I should be able to dream better than this." Realizing she'd spoken out loud, she glanced at Hart's side of the bed, ready to apologize for waking him.

His side was empty.

With a glance toward the adjoining bathroom, she realized he was not in the master suite. Curious, she got up and went out into the hallway, listening, thinking he might have gone downstairs for a midnight snack.

Both of them had been having trouble sleeping, so perhaps he went in the family room to watch late night television where the noise wouldn't disturb her.

She peered over the stair rail, and saw that all was dark and silent downstairs.

Realizing where he might be, she peeked in Andy's room.

Hart was curled up on Andy's bed, hugging Andy's pillow, sleeping.

She watched him a moment, and decided that she'd go to the grief support group with him, as he'd requested.

It was a small favor to do for the father of her son.

Yolanda and Marybeth crossed the church parking lot with a few others who had just attended the small suicide support group that met weekly in one of the church's classrooms.

"I think that was very helpful," Yolanda said. "Don't you?"

"I'm not going back."

"But why? They all liked you so much. And you were very articulate when they asked you to tell them a little about yourself, and what happened with that Powell boy. No one blames you about him."

"Did you know that when Naomi killed herself, Robbie called me? He was so upset. He came to see me. Cabot found out, and I don't think he's ever forgiven me. He thinks I reached out to Robbie for comfort but actually it was the other way around."

"Did you and Robbie–?"

"I didn't betray my vows to Cabot if that's what you're worried about."

"Well, that's good, honey. And when you get to know the people in this group better," Yolanda said, glancing back at the church, "I bet they can help you with the way you feel about Naomi, too."

"I don't think it's the right group for me."

"You need to have someone. I have to get back home tomorrow."

Marybeth looked at her, feeling sorry that she couldn't be what her cousin wanted her to be, and couldn't say what Yolanda wanted to hear. "I'll find an online group, okay?"

"Great idea! We can look on the internet together and sign you up. Or whatever you do."

"All right, Yolanda. But let's go have lunch together now. Just the two of us. That would be such a treat for me. And we won't talk about anything serious."

"Okay, honey."

"Mexican sound good to you? I know a little place where it's all homemade style."

An hour later, Hart pulled into the same church lot Marybeth had just left, and parked. "I have to admit I'm feeling a bit nervous about this."

"You and me both," Jemma muttered as they headed toward the classroom where a few others could be seen in the doorway.

As they approached, an attractive middle-aged woman stepped up to welcome them. "I think you must be new. I'm Tracey. I'm the group moderator."

"I'm Hart, and this is my wife Jemma."

"Come on in, you two, and grab a cup of coffee. Help yourselves to cake and cookies. I'm a baking fiend and always bring enough for an army. Usually there's only about eight or ten of us, though. We'll get started at the top of the hour." She glanced at her watch. "Six minutes to go."

"Thanks," Hart said and put an arm around Jemma's shoulder as they headed inside.

A dozen chairs were placed in a semi-circle, and after getting coffee, they sat down.

Tracey came in and shut the door. "Let's go ahead and get started. Hi everyone, I'm Tracey and I'd like to welcome you all to this grief support group. It's informal, but we do ask you to raise your hand when we start sharing, so it doesn't become a free-for-all. Each of us has a unique contribution to make to the group. I started attending after my husband died, and I've ended up coming back week after week even though it's been over a year, because I like to share with others that you really will feel better." She glanced around at the eight people seated before her. "Grief cripples us. Let the group be your crutch while you heal."

After Tracey finished, she invited people to share, and Jemma listened idly as others in the room told the group about their losses and how they were coping with their sorrow.

When everyone but Hart and Jemma had shared, Tracey looked at them. "You don't have to say anything, but it will help us get to know you, and that way we can all be in this together. You know the saying, I'm sure: Troubles shared are halved and joys shared are doubled." She waited a moment, but they sat in silence.

"That's okay," Tracey said. "I didn't say a word the first few meetings I went to. Jump in when you're ready. You know, when my husband died, I developed a backache that got worse every day. I realized that grief crumples us inward. We hunch over in pain, clutching our broken hearts. Think about it-- how your step drags, the zest in your walk is gone, your voice sounds flat, the exuberance in your laughter is a memory. We even rub our foreheads like we could erase the pain. It seems impossible we used to spring out of bed, happy to see a new dawn."

"I know what you mean," Hart said impulsively. "That's happened to me." He reached in his back pocket and took out a folded paper.

Surprised, Jemma whispered, "What's that?"

He stood up, saying to the group, "I wasn't sure what the format of the meeting would be, so I wrote something down and I might as well read it to the group."

200

"I can't wait to hear it" Tracey smiled at him.

Jemma's antennae went up. She recognized when another woman was looking at her husband that way, but was surprised to encounter it here, of all places.

Seeming oblivious to Tracey's flirting, Hart began reading, "We say time heals all wounds. Time marches on. Only time will tell. There's another truth about time: we can't stop it. It eventually leads to the day of our own death. Time gave me nearly sixteen years with my son. What a gift! I am trying to focus on the gift." He shoved the paper in his pocket and hurriedly sat down.

"Beautiful." Tracey dabbed her eyes. "That touched my heart."

Jemma felt her temper simmer.

"And what about your wife?" Tracey asked. "Anything to add, dear?"

Jemma leaped up, fueled by fury. "Sure, thanks, Tracey," she said, in a shotgun delivery that had people near her recoil a bit in surprise. "I was looking through old photo albums when our families were in town for the funeral. My husband put together a slide show for the service. I came across a note my son wrote on a Mother's Day snapshot of the two of us, from a few years ago. It was the same year he gave me a sand castle ornament and that's in the picture with us. The note said: 'You're a wonderful Mom. The best!' The best? Not exactly the appropriate word for me anymore: I let him die. If we hadn't argued, if I hadn't let him run on ahead, he would have been safely with me when That Woman's car ran a stop sign. We would have continued our run and gone home for dinner. Don't worry. I'll get to the point. How do I stop all these 'What if's' from ripping my heart out?" She looked around, seeing that her loud angry share had startled everyone.

Hart stared at her.

Jemma picked up her purse. "I'll wait in the car while you guys finish."

Tracey said, "Oh, I can give him a ride home if that would be more convenient. It's kind of a hot day to sit waiting in the car. Don't you think?"

Expecting Hart to refuse and get up, Jemma was stunned when he remained seated. He handed the car keys to her, then turned to Tracey.

"Thanks, Tracey, I'd appreciate a ride. I'm finding this group helpful and I don't want to leave yet."

Jemma walked out, feeling that something monumental had just happened, but not wanting to examine it more closely.

When Jemma parked Hart's car in the garage, she thought of the golf clubs that Hart had hidden for Andy's sixteenth birthday, and quickly found them. For a moment, she thought of leaving them alone and untouched, but then she hefted the bag and shoved it in the trunk of her own car, slamming the lid with a resounding thud.

Before she could think too much, she ran in the house and changed into shorts, grabbed a Dodger baseball cap and hurried back to the car.

About twenty minutes later, she parked at the Sepulveda Basin Recreation Center, near the golf practice range. Although Jemma had never been there, she remembered seeing the sign when they drove past or came to the park over the years with Andy, or to see the cherry trees in bloom around nearby Lake Balboa.

As soon as she paid, she entered the fenced area, set down the bag of golf clubs, grabbed one from it and began hitting balls. She was focused entirely inward, on her anger.

She grabbed another club, and started to swing.

"Excuse me?" A tanned, graying man in his fifties approached her. "That's a putter."

Ignoring him, Jemma hit the ball. It didn't go very far. She frowned.

"You're using the wrong club," he said. "You can use all the drivers in the bag--the ones with the big heads--but don't try a putter when you're going for distance."

She looked at the clubs. "Oh. Thanks."

"Sure." He smiled at her. "I would ask if you come here very often, but I think maybe the answer is no."

"That's right." She selected a driver and swung, trying to hit the ball as far as she could. The hitting distance went up to 250 yards but her ball stopped far short of that.

"I'm a realtor so I get to come here whenever I'm in between appointments. My office is in Encino, which makes it convenient."

She kept hittings balls, her anger at the world not abating.

"Well, I see you're busy," he said, undeterred. "Have fun. Hope to see you again. I'd be glad to help you with your stance and swing anytime."

She nodded curtly, knowing she was being rude to someone who was probably trying to be friendly and helpful, but not finding any place in her heart where she could care about a stranger's feelings.

Yolanda came out of the guest room with a manila envelope and found Marybeth scrubbing the stove in the kitchen. Glancing out the window, Yolanda saw her husband Tom helping Cabot with a gardening project. "I was packing and realized I forgot to show you these drawings."

Marybeth looked up. "Have you been taking an art class I don't know about?"

"I decided to host a contest," Yolanda said.

"When did all this start?"

"I got local art teachers and students involved—over the past week or so. I didn't want to intrude by telling you about it, honey."

"Yeah, the timing sucks all around, doesn't it? I'd love to see them." Marybeth took off her rubber gloves and they sat at the kitchen table.

Yolanda spread out a dozen drawings, all of them featuring rabbits.

"Oh, these are so sweet," Marybeth said. "The artists have a lot of talent."

"Middle school kids. I have the feeling I'll want to do this every year, during the school year too, instead of just summer sessions. There'll probably be a stack waiting when I get home. More come in the mail every day."

"But what made you think of doing this?"

"I wanted to draw attention to the rabbit rescue adoptions, and I thought a little contest of some kind might help. Most people know about dog and cat adoptions, but unwanted pet rabbits need homes, too."

"What a great idea. What does the winner get?"

"A homeless rabbit, of course!"

Marybeth smiled. She looked through the drawings and then came back to one and lingered over it. It showed a small brown rabbit hunched inside a golden cage, looking out the partially open door at a beautiful field of clover and daisies.

"You like that one, honey?" Yolanda asked.

"Why doesn't she leave?"

"Excuse me?"

"Why doesn't the little rabbit hop outside the cage and go enjoy the field? You can see from her eyes that she wants to, more than anything in the world. She wants to push that damned door open and leap out. So why doesn't she?" Marybeth put the drawing down, and looked at Yolanda, desperate for an answer. "The door isn't locked. It's not even latched. It's open. Why doesn't she nudge it with her little nose to open it the rest of the way, and then hop out?"

"Oh, *pobrecita.*" Yolanda grabbed Marybeth's hands and held them tightly in her own. "Are things really that bad?"

"That day, when I was in my car–"

"You mean the day of the accident? I thought you didn't want to talk about it."

"Cabot interrogates me constantly. I'm sick of talking about the details and what I might possibly have done differently other than killing myself before I got in the car–"

"Don't talk that way," Yolanda said. "Please, it scares me."

"I'm sorry. I couldn't tell Cabot this because I knew he wouldn't understand. He'd mock me for hearing voices when no one was there."

"Well, that happens to me sometimes," Yolanda said with a little chuckle, trying to ease the tension.

"I heard a small voice," Marybeth went on intently, "saying 'Take it easy!' but I was so mad at Cabot for making me late, and mad at myself for not putting the top up and ruining my hair, and wanting so badly to get to the audition, get a part and get <u>money</u> so I can afford to leave him–"

"You're planning divorce, Marybeth?" Yolanda was aghast.

"Don't act like nobody at your church ever gets divorced. Would you prefer for me to be miserable and properly married?"

"Of course not, but–"

"It's not going to happen any time soon," Marybeth muttered. "I have to get a job, make some money. But all I know is acting. I dreamed last night about circles and wheels. I was on stage but no one listened to me. My voice was a whisper even when I tried to shout. All around me on the stage, the other actors chatted among themselves, animated by excitement. But their backs were turned against me.... Who would want me in their film now? The way I look?"

Yolanda touched Marybeth's cropped hair. "It'll grow back and you'll be able to style it like I see in the magazines. What I'm worried about the most, Bunny, is that you are so very sad and unhappy. You've always been sweet and vulnerable, and I guess Cabot took advantage of that. I didn't know. I didn't realize--"

"I'm afraid to drive," Marybeth blurted. "A voice told me to take it easy, but I didn't. I was swerving around because of the broken tree branches in the road and the next thing I knew, I looked up into the sun and say that boy running and he ran right into my path!"

"I noticed how carefully you drove when we went out yesterday. That happened to Tom when he had a bad accident. Just take it slow, start off with short trips to the grocery store. Try not to be too nervous. It'll be fine, honey. You'll be back to your happy-go-lucky self one day soon, and all the darkness of the past two years will be behind you, a memory you've shut away."

Knowing Yolanda would be upset to hear an outpouring of all the guilt she carried, Marybeth said, "I don't know if I'll ever be happy again."

Behind them, Marybeth heard the men's voices as they approached the kitchen door from the back yard. She sat up straighter and swiped at her eyes. "I'd better get back to that stove of mine! I spattered grease cooking breakfast and didn't get it all up. Cabot hates it when I leave messes instead of cleaning them thoroughly and immediately. I know he's right." She hurried to put her rubber gloves back on and was at the stove scrubbing when Cabot walked in.

"Hey, that's the way I like my women," he said, laughing. "Hot, sweet and creamy. No wait, that's the way I like my coffee. I mean barefoot, pregnant and in the kitchen."

Marybeth's smile was tight.

"Are you–?" Tom looked at her, confused.

Marybeth shook her head and darted a look at Yolanda.

"Not yet she isn't," Cabot said, "but not for lack of trying. Hey, how about a beer, Tom?"

Seeing the look on Marybeth's face, Yolanda gathered the drawings and put them in the envelope. "We need to hit the road, Tom. I got us packed and we should push on." The look she sent her husband prompted him to nod in agreement.

"It's been great seeing you both," Tom said, then corrected himself, "under the circumstances, I mean."

"Thank you for coming," Marybeth said. "I appreciate the support."

"Could've happened to anyone, *querida*," Yolanda said firmly. "Put it behind you now."

"Twenty years ago," Tom said, "my car hit a guy on a motorcycle. He lost his leg. Nothing I could change, no matter how much I prayed. Took me a while to feel okay behind the wheel again, but soon I was driving like regular. What you need is...Oh, I don't know, Bunny. I don't have any answers. I wish I did. I guess what I mean is to find something to engage your interest."

"Exactly what I've been telling her," Cabot said. "Get back to normal, for God's sake."

Yolanda shot him a withering glance.

"You better start seeing that therapist again, Marybeth," Cabot said. "This time, for real. I'll take you and pay them myself. No more skipping out on appointments to go play hooky or whatever you did with all that time and money when I thought you were getting help for your problems."

At home, Jemma showered and changed, and fixed herself a sandwich, all the time darting glances at the clock. Hart was still not home from the grief support group. She checked her phone for messages. Nothing.

By the time she heard a car pull into the driveway and stop with the engine idling, she was fuming...and yet annoyed with herself at the same time. After all, he had the right to speak to someone and get help for his bereavement issues. Didn't he?

She didn't want to be seen waiting for him, so she sped into her study, and sat at her computer just as she heard his key in the lock.

After calling out a goodbye to Tracey, Hart shut the front door and poked his head in Jemma's study. "Saw your light go on."

"Thought I'd answer some of the emails we got. So many people sent sympathy e-cards and I should send thank you's. I'll sign your name."

"Thanks."

"I already ate," she said.

He glanced at the clock on her wall. "Oh, yeah, I guess it is kind of late."

"The meeting went a long time?" she asked casually. "Glad I didn't stay for the whole thing after all."

"Actually, it ended a few minutes after you left."

"Did it?"

They looked at each other.

"I stayed after," he said, "talking to some of the others for a while."

"And then Tracey gave you a ride? Did her car break down?"

"We stopped for a bite to eat. She was telling me about her husband. He had cancer and was in hospice care for over a year. Really sad. Seemed like she needed to talk about it."

"And you offered a shoulder to cry on?"

"Don't be like that, Jemma. There wasn't anything–"

"She's a predator! I wonder if her husband even died, or if she just finds it easier to pick up guys when they're vulnerable from grief compared to cruising the bars for dates."

"She's nice, Jemma. I think you'd like her, if you gave her a chance."

"I can't believe you fell for all that teary-eyed praise she gave you."

"Some women are able to show their emotions," he said.

"So many times, Hart, I wanted to reach out to you but–"

"Let's not try to take a different path. Your anger is dragging me down when I'm trying to lift myself up and out of this hell hole of grief."

"I miss all the noise and movement around here." Jemma shuddered, remembering. "The sound of his sneakers pounding up and down the stairs. The humming and whistling while he had on headphones and didn't realize how loud he was getting, singing along or tapping the beat."

"You wouldn't let him be a teenager. You wanted him to be a mini-you."

"That's unfair. I didn't do that. Accusations won't bring him back."

They glared at each other, and the silence between them grew heavy.

She got up. "I think we better stop now. Before one of us says something irreparably cruel."

"In all the years we've been together, Jemma, I've never done anything I'd be ashamed to tell you about. I get offers all the time at the restaurant. Women are always flirting with me, coming on to me, giving me their phone numbers. I wear my wedding ring, and I never pretend that I'm available. You've picked a strange time to accuse me of being unfaithful. And I have to tell you–it hurts." He turned and left the room.

She heard him going slowly up the stairs.

Sinking back in her chair, closing her eyes, she wished too late that she'd kept her mouth shut.

Marybeth dreamed she was walking in a beautiful garden filled with tropical plants and bright flowers. She reached up to pick a flower growing from a tree, and a tiny ruby-throated hummingbird perched on her fingertip, clinging to her fingernail. The little jewel-like bird stayed all day with her, as she explored the garden, alone and at peace.

She came around a curve in the path, and saw a small waterfall cascading into a pond where fish, turtles and frogs lived. A bench was next to the pond, so she sat to enjoy the vista.

The hummingbird was still perched on her fingertip, and she felt so happy.

After a moment, she heard a soft whirring noise. A bright blue bird unlike any bird she had ever seen, eight inches long and two inches wide, flew toward her although it didn't have wings. It was a flat rectangle in shape, and had long talons at the top and at the bottom. There was a tuft of blue feathers at the top, so she assumed that was its head. The bird clung to her shoulder with one set of claws, and her breast with the other. The talons bit into her, hurting her, but she didn't know how to make the bird fly away.

Alarmed, she asked the hummingbird for advice, and felt rather than heard the tiny bird explain that this was a dragon bird and it was good luck. The pain would lead her to happiness, but only if she allowed it to stay and didn't try to pry it off.

When she woke up, Marybeth automatically reached for her dream journal and wrote swiftly, although she suspected that she would not soon forget the details of this strange dream. She found it comforting, somehow, that the dragon bird recognized pain was an omnipresent part of her life.

She wished she could hold that sense of happiness she'd felt in the dream, but it was already fading.

Chapter 14

"Why didn't you warn my mother?" Andy wheeled on Qaletaqa, outraged. "Your own granddaughter!"

Qaletaqa looked at Andy.

They sat together on a hilltop in Griffith Park.

Joker lay sprawled at Andy's side.

"You blame her for your death, Andrew? She didn't force you to run off. You did that on your own."

"I had to get away from her. All that stuff she kept needling me about--"

"What makes you think she was not warned to change her behavior? She was given advice—including strong suggestions from her husband–that she chose to ignore."

"Then someone should've tried harder to get through to her."

"Free will means there is always a choice, Andrew. Humans are stubborn, as a whole, and barrel ahead without stopping to take all input into consideration, whether it's an intuitive thought that arrives in the dream state, or something that is read, or a piece of advice from another person. Emotions and wishful thinking drive human behavior far more than rational thought or logic."

"Wait. Back up. You mean she was warned in a dream not to keep hounding me about that thing–that arrest?"

"It is not always so direct, Andrew. We have to do things in a more roundabout way so the concept is not rejected. The power of the human mind to resist is--"

"But you plant ideas, right? You plant thoughts in people's dreams. That's what a Dream Spinner does."

"Suggest would be a better choice of words than plant. We don't seed foreign ideas against someone's will."

"Gabriella has been explaining stuff like universal laws and all that. Law of attraction, which I've heard of, of course, but I guess I never really understood the real power of it. But it sounds like what you're saying is that I brought it on myself, that my mom and I both did."

"It's like the saying in Las Vegas, Andy. The house always wins. In life, the law of attraction always wins. Your attention is like a tractor beam, bringing both good and bad experiences to you, depending on the nature and focus of your thoughts."

"I'm trying to send my mom messages in her dreams, but I don't think they're getting through to her."

"Keep working with Gabriella. There's more to it than you might think."

"I'm the only one who can send her dreams, aren't I?"

Qaletaqa looked at him, understanding this was all new. "Do you think that Gabriella's team is the only one? There are more Dream Spinner teams than you might imagine. It is not a new project. There are also rogue spinners, who strike out on their own, with their own agendas."

"Well, shit." Andy sighed. "That complicates things, doesn't it?"

"Let's get back to that issue of blaming your mother for what happened."

"Issue?" Andy gaped at Qaletaqa, surprised to hear him use the modern term for problem.

Qaletaqa shrugged, amused.

They moved on to Forest Lawn, where an interment ceremony was in progress. Gabriella joined them and indicated the closed casket. "Anyone we know?"

"You won't be meeting this one soon," Qaletaqa said. "He was a wise old soul, and has already advanced to a higher level than we are on."

Andy frowned, taken aback.

"You thought this was as good as it gets?" Gabriella asked, teasing.

"I guess I didn't think much about it. No way this gets boring, not like the bungee jumping." He looked around the cemetery curiously.

"Over one hundred and fifty thousand departures each day," Qaletaqa said.

"Whoa!"

"He means worldwide, Andrew," Gabriella said. "Not just in Los Angeles."

Andy nodded sagely, pretending he knew that.

Qaletaqa said, "Everyone--whether a believer in the after-life or not--discovers that death is simply a doorway."

"Many people think that at death you magically become a person without flaws," Gabriella said, "and you enjoy eternity like one long garden party. As you are discovering, Andrew, you are the same person you were when you were alive, but now you can see more readily where you need to grow spiritually. You understand that we are all on a path to develop higher and higher awareness, and we return to earth lifetimes to enjoy the experience of creativity, or to test ourselves with a lesson we want to master."

"Listen, Qaletaqa," Andy said hastily. "If it's a doorway, can I go back? It would be faster than all this dream spinning stuff. All I need is about an hour and I could explain to my mom that she doesn't have to grieve anymore, and she should get back with NASA and go be an astronaut. Do that special project of hers."

"I cannot allow it," Qaletaqa said. "Your life as you knew it is over, Andrew. I'm sorry."

"Please? My mother needs–"

"She has her own journey to follow." Gabriella smiled at him, understanding.

"We will help her as much as we can," Qaletaqa added, "but we cannot intervene the way you would like."

Andy looked at them, hiding his frustration. "Figured it couldn't hurt to ask."

Privately, he grew determined to find another way to help his mother.

Marybeth sat with her laptop in the gazebo, and logged in as "bunnygirl" at the suicide support forum that Yolanda had helped her find. She avoided any reference to her real name or where she lived. The avatar she picked was a drawing of a girl with shocking pink hair and big sunglasses. She noticed that some users posted photos of themselves and freely gave their names and email addresses for others to contact them, but she preferred anonymity.

After reading a few of the posts, she decided to introduce herself and see if she got any replies.

"Hi everyone," she typed, "I'm new at this forum. I've got two attempts on my record, and the experts say that means I'll try again. The first time was a few months after I got married, which was nearly two years ago. My best friend killed herself and I felt so awful about it that I decided to do it, too, but I couldn't even do that right. Then I found out I was pregnant, so I knew I needed to live for my baby even though I had already realized my marriage was a mistake. But my little girl died at only three months old from SIDS, and I knew God was punishing me for not being able to save my best friend when she was so unhappy about something bad that happened to her. So in a low moment, I decided again to end it. But--again--I guess I wanted to live or I would have succeeded. Something happened recently that makes me feel very sad, upset and guilty, and my husband makes a point of locking away anything sharp. He watches me like a hawk, but he's also pushing me to get pregnant again. I tried going to a therapist but it didn't help much. My baby's birthday is coming up and she'd be one year old if she had lived. My older cousin said I should have support right now, so that's why I'm here–to please her, actually. Sorry if I'm rambling. I'm nervous about sharing all this online."

When Lulu visited, she had offered repeatedly to help Jemma sort and pack up Andy's bedroom, and any other areas of the house where he had personal items that his parents might want to put away. Jemma had refused each time.

But now, having fed his fish and once again studiously avoided looking at his shelves and the other evidence of his life, she decided to get the task over with.

She did the easiest things first. She stripped the bed, bundled the sheets and comforter together and put them outside the door. She'd take them down later to the laundry room, planning to wash everything and then donate it to charity.

Keeping her mind as blank as possible, she remade the bed with spare sheets and a coverlet she had used at one time in the guest room. That done, she tackled the dresser drawers, and filled Hefty bags with socks, underwear and t-shirts for giveaway.

Hart stood in the doorway, aghast. "What the hell are you doing?"

"You said you want to sell the house. Do you think the new owners want this room to be intact?"

"It was an idea I tossed out for further discussion. Why? Do _you_ want to sell?"

"This will always be Andy's house. The house where he lived. No matter who is here. But I can't keep being here with his room waiting as if he's going to come in the door at any moment. I won't be one of those mothers who creates a shrine to sit in and remember the last sixteen years." She tapped her heart. "It's all in here anyway."

"You're not throwing everything out, are you?"

"I'll box up all his personal things and we can take our time with it. I wouldn't put everything in the trash."

"Then why–"

"I can't keep doing this, Hart." She glanced at the coral tank. "I don't want his fish to die, but if it weren't for them, I wouldn't come in here. I'd shut the door and leave it all alone."

"I could feed the fish."

They looked at each other a long moment, knowing that wasn't the real issue but not wanting to go any deeper.

"Remember his first tank?" She looked wistfully at a photo on the wall of Andy at age ten proudly displaying a small fish tank with two tiny tropical fish in it.

"He saved up his birthday and Christmas money–"

"And did extra chores to earn the rest he needed."

"But then he was disappointed to discover he could only have two fish in a saltwater tank that size." Hart walked over to the 55-gallon aquarium. "He sure did love this thing. Brought him a lot of pleasure, watching the fish and tending their needs." He picked up the algae scraper's magnet and lined it up with the scraper inside the tank, then slowly moved the magnet around, scraping off a thin film of green algae here and there.

Jemma watched a moment. "He always said it was important to keep the glass clean so the fish could see out. Remember?" Her hands were still sorting clothes but her mind was not on the task and she began absently putting socks back into the drawer.

Hart nodded. "He was such a good kid–"

"Most people would do it so they could see in. He always put a spin on things, didn't he?"

They looked at each other, silently sharing memories of their beloved son.

"Why don't you take the tank to the bistro?" she suggested impulsively. "It would look fantastic in the reception area and you could order a plaque for it, naming it Andy's coral tank. That aquarium store where we got this could handle the move and set it up again." She looked at the fish and saw the blue tang darting around dizzily. "You'd like that, wouldn't you, Dory? Lots of new faces looking in at you instead of our sad ones."

Hart brightened. "I'm going to name the caramelized apple tart after him."

"He loved those tarts." She went to him and placed a hand on his arm. "You were such an amazing dad for our son, Hart. I can't thank you enough for that. I know I probably didn't verbalize it much over the years, but you made the life I wanted possible, with all the sacrifices you made. I know you could've opened the bistro sooner, if I'd been the one at home with Andy when he was younger and needed someone around more. I appreciate that you let me pursue my dreams at the cost of your own."

"They were *our* dreams, Jemma. We worked on them together. I've never known anyone as smart as you. Your brilliance dazzled me from the start. You dropped into my life like a star that fell from another galaxy and you made me want to be my best. I didn't want to let you down."

She looked at him a moment, and then spoke quietly. "This is beginning to sound like a final summing up of a project that's been successfully completed."

He fell silent.

She looked around at all the familiar things. "Let's get started. And let's promise each other that we will only say kind things from now on. This is going to be hard enough without getting into recriminations. Let's make our memories of Andy sweet ones."

He nodded, and for a moment, they walked around Andy's room, silently touching items here and there, each reliving precious memories. And then they got to work, sorting and packing.

After an hour, he said, "I should get going to the bistro. Let's take these bags down to my car and I can drop them off at the Goodwill store before they close."

"Good idea." She smiled at him, but realized they were standing yards apart, rather than falling into each other's arms to offer comfort.

The marriage had died, along with their son. And both of them knew it.

Sadness washed over her, and she felt like putting her arms around her husband's neck and insisting they could work things out. Inside she knew that everything between them had shifted, like it had when she officially became an astronaut-candidate. It occurred to her that not only would nothing ever be the same in her marriage, it would never get any better than this.

The glue that held them together was gone and they didn't know how to reconnect without Andy.

Jemma felt it was only a matter of time before they both admitted it, and then took the next step. But that wasn't going to happen today.

She glanced around at the rest of the room. "That's enough for now."

Across from Griffith Park's south entrance, Gabriella and Andy approached the William Mulholland Memorial Fountain. "Many years ago," she told him, in answer to a question he'd just posed, "I came to Hollywood to work with an Italian writer. He was working on a movie."

"But I thought you were in Italy."

"I had already died, near Rome. My assignment was to help the writer, by inspiring him in his dreams. Then I discovered the community here at the park and decided to stay."

"Man, this is the craziest after-life." He danced up and around the tiers of the fountain, holding an imaginary an umbrella. "Hey, I'm Gene Kelly." He sang out, "'I'm singin' in the rain!'"

She tried to engage his attention and continue her instruction. "While working with the writer, I also inspired Cary Grant to switch roles with David Niven. They were working on 'The Bishop's Wife' and David was going to play the role of the angel, but we knew Cary was right for the part and gave nudges in the right places. The film inspired many people to think more carefully about what is important to them, and I advanced."

He stopped dancing and pointed at her silver armband questioningly.

"There are many opportunities here for service. Some people think this is just The Big Sprawl, but I like L.A."

From the top of the fountain, Andy waved to all the cars whizzing past. He sang out, "I love L.A." He held his hand to his ear, like he was trying to hear their response. "Come on, that's your cue, you're supposed to shout out: WE LOVE IT!"

"Get down, Andrew."

Laughing, he continued dancing. "Come on, everybody! You know the words! Or at least some of them! I love Randy Newman but his lyrics are kind of hard to recall on this one."

Gabriella appraised him as he played in the water, singing to himself. "This is all a game to you."

Andy shrugged. "Might as well enjoy my death. You and Qaletaqa won't let me do the things I want, and the dream spinning doesn't do any good for my mom. So why not!"

"You argued with your parents over selfish matters, and cried over broken castles made of sand."

He grew still, disgusted by the dawning realization. "You were there?" He leaped down. When she nodded, he said, "If it wasn't for you, I'd be alive!"

"Think about that last day. What do you remember? A small voice, perhaps?"

"No...Wait...Yeah. I had an urge to look for traffic. But...I...I ignored it. That was you? You could've tried harder, Gabriella! How about this: 'Andy! Heads up! There's a CAR coming!' Ever think of that?"

"You led a pampered life. You have no *concetto*. No...concept what life was like for my family. My friends. Millions more...." During this, her flowered dress abruptly transformed to a plain, much-mended dress, revealing her as the scrappy survivor of war-torn Italy and ultimately its victim.

"When did you die, anyway?" he asked. "And how?"

"It was 1942. My sister and I left Rome and hid in a barn in a small village, trying to escape marauding soldiers. But they found us."

"You're not one of those girls obsessed with talking about how they died, so I thought it wasn't important to you. Forgive me if I was supposed to beg you to tell me."

"Everybody has to learn to let go of anger and hatred, Andrew. I was filled with rage when I arrived in 1942, because my sister and I were raped and killed by those soldiers, but my guide told me I could recover if I helped others who died in an accident, disaster or bombing. In that way, I healed. My sister quickly reincarnated three more times--still filled with hurt and rage, and so she repeated similar events in each new life and died young each time."

"And she's still alive?"

"No."

"But it sounds like she's having a hard time. Even here? I mean, even though she could be happy now and create a heaven here for herself?"

"She was very bitter about men, and in each lifetime gravitated toward the ones who prove her belief was correct."

"So you hope she'll finally get it that guys can be good or bad?"

She studied his face, as if searching long and hard for something she couldn't find. "When I first became your spirit guide, replacing the one you had during your first few years of life, you were praying fervently that your dog Joker would be found. He'd gotten out of the yard because you left a gate open."

He walked closer to her. "I haven't thought of that in–"

"You asked for help."

"And you came?"

She nodded. "And when Joker died, I told him that it would not be long before you arrived as well."

"Hold on a minute! You KNEW–"

"There was a strong probability you would die as a teenager. I did not know any details." She watched him angrily stomp about, muttering to himself about betrayals. Sorry for him, she said softly, "Andrew. I feel richer for each goodbye in my life. Do you feel anything but sorry for yourself?"

"I'm not sorry for anybody. And I don't need you."

"All you want to do is play when there is vital work to be done. Don't you wonder why it is that we remain on this dimension, so close to the human plane? Because we take joy in helping them. Stop wasting my energy, Andrew. Find someone who'll be impressed by your few good deeds. When you are ready to become a serious student, you'll know how to find me. Your thoughts are still so earth-bound. Wake up and realize all you are capable of doing."

He strode away.

"That's right, Andrew," she called out after him, frustrated. "Run away whenever there is something you don't want to discuss."

Outside the Griffith Observatory, Andy sped up the curving staircase, past plodding tourists. He ran up to Qaletaqa, whose back was turned, and called out, "Gabriella's driving me crazy!"

Smiling to himself, Qaletaqa faced him. "Interesting, Andrew. That is what she tells me, about you. But the telling takes longer in Italian."

"I want to know more advanced stuff about being a Dream Spinner."

"Have you mastered the basics yet?"

Andy glared at him.

"I understand your impatience," Qaletaqa said. "Let me tell you something about the dream state. Humans identify themselves with their physical bodies, and when they sleep, they think that is merely a time to refresh for the next day's work."

"It's not?"

"Of course it does serve that purpose, but an even more important function of sleep is that each person's true self–the spirit or soul–can visit a different stream of consciousness during those hours. It is a time of growth, of stretching and reaching out. But most people do not remember it because they've been conditioned to think of dreams as entertainment. Or, if it has frightening elements they do not understand, as a nightmare to be hastily forgotten."

"I never gave it much thought, to be honest. I know some girls at school would talk about writing down their dreams and trying to figure out what they meant. Seemed like they were mostly interested in finding out what their future would bring. Like who was their soul mate or something."

"You can use dreams to help you plan. People also unconsciously color the dream's details when they wake up so it fits more readily into their daily activities and what they know and believe about life. Even if a message is there from a Dream Spinner, the symbolism we intended can be easily lost when the dreamer tries to be too logical."

"Logical? Like my mom, you mean." Andy looked at the city, and the glittering Pacific Ocean in the distance. "Do you think I can get her to reconsider her decision to quit NASA?"

"Do you believe it is worth a try?"

Andy nodded.

"So do I." Qaletaqa touched his arm, and Andy felt a surge of energy. "I'm counting on you, Andrew. Don't let us down."

Andy felt a new sense of confidence. "I'll make sure she gets the right message."

"You don't have proprietary rights for anyone's soul but your own," Qaletaqa said, smiling to soften the rebuke. "Don't forget that. It is an important factor to understand."

Marybeth and Cabot stood outside a French bistro, *Café Réflexions*, studying the menu posted by the door. Several customers went inside, chatting.

Marybeth scanned the menu to be sure there were vegetarian choices for herself. "It looks good." She waited for Cabot to announce his opinion, hoping he'd approve.

With a shrug, he opened the door and they went in.

Cabot glanced around.

The bistro was full. In keeping with its name, there were mirrored surfaces everywhere. A shallow stream, holding narrow trees in clay pots, meandered throughout the seating areas, creating private spaces. The effect was like a park, made larger by the multiple reflections.

Marybeth gave Cabot an encouraging look, hoping it would prompt him to give his name to the hostess, whose name tag read "Tracey."

Tracey, newly hired by Hart to work here in his bistro after meeting him through the grief support group, smiled at them. "Two for dinner?"

After Cabot gave his name, she glanced over the seating chart. "It'll be a few minutes. I'm sorry for the delay but everyone loves the desserts here. Personally, I love the chocolate tart but I've tried everything on the menu and it's all amazing. But what happens is they linger over a second cup of *café au lait*. I love it with the hazelnut flavoring added."

"That all sounds so good," Marybeth said.

"Ever heard about 'too much information'?" Cabot grumbled as he turned away.

They hovered near the door with others waiting to be seated.

"Couldn't get out of going," Cabot said abruptly.

Marybeth knew what he was talking about. "I never told you to stay home with me. I know your trip to Cleveland is important. It's been planned a long time."

"But next Wednesday is–"

"I know what the date is, Cabot."

"You shouldn't be alone. It's not safe. Get Yolanda to come–"

"I don't need a babysitter."

He looked at his watch and made an impatient noise.

Tracey noticed and called out, "It won't be much longer, sir."

Turning away, Marybeth noticed an aquarium, unaware it was Andy's coral tank because the plaque wasn't on it yet. She went closer, and watched the tropical fish darting around. "Hello, Nemo," she said to the small orange striped clownfish hiding in an anemone.

A man waiting to be seated noticed the fish, and commented to his date, "Oh, that tank's new. Nice."

Cabot looked at the diners and saw no one was getting up yet. He sighed loudly, showing his displeasure. He looked at Marybeth and jerked his head toward the door.

She was disappointed, but followed him out.

The door to the street closed softly behind them.

Moments later, Hart emerged from the kitchen in his chef hat to meet-and-greet customers. He did so with warmth and friendliness, but less exuberance and bonhomie than before Andy's death.

Andy caught up with Gabriella as she entered the park. "I'm sorry. You're right. I have a bad habit of tearing off when I'm annoyed. I apologize."

"Apology accepted. It's good to recognize your own patterns, so you can grow past the behavior habits that block you. I have to point things out to you. It is part of my job, Andrew."

He thought a moment. "Then let's continue our lessons about being a Dream Spinner, okay? I do want to learn."

"*Benissimo.*" She began strolling, her arm linked with his. "With each inspiration, you breathe in God. The Divine Mind. The Creator. Pure Consciousness. Whatever name you like to use is fine."

"They all mean the creative field, pure energy, eternal love."

"So you <u>have</u> been listening!" Her smile was wide. "Some ideas are particularly appropriate for a specific type of human mind to appreciate, grasp and develop further. That is why it often seems several people have the same idea at the same time in science, math and the arts. But always there is free will."

"You mean choices."

"Free will is at the heart of the human condition. That's why we have beautiful music, literature, art and architecture. But it is also why there are wars and poverty and crimes against humanity."

"You're saying the accident was my fault because I didn't listen to your voice in my head."

"The accident was–" she paused, helpless for a better word– "an <u>accident</u>, Andrew. Yes there were contributing factors from all involved, from your angry thoughts, from your mother's frustrated determination to resolve what she saw as a problem to fix what had gone wrong between you, from the driver's thoughts as well, of course. No one was acting deliberately, but the confluence of anger and thoughts of a lower nature all combined that day. But, remember this, when you are born, the date of your return here is not yet written in stone, but you always come and go on a round trip ticket."

"I never thought of it that way. But still, I kind of thought I'd stick around as a human till I was an old man."

"Try not to dwell on regrets, Andrew. It will block your energy, and you need it to contact your mother."

"You mean we can try again?"

"Unless you'd prefer to put it off?"

"No, no, let's definitely... Oh, you were kidding me."

"We will attempt to send her a message when she goes to sleep tonight."

"I've got an idea that can't possibly fail," Andy said. "Wait till you hear about the images we're going to send her. I've worked it all out. It's perfect, Gabriella!"

Chapter 15

Andy sat quietly with Gabriella. He calmed his mind, as she'd taught him, and waited for her signal. At her nod, he began spinning a dream for his mother.

"Your goal of being an astronaut started when you gave a school report on women and NASA," Andy said, using energy vibrations to transmit images to his mom along with the words. "But now, imagine you are traveling back to before you were born. It's 1955. Jerrie Cobb flies across the sky in a twin-engine Aero Commander. See her fly back the other direction on another day, this time in a B-17 Flying Fortress. Jerrie sets world speed records. Top female pilot. A natural choice for America's new space program."

Gabriella smiled in approval and indicated he should continue.

"See the desert, with a building on the horizon. It's 1961 now, at Lovelace Clinic in Albuquerque, New Mexico. Outside the building, women enter and exit in ones and twos.

Twenty-five outstanding U.S. women aviators are being secretly tested for the unknown hazards of space. Jerrie Cobb, Wally Funk, and other women endure rigorous tests administered by Dr. Lovelace and a nurse. Jerrie and the other women pass physical and psychological tests as hard, or harder than ones given the men–and they complain less!"

His excitement built, and he talked more rapidly. "They're actually cheerful about it. Sensory deprivation tanks. Noise tolerance tests. Spinning dizzily on a mechanical contraption. Being strapped to tables that tilt alarmingly. Dropped into water tanks."

With a gesture, Gabriella urged him to slow down.

He went on, in a more moderate tone, "Jerrie Cobb gets eighteen needles stuck in her head to measure brain waves. Another day, she swallows three feet of rubber tubing. The women who qualified for space travel were later dubbed the 'Mercury Thirteen.' See the faces of the thirteen women. You know their faces. You wrote a book about them! Despite two years of hard work with no pay, the women's project was abruptly cancelled--right before their flight simulation tests. Jerrie Cobb hangs up a phone, stunned. The approved astronauts had pushed NASA and Congress to agree that all astronauts must be military jet pilots–"

Gabriella looked surprised to learn this.

"–A position barred to women then. Now see the sky at dawn. It's 1963. See a news headline: Russian Woman Orbits Earth 48 Times. Look up and see the Russian space capsule Vostok 6 as it passes by, in orbit." He paused, then went on more firmly, "You <u>know</u> Russia sent up the first woman. You <u>know</u> Russia planned to send up an all-female crew. IT NEVER HAPPENED. Not then. Not ever, MOM!"

Gabriella gave him a warning look.

He mouthed the word "Okay" grudgingly.

"It never happened," he repeated quietly. "And the door that slammed against American women aviators didn't open for another twenty long years. Now it's 1983. Astronauts of Space Shuttle Challenger STS-7 walk out of crew quarters. You see Sally Ride waving to all the reporters. Ride, Sally Ride! The first American woman in space! The first one!"

With a quick frown, Gabriella sent him a questioning look, her hands spread, meaning, *How much longer?*

He wondered swiftly if he needed to cut this short. He was nearly finished, though, so he held up his index finger, asking for one more minute.

As she nodded, he hurriedly continued dream spinning. "Now it's 1999. See the Space Shuttle Columbia slice through the sky. See Lieutenant Colonel Eileen Collins. The first woman in the world to both pilot and command a space shuttle! And now it's the present day. Look what you're doing in spite of all the changes at NASA. See Dr. Jemma Malotki command the first <u>all-female</u> space mission…You can do it, Mom! You can! I'm so sorry--I didn't mean to jinx it!"

Jemma showered, letting the hot water stream across her face. She couldn't stop thinking about the potent dream she'd had last night. Seemed like it went on for hours, with one vivid image after another. She even felt that Andy had been speaking to her, but of course that was nonsense.

While drying off, she thought about the women of NASA, including the ones who never got a chance to go into space. They qualified in every way except gender, but now it was ordinary to see a woman on a launch, even though she might be the lone female in the crew.

Toweling her hair, Jemma reflected that if she dropped out of the space program, it would hardly make a ripple.

So many others had been forced to give up their dream of a shuttle mission. Some were applying for commercial flights, while others hoped to be part of an international team, which was the avenue she'd been pursuing. It wouldn't matter to anyone if she simply quit.

But still, she thought as she dressed, *no one has done what I want to do, what Fran encourages me to do. Even the Russians never did get around to it.*

Her heart stirred with an excitement she hadn't felt since before Andy's death. Fran was right to say that Andy would be disappointed if she turned down NASA after working so hard for her place on the astronaut-candidate roster and enduring a year of the rigorous training required to qualify for the astronaut corps.

What message would she be sending those students she talked to about not giving up on their dreams? She thought of the young girl seated next to her on the plane from Houston recently. The girl had followed up on Jemma's suggestion, and emailed photos of her landscape paintings. They were good, darned good, and Jemma wrote back a couple of times to encourage Savannah to persist with her goal of being an artist.

What would that eager girl think of herself and her own goals, if Jemma quit now?

Thoughtfully, while hanging up the towels and neatening the bathroom, Jemma decided to go downstairs and call Fran.

She'd re-commit herself to the training program, and meet with her contacts at the Russian Federal Space Agency.

Hart got out of bed and stretched. "Finished in the bathroom?"

"Yep, it's all yours. I'm going down to get some work done."

"Did something happen, Jemma? You look different. More like your usual self."

"I feel a little better today. I do. I think you're right--day by day you can feel less battered by grief, and more in charge of your life again. Feels...good."

He crossed to her, his arms starting to reach out as if for a hug, but he let one arm fall to his side and simply patted her on the shoulder. "Glad to hear it, Jemma. I've been concerned about you."

A few blocks away, Cabot was unloading a grocery bag. "And here's the milk you asked for."

Marybeth looked up from making his breakfast. "I...thank you."

He grabbed her ass. "Anything for my baby."

She felt cold inside, shaky at the very idea of pointing out an error, but she was determined to do things differently, to stop bowing to the idea that she wasn't allowed an opinion or a say-so in life, and so she spoke up. "I asked for regular. Dear. Not skim."

He turned, his eyes widening in surprise. "What did you say?"

"Um, I said that I asked you to please get me a carton of regular milk. But you got skim."

"The skim is better for you."

"In other words, you decided you knew best?"

He chuckled. "Isn't that what a husband is for?"

"I don't like the way skim tastes on cereal."

"You could stand to lose a couple pounds, Marybeth."

"I only use a small amount on cereal. It's not that many calories." She stopped herself, realizing two things: one, she was defending a preference she was entitled to have as if she wasn't entitled to have it, and two, he was doing that crazymaking thing on her again, twisting things around. "You said I'd be perfect if I gained five pounds."

Cabot laughed. "And you went overboard as always and gained ten."

Marybeth knew to a certainty that she had gained five pounds, and no more. For a moment she felt confused, but then realized this was yet another game he was playing, probably not even aware he was doing it, but with the overall intention of controlling her. Even though she could see what was going on, she still felt sick inside, tense and uneasy.

Shoving aside the whole issue, she asked brightly, "Did you want maple syrup with your waffles, or that new blueberry syrup you haven't tried yet from the gift basket your client sent?"

He looked at her. The silence between them became oppressive. The hissing of the waffle iron seemed unnaturally loud.

She fumbled with the lid of the waffle iron, opened and it forked out a beautifully golden puffy waffle to place on a ceramic plate she'd already warmed in the microwave. "I fixed you a little pitcher of melted butter, just the way you like. It's the unsalted kind, sweet butter so that—"

"On second thought," he interrupted, "waffles sound too heavy. Mind fixing me two poached eggs and rye toast? I'll be at my desk. Bring me a tray, okay, baby? You don't mind, do you?"

"Of course not. Dear. I'll bring you a tray." She hesitated fractionally. "Want anything else with that?"

Andy fretted that the dream he spun for his mother might not be enough to motivate her. He went in search of Qaletaqa. "I think I did a pretty good job," Andy said after explaining the dream in detail, "but I want you to do me a favor."

"What is that, young Andrew?"

"Spin another dream. Make sure my mom gets it–"

"We need to wait and see how she responds to the dream you--"

"My mom wanted Jerrie Cobb to go up in space back in the late nineties when John Glenn got to go up as a senior citizen. Lots of people petitioned for it to happen. I remember seeing pictures of me as a little kid going door to door with my mom in our neighborhood, getting people to sign a petition. Jerrie even said she'd go on a one-way trip--she just wanted to finally be able to go!"

"I understand."

"I found out that Jerrie spent many years doing missionary work in the Amazon, flying small planes with medical supplies. She got nominated for a Nobel Prize!"

"I am familiar with her story," Qaletaqa said. "Jerrie faced many obstacles and persevered in service to others. Your mother will learn to face–"

"These women fueled my mother's ambition for years. Not just years–her whole life. Until I stepped off that curb. I <u>have</u> to fix this, Grandpa. Don't you see? I have to!"

"Laws of free will demand that we—"

"I'm sick of all the rules!"

"Enough," Qaletaqa said. "I forbid you to interfere in your mother's life. It is hers to live, not yours."

Andy looked at him resentfully, and turned away, muttering, "Some great-grandfather you turned out to be." He yanked at the buffalo nickel and tossed it with its chain toward Qaletaqa.

Qaletaqa caught the necklace easily and watched Andy stride off.

All his life, Andy had been known as a team player, but the rest of the team kept telling him he couldn't and shouldn't do what he <u>knew</u> he must: Make amends to his mother and set things right that he had caused to go wrong in her life.

Having waited out of sight, Gabriella joined Qaletaqa. "Boys will be boys, isn't that what people say? He will cool off."

Andy sought out the gray girl he'd talked to before in the Gray Zone. "You've got to help me," he called out as he approached her stone grotto. "I thought everything was going good, but I need to be positive it turns out right."

"And you're, like, shocked you didn't do things perfectly the first time, boy scout?"

"Cut it out, okay? I need your help."

"What's on your mind?" Naomi feigned an elaborate yawn. "Need to know where to get the latest designer jeans at a discount?"

"What do you know about rogue Dream Spinners?"

Her eyes flickered, but she shrugged. "Who says I know anything?"

"Can you make objects move? Make the lights flicker and stuff like that? I need to send a message that someone will realize means I didn't die. You know how, right?"

"*Moi?*"

"Please. There isn't anyone else I can ask."

"Poor baby. Bad things happen to good people all the time, don't they?"

"You know, you've really got an attitude problem. How come you knew my name the first time we met? But I don't know yours. What is it?"

"Cleopatra."

"Thanks anyway," he muttered bitterly, turning to go.

She let him walk away a few steps and then she said softly, "Wait."

In a rush of anticipation, Jemma hurried down the stairs, carefully averting her eyes as she passed the photo gallery with all the smiling faces of Andy through the years.

At the bottom of the steps, she turned left, heading toward the kitchen to get a cup of tea before going to her study. She passed the narrow table beneath the portrait of Andy and Joker that Lulu painted. Out of habit, she glanced at Andy's portrait.

He winked at her.

She stared, open-mouthed.

Baffled, she changed direction and walked slowly into her study. Her glance took in the array of science books and awards on her walls, a tangible reminder of the life she carefully built for herself brick by brick on a solid foundation of provable facts.

Turning on her laptop, she did an internet search on the keywords "grief + hallucinations." The resulting web site links numbered in the thousands. After about an hour of reading, she came across an article titled "After Death Contacts."

She leaned forward more intently, as she read about such phenomena as rooms filling with the scent of a loved one's favorite perfume or flower, their lost articles suddenly turning up, photographs of the deceased moving to a different location or even speaking or smiling as you passed.

Clicking to close the web site, she decided that, of course, she'd imagined the winking.

While dialing Fran's private number, she hummed tunelessly to herself, knowing this was the right choice. Everyone said it helped speed up the grieving process if you got back into your regular work routine. She couldn't hang around the house day after day. It was unhealthy and unproductive.

The call went to Fran's voice mail, so she left a message, "Hey Fran, it's Jemma—I should say Dr. Malotki as this is an official call—and I'd like to talk to you at your earliest convenience. Give me a call as soon as you can. Thanks. Talk to you soon."

She debated calling Fran's office number, but decided to keep this conversation more private for the moment and wait to hear back on Fran's cell. Meanwhile, she went to the kitchen for that cup of tea she'd planned before getting waylaid by her imagination.

As she passed the portrait of Andy, it abruptly tilted to the left.

Bewildered by the sudden movement, she straightened it and kept going to the kitchen.

A few minutes later, returning to her study with a NASA logo mug of steaming green jasmine tea, she glanced at the portrait, hanging straight on the wall.

It immediately tilted, to the right this time.

With a quick glance around she verified that the chandelier over the dining table was motionless. No other pictures moved. Nothing swayed.

She called up the stairs, "Hart? Did you feel anything?"

He came to the head of the stairs, buttoning his shirt. "Earthquake? No. You're imagining things, I guess."

Troubled, she straightened the portrait, went to her study and set down the tea. Her phone rang. She looked at the Caller ID and saw it was Fran calling. Feeling a rush of uncertainty, she let it go to voice mail.

Hart left for the bistro, and Jemma spent the morning going through her NASA files, forcing herself to concentrate.

Needing a break, she went to the kitchen, intending to grab a container of yogurt for lunch. As she passed the living room, she heard the piano playing the Beatles' song "Hello, Goodbye" that Andy had been learning. Whoever was playing it even hit the same wrong note Andy always did.

Racing to the piano, she got there as the music stopped. She touched the piano bench. It was cool. No one had been sitting there. There was no one in the living room. "I don't know why you say goodbye," she sang the lyrics softly, "I say...hello." Sinking into a chair, she dropped her face into her hands, wondering in despair what was happening to her sanity.

Restless, Jemma went to the kitchen and discovered they were out of yogurt. They needed a few other things, so she got in her car and drove to the grocery store.

On the way home with groceries, Jemma abruptly turned to take a different route than normal, not planning to do so, and approached an arts and crafts fair being held at a local park. Not knowing why, she pulled into a parking space and began walking around the booths and exhibits at the fair.

She turned a corner and saw a booth where a bearded vendor stacked New Age books and CDs for sale. A string of crystal prisms he'd hung between two poles glittered in the sun. But Jemma saw something else and she was mesmerized. Standing a few yards away, she stared at a green lava lamp and its undulating blobs.

The vendor noticed her interest and beckoned her closer. "You like lava lamps? It represents the cycle of life. See how the blobs grow? Then they disappear. But just as you think they're gone, they bubble up again and create new blobs of color."

Jemma had never liked lava lamps. When she was dating Mike years ago, he'd tried to buy her one for Christmas and she scoffed, telling him it was too ugly and she didn't want one. She still felt that way about lava lamps, but found herself asking, "How much?"

He smiled. "Not for sale. It's just decoration." He rummaged under the booth table and pulled out a box with a red lava lamp on the cover. "Here's a brand new one."

She opened her wallet and pulled out a twenty dollar bill. She indicated the green one that was plugged in. "I want this one."

"It's a vintage sixties Lava Lite. A necessity for every space-age bachelor pad."

She looked a question, meaning: *How much?*

He laughed and tossed out a wild figure, "A hundred."

In compromise, she counted four twenties into his hand.

He shrugged, unplugged the lamp and wound the cord around it. As he handed it to her, a sudden breeze passed through the crystal prisms and played a haunting melody. Hundreds of facets caught the sunlight and created rainbows.

At the next booth, kids and adults were lined up for face painting. A mother with a sun and moon design painted on her cheek glanced up to admire the chiming, sparkling crystals. She came over to the New Age book display and noticed the various titles. "After my mother died, my dad suddenly found her starburst pin. It had been missing for years."

The vendor pointed to books about getting messages from beyond. "Lost objects suddenly found. Just like getting a postcard from someone on a long journey."

Hugging the green lava lamp, still feeling confused why she had felt compelled to buy it, Jemma stared up at the crystal prisms.

Jemma hurried into the kitchen from the laundry room and grabbed the cordless phone on the third ring, thinking Hart might be trying to reach her. The lava lamp sat on the counter, with its plug dangling free. She answered the phone, but it turned out to be a solicitor selling carpet cleaning services.

After hanging up, she went back to her chores, and loaded the washer. She added detergent, but when she picked up the bottle of fabric softener she discovered it was nearly empty. She drained it into the cap, needing more.

Searching cupboards for Downy, she saw Andy's backpack on a shelf. Startled, she took it down, opened it and saw the catalog he had put in there. She pulled it out, frowning but curious, and then stared in bewilderment at the picture of a green lava lamp he had circled.

Feeling puzzled, she returned to the kitchen and looked at the lava lamp on the counter. It was an exact match to the one in the catalog.

She didn't touch the lamp or plug it in, but as she looked at it, it turned itself on, heated up and started blobbing.

She stared, confounded.

In the Gray Zone, Andy let out a whoop. "We did it! High five!"

When she didn't make a move, he grabbed Naomi's hand and slapped it with his.

Naomi backed away, as if his touch had hurt.

He was too excited to notice her reaction or question it. "Now she has to understand that I'm still around but she just can't see me like she used to."

"Give me four!" Andy shouted to his dog. He glanced down and around, frowning to see that Joker wasn't with him. "Where are you, boy?"

"Looking for someone?" Naomi asked, bored. "He must be a short guy."

"My Golden Retriever. Joker. I thought he was with me. Now that I think of it, he never comes in here when I do, but he's always there again when I leave. I wonder why."

"Oh my, the dramas of the after-life never cease. A missing dog. What will happen next. Stay tuned to this awesome broadcast from Hollywood."

"I didn't say he was missing," Andy snapped. "I said he doesn't come into the Gray Zone."

Naomi looked at him for a long moment. "Smart move on his part. You might want to follow his example."

Marybeth dreamed that she was packing to leave. She felt a sense of urgency, and hastily threw clothes in bags, then grabbed a picture of Naomi and stuffed it in with silky scarves that kept slipping out and tangling.

Struggling with the bag's zipper, she saw a woman come in and say, "Quick! He's waiting in the car."

"But I'm almost ready," Marybeth said. "We can't just leave everything!"

"It's not important. He's getting pissed."

Marybeth fussed with a zipper, trying to put more of her clothes in an already bulging bag. "At least let me turn off the lights and make sure it doesn't look inviting to thieves if they look in a window."

"Would you hurry!"

Marybeth woke up suddenly, with the dream still lingering, and her heart beating fast. Had she been dreaming about leaving Cabot? Who was the woman? And what man was waiting? Maybe the people were Yolanda and Tom, helping her escape?

Feeling weary and drained, she got up and went into the kitchen to make a cup of green tea. It was the only caffeine she allowed herself, and she was momentarily tempted to drink a cup of Cabot's strong coffee, still warm in the pot. He was outside, building a garden trellis for flowering vines to climb.

While sipping her tea and eating a piece of whole grain toast, Marybeth flipped through the community newspaper. She spotted a small display ad for a woman attorney who offered a free one-hour consultation.

Forcing herself to take an action instead of feeling nervous even thinking about it, she hastily picked up the phone, called and made an appointment, her attention on Cabot's location throughout so he couldn't inadvertently eavesdrop.

When Marybeth got to her appointment, she was pleasantly surprised to find a soft-spoken woman who made her feel at ease right away.

"The reason I called," Marybeth said, "is I'd like to find out what some of my options are."

"For–?"

"Um, divorce. I've been married two years, and it was a mistake. Definitely. But I can't afford to leave. I'm an actress but I haven't been getting parts lately. I don't have an income and I don't have any money put aside in my own name. I had an inheritance but when we got married he convinced me the smart thing was to give him half to invest with his other projects."

"I see."

"The thing is, I want to do this quickly, before I lose my nerve. And I'm afraid if I suggest divorce, he'll talk me out of it. Even if he agrees, if I have to keep living with him until I can afford a place of my own, he'll make my life hell. So I want to say to him 'I'm moving out' and just do it."

"Do you have shared assets, such as cars, a house?"

Marybeth nodded, and explained more details in answer to the attorney's questions.

An hour later, she left the attorney's office, downhearted. Her finances were too enmeshed with Cabot's to make a quick move feasible. She had signed a pre-nuptial agreement, and on top of that, when they bought the house to fix up, he said it was only fair that she put all her savings toward the down payment. That included the remainder of her inheritance from her grandmother. He was putting in money of his own, so she agreed that his idea was fair, and even thanked him for not expecting her to pay half.

"Pay half!" she muttered to herself as she got in her car. She felt like a fool. She'd done all the things that women's magazines warned you not to do when you got married. She gave up her independence and she gave up her separate bank account. Instead of thinking about her future, she had rolled everything she had into their new joint checking account and from there Cabot withdrew funds to open escrow on the house she hadn't even wanted.

Driving home cautiously, Marybeth thought of that bunny drawing Yolanda had shown her. *A bunny in a gilded cage,* she thought. *That's what I am. And the house isn't even that fancy.*

The one solution the attorney mentioned that made sense was to keep quiet for now about wanting a divorce, get a job and save the money to finance her move.

But what kind of job could she get?

She was discouraged about her chances to get hired through an audition, but she wasn't qualified for anything else that would pay as much money as quickly as she wanted it.

Jemma stood at the master bedroom window, staring out at the swimming pool, reliving times she'd played in the water with Andy. Hart was probably right about selling the house. It wasn't that she wanted to abandon her memories, but it was too painful to have them in her face on a non-stop basis.

Hart entered behind her and joined her at the window to see what she was looking at.

She didn't turn. "I saw a movie a few years ago, I forget what it was called, something that was playing on cable in a hotel room when I was at a conference in New York. It was a historical drama. Native warriors took their captives from another tribe and tied them to upright poles, and then slowly scraped their skin off in long narrow strips, using razor-sharp clam shells."

Hart winced.

"I feel like I'm one of those captives," she said. "I never knew there could be pain like this.... Every breath I take catches. Every nerve knows my son is gone."

"I thought you were feeling better." He looked at her.

She shrugged. "Who am I kidding? I feel like shit, and I can't even trust my own sensory perceptions."

He waited for her to explain, but when she remained silent, he said, "Lately--before this happened--I found myself thinking what kind of girl he'd marry. Maybe someone we'd welcome as the daughter we never had...because you only wanted one child and insisted--"

"Don't, Hart. Please don't." After a moment of tense silence, she said, "Did I ever tell you about the time I saw a video of a heart-lung transplant?"

Hart blinked. "What's that got to do--"

"Somebody I met on the plane flying to Houston one day told me he had directed a technical video for the first time and he had a rough cut. They were still editing it and he wanted my opinion. He gave me a DVD and later I watched it, and sent him an email that it was good. I made a couple of suggestions for editing it tighter."

"I don't think I'd like to see something like that. Too graphic. Even though I'm a chef, I've never been into butchering."

"I couldn't get the images out of my mind for the longest time. You see, after the defective heart and lungs are removed, the patient's chest cavity gapes wide open. You think to yourself, well, how can this hollow man still be alive? But then you see gloved hands reach for the donor organs, and the cavity is filled up again, and the camera pans back to show the draped patient, breathing and alive. The operation is a success."

"I don't know why you--"

"I am that person on the table, Hart. I'm waiting for something to fill the core where the heart and breath of my life used to be. And a brain transplant might be needed any day soon as well." She sighed. "At least the patient in the video was anesthetized first."

"People keep saying the pain of new grief will slowly get duller," he said. "Like an old knife, I guess. But I know it'll always be able to slice me to the bone."

"It hurts just to wake up each day."

He nodded, agreeing. "When I look at you all I see is the place beside you where our Andy should be."

She could barely breathe. More to herself than to him, she whispered, "Empty spaces are the hardest."

"Fran called just now. Didn't you hear the phone? She said you were trying to reach her, but you don't answer your cell. She asked if I knew what you plan to do. About NASA. She's getting pressured for an answer. They need to know if you're in or out. People on the waiting list want your spot."

Her eyes closed briefly. What was there to say about old dreams? She looked out the window again. "I don't qualify anymore. It wouldn't be safe to have me on a mission."

After the incident with Andy's portrait winking and moving on its own, compounded by the piano playing itself, Jemma couldn't avoid analyzing what would happen if she were in the midst of an important task in space, and had a hallucination, or believed she was pushing the right button but instead caused a malfunction or shut down the life support for one of her team mates.

"Are you sure–"

"If Fran calls again," Jemma said, "tell her I'm not going back."

"If that's your decision, then I think she should hear it from you."

"Do you think I'm wrong?"

"In all the years we've been married," he said, "you've never asked for my advice. I don't know what to say."

"You're right. Sorry." She tried to laugh. "I guess it's a sign of how mixed-up I feel."

He studied her. "There's something I want to tell you."

She waited, looking out the window.

"I'm going ahead with that cooking show. The network liked my proposal, and they said I'm good in front of the camera. I think it's what I need to move forward. Andy was excited for me, and I can do this in his memory."

"I'm happy for you, Hart," Jemma said sincerely.

He looked at her, studying her profile. "There's something else. Might as well get it over with now. I know there's never going to be a good time to say this."

"What?"

"I'm leaving," he said.

She gave a sudden start, but still did not turn from the window to look at him.

They'd always enjoyed a relaxed companionship with endless topics to discuss. About raising Andy, about redecorating the living room, about where to put the Christmas tree for a change. They had careers they loved, and each respected the other's abilities, talents and ambitions. There was always something to talk about. Always.

And yet, now, when they should be offering solace, they didn't have anything to say to each other aside from, apparently, *Goodbye.*

There would be time enough later for the details about ending the marriage and what to do about the house.

She knew he was awaiting her reaction to his announcement that he was leaving.

So, for now, she said without making a move towards him, "And I should be trying to stop you."

Jemma went to the driving range and got some of her pent-up feelings out by whacking the golf balls for an hour.

She had kept her medical record scrupulously clean for many years, so that NASA would have no reason to reject her application. And now, here she was an astronaut-candidate, in the midst of final training, aiming for a slot on an international team, and suddenly she'd become mentally unstable.

It broke her heart, knowing this, and she knew, too, that she could never admit it to anyone.

She shoved the clubs back in Andy's bag–the golf bag he'd wanted for his birthday but never got to use–and put it in her car.

Moments after she drove away, Mike McLeod pulled into the lot and got out with his clubs to spend an hour unwinding by hitting golf balls.

After his wife moved out, Mike hadn't bothered fixing up the house other than what was needed to make it livable. She took most of the furniture and paintings but he hadn't cared enough to argue about any of it.

When he had asked Nikki why she was asking for a divorce, Nikki said she needed to find her own space. That was all. Her own space, like something you heard on a daytime talk show. The woman wanted space, and his long absences from home while shooting on location hadn't provided it?

No, she had admitted, vaguely.

Then he heard gossip via a mutual friend, that Nikki had wanted to leave for several years, but hadn't felt there was enough money to bother splitting in half.

His recent success in the film industry had apparently made the bank account large enough for a divorce to be worthwhile.

The phone rang, with a call from his friend and producer, Simon.

"Bad news," Simon said. "We lost our Cerise."

"But what happened? I thought they were on schedule."

The actress Mike had signed for the role of Cerise was in production on a drama being filmed on location in Nova Scotia.

His own film, "Seven Funerals," was scheduled to start rehearsal after her completion date on the other project.

"She got the mumps. Don't ask me how. Like a curse descended on her from above. They have to wait for her to recuperate, then continue shooting their own film, and we're shit out of luck as far as our schedule goes."

They talked over the idea of waiting for her, and decided against it. Lawyers would handle the details, but Mike would call Penny Sheridan, their casting director, and find a new Cerise.

Thinking about all the headshots he'd seen, and the parade of actresses who auditioned, he remembered that one he'd been interested in, who had not shown up.

After ending the call with Simon, Mike got hold of his assistant. "Hey, Rodney. We need to re-cast Cerise. There's somebody I want you to get hold of. A no-show. You'll probably remember who I mean. The one with the vulnerable eyes."

"Oh, yeah. You mean Marybeth Lacroix," Rodney said. "I'll get right on it."

Marybeth huddled in a corner of the gazebo, her favorite place of late. She'd sit there for hours on a cushion, and stare into space.

Cabot tried to get her interested in the house. He brought home decorator magazines, paint samples and swatches of fabric for new living room furniture to order if she wanted. He made every effort to accommodate her poor appetite, ordering food delivered or picking it up from delicatessens, hoping to stimulate her.

All to no use. She had lost interest in normal activities.

The one thing he had not tried, he admitted to himself, watching her from the master bedroom window as she stared at something invisible near the birdbath, was to encourage her to go on auditions.

He looked down at his hand, which held her cell phone.

The parrot on Cabot's shoulder tilted its head and imitated the sound of a phone ringing.

Cabot reached in his pocket and fed the bird a sunflower seed. "Good boy. That's right. And what do you say when the phone rings?"

The parrot said, "Hello."

Pacing in her study, Jemma held the phone to her ear and waited for Fran to answer.

When she did, Jemma said, "Take my name off the list, and let someone else take my place. Don't try to talk me out of this. My mind is made up."

There was a long silence at Fran's end.

"Fran? Did you hear me? You there?"

"I'm here. This is a huge step to take, Jemma. And I want to be sure you've thought it out completely before I make it official–"

"I have!"

"But I think it's an impulsive reaction to your bereavement," Fran said over the phone. "I'm going to make a suggestion, Jemma, and I hope you know I have your best interests at heart. Go away for a few days, where no one knows you. A spa resort hotel where they'll pamper you with massages and great food and movie rentals in your room. Don't take work or heavy reading along with you. A real getaway. Will you do that? And keep in touch?"

After a heated discussion, Jemma finally agreed to Fran's terms.

Chapter 16

Gabriella looked at Andy as if she didn't trust herself to speak, and then finally asked in measured tones, "What have you done?"

Even though she didn't yell, Andy could sense she was upset. Stalling for time, he said, "The dream spinning went okay, didn't it?"

"Stop congratulating yourself on a job well done. Stop applauding your cleverness for a moment. Stop and think."

He started to ask what she meant, but instead he grew still...and awareness seeped in. He looked at her, panicked. "She thinks she's hallucinating?"

Gabriella nodded.

"But I was just trying to help!"

"And did you hear about your parents?"

Andy waited warily, afraid to hear the answer.

"They are getting a divorce."

He felt stunned.

Everything was a big mess, when he'd thought he was doing such a good job.

Morose, he wandered off, ignoring Gabriella when she called out to him.

He didn't call Joker to go with him. The dog turned and left with Gabriella.

Following Fran's advice, Jemma arranged to get away to the desert for a few days. Maybe the hallucinations were caused by being in the house too much. Each room was filled with so many memories of Andy they seemed to hang in the air and made it too thick to breathe.

Upstairs, she packed a duffel and left.

Driving to the Van Nuys airport, a general aviation facility for corporate jets and small planes that served the Valley area, she made a mental list of calls to make and errands to take care of when she got back from her spa trip. She'd need to meet with Hart and an attorney, meet with a realtor about putting the house up for sale, and start looking for a condo or apartment if she decided to stay in L.A.

She realized she was tensing up, and driving too fast. Since the accident, she had become a more cautious driver, hesitant to change lanes until there was more than adequate space to do so, and vigilant about coming to a full stop to the count of three at stop signs--rather than the more common "California roll" in which you lift your foot off the accelerator as you approach the sign, glance for cross traffic and if there's none, hit the gas and keep going.

When she got to the Van Nuys airport, parked and walked to the terminal, carrying the duffel, one of the mechanics recognized her. "Hey there! Haven't seen you in a long time," he called out. "Thought maybe you quit the flying club. How's that boy of yours?"

"Hi, how're you doing?" she called back, pretending she hadn't heard the question. She hurried past, plowing through the immense waves of heat curling up from the concrete.

By the time she was airborne, Jemma knew this trip had been a mistake. She barely took in the scenery as she flew to the Palm Springs airport, and then taxied in.

The more Andy dwelled on the mistakes he'd made and how miserable he felt, the grayer he became, until it seemed natural to drift into the Gray Zone and join the others who were as gray as he now was.

He sat cross-legged with them in the shadows, complaining bitterly. He didn't notice that no one was listening to him because they were blathering nonstop about their own woes. He explained in exhaustive detail how hard he had tried to help his mother and how unfair it was that things had turned out the way they did.

After a while--he didn't know how long in Earth time--he wandered off alone past the grottoes and caves, and squatted in a cage that had been built for monkeys long ago, feeling at home in the dank and swirling mist. He didn't have a headache this time because he was now vibrating at the same frequency as the negative atmosphere in the Gray Zone. He leaned against the bars, morose.

Just outside in the park area, beyond his ken, Andy's dog Joker whined and paced as if he sensed Andy within.

At the dog's side was Naomi. She was spending longer stretches outside the Gray Zone, wanting to change, but finding that she always ended up inside no matter how much she promised herself she wouldn't go back. She struggled to understand why she couldn't seem to do things differently.

Now she tried to see in past the smoke and gloom. She knew there were peepholes here and there, whose locations changed frequently, and she searched for one without luck. It occurred to her that she could go in as a visitor, as Andy had before, but she shrank from entering, afraid it would be too hard to get out again.

Leaning close to the bars of the Old Zoo, she yelled, "Andy! Andy Powell! ANDY!"

She knew from experience that the noise level inside was intense, with people moaning, crying, jabbering incessantly to themselves and clanging against bars. But from this side, there was silence.

Joker whined.

She'd known he was Andy's dog as soon as he ran up to her, circled and ran off, then lumbered up to her again, making it clear he wanted her to follow him. But she hadn't expected the dog to lead her to the Gray Zone, and now that she was here she didn't see how she could help.

"Sorry. You're a nice dog but you picked the wrong rescuer." She patted him and saw his name on the heart-shaped tag dangling from his collar. "Joker. Pleased to meet you. Are you trained?...Sit."

He sat, and looked at her expectantly.

Across the picnic area, a dog obedience class was in session. She watched the humans trying to train their dogs, and got an idea. She turned back to Joker. "Bark!"

He wagged his tail.

"No? Don't know that word? Okay. How about...Speak!"

Joker barked. Once.

Encouraged, she said, "Louder, Joker! SPEAK! SPEAK!"

He caught on and came to his feet.

He barked over and over again, and...

In the obedience class, thirty dogs on a down-stay command leapt up and began barking like alarm bells had rung. The dog owners tried frantically to control their pets, and the instructor strode up and down the ranks, calling out, "Down! Quiet! Stay! Enough!" but none of the dogs paid heed.

They were following Joker's lead, and he didn't stop barking.

Within the Gray Zone, a sound of muffled barking penetrated the gloom.

Andy slowly looked up. Then stood.

He followed the sound through the shadows and smoke and located a peephole.

He saw Joker outside, barking.

"Joker!" he called out. "Here I am! Good boy." Then Naomi moved into view and Andy's jaw tightened. "You knew that would happen--you knew she'd think she was hallucinating!"

Naomi made a gesture to the dog, and Joker fell quiet.

The other dogs abruptly stopped barking, and the obedience class resumed, with the humans baffled what the ruckus had been about.

Peering into the shadows, Naomi tried to see which smoky shape was Andy's. "I know you're angry with me, Andy, but you have to understand–"

"You knew who I was when I first approached you, begging for help. You must've been laughing inside at what a sucker I am!"

"It wasn't like that–"

He didn't want her excuses or explanations. He slammed a fist through the peephole. "You owe me!"

Reluctant to go in, yet knowing it was the best way to approach him, she slipped through the bars and squatted beside him.

He greeted her with cold silence.

"Well, hello," Naomi said, trying to coax him to be friendly. "What brings you in here, looking like you need Grecian Formula all over? Been a bad boy lately? Or couldn't you stay away from me?"

"Beat it," he mumbled.

"Hey, that's my line," she said. "Know something? You're not a bad guy. I kind of like you."

"I'm thrilled."

"Where's the chipper, perky boy scout who was out to save the world?"

"Why didn't you warn me I was doing too much?" he asked, not looking up. "You egged me on. Now my mom thinks she's insane. And my parents are splitting up."

Khaki wandered past, did a double take and returned to accost Andy. "Hey, dude, never thought I'd see you looking that color! Last time I saw you, Gabriella was leading you around by the nose."

Naomi gave a start, but hid her reaction to the name.

"I heard a rumor you were in here," Khaki said, "but I didn't believe it."

"We were talking," Naomi pointed out coldly.

"You're invited too, Gray Bitch," Khaki said. "Hurry up and let's go."

"I'm a total screw-up," Andy mumbled to himself. "I'm not just a nerd. That was bad enough. Everything I do is useless. What's the sense of even trying?"

"Time for Mardi Gras in Rio!" Khaki grinned. "Gorgeous topless babes. You can have one on each arm. Or three. It's a blast. You'll dig it. Come on, Andy, let's split this dump."

"Do you want to go to Rio with him, Andy?" Naomi asked.

Andy retreated further into the cage, his back turned against them.

"Go away," Naomi said to Khaki. "I'll handle this."

Cabot crossed to the front door with a suitcase. His hand on the knob, he turned it slowly and looked at Marybeth.

She wore a long summer robe, and kept nervously knotting the sash and then untying it, over and over.

"Don't be alone tomorrow," he cautioned.

His tone infuriated her. She crossed her arms, tucked her hands under so the scars on her wrists didn't show.

"I should've asked Yolanda to come stay with you," he said.

"I told you a hundred times, I don't need a babysitter!"

He looked at her evenly, and then used one of his favorite weapons: silence.

She tried not to fidget under his steady gaze, tried not to feel like an errant school girl called before the principal, but more often than not in the past, his strategy worked quickly, and she'd leap into appeasement mode to soothe and assuage whatever imagined insult had raised its head between them, and then Cabot would be mollified, at least for a few days.

It seemed to Marybeth that Cabot always managed to include a vestige of truth in what he said, but then twisted it in such a way that she felt confused, as if "up" had suddenly become "down" and yet she wasn't supposed to notice that Cabot had manipulated gravity for his own secret purpose.

Yes, it was true that tomorrow would be a challenge for her, but he was making it seem that she'd fall apart, that she needed to be guarded, watched like an asylum inmate.

The silence unnerved her, as always.

But, unlike other times, she was not in her default appeasement mode. Not even close.

"Why does everything have to be a battle with you, Cabot?"

He gave a start, taken aback by her quiet attack.

She felt her breath quicken. "You act like winning is the most important thing in the world even when you have to invent a problem to fuss over. You get your teeth in it and you just can't let it be, can you? You just have to dig and poke and prod until you get a rise out of me. Then you get all smug that your crazy wife is upset and moody, and you get to pretend you are the poor put-upon husband and nobody realizes how much you endure behind closed doors."

"Invent!" He spluttered. "I invent problems? Look in the mirror, Marybeth, to see the one who's got a wild imagination."

"Have a nice trip, Cabot." She flung the door open.

In the driveway, an airport shuttle van was waiting.

But there was something wrong with the path from the door to the driveway.

Cabot frowned. He pointed at the path between the rows of rosebushes they'd planted. "What is all that?"

"I don't know...." Shocked, Marybeth walked outside on his heels.

The path was littered with rosebuds. Dozens. Two hundred or more dainty rosebuds.

Cabot dashed from one bush to the next. "Every goddamned rosebud. Cut off. Twelve rosebushes. How many buds on each bush? They won't bloom now. They have to produce new buds. Probably six weeks before we see more buds. Maybe longer. And then they have to open before we can enjoy roses. My roses." He looked at her steadily, accusingly.

She realized what he was silently saying. "I didn't do it!"

"Why did you buy those scissors, Marybeth?"

She unconsciously touched her shorn hair.

He stepped toward her, looming larger.

She quailed. Her hands slipped into the pockets of her robe, as if wanting to hide their own trembling. Her fingers curled into tight fists, her nails biting into the soft flesh of her palms. She clenched her fists tighter as if that would give her strength to stand up to Cabot.

He'd never hit her. But maybe today was the day that he'd cross that invisible line.

Cabot said flatly, "You knew how much these roses mean to me. Would it have made a difference if I'd ordered white instead of pink? Is that what this is all about? Some kind of power play to show your displeasure with my color choice?"

"I DIDN'T DO IT!"

The van driver gave a beep of his horn. Other passengers in the van made motions to mean *Hurry up!*

"People are waiting," Cabot said coldly, "and I've got a plane to catch." He grabbed his suitcase and deliberately stomped over the rosebuds to reach the van. He glanced back over his shoulder. "And you claim that I invent problems?"

She watched him leave, then examined the devastation. Each bud had been snipped at the neck, leaving its stem still on the rosebush. If the buds had been cut off with their stems intact, there might be a chance of salvaging at least some of them in water. But this was hopeless.

After she got dressed in shorts and a halter top and sandals, she swept up the flower buds and put them in the trash, whispering over and over again to herself, "I didn't do it. I know I didn't."

Inside her room at the resort hotel, Jemma opened the draperies and peeled back the sheer curtain to look out. She'd been given a ground floor room with its own enclosed patio overlooking one of the swimming pools. She could see the steam rising from the water, and knew its source must be an underground hot spring.

A woman glanced up from the water, smiled and beckoned Jemma to come out.

Lost in thought, not being intentionally rude, Jemma let the curtain drop and turned away.

After setting up her laptop, Jemma emailed Fran to let her know she had followed her advice, then got a bottle of mineral water from the mini-bar.

Behind her the laptop screen flickered strangely.

When she returned to it, her monitor showed an archived article from a local newspaper. A black and white photo of Naomi Valverde was captioned: "LOCAL STUDENT, DEAD IN DORM ROOM."

Unsure why she was intrigued, Jemma read the article, and then picked up her phone.

From a safe distance, Eric Blum watched Marybeth clean up the mess he'd created for her to find.

He was seated on his bicycle, one foot braced on the curb.

As she swept up the rosebuds, clearly agitated, he smiled grimly.

Jemma made a few calls. Each time she was referred to someone else who might be able to answer her questions. She hung up and sat staring at another name and number to call, not sure why she was going to all this trouble.

When Jemma traveled, and in business, she used her professional name of Dr. Jemma Malotki, and so it didn't occur to her to use the name "Powell" at any time in these conversations.

She picked up the phone again. Looking at her notes, she dialed, and when a woman answered, she said, "Yolanda? You don't know me. My name is Dr. Malotki and I got your name from a reporter at the local newspaper. Could I...Yes, that's right. I'm a...writer and I wanted to talk to you about your cousin's death last year...Sure, I'll come over in the morning. Give me the directions."

The next day, knowing Cabot was expecting a check from a client, and not wanting to be responsible for it, aware he'd accuse her of leaving the mail too long in the curbside box and allowing someone to steal it, Marybeth hurried outside to the mailbox after seeing through the bedroom window when a neighbor got their own mail and went back inside.

It was the type of metal box on a wooden post that was commonly used for the mail carrier's easy access without the need to get out of the postal delivery truck.

As she leaned to open the dropdown flap of the metal box, she shaded her eyes with a hand to peer in for the mail.

She staggered back, repulsed.

Inside the mailbox, on top of a stack of letters, catalogs and advertising flyers, was a wooden rat trap, the common spring-loaded variety. Caught in the trap was a large rat, dead and bloody, its neck crushed by the metal bar.

Taped to the rat was a handwritten note in bold red ink that read: "U R Next!"

Not knowing what else to do, having no one she could call, Marybeth ran into the kitchen, got a pair of aluminum serving tongs and a black plastic garbage bag. Facing the mailbox with her eyes closed, she counted out loud, "One, two, three!"

On three, she opened her eyes, grabbed the trap with the tongs, dropped it in the bag, dropped the tongs in with it, tied the bag and sped to the trash bin at the side of the house, her heart racing, trying not to breathe, holding the bag as far out in front of her as possible. She deposited the bag in the bin and slammed the lid, shuddering with disgust.

Later, before her courage could ebb completely, while holding her breath and keeping her face averted, she sprayed the mailbox and all the mail inside it with Lysol, and ran back in the house.

Even later, knowing she'd allowed a far longer drying time than was needed, she forced herself to go back out and finish the task.

Crying softly to herself, her hands shaking, she put on rubber gloves and gingerly removed the stack of mail, knowing she'd have to sort it quickly for anything important before she could discard it, along with the gloves.

All the while, she could only wonder who was torturing her this way. When the shock of the graffiti vandalism had worn off, she'd allowed a tiny suspicion that Cabot had done it himself. Even the rosebuds could've been cut by him while she was sleeping. But this? Cabot's out of town, she reminded herself. He could've paid someone to do this, but why? For what purpose?

It crossed her mind that the parents of the Powell boy might be to blame: maybe in their grief they were seeking vengeance. And yet, knowing the pain of losing a child herself, she didn't understand how any parent could be so wicked and cruel.

Marybeth realized how strange she must look, collecting the daily mail with rubber gloves and brandishing a spray can of germ-killing deodorizer.

She glanced around, hoping neighbors were not watching her from behind shuttered windows.

A thought occurred to her: *I can't tell Cabot about this.*

Jemma parked the rental car at the address Yolanda gave her, but checked the slip again, confused. A rabbit rescue adoption was in progress in the open garage. Domestic rabbits of all colors, sizes and varieties were in large wire enclosures. People with name tags identifying each of them as a "Bunny Rescue Volunteer" wrangled bunnies as well as visitors of all ages.

As she approached, Jemma wondered which woman was Yolanda.

Seeing the woman who looked lost and paid no heed to the rabbits, Yolanda came up to Jemma with an outstretched hand from beneath the large black rabbit she held. "You must be Dr. Malotki. I'm Yolanda Gomez." Yolanda called to one of the volunteers. "Diedre? I'm going inside a few minutes. Give a holler if you need me."

Sitting in Yolanda's kitchen, Jemma did not disavow Yolanda of the notion that she was a writer doing research on college suicides. Yolanda practically filled in the blanks herself and Jemma went along with it, sensing it would be easier to ask questions than if she talked about Andy's death or explained she had no rational clue for why she was interested in the life and death of a girl named Naomi.

Yolanda settled the black rabbit on a chair by itself, and poured Jemma a glass of lemonade. Indicating the rabbit, Yolanda said, "They don't like as much handling as people think."

Jemma took a sip of lemonade. "I didn't know that."

"They're defenseless creatures," Yolanda said, "living in a world of predators." She went on about the various personality traits of pet rabbits, then segued into Naomi's desire to be a social worker and how shocked the family had been when the girl committed suicide while at college.

"So she wasn't depressed a long time or tried it before or–?" Jemma wasn't sure what questions she should be asking in her role of writer.

"Not that I know of. I thought Naomi was happy at school. I hadn't returned a call she'd made, and you can imagine how much I kicked myself for that lapse afterwards."

"I can imagine how you must've felt."

"But listen to me, going on and on," Yolanda said. "I bet you want to know what's different about Naomi's story or you wouldn't be here. The reporter didn't put it in the newspaper article–his editor called it too New Age–but he obviously mentioned it to you or you wouldn't have come to interview me."

Jemma hadn't learned anything unusual, but she nodded.

"A few weeks after the funeral," Yolanda explained, "I was helping her mother, who is actually my father's stepsister, so Naomi and I are only step-cousins but the family is a big blend of what we call cousins and we love each other more than lots of blood relatives do--"

Jemma shifted impatiently, and Yolanda came to the point.

"We were sorting Naomi's belongings in her bedroom at home–"

"Not an easy task," Jemma interjected, thinking of Andy's room.

Yolanda looked at her curiously but Jemma was not forthcoming.

"The room filled with the scent of fresh gardenias," Yolanda said.

"Were they blooming outside?"

"Gardenias. During a time of year when they don't bloom outdoors. You can't even find them at nurseries to buy when this happened. Naomi's favorite flower. Not the smell of perfume or candles, but real flowers."

"You were thinking about her and remembered–"

"We both imagined the same thing? It got so strong we had to open a window. But it wasn't scary. It was a sign that our *querida* Naomi is not really gone. I went to church that day and lit a candle for the repose of her soul. I know suicide is a sin, but I know my Naomi and she must've had a good reason for what she did." Yolanda dropped her head and studied her hands. "I know she's not in hell, burning with damned souls. If anything, she's in purgatory, repenting."

Jemma surreptitiously looked at her wristwatch. The notepad in her lap was unused, her ruse for coming here forgotten.

She glanced around, and noticed a framed photo of a young woman with long straight blonde hair, her face obscured because she was up to her eyebrows with an armful of rabbits. Jemma couldn't help smiling at the charming picture.

Seeming to recollect herself, Yolanda peered out the door into the garage at the bunny adoption. "I should get back to work, and let you go write your article." She went to a desk by the stove and jotted down a web address from a note she found in her purse, then handed the paper to Jemma.

"This is an Internet group for suicide support," Yolanda said. "You'll have to sign up like a member. Don't take advantage of things they think are private. But I'm sure I don't have to tell you that. I just thought it would be a good resource for your article."

Jemma recollected her mission, and scribbled a few fake notes on the blank pad she'd brought as a prop. "If you don't mind my asking, did the family ever discover why Naomi did it?"

"She was real upset about something. The only person she told was her best friend, actually a cousin of both of ours. When she died from an overdose, what else were we to think?"

"But it could have been an accident?"

Yolanda looked at her. "The police said her last journal entry sounded like a suicide note–she was very depressed--so we all believed.... Oh! I wonder if you could be right. That would mean so much to the whole family, to find out she did not commit suicide."

Jemma walked toward the door, Yolanda at her heels.

"Of course it doesn't bring her back," Yolanda continued, "but I for one, would feel so much better. An accident is easier to accept."

Stopping at the door, Jemma looked at Yolanda. "Is it?"

Without explaining, without waiting for a response, Jemma left.

At home, Marybeth finished her solitary bowl of soup at the kitchen table, put her dishes in the dishwasher and wandered into the living room.

She knew she was inviting depression, and that the therapist she used to see would scold her, saying *You're setting yourself up for a breakdown, Marybeth, when you do these things. Why do you participate in your own despair instead of taking action to lift yourself out of it?*

But she was drawn to a framed wedding photo of herself with her Maid of Honor, her cousin Naomi, a lovely brunette with an impish grin and sparkling brown eyes.

Touching Naomi's face in the picture, Marybeth thought of the years growing up together in Palm Springs. Looking at the photo, missing Naomi deeply, Marybeth began to cry.

Determined to fight the impulse to do what Naomi had done, Marybeth posted a message from bunnygirl at her suicide support forum: "Anybody there? I really need help."

She stared at the screen and tugged at a short lock of hair, waiting.

After soaking in the hot mineral water pool at the hotel, Jemma swam laps in a fresh water, unheated pool, then showered and ordered dinner from room service. She ate alone in her room, watching television without paying attention to what was on. Realizing she was falling asleep watching TV, a habit she'd always scolded Hart for, she turned it off and got into bed.

In the darkened hotel bedroom, Jemma slept fitfully, dreaming she heard a tinkling lullaby.

Outside the ornate gates of Forest Lawn cemetery in the Hollywood Hills near Griffith Park, Qaletaqa approached the heron pond with a small handful of pebbles. Bronze statues of tall herons were in the center of the circular pond and fountain.

He tossed a pebble into the water, and observed the ripples.

Gabriella joined him. "So many lives, each person thinking they act alone. We are all connected, though, aren't we?"

He tossed another pebble.

The ripples intersected.

In the Gray Zone, Naomi shook Andy's shoulder.

He shot her a cold look.

"Get up! I need you."

In a guttural whisper, he said, "Leave me alone!"

"You're a runner, right?"

He shrugged, barely nodding in agreement.

"Then put your running shoes on!"

"Why should I do anything for you?" he snarled. "You screwed up my–"

"Shut up. Just come with me."

He noticed that she was dressed in a track suit and running shoes.

She crouched, as if at a runner's mark.

Intrigued, he stood up and did the same, and was instantly dressed as she was. Both were still gray, head to toe.

She glanced over at him and nodded briskly.

They sped off, side-by-side.

Marybeth looked out the master bedroom window at the gazebo as the lullaby wound down and came to a stop.

In her hand she held a TV remote control.

Barely glancing at it, she pressed the button to replay the video.

The scars on her wrists seemed to glow in the moonlight streaming in the window.

Andy and Naomi ran on a straight line with no regard for physical obstacles.

A dog woke up, looked their way and bristled.

They bore through a fence and across a backyard.

Everything was a blur.

They cored through the wing of a house where a weary mother paced with her colicky infant.

When they cut through a suburban bedroom, Andy saw a familiar figure, playing a video game. "Eric–!" he called.

Naomi grabbed his hand, pulling Andy along. "Faster, faster!"

Behind Marybeth, on the bedroom TV monitor, the home video played.

Cabot's voice came over the speakers, talking as he filmed Marybeth entering their apartment with their newborn daughter. Then, in the nursery, Cabot's hand reached out to wind up a crib mobile. It played the same lullaby Jemma was hearing in her dream.

Naomi and Andy watched Marybeth for a moment from outside and then entered the room.

Naomi ran to Marybeth's side and tried to hug her.

"Wait," Andy cried. "I know her." He wheeled on Naomi. "Why did you bring me here--to <u>her</u>?"

Looking up, Naomi said to him simply, "I was right. She's at risk. Let's go!"

They zoomed towards Andy's house. No lights were on. They stopped at the front door.

"What the hell is going on?" he demanded. "You know where I live?"

Naomi frowned. "She's not home."

"You know my mother?"

Ignoring him, Naomi thought a moment until she had a new plan. "Come with me!" She ran off.

He caught up to her, and almost at once they were at the Van Nuys airport.

Again, Naomi halted, and looked around, baffled. "She was here. But–"

"She flew somewhere." He thought a moment. "Palm Springs. She's at a hotel."

"You know which one?"

He looked at Naomi, hesitating. "Are you going to hurt her?"

Impatiently, she shook her head. "Take me to her. Now!"

"But–"

"Do I have to spell it out? Time is of the essence, boy scout!"

She ran circles around him to prompt him to get moving, and he finally took off in the direction of the desert.

She ran at his side, both of them as swift as the wind.

In Jemma's hotel room, she gave up on sleep, turned on the bedside lamp, plumped the pillows and lay in bed with her laptop, looking at the note Yolanda gave her.

She joined the support forum under the name "flybynight," with no personal information about herself, and then browsed recent messages. She saw several posts from someone called bunnygirl and came back to the name, idly curious.

Then she logged off and signed into her email account, where she began checking mail and sending out a few replies.

Marybeth cried out and flung the remote. She moved closer to the TV, and reached out to the screen to caress the baby's face. "Happy Birthday, my sweet Stephanie," she whispered.

Her thoughts plummeted into an abyss of guilt, shame and blame: *It was my fault! I don't know what I did wrong, maybe I shouldn't have put you on your stomach to nap! If only I could go back and have another chance, I'd keep you safe....*

Letting the video play to its conclusion, she walked as if staggering in the desert and took her grandmother's old Bible from her night stand.

With trembling fingers, she turned onionskin pages, tearing a corner in her haste to find an appropriate chapter and verse.

In Jemma's hotel room, she sat at the computer, her head nodding as if she was about to fall asleep.

Andy reached out eagerly, trying to touch her.

"Never mind that, Andy," Naomi said.

"Why are we here?"

"I've seen how good you are at dream spinning already, and you were great at moving objects. You must have an amazing connection with her."

"What's that got to do with you?"

"Get a message to her! She's the only one who can receive it and know what to do with it right now."

"But–"

"Please?" She looked at him a long moment, and something between them shifted from all the sparring to a new, growing trust.

Holding her grandmother's Bible, Marybeth paced outside in the dimly lit back yard, growing more despondent with each step.

She wore a long sheer gown, too thin to provide any warmth, but she didn't go back inside for a blanket or robe. Even though it was summer, the temperature had dropped at sunset, and she felt chilled.

The automatic lawn sprinklers popped up and sprayed her legs.

She moved in one direction, then another, like a child uncertain how to escape the water. From across the yard, a Rainbird sprinkler head ratcheted a stream in an arc towards her.

She stopped moving and stood like a statue in the center of the yard.

Hugging the Bible to her chest, she kept it dry with her arms as the shower struck her.

In agony, she raised her face to the heavens, as if this cold baptism were her due.

Andy whispered in Jemma's ear, "Tell bunnygirl that her cousin did not commit suicide. It was an accident. An accident. Not suicide. Tell bunnygirl this. Do it now. Write her. Get up and write to bunnygirl, Mom."

268

He glanced up at Naomi and she nodded anxiously.

He repeated the message.

And then he backed away, hoping it would work.

In her kitchen, dripping water, Marybeth rattled the drawer that was the only one with a padlock on it. It was the knife drawer. Only Cabot knew the combination. Only Cabot could open it, but even if he were at home, she knew he wouldn't. He thought he was protecting her, protecting the young bride who still had the potential to produce a son for him.

As she moved, water sprinkled the floor with each movement as if a priest were blessing the faithful.

The Bible was on the counter.

The refrigerator hummed quietly.

She went from one drawer to another: yank open, bang shut after a quick survey of the innocuous contents. Spatulas. Dish towels. Spices.

On the counter, there was a sloppy pile of old mail, including a solicitation letter from a research foundation on SIDS: Sudden Infant Death Syndrome.

The refrigerator hum abruptly stopped.

In the sudden stillness, the parrot whistled loudly from its cage and called out, "Hello!"

Marybeth jumped.

Running from the room, she hurried down the hall to the master bedroom closet and took down the purse she'd hidden.

Inside were the seven bottles of sleeping pills she'd bought online. She snatched a tissue from the box on the bathroom vanity, opened the bottles and shook the pills out. Holding the tissue bulging with pills, she looked around for a glass to fill with water.

In the bedroom, she found a vase, ran back with it to the bathroom sink, took out the flowers, dumped the water and swiped at the slimy residue with a paper towel before filling it with fresh water from the tub.

She put a few pills in her mouth and took a gulp of water, but gagged on the stench and taste of rotting vegetation. She spit it all out in the sink.

As she started crying, overwhelmed with pain, she caught sight of herself in the mirror. For a moment, it seemed a stranger looked back and she sensed a small voice in her head, whispering gently, *Ask for help and you will find it.*

Her breath caught.

She started to try again with the pills, but then emptied the tissue into the toilet and flushed all the pills before she could change her mind.

Running out of the room, she snatched her laptop from the kitchen table, took it into the living room and placed it on a couch cushion. Standing, she logged into the suicide support forum and saw that no one had replied to her earlier plea for help.

She started to sign off, disappointed, but remembered that voice in her head, and so, while typing rapidly, she slowly knelt in front of the computer, almost as if it was a shrine. *Anybody there yet? I need help. Please, please, someone answer me....*

In her hotel room, Jemma gave a start. She'd dozed off with the computer still on her lap. She glanced at the clock. It would be dawn in a few hours.

She yawned, and reached to turn off the laptop. Her jiggling movement made the computer wake up. The wallpaper on her monitor was a photo of her with Andy. She looked at it, missing him. At once, she frowned, sensing that something was wrong. She touched the back of her neck, and had that prickly feeling of tiny hairs standing on end. Without planning to, she logged onto the suicide support forum and saw the urgent message from bunnygirl. She read it, stared at it in momentary confusion, then was galvanized into action. Straightening, Jemma saw the status for bunnygirl was "ONLINE."

She sent an Instant Message from flybynight to bunnygirl: "What's going on? Talk to me!"

Right away, as if clutching a lifeline, bunnygirl replied: "I can't stand the guilt!"

Watching the screen over Jemma's shoulder, Andy and Naomi exchanged a look of hope.

Jemma paused, searching for strong words. The right words. She typed: "Don't do anything rash." But she deleted it, hesitating what to say that would be helpful instead of patronizing.

Naomi told Andy, "Tell her to call bunnygirl on the phone."

Andy relayed the message to Jemma.

Jemma's fingers hesitated over the keyboard and then typed swiftly: "Give me your phone number."

In Marybeth's living room, she clutched the phone so tightly her knuckles were white as she talked on into the early morning hours with her new Internet buddy, known only as flybynight.

"Everyone has guilt, bunnygirl," Jemma pointed out gently, after letting the other woman ramble on about her near-brush with suicide not just tonight but on two other occasions, when her baby girl died and also when her cousin had killed herself. "I'm sorry about your baby, bunnygirl. SIDS has so many factors. I hope you can learn to forgive yourself."

"My cousin killed herself and I was too weak to join her."

Prompted by Naomi, Andy leaned in and whispered urgently into his mother's ear, "Tell bunnygirl that her cousin's death was an accident. Not suicide."

"I met someone today," Jemma said into the phone, "and she thought a member of her family committed suicide. But when we talked about it, it became pretty clear that it had been an accidental death. Is that possible in your cousin's case? That it was an accident, and not suicide?"

"Oh!" Marybeth gave a little cry. "Do you think so? She took pills."

"Overdoses are often accidental. Maybe she was trying to get relief from feeling depressed and she took too many pills by mistake, only wanting to sleep a little or feel better. Just because the police labeled it suicide doesn't mean it was actually intentional on her part."

"I have the sudden feeling you're right." Marybeth grew excited. "It makes so much more sense to me now. She told me that a guy she dated casually was pushing her for sex, and when she refused him, saying they didn't know each other well enough yet, he raped her."

"Unfortunately date rape is not rare," Jemma said. "But suicide isn't genetic, bunnygirl. Your cousin's death doesn't mean you have to die when you are sad about something."

"But I did something else I can't live with," the voice from the phone whispered.

"Whatever it was," Jemma said, "no matter how bad it seems, it can't be worth killing yourself." She felt sorry for bunnygirl and all she'd endured and survived, then realized she had experience to share because of what she had gone through after Andy died.

"When other people are counting on you," Jemma told bunnygirl, you have to keep going anyway. No matter how you feel inside. If you can keep going, a day at a time, focusing on a task or your work, slowly you'll be able to put your sadness and depression in perspective."

"All my life," Marybeth said, "it's made other people happier when I smile. So that's what I do! Even when I feel like crying inside, I smile and I pretend. But…sometimes I just can't take it anymore. I feel so fake! And if I told anyone how I really feel, I know they'd be so disappointed in me. They'll be better off if I just get out of their lives."

"Think it through. It won't matter how sorry they are. You'd be dead. The end." Jemma said into the phone, "I lost someone precious to me recently. Think of your parents, bunnygirl. Or your friends. How they would feel. I would be saddened too. Chatting with you helps end my own loneliness."

In Marybeth's backyard, water in the newly restored fish pond rippled gently.

In the living room, she stood up, exhausted. "I don't know how to thank you," she told her anonymous savior.

Jemma drew open the hotel draperies. Bright light streamed in and shone on her tired face. "I'm glad I could help. See you at the message board, bunnygirl. Take care of yourself."

She hung up, deeply affected by the call.

Andy watched her, filled with admiration.

Naomi held out a hand to him. "We need to go now."

Looking at his mother, Andy said, "I don't think she knows who bunnygirl is."

"Are you going to tell her?"

"No way. I'm not going to be the one to let her know she just helped the woman who killed me. You do it, if you want. But you don't know her temper like I do."

Jemma looked out the window, rubbing her arms as if she felt a sudden chill.

"She needs to say yes to NASA," he said thoughtfully. "She needs to finish her training so she can fly in space." He looked at his companion. "As long as we're AWOL, want to swing by Houston? Won't take long."

"I didn't have any other plans anyway."

"By the way," Andy said. "You've known my name all along, but you never told me—"

"It's Naomi."

Chapter 17

The moment Marybeth began reading the pages from the script of "Seven Funerals," she knew she wanted the part of Cerise.

She wanted it badly.

A tingle ran through her. If she could convince the powers-that-be that she was capable of handling this challenging role–the part of present-day Cerise as well as six earlier reincarnations of the same soul–she would finally have something significant enough to pull her back into the living world.

Gone was the motivation that had led her to accept the second chance to read for Mike McLeod. She'd seen it as a way to make money. But now, she simply had to play Cerise and that was all she cared about. She would do it for free if that was the only way she could get hired.

When she had walked into the audition that morning, she'd been strangely calm, so confident in her reading that it seemed the role of Cerise was merely another aspect of her own persona.

Mike only waited to confirm his decision with Simon, as a courtesy, and then Marybeth's cell phone was ringing before she reached home.

She said yes, with no hesitation.

She got the part of a lifetime.

She knew this film was going to be her salvation.

After Andy paid an anonymous call on Fran, whispering into her ear, Fran felt the urge to pick up the phone and dial Jemma's cell.

When Jemma answered, Fran said, "I have a challenge for you, Dr. Malotki."

"What kind of a challenge?" Jemma was taken aback. Fran was generally brisk but this sounded like a gauntlet had been tossed.

"You say you want to quit."

"That's right."

"Give up your lifelong dream of space travel."

"It's for the best." Jemma shuddered, thinking of the hallucinations.

"If you want to hand in your resignation," Fran said firmly, "you'll have to do it in person."

"But--"

"You don't get to stay at home and hide from your destiny. You must come here, to the Johnson Space Center. Walk the halls, see the people you know here, and then tell me to my face that you don't want to be an astronaut. I'll see you in my office at noon tomorrow."

Qaletaqa held out the buffalo nickel and chain Andy had thrown at him one day in anger. "Take it to her."

Andy stared, wondering what the catch was. It was probably some kind of test.

His great-grandfather smiled. "Before I change my mind."

Andy took the necklace and fastened it. "But how will she know it's from me?"

"That is up to you to manipulate."

276

Jemma packed for the last-minute trip to Houston, then went downstairs to wait for the Town Car that would take her to LAX.

She glanced at the portrait of Andy and Joker, relieved to see that it didn't start moving on its own.

But she saw something on the table, below the picture, that had not been there before.

It was a buffalo nickel on a silver chain.

She picked it up and studied it.

Even though it looked exactly like the one her grandfather had given her years ago, and that she had given to Andy, she knew it couldn't be, because that one had been lost at the accident scene.

A skeptic to the core, she examined the Indian head nickel carefully, and was surprised to see the initial "Q" scratched on the reverse side, on the buffalo, just the way she remembered.

But something new had been added, an "A" scratched on the surface, so that it read, "Q & A."

Just like getting a postcard from someone on a long journey.

Could it be that her son had sent a message that he survived death? And since the buffalo nickel he'd been wearing at the time of his death was directly beneath the picture of Andy with his dog, did that mean he was reunited with Joker?

She wasn't totally convinced, but it was beginning to seem at least slightly plausible.

"Qaletaqa and Andy," she murmured, looking at the Q&A scratched on the buffalo nickel. Or...*Questions and Answers.*

In Fran's office at NASA headquarters, Jemma studiously avoided looking at the wall of framed photos, and especially that vacant space Fran had said was waiting for Jemma's own picture once she was an astronaut.

"Go ahead." Fran crossed her arms. "Tell me you're quitting."

Jemma heard voices in the corridor and glanced out. Other astronaut-candidates strolled by, busy with their lives in the space program, the life she had wanted for herself for so long. "I–"

Fran held up a NASA baseball cap. "Does this mean anything to you?"

"What?" Jemma turned and saw the cap. "It has the same logo I got for Andy my last trip here, before he--"

Fran said, "He showed me which cap."

"Pardon me?"

Fran put on the cap, backwards. She gave Jemma a comic salute, a perfect imitation of the way Andy had done it, and called out, mimicking his tone to perfection, "My mom, the astronaut!"

Tears sprang to Jemma's eyes. "Why are you–? How did you–?" Jemma sat down heavily in the nearest chair.

Fran explained, "I was minding my own business, taking a cat nap at my desk like I often do in the middle of the day with my door closed. And when I woke up, it felt like I had been watching a film clip of Andy, and I had the urge to share it with you. It's the reason I asked you here. Wait. There was something else."

"There's more?" Jemma asked.

"Andy said he didn't mean to jinx it."

"Oh...." Jemma was overwhelmed with a flood of thoughts and memories.

"That means something to you?"

"Hart had already gone into the kitchen with the box of Gulf shrimp I brought him. Andy and I were alone. Nobody could've told you about this but me."

"Or Andy," Fran pointed out.

Jemma thought, *More evidence.*

So many coincidences, but also so much proof. As a scientist, Jemma knew when to stop demanding yet another item of verification when the results were conclusive.

"When he put the cap on, just like that," Jemma said, "and saluted exactly the way you did just now, I teased him that I was determined to have a mission and he'd better not jinx it by clowning around."

"So, Dr. Malotki," Fran said, picking up a file folder with Jemma's name on it. "Did you wish to formally submit your resignation to the program?...Or... not?"

Jemma touched the buffalo nickel at her neck and in a moment of reflection that turned her whole life on end, she realized in a rush that all the incidents she thought were hallucinations were Andy's way of helping her understand there is more to each person's consciousness, each person's <u>existence</u> than what can be seen by humans.

She took a deep breath, and slowly exhaled, then said to Fran, smiling through her tears, "I think you know the answer."

Andy and Naomi returned to Griffith Park.

"Thought you'd always be in black and white," he said, "but it looks like Ted Turner colorized you."

"You, too," she said. "And we've both got bronze armbands now."

They looked around, realizing that with their advancement, their awareness of their dimension was enhanced too. They noticed flowers they had never seen before, and an incomparable beauty everywhere. Colors were more vivid, fragrances in the air were sweet and lovely.

Naomi stopped in front of a large bush with glossy dark green leaves and saucer-like creamy white blossoms. "Gardenias--my favorite!" She plucked one, inhaled its exquisite fragrance, and then tucked it in her hair.

"This really must be paradise," Andy said, looking around. He felt humbly grateful for everything he'd learned, and made a silent commitment that he would continue to grow and advance. He knew that he would awaken more and more to his soul's true life, as long as he remained willing to evolve his consciousness.

"Thank you for helping with my cousin." Naomi picked another fragrant blossom and offered it to him.

He accepted it. "You could've asked, instead of tricking me."

"I knew what she did to you."

"She was driving the car that day--"

"And that means Marybeth is the reason you're here. I figured you must hate her. I saw a chance of helping her, and so, yeah...I used you. I couldn't let you make the connection between her and me. So I took a chance, and it worked."

"You're not even sorry for what you did to me?"

"Don't you see, Andy? I wasn't sure I could trust you."

He nodded, realizing that made sense.

"Marybeth was going to kill herself over your death, like she attempted over mine. But we intervened, using your mother as the messenger of hope."

They passed the Gray Zone, but did not go in.

They strolled past it to the boulders and dry creek bed. He noticed someone at the picnic tables, waiting.

It was Gabriella. As she stood and lifted a hand in greeting, her costume changed into a sporty two-piece dress in a citrus print. She wore spotless white net gloves and a tiny yellow hat with a dotted veil that grazed her wide dark eyebrows.

"Hey, Gabriella–" he started toward her. Then he realized that Gabriella and Naomi were hurrying to each other.

"*Ciao, bella,*" Gabriella said when Naomi reached her. They embraced.

"Hold on a sec!" Andy cried. Pointing to Naomi he said, "<u>You're</u> the sister she's been telling me about? The one who kept reincarnating and hooking up with the wrong men and dying young?"

Smiling bashfully, Naomi nodded. "I have a stubborn streak, I guess."

"What are you going to do now?" Gabriella asked Naomi. "Reincarnate again? Or do you feel you have finished that path?"

"Thanks to Andy," Naomi said, "I'm done with that lesson."

"Me?" he asked. "What'd I do?"

"You helped me learn to trust men." Naomi turned to Gabriella. "I want to be a greeter, and welcome the ones who come over like I did--hurt and disoriented."

Marybeth met her co-stars, Seth and Adam. The three main players were in their mid-twenties, and felt on top of the world, starring in a film by a director who was moving up fast in Hollywood.

Mike explained, "Time Traveling Vale--played by Adam--jumps back and forth in time. But each time when he returns to the present, Cerise is still here. So he needs to travel further back. He must have missed a shared lifetime or she would no longer exist. Vale is trying to purge her from his soul, Adam, so keep that in mind. And Seth as you enact the contemporary Vale in each time period, in every scene with Cerise, whether it's the desert nomads sequence or when you are Irish immigrants to America, remember that she is the love of your life."

Behind Mike's back, Seth ogled Marybeth and mimed French kissing.

With an inward groan of revulsion, she looked at the script in her hands. "When will we start rehearsals?"

"I'm going to Phoenix this weekend for my parent's fiftieth anniversary," Mike said. "We'll start Monday when I get back."

Andy located Qaletaqa about fifteen miles from the zoo, at the San Gabriel Mission, sitting in one of the bell wall niches.

He joined him, and they flanked the largest of six bells. "Is this where you go when I can't find you?" Andy asked, not surprised when Qaletaqa did not respond.

They watched as a group of people approached the church entry from the parking lot. A young couple carried their twin infants in christening gowns.

"Let's join them," Qaletaqa suggested.

Inside, they sat in a pew behind the humans.

Andy admired the hammered copper baptismal font.

"It is nearly two hundred and fifty years old," Qaletaqa said. "This mission has been here a long time, named for the Archangel Gabriel."

"The one with the trumpet, right?"

"Gabriel is one of the three angels named in the Bible. He is known as God's herald and messenger."

"So our Gabriella was named after an angel," Andy said. "I know she'd ask me if there's more to it than that, more than the quick answer."

"Is there?"

"Well, she's been a messenger to me, and to Naomi. Helping us. And I guess the lesson would be that all of us are messengers, either carrying impressions of love or of fear. We have an impact on people around us, even when we might think we don't make much of a difference at all."

"I am proud of you, great-grandson." Qaletaqa indicated the infants being baptized. "Did you know that Earth's birth rate is over three hundred fifty thousand a day?"

"But at the cemetery that time with Gabriella, you said that a hundred fifty thousand people die each day. So where do the extra two hundred thousand come from? Every day, day after day?"

"An enigma for others to explain," Qaletaqa teased.

"Houston, we've got a problem in paradise!"

Qaletaqa asked as they left together, "Have you thought about the mistakes you made, being a rogue spinner?"

"Yes, sir. And I know what I want to try now, to help my mother."

"You are not giving up?"

Andy looked at him a moment. "I'll try love."

Qaletaqa waited patiently for him to explain.

"When I did my Life Review," Andy said, "I felt a loving presence surround me. When you told me that love is the most important thing, I took it to mean ordinary human love, like the love I feel for my parents and friends. That's good, but love's even bigger than that. It's all about love of creating, love of expanding, love of developing... of <u>growing</u>. The universe is all about love, isn't it?"

"Let right action flow through you, and that is your true function--"

"How do I figure out when something is right action?"

"--And when you discover your true function, Andrew, let <u>love</u> flow through you. It will flow you into wholeness."

"Okay, so here's what I was thinking, and you tell me if it's the right thing." Andy hesitated, realizing he should be perfectly honest. "Actually, I already did something maybe I should tell you about."

"I suspected as much, Andrew. I already know about the buffalo nickel, of course, and also about Fran. Continue."

Relieved, Andy said, "This guy Mike. That my mom almost married before she met my dad. Will he make her happy?"

Qaletaqa looked at him thoughtfully. "I know Mike."

"You do?"

"I met him when he was a boy. He's a fine man now. Excellent choice."

"So...do I have your authorization?"

In the baggage claim area at Los Angeles International Airport, luggage from the Houston flight tumbled down the chute and slammed into the sides of the moving carousel.

Passengers jostled to claim their bags.

Jemma stood apart from the crowd, finishing a magazine article. She glanced up now and then to check for her bag, feeling no hurry. It felt great to be back on track with NASA, and now she'd begin taking care of the details of her divorce before returning to Houston for the final stage of astronaut training.

At the next carousel, passengers from an incoming flight from Phoenix began gathering. Mike McLeod had gone home to visit his parents for their fiftieth wedding anniversary, and his golf clubs bag was one of the first to come down the chute.

He hoisted his carryon luggage over one shoulder and wheeled the golf clubs toward the exit, passing Jemma as she bent to put the magazine in her own carryon.

Mike found the chauffeur holding a hand-printed sign that read: "McLeod." They went outside and he got into the back seat of the Town Car while the driver stowed his luggage in the trunk.

Jemma glanced out the window as a black Town Car pulled away from the curb, hoping her own chauffeur would pull up soon. Her flight had landed early and she might have to call the company. She spotted her suitcase and moved towards the carousel.

After Lulu had gone home after Andy's funeral, Jemma went back to that same gym and spa they'd visited, to enjoy another massage, and then decided to join the gym as Lulu had suggested.

Wanting to keep up her daily exercise routine, she went there now and worked out on the equipment and free weights for nearly two hours. Sweaty and exhausted, she headed for the shower stalls in the women's locker room, but they were all in use. Rather than waiting, she decided to go home grungy and shower there.

Moments after Jemma drove away, Mike pulled into the parking lot and went in the gym for a workout on the equipment.

Andy felt discouraged by these continued near-misses, but he did not give up.

At a book fair held on the grounds of a local university, Jemma made her way further down the aisle toward a display of first editions. She'd stopped at the outdoor fair on an impulse, after seeing signs advertising the event.

Tents and booths were filled with browsers and shoppers, and it looked like the fair would be a successful fundraiser.

Behind Jemma, a young mother pushing a double-wide baby stroller knocked into a tall rack of books. It fell over with a crash and blocked pedestrian traffic.

At the noise, Jemma glanced back.

Mike turned a corner to enter the first editions aisle from the other end.

Behind him, a workman was pushing a dolly heaped with book cartons. One of the wheels caught on a seam in the temporary walkway. Cartons spilled across the path, blocking traffic.

Mike glanced back at the noise.

Unaware, Jemma and Mike were trapped on the same aisle of booths.

Jemma went into the rear of the first editions tent, exchanged a polite comment with the bookseller about the crowds and the heat, and bent down to see hardback volumes shelved near the ground. She didn't see anything she cared enough about to pay top dollar. Coming forward, she squeezed past browsers looking at books arranged on a table, and paused to see if there was anything of interest.

Approaching the first editions tent, Mike slowed to let young parents pass him with their toddler.

On the table, Jemma spotted a first edition of *No Good-Byes* by Adela Rogers St. Johns. Curious, recognizing the name of a famous journalist from years ago, she reached for it, feeling an irrepressible urge to read this book.

On the other side of the table, Mike spotted the book and reached for it at the same time. His hand grazed hers, but his attention was on the book cover and a sudden urge to pick it up.

Jemma quickly spoke up to claim the book for herself. "You don't really want this, do you?" She was intrigued by the book's subtitle "My Search into Life Beyond Death."

Mike looked up, startled. Seeing Jemma, a smile came to his lips in an instant and he gazed at her with the eyes of a man whose love was undiminished by the years since their parting. "Hot Wings? Is that really you?"

Her head flew up.

She stared at Mike, speechless.

Meanwhile, another customer reached for the book.

Mike noticed, and snatched it with an apologetic smile. He said to Jemma, "Let me get this for you."

"But you were reaching for it, too. Don't you want it after all?"

"The title caught my eye. No particular reason. It's yours." He handed the book and money to the bookseller.

While waiting for the transaction, Jemma and Mike looked at each other, sizing up what changes the past twenty years had wrought. When they were ready to leave, he used the crowd as an excuse to touch Jemma's shoulder, guiding her to the walkway.

They strolled away together, skirting the spilled cartons now in the process of being cleared.

Each surreptitiously looked at the other again, and got caught doing it. An awkward silence. Both started to talk at once, and they laughed. He indicated she should go first.

"I was going to say, you haven't changed much, Mike. You look great."

"So do–" he automatically started, but then his observant eyes picked up the sadness she couldn't hide. He'd always been able to detect her vulnerability despite her seemingly carless layers of armor that she put up between herself and the world. It was still there, hidden at first glance by an air of capability and self-assurance. And yet, he sensed a deep sadness in her that he couldn't recall ever witnessing, not even when she had broken their engagement.

"Jemmie?" he asked gently. "Is something wrong?"

She shook her head. "I'm fine. Fine, Mike."

"Do you have time to get a coffee or a drink? Not here," he added, indicating the booths of refreshments. "The serendipity of meeting out of the blue like this deserves something more celebratory."

Seated at an outdoor bar at the crowded Universal City Walk, with a tray of assorted appetizers in front of them, Jemma asked Mike, "Did you ever write that novel, like you wanted?"

He laughed. "Spent two years on it, barely scraping by financially but writing feverishly every day until I had an eight hundred page novel."

"Isn't that kind of long?" she asked tactfully.

"It was a mess. I got it out of my system though, and maybe someday I'll self-publish it so I can have the satisfaction of holding a bound copy in my hands and then display it on my bookshelf."

"I'd love to read it."

"It's a daunting task, but thank you. What I learned in the process, though, is that I think visually much more than with the written word. I got into writing screenplays and eventually sold a few. A couple years ago, after seeing all the changes made to a script I'd written–the movie on screen was nothing like the complex characters and story I'd created–I decided the best way to protect my stories was to direct them myself. So now I'm a director, too."

"Looks like it suits you. How about marriage?"

"Right now?" He looked around. "Where's the wedding chapel?"

She grinned in spite of herself. "Silly. I meant, are you married?" As he shook his head in reply, she asked, "Well then, have you been, or–?"

"Three strikes. To be completely frank, I did my best to marry your opposite each time, and I got bitten—each time." He shrugged, dismissing the past. "What about you?"

"Just initiating the divorce process, actually. First time."

"Oh. I'm sorry. That's never fun, but you'll get through it. Are you okay with it? I mean, was it your idea or–?"

"Mutual decision in the midst of inertia over whether to keep trying."

Their glasses of wine were nearly empty before Jemma found herself creating a more serious turn in the conversation.

"It wasn't you," she blurted, and kept going before he could interrupt. "It wasn't the relationship. It was the timing. And I was young, ambitious, driven."

"You were intent on creating a blame-free, flawless resume for NASA," he put in, nodding. "I'd never known anyone with your degree of commitment to righting a wrong in history's pages. Still haven't met anyone more focused on that task. Even at age thirteen or fourteen, you were intent on that one specific goal, and all I could do was stand and watch and pay for two tickets to the movies because you didn't want to get caught sneaking in with the other kids to see *E.T.* or *Tootsie* or whatever was playing back then."

"You always went along with what I wanted, didn't you, Mike?" She looked at him curiously, having never really focused on all he had done to support her during those long school years they'd spent together.

"I made a vow early on," he said lightly, "to protect you from censure."

She toyed with her empty glass, twirling the stem in her fingers. "I just didn't know how to make it all work. It felt wrong to ask you to wait indefinitely for me to—"

"I understand. I do, Jemma. Don't beat yourself up over this anymore, okay?"

She looked at him with a wry smile, knowing he was the only one who would've guessed her guilty secret. "Okay, I won't. Remorse never gets you anywhere, does it?"

"But that's not the reason for the sadness in your eyes. I'm not egotistical enough to believe you've been mourning our broken engagement all this time."

While waiting for her to breach the silence, he gestured to their passing server for two more glasses of wine.

"I…my son died, Mike. I had a son, a teenager. And, there was a terrible accident."

He took the glass from her, held her hands in his and looked at her gently. "Tell me about it."

And so Jemma unburdened herself. She told Mike about Andy's death, about the argument that preceded it, and how she couldn't let go of her rage about what had happened. While talking, she shared family photos from an album on her cell phone.

"And you blame yourself."

She gasped, startled to hear the words spoken out loud by someone who knew her.

"All my life," she said, trying to be totally honest with Mike about what had happened that day, "when I have a problem to resolve, I deliberately place it in front of my mind at bedtime and request assistance so I'll know what to do the next day."

"You pray?"

She scoffed. "I ask for help from a higher intelligence. My own, or who knows. But that night, the night before the accident, because of Andy's arrest, I was too angry and…"

"Distraught?"

"I couldn't think straight. My son, sabotaging his success with a stupid act. I lay awake most of the night, fuming. Finally fell asleep just as dawn was breaking."

"So you got up even madder than before. Instead of calming down, you gorged on the anger all night long."

"I'd hate to admit this to anyone else, but...yes."

"Whatever we pay attention to always seems to get bigger, doesn't it? In my marriages I didn't think I was expecting failure. I thought it would work out each time, but I never picked a woman I was in harmony with. Failure was inevitable."

"I'll never forgive myself for that day," she said, still thinking of the accident. "And I'll certainly never forgive That Woman."

"I understand your feelings, Jemma, but that poison corrodes your heart. Try to let go. Forgiveness doesn't mean what happened has your approval or that you stop loving Andy. It means you release the past to the past."

"You make it sound easy."

"I'd love to talk to you more. Are you sure I can't take you to dinner?"

"It's been a long day and I'm kind of tired."

"Something else on your mind?"

"Never could fool you, Mike. That last day, Andy and I were arguing–"

"What about?"

"--or rather, I was attacking him over what he'd done and trying to get to the bottom of it, and he was trying to get me to back off. My son died believing his mother didn't think he was good enough."

"It's a waste of time spinning a final conversation in your mind," he said, "when you can't change a word of it. Trust me, I know about that process first hand."

She looked at him, guessing he was referring to their own final conversation that day she'd broken their engagement. Rather than rehashing that whole episode, she teased, "Since when did you become a life coach?"

He laughed. Their teasing had always been of the gentle variety, without malice, barbs or condemnation to shred the other's dreams.

"In my line of work," he explained, "I'm babysitter, therapist and stern parent all rolled into one. Jemmie, it's amazing to see you. I don't want to let another twenty years pass before the next time."

"I'm impressed you can forgive me for what I did back then, but I've got so much going on right now with NASA and...Listen, thanks for the book, but I better get going."

"I didn't mean to upset you, Jemmie. I'd like to see you again," he said. "Just as friends if it sounds like I'm moving too fast."

"I can't handle a new relationship right now."

"Ours is hardly new, Jemmie. Neither of us is on the rebound. How can we be? Don't you remember?"

"That was a long time ago!"

"But we're the original <u>bound</u>. Maybe we had to take our separate journeys," Mike added thoughtfully, "to learn what we needed to know so we'll really appreciate each other this time, and not mess it up."

"Being Andy's mother was such a gift. Hart called it that, and he's right. A gift. I forgot to even ask–do you have kids?"

"It turns out that weird soccer injury in high school made me sterile. So, you see, marrying Hart allowed you to experience motherhood. Would you say that it changed you, in a good way?"

"Definitely."

A gaggle of teen boys ambled towards them, laughing and joking, full of life and vigor. One of the boys resembled Andy in his coloring and build.

Jemma turned her head to follow the boy with her eyes.

Having just seen photos of Andy, Mike guessed what was going through her mind. He leaned across the table with a napkin and wiped her tears so tenderly her bones almost dissolved.

She looked at him, her resolve melting. It felt like she'd just been kissed thoroughly. She grabbed her bag for paper and pen, and jotted her phone numbers for him. "But we have to take it slow, okay?"

"Right. Nothing hot and heavy." He smiled. "Do you play golf?"

"I've hit a few balls a couple of times at a practice range."

"The one at the Sepulveda Basin?"

"Why, do you go there, too?"

He nodded. "I wonder how many times our paths have just missed each other? I guess we'll never know. We'll go there together one day, when we have time. But for tomorrow, how about an innocent picnic in the park?"

The white letters of the Hollywood sign loomed in the near distance, and two hikers approached the crest of the trail from below. Jemma and Mike, climbing with daypacks, came up side-by-side.

When they reached the top, Jemma gave a small gasp of surprise and delight, and slowly turned, taking in the full view of the Los Angeles basin and the hills around it, as if she was finally waking up from the immense grief of losing her son.

After finding a place to sit, they took their picnic out of their backpacks.

"My parents will be tickled you're trading that old homemade Halloween costume for a real space suit," he said, alluding to a strange outfit she'd cobbled together out of aluminum foil and cardboard boxes the year they were in ninth grade.

"And you're making real movies."

He grinned wickedly. "I still have our old videos, *shweetheart.*"

"I thought you destroyed all that long ago."

"Today even the raciest among them would only be rated PG-13."

Further down the trail from their picnic spot, and across Runyon Canyon, Andy, Qaletaqa and Gabriella moved towards the Bronson Caves, one of the sites where Mike would be filming "Seven Funerals" although Andy wasn't aware of that fact.

They headed to the face of a cliff where a rock climber was stranded. His cries for help had been reported to 9-1-1 and now a helicopter hovered while lowering a rescue team.

The rescuers clambered down the cliff and began fastening the climber into a safety harness.

Andy watched with interest. But now, distracted, he looked searchingly in the direction of Jemma's picnic. He grew excited. "My mom is up there! I know she is!"

Gabriella looked swiftly to Qaletaqa for guidance. He made a cautionary motion and shook his head. She took Andy's arm and the trio moved on.

At the top of the hiking trail, made curious by the presence of the helicopter, Mike and Jemma moved to the edge of the hilltop and watched the successful rescue of the climber.

Jemma rubbed her arms, feeling a sudden chill.

"What's wrong, Jemmie?"

"Just...sometimes it feels like Andy is so close, I could reach out and touch him. I know that's crazy."

The helicopter flew off with the rock climber safely on board.

Mike gave a rueful grin. "Some guy found to his dismay and chagrin that he needs a helping hand. He can't do it alone anymore." He looked at her and slowly held out his hand, his expression entreating.

She felt overwhelmed by sudden emotions. "I've got so much going on–"

"Me, too. We'll take turns being strong for each other."

After a moment, she smiled and accepted his hand.

"You'll have to throw me bodily off this hilltop if you want me out of your life now, Jemmie. We were meant to meet again. I won't walk away without a promise you'll agree to call me from Houston."

She began packing their lunch trash. "Maybe an email now and then would be okay."

As they walked down the hill, he told her more about his production schedule and explained why he wouldn't be able to fly to see her in Houston until later.

"After we finish shooting," he said, "I'm going to take a week off before we go into post-production, because then I'll be tied up long hours again every day until we've got it in the can."

"Which means we should shake hands," she said, "and agree it was wonderful seeing each other after so long but we've got crazy schedules and there's no way–"

"There is always time in life for things that are truly important." He held her hand as they negotiated a rocky part of the climb downhill. "Let's make time for us, Jemmie, to at least find out if there is any spark still there. I feel it already. I think we owe it to our old selves, don't you?"

While they walked toward the parking lot near the bottom of the trail, she asked him to tell her more about his movie.

"The most important character is Cerise. I discovered an unknown and she's perfect."

"Tell me the story." Jemma was caught up in his enthusiasm and delight over finding this "Cerise" character.

"It's called 'Seven Funerals,'" he said, hesitating, mindful of her recent loss.

"Sorry, doesn't sound like something I'll rush to see."

They reached his car. "It's not really about funerals. It's time travel and shows the relationship between these two people in various incarnations. They're soul-mates, you see. It's a comedy-drama. Uh. Actually kind of a romance. But with a lot of adventure."

She looked at him curiously, wondering why Mike was stumbling over himself, and now seemed reluctant to expound. She prompted him with a look.

Hesitantly, he said, playing with the keys, "This guy...the male lead–"

"Whose name is–?"

"Vale," he said reluctantly, then rushed on. "He's miserable. Can't get his first love out of his mind and so he builds a time travel device with a lot of computer parts and–"

"Vale," she repeated. "As in Michael <u>Valenski</u> McLeod? And you named the heroine Cerise–?"

"How could I ever forget that time your dad had business in Tucson and on the way home he stopped at a cherry farm and then--"

"He brought home enough cherries to start a pie industry."

Mike laughed. "And we ate so many--"

"Our lips turned dark red...."

They had been fourteen, and already shifting from being playmates to something they hadn't yet identified. That day, after eating far too many of the luscious cherries, Mike had kissed her for the first time. After that turning point, their feelings developed into a love they both had thought would last forever.

"It was my first real kiss," he said, as if he'd also been reliving the memory.

"Mine, too." Not sure if she should be angry or flattered, she added, "Think I don't know *cerise* is the French word for cherry? Your movie is all about us, isn't it?"

"It's not biographical, Jemmie. No one will see Cerise and think she's you. I promise."

"You'd better be right, Michael." She darted a mischievous look at him. "Or should I call you 'Vale' from now on?"

He kissed her warmly, then opened the car door for her.

Chapter 18

At the kitchen table, Marybeth studied her lines for "Cherokee Cerise." Beside her was a call sheet for "Seven Funerals." The next scenes they'd be shooting were part of the two sequences depicting "Cherokee Trail of Tears, 1838" and "Stalking at Frontier Cabin, 1867."

Outside, day laborers helped Cabot build a backyard patio. Cabot looked at his watch, tapped on the kitchen window and yelled in to her, "Told you to feed these guys, Marybeth. They're getting hungry."

Feeling bolder now that she was working and he couldn't honestly complain that he paid for everything, she called back cheerfully, "Plenty of food in the fridge!"

He put his face against the window. "You want to come out here and supervise while I fix lunch?"

She looked at him with growing resentment.

"I'm paying them by the hour," he added.

"And I'm getting ready for the scenes we're shooting tonight!"

"By. The. Hour." He turned away.

She slammed the script on the table and got up.

Opening the fridge, she flung sandwich fixings onto the counter, hating herself for not taking a stand.

Later, during the filming, Marybeth, dressed as "Frontier Cerise," nervously backed away while Adam as "Time Traveling Vale" stalked her.

Mike watched the action on a monitor.

Time Traveling Vale said to Cerise, "The other day...I think it was on a talk show...this guy said forgiveness is what'll break the chain that binds us."

Cerise bumped against the rough door of the frontier cabin and groped behind her back for the latch.

She stared at the stranger in growing terror, not understanding what a talk show was or why he was there or even why he looked so much like her husband when he'd already explained they were not twins.

"Sorry, love," Time Traveling Vale said, "I can't wait around till forgiveness finally kicks in." He whipped out a pistol and took aim at her.

A sharp noise came from the pool equipment in Jemma's backyard as the pool lights switched on.

The rippling water glowed eerily.

A slim figure passed through the shadows, stopped at the pool's deep end, slipped off a long robe and poised at the edge...

Jemma made a clean dive into the swimming pool.

Inside NASA's Weightless Environment Training Facility, known as WET-F, water streamed from a helmeted figure as it emerged from the half-million gallon swimming pool.

A technician removed the helmet, revealing Jemma's smiling face.

She gave a thumbs up.

Thoughts of Mike sustained Jemma during their times apart while she trained to be an astronaut and he shot his film, but sometimes she felt uneasily superstitious that something would go wrong again between them.

They talked on the phone every night, and used the calls to not only reminisce over the years they'd shared in Phoenix, but to catch up on the twenty years they had been apart.

This night, she yawned and stretched, ready to go to sleep, knowing the two-hour time difference meant Mike was probably still shooting.

Her cell rang and she grabbed it. "Hey, honey."

"Things going okay today?" he asked.

"Fun and games. I got to go in the G-force machine."

"You hate that–"

"But I didn't pass out. Feeling very proud of myself. And how was your day? Shooting going well?"

"Taking care of some indoor shots at the studio. Working with Irish Immigrant Cerise and Time Traveling Vale, set at Ellis Island in 1902."

"Funny, I don't remember that year with you."

"Wait till we get to the swashbuckler scenes, and the sword fight where Cerise is dressed like the cover of a bodice-ripper historical romance. I'd love to see you in her costume."

"I'll be glad when I can come to the set and see you working."

"Cerise is such a natural. She takes direction really well. I wish the whole cast was that easy."

"Problems, dear?"

"Nothing I can't handle. The guy playing Present Day Vale is kind of an asshole."

"Oooh, is that a Freudian slip about yourself, Mike?" She laughed.

They chatted a half hour longer and then Mike said, "I better let you get some sleep, Jemmie...Talk soon."

"Something else on your mind?" she asked, hearing that hesitation in his voice.

When he felt he could get away with it, he talked to her about forgiving the driver who caused the fatal accident, but no matter how carefully he broached the subject she flared and said she hated That Woman for what she had done. Even when he said he didn't mean she should do it in person or a letter, but only in her own heart, to release herself from the chains of hate, she got annoyed and changed the subject.

He was too tired to deal with it tonight, so he merely said, "Nope. Love you. Sweet dreams."

On a three-day holiday weekend they both had free, she flew back to L.A., called Van Nuys airport and arranged for the use of a Cessna. She wanted to fly Mike up to Mammoth, in the Sierra Nevada range in California. It would've been at least a five-hour drive, longer if traffic was bad, and they didn't have enough time for that. "Besides," she'd added to Mike, "you wouldn't expect someone you call Hot Wings to drive, would you?"

While flying, Jemma said, "Feels like we're running away."

"Like when we were ten," Mike agreed, "but that time we only got two blocks before hurrying home, scared we'd get lost."

"I don't feel scared anymore." She smiled at him.

The resort area included mountains for hiking in summer and skiing in winter, a lake for boating, and a village filled with shops, inns and cafes.

It was autumn. There was no snow yet, and none predicted, which suited her fine because it meant there was minimal risk of getting snowed in. They were able to rent a cabin, and take long walks past fragrant pines and singing birds.

300

When browsing the shops one morning after breakfast, she spotted scented candles. Picking up one labeled 'Sensual' she said, "We should probably stock up on these. I'm not a teenager anymore, Mike." She glanced toward a mirror and absently touched the crow's feet at her eyes.

"Stop comparing us to <u>them</u>."

She looked at him questioningly.

H leaned in close and whispered, drawing her into a private world with his voice and the intimacy he promised, "Those kids we used to be. Let them slumber unaware of what mature adults do together."

Later, in their cabin, logs in the fireplace burned low. They kissed, and he smoothed her rumpled hair.

After a few moments of easygoing silence, Mike took an old snapshot from his wallet.

"What's that?"

"Look what suddenly turned up in my desk at home. I thought I'd lost this years ago, but I opened a drawer while packing for this trip, and there it was, on top of some papers."

He showed Jemma a photo from their trip to the Hopi reservation when they were eleven. In the photo, he and Jemma stood on either side of Qaletaqa, who had his hands on their heads. "Looks like he's giving us his blessing."

"It does, doesn't it?"

"Even back then," he said, "a wise old Hopi knew we belong together. I wish we could stay here forever like this."

She murmured her agreement, snuggling up against him contentedly. "I love hearing your voice in my ear."

"Yours has been in my memory for so long, I have to pinch myself to be sure I'm not dreaming.

They watched the glowing embers, in complete harmony with each other and their love.

"I've got an idea, Jemmie."

"Back to bed <u>again</u>?" she teased.

"That, too, but I was wondering if you can squeeze another day out of your break from Houston?" When she nodded, he said, "Visit me on the set when we're back in L.A. I'll tell Rodney to watch for you. Actually, let me put his number in your cell so you can call him later for directions."

Not far from the Hollywood sign, north of Franklin Avenue, a portion of Griffith Park juts down into a residential area. There's a parking lot where day hikers can leave their cars and a small tree-shaded park with a creek that's dry most of the year.

Hiking further in, you reach the Bronson Caves, up against a cliff in an area that has been used for countless TV westerns and as movie locations, even being filled with fake snow at least once for a winter scene.

The cliff above the honeycomb of caves was where the rock climber had been rescued while Jemma and Mike picnicked.

"Seven Funerals" was on location here, taking advantage of the natural environment for different scenes. In one direction were the rugged natural caves they were using for most of the scenes involving Vale's travel to prehistoric times when he first met his soul mate Cerise.

With a ninety degree turn, the camera then had a view of the wild west with scrub brush and a newly made clearing containing the false front of a pioneer cabin dressed for the scene they were shooting this morning. Indoor shots took place at the studio.

In the pioneer sequence, Time Traveling Vale succeeds in killing the 1868 incarnation of Cerise, and now in the scene they'd be shooting this morning, her husband, pioneer Vale, played by Marybeth's least favorite cast member, Seth, mourns over his wife's open coffin.

Just thinking about playing this scene gave Marybeth a sick feeling, but she knew it was important to get in character, and follow Mike's direction.

Mike cut the action only moments into the scene. "Seth. You're soul mates, for God's sake. Don't whine and wring your hands. You're a rugged frontier man who lost his wife. His business partner. The helpmate whom he counts on to raise the children, churn the butter, bake the bread and use the plow. You're in agony. Your whole lifestyle has been affected. So it's not the timid 'Come back to me' that you keep giving me, okay?"

He waited until he got a nod and at least a glimmer of understanding from Seth.

Mike went on, "It's 'COME BACK TO ME!' Got it? We need to get this in the can. Seriously. I didn't think we'd still be shooting this scene today. And we've got another scene to shoot after the lunch break."

"I know the schedule," Seth said, furious.

They did another take.

Marybeth lay motionless in the coffin and willed herself into a meditative state, barely hearing Seth speak his lines in a hoarse voice that was filled with agony, "Our time together was too short. Come back to me!"

And then she was vaguely aware of Mike calling "Cut! That was great," and then strong hands helped her up and out of the coffin.

She stood there, trembling, then hurried off to get out of the homespun dress that was heavy and hot.

During the lunch break, Marybeth sat in a chair in a kimono, not in costume or wig yet for the role of Prehistoric Cerise. She stretched to get the kinks out of her neck, opened her laptop and checked messages at the suicide support forum.

By her side, on the ground, was a cold drink in a can. In a few minutes, she'd get up and change in her trailer.

Seth, already costumed in a loincloth for his role as Prehistoric Vale, sneaked up behind her and looked over her shoulder to see what she was doing. He saw the user name bunnygirl.

She sensed his presence and turned in annoyance. "Go away, Seth." She shut her computer before he realized what the site was about.

"Oh, hey, bunnygirl, don't hop away. I'm not a big bad wolf, am I? We'll be snuggling on a bearskin in the cave later on. Let's rehearse." He made sure no one of importance was looking when he nuzzled her neck.

Hating him, but fearing that if she made a commotion Mike would think she was difficult to work with, she resignedly got up with her things.

"Hey, baby," he crooned. "You like all our love scenes too much to be faking it." He grabbed her ass.

She didn't hesitate. In one motion, she turned and flung her cold drink in his face.

Seth sputtered and furiously wiped his face on his bare arm.

She floated away, giddy with private triumph for standing up to a bully.

When Jemma arrived at the set that afternoon, the film equipment and crew members inadvertently blocked her view as she approached the caves.

Rodney indicated cables as he escorted her. Whispering, he said, "Watch your step."

Then people moved, going about their jobs, and Jemma had a clear view of the scene being filmed, and for the first time got to see Cerise. It was the fourth take, and expected to be the last now that a few problems had been resolved.

Her brow creased. Perturbed, she stared at the actress dressed in animal skins and wearing a long red wig meant to look like hair that had never seen a comb or conditioner. There was something familiar about the dirt-smeared face, but she couldn't put her finger on it. Who did the woman remind her of?

She continued watching, trying to inch closer, but blocked by equipment and knowing she mustn't cross into the camera's range.

It was interesting to see all the people who stood outside the frame of what the audience would eventually see on screen. Jemma found it amazing that actors could concentrate on their lines and not be distracted by all the eyes watching.

Then Mike called, "Action," and the A.D. repeated it, and the actress started moving as if she was alone in a field.

Jemma got caught up in watching as the brief scene unfolded.

Prehistoric Cerise snared a live jackrabbit, pretended to kill it, held up a fake dead rabbit and began skinning it with a sharp piece of shale.

As she finished, Mike called out, "And...Cut!" He went over and conferred with the actress. Then he nodded and gave her a pat on the shoulder.

The actress turned and smoothed the artificial hair off her face.

Jemma was thunderstruck to recognize the woman whose car struck Andy. Her blood ran cold.

Marybeth glanced up and saw Jemma staring. She sagged, sucker-punched.

Mike missed this interplay and sauntered over to greet Jemma. "Glad you could make it!" He leaned in to kiss her.

She slapped him. "You set me up!"

He touched his cheek, dumfounded.

Cast and crew stared.

Mike impatiently waved everyone off. "Ten minute break."

Marybeth remained where she was, frozen.

"When were you going to tell me?" Jemma demanded.

Mike was at a loss. "Tell you what?"

She pointed to Marybeth. "Don't pretend you didn't know your precious Cerise killed my son."

The astonishment on Mike's face was genuine, but Jemma was too angry to notice.

"I didn't–" Mike began.

"Why didn't you have the honesty to admit you hired Marybeth Garner–"

"Garner? Her name is Lacroix." He shook his head in confusion. "I'm always so careful around you, not wanting to offend because of my 'Seven Funerals' title, and knowing you hate it that I based the premise of the story on my attempts to get over you. I didn't think of rattling off all the actors' names for your approval." He felt unfairly judged. "This is the first mention of a Marybeth I've even heard from you. You never call her anything but 'That Woman'–"

"You never call her anything but Cerise. You deliberately manipulated me into your whole 'forgive and move on' feel-good scenario."

"Let's sit down and talk calmly." He gestured for Marybeth to join them.

Marybeth ran to her trailer.

"A lot makes sense now," Mike said, thinking out loud, not realizing how his words could be misconstrued. "All the times she seemed depressed. Her hatred of getting in the coffin. Her moods–"

"HER moods?"

"I'm sorry, Jemma, but I didn't know." He gave a short harsh laugh. "I know a little about forgiveness, Jemma–"

They both knew he meant the day after college graduation when she'd taken off her engagement ring and claimed she didn't love him enough to get married.

Now she said heatedly, "I will never condone what she did–"

"No one expects you to, Jemma. But you can't change what happened." He looked at her, and tried to think of a way to mend emotions that were fast shattering. "You can't go back," he said more gently. "Life isn't a time travel movie."

She backed away. "Don't call me again, Mike."

She spun on her heel and left.

He watched her go, feeling helpless.

In agony, he whispered the lines from his screenplay, "But our time together was too short. Come back to me...."

Andy's head whipped up as he reacted to the breakup.

All the things he'd done to bring them together, thinking he was going to help make his mother happy again, had been for nothing.

Moments after Jemma hurried past Marybeth's trailer, Seth approached and called out, "Bunnygirl! Come out and play! I've forgiven you for throwing that soda at me. No hard feelings. Let's rehearse for our big love scene next week when you play Nomad Cerise and I get to be your secret Bedouin lover!"

Jemma was already out of earshot, and didn't hear him use the name "bunnygirl."

That night, Jemma sat at the computer, trying to stay distracted so she wouldn't think about Mike. He'd already called three times, but she didn't pick up.

At the same time, Marybeth was also at her computer, at the kitchen table, finishing a note to her cousin Yolanda, explaining that she'd come home upset and Cabot had been annoyed with her for not feeling like going out to dinner.

He marched off to bed early, giving her the cold shoulder.

Realizing it was getting late and she might as well sleep in the guest room and let Cabot pout by himself, she started to get up.

But then she noticed a pop-up on her screen, alerting her that flybynight was online at the forum.

She sat and sent an Instant Message, asking if her new buddy was free to chat. The answer came back to go ahead, and so she wrote what Cabot told her about being too sensitive, adding, "I shouldn't have told him about the woman who caused a terrible scene where I work. It turned out she's dating the guy I work for. It really upset me."

Jemma typed back an IM to bunnygirl: "What happened?"

Marybeth huddled over her computer, her shoulders tight with anxiety as she typed: "My car hit a teenage boy. He died. His mother came on the set. I mean, where I work. I feel so guilty."

The blood drained from Jemma's face.

She ran a harried hand over her forehead. *It couldn't be!*

She pressed her fingertips to her lips, frantic to force her thoughts into a semblance of logical order.

In her own house, a few blocks away, Marybeth looked at her screen and waited for a reply, wondering what happened.

Maybe flybynight was having computer problems.

Jemma clenched her fists, stunned, trying to breathe. Her hands were trembling as she typed: "Is your name Marybeth?"

She watched the screen just long enough to see the reply from bunnygirl: "How did you know?"

Instead of sending an answer, Jemma yanked open a file drawer.

She took out the unmarked manila folder in front, and flipped through it. Insurance reports. Legal correspondence. Finally, the original accident report.

She jotted down the driver's home address, grabbed her keys and hurried out.

Marybeth decided she might as well give up.

It looked like flybynight had been called away.

In her car, Jemma slowed to check house numbers and then pulled up in front of Marybeth's house and parked at the curb.

She raced to the front door.

She rammed a thumb on the doorbell and held it there.

At the sound of the doorbell, Marybeth leapt from the table, startled.

They rarely had guests, and hardly knew the neighbors.

As she hurried out of the room, the laptop still showed her last IM to flybynight: "How did you know?"

The doorbell kept ringing.

She dashed to answer the door before Cabot complained.

Standing on the porch, Jemma watched as the porch light came on and then the door opened a few inches.

Marybeth peered out at her.

"You're bunnygirl." Jemma pushed past Marybeth into the house. "Three guesses who I am."

Marybeth shrank back, her thoughts in a whirlwind of confusion.

Cabot strode out of the bedroom in his boxer shorts, annoyed. "Who's there this time of night?"

Jemma and Cabot stared at each other, strangers. He gave the two women a curious look but went back down the hall to the master bedroom and slammed the door.

Jemma kept walking towards Marybeth, driving her backwards into the living room, where Jemma glanced around with cold curiosity, finally seeing where That Woman lived.

Out of a photo display, three slammed her, one by one: Yolanda. Naomi. Yolanda's photo of a young woman with long blonde hair holding an armful of bunnies up to her eyebrows.

Her mouth agape, Jemma crossed to the bunny photo and picked it up. "This is you? Hiding behind the rabbits? A defenseless creature?" She slammed it face down. "Behind the wheel of a two-ton weapon!"

She looked at Marybeth, cowering in a nightshirt, her short hair in pixie spikes, her delicate features drawn in confusion. For once, logic failed Dr. Jemma Malotki Powell. "I don't understand what's going on."

Neither did Marybeth, but she couldn't speak. All she could do was watch this crazed woman stomp around her living room in a rage, and wonder how there could be such a horrendous coincidence on top of all the other disasters in her life, that the one person who had befriended her in the suicide support group should turn out to be the mother of the boy she'd killed.

Marybeth interrupted her own thoughts. "Please don't hit me."

Jemma was startled into awareness of behaving like a virago. "I wasn't planning to." She picked up a framed photo of Marybeth on her wedding day, waltzing with her father.

The silence became agonizing.

Marybeth perched in her favorite wingback chair and hugged her knees. Finally, she said, barely above a whisper, trying to remember this woman was also flybynight who was so understanding and gentle with her online, "Don't you ever feel like...like you want to climb right out of your own skin? Just fly away like a little bird. And not look back. Not ever have to look back."

Without replying, Jemma looked over Marybeth's collection of classic DVD movies. "You think if you kill yourself you'll wake up on a pink cloud..." She picked up a Cary Grant movie–*The Bishop's Wife*-- "... and dance the night away with an old movie star." She set the movie down.

They looked at each other a moment.

"I don't know what else to say," Marybeth said at last, "except I'm so very sorry–"

Jemma let out a long broken sigh.

In a way, she felt sorry for the young woman, who was obviously upset and remorseful. "There isn't anything you <u>can</u> say."

Glancing again at the wedding photos, Jemma added, "But my son won't be dancing with me on <u>his</u> wedding day."

The next day Jemma had to travel again, and after a sleepless night, she boarded the plane, thoroughly cross at having been delayed by a random security check of her shoulder bag and carryon, and then a further delay for mechanical reasons related to the air conditioning before they were allowed to board.

When she finally got on the plane, she found her seat, shoved her carryon into the overhead bin and sat down like this was the dentist's chair and they had just run out of Novocain.

She buckled up and ignored the perky Texas college girl beside her who tried to strike up a conversation.

It was a full flight to Houston.

There was no other seat Jemma could move to and the college girl didn't understand the meaning of, "I'm not interested in conversing, I'm going to rest."

The sorority girl's mouth didn't take a rest the whole flight.

Chapter 19

A ll Jemma could think of lately was that she was glad she hadn't made a grand gesture and given up her career for Mike, because that would mean she'd have nothing now.

She threw herself into her work, excelling at everything she had to do, and then looked around for more ways to prove she was ready to command a mission.

"Slow down, honey," Fran whispered one day, as she managed to catch up with Jemma in a hallway at the Johnson Space Center.

Jemma smiled grimly. "You're the one who told me work would help me handle my grief." She glanced through a file, barely paying heed to Fran's invitation to a barbecue at her house that evening.

"I'm celebrating the mission and it won't be the same without you," Fran added.

"It's kind of last minute–"

"I've been telling you about it for over a week. You're the only one who hasn't replied."

Jemma stopped as that last comment sank in. "I'm sorry, Fran." She closed the folder.

"I know, Jemma," the older woman said, patting her shoulder. "You can't stop thinking about Mike." She gave Jemma a paper with the directions. "And don't be late."

That evening, driving a rental car, Jemma consulted Fran's directions and turned onto a residential street.

Spanish moss dripped from gnarled oak trees on both sides of the curb. She could see from the addresses that the house she wanted wouldn't be in this block.

Going the posted speed limit, she came to a 4-way intersection. There was no stop sign, no signal, and no traffic so she sailed through without slowing.

Then an oncoming car passed her.

Glancing idly in the rearview mirror, Jemma saw the other car's brake lights come on at the intersection. And she saw why: There <u>was</u> a stop sign.

Stunned, she pulled to the curb.

Leaving the engine idling, she twisted to look out the back window. There was a stop sign on her side of the street, too. Thick oak tree branches and Spanish moss had obscured it from the front when she approached it.

Aghast, she sat in the car, staring out the windshield as the implication of running the stop sign struck home.

"You're not yourself anymore," Cabot said over dinner. "You've become this Cerise person instead."

"I'm sorry," Marybeth said automatically. "Sometimes it spills over. I'm studying her characteristics so I can get the nuances right."

"Characteristics? More like character tricks, always trying to sway my opinion."

"What are you talking about?"

"I saw what you did."

"What are you talking about?" she repeated, more calmly than she felt.

"You moved that vase."

"What vase?"

"That vase with the pointy lid. Tall vase with a green paisley design."

"The ginger jar?"

"You moved it out of the living room."

"I was just changing things around a bit," she said, "seeing what fits where the best, and I thought it looked better in the guest bedroom. The colors go with the new wallpaper."

"So you shove it off in the guest room. The vase that I bought you."

"I'm sorry, Cabot. I didn't realize it would be a big deal. I'll move it back to the living room."

"Don't go doing it on my behalf." He got up, scraping his chair back noisily. "Too late, anyway, now that I know how you feel about it."

"But I don't feel any different about it!"

"You never liked it, but you didn't have the balls to say so when I gave it to you."

"That's not true, Cabot. I like the paisley and I like the colors. I like the ginger jar."

"You are so freaking busy making sure everyone knows how talented and sweet you are, but at home you're a cold bitch. I'm the one who has to live with you, Marybeth."

She stared at him a long moment as he stomped away.

She watched his retreating back, thinking hard about what he'd just said, claiming she was impossible to live with.

Thinking... *It's time I do something to change that.*

As she jetted towards Los Angeles, Jemma slumped in her seat, her thoughts inward, barely aware of the purchased sandwich she ate, or the polite comments she made to the man next to her each time he asked to get past her to reach the lavatory, or the reply to the flight attendant who wanted to know if she'd like headphones.

Marybeth called the attorney who had given her a free consultation. "I'm ready to file for divorce," she said firmly. "I found a garage apartment I can rent month-to-month, and I'm moving into it the first of next month."

When she got home, Jemma dropped her purse and suitcase and carryon in the foyer, and went immediately to the kitchen to make a phone call from a number she'd scribbled in her agenda book that time in the desert resort hotel when she'd called bunnygirl.

She reached Marybeth's voice mail, and left a crisp message with a return number to call, saying she wanted to meet for lunch at noon the next day and discuss something.

That evening, Marybeth retrieved her phone messages.

Her heart sank when she heard that flybynight, the Powell boy's mother, wanted to meet for lunch.

Knowing she had to force herself to do this and not hide from reality, she thought of places to eat in the area.

They all brought up bad memories of Cabot nagging her about what was on her plate and telling her she needed to eat meat, needed to gain weight, needed to lose weight, needed to be doing the opposite of whatever she was doing.

Then she remembered the French bistro with the big fish tank and that friendly hostess who told them about the desserts.

Cabot didn't have a chance, there, to make snide comments about what Marybeth ordered for dinner because he'd walked out.

Thinking of this, she realized it was a good choice, and at least she'd have that friendly hostess to draw some positive energy from.

She'd need all the courage she could muster to meet with Mrs. Powell.

The next day, precisely at noon, Jemma entered Hart's bistro, feeling somewhat dazed that Marybeth had chosen this particular restaurant out of hundreds in the area.

She scanned the dining room until she found Marybeth, alone at a table. Still bewildered, she took the seat across from bunnygirl, and asked, looking around, "Why did you choose this place?"

"My husband–soon to be ex, I should qualify--and I tried to eat here one night but it was crowded. I thought the menu looked good. If it's not all right, we can go someplace else."

"This is fine."

Behind Jemma, having been on the phone when she came in, Tracey hurried into the kitchen, and returned almost immediately with chef Hart at her heels.

He came to Jemma at once and kissed her cheek. Although Hart had aged greatly since Andy's death, he looked at peace.

Jemma stood up and gave him a hug.

Glancing over at one of the many mirrors of *Café Réflexions* for a moment, she saw Andy appear between them and look lovingly from one to the other, and then vanish.

She blinked and looked again, but saw only her own reflection with Hart.

Marybeth glanced at Hart and didn't recognize him from the day of the accident.

Both had changed greatly since then. She was no longer the helpless, scared young woman with scarlet hair tumbling to her shoulders in curls, but a sophisticated actress with a highly anticipated film that would be in theaters soon. She smiled politely at the chef.

Jemma realized he didn't know who her lunch guest was, and decided against introducing them. It would only cause more pain, and they had all experienced more than enough of that. She was gentle with him. "Make us something special, okay?"

He thought a moment, then brightened. "*Sole veronique.* It's not on the menu, but the fish is fresh, the grapes are plump and sweet. You'll love it." He returned to the kitchen.

Marybeth looked at Jemma with trepidation, wondering why she had asked to meet again, but not wanting to be the first to speak.

Jemma took a warm roll from the basket, broke it open, began buttering it, then set it down, uneaten. "I know it was an accident."

Across the table, Marybeth gave a small intake of breath, then exhaled softly. She had never expected this, but she knew all at once that this was the final thing she needed to hear in order to heal and move on with her life.

"And both of us would turn back the clock," Jemma said. "If only we knew how."

She hesitated, then got up and went around the table.

She rested a hand on Marybeth's shoulder in forgiveness.

Andy approached Qaletaqa. "Is it okay if I get back on the Dream Spinners team? There's someone I want to help."

Qaletaqa looked at him a moment, smiling. "Yes, Great-grandson, you may be on the team, and we are fortunate to have your warm and generous spirit with us. Now, go. Why do you stand there gaping? Run and help your friend Eric."

"But how did you–" Andy stopped, laughing. "I bet you've known everything the whole time."

Qaletaqa shrugged, amused.

Eric awoke from a sound sleep, frowning thoughtfully about the dream he'd just had. He got up, dressed, spent a few moments writing something at his desk, and then hurried out.

He rode his bike to Marybeth's house and put the note in her curbside mailbox on top of letters that were just delivered. Questioning the impulse, he started to take his note back, but firmly shut the mailbox door and rode away.

As he biked toward home, feeling lighter and freer, he passed a homeless man shuffling along the street. Eric stopped, took off his stolen divers watch and handed it to the man.

The man grinned. "A watch! Now I'll know when *Dancing with the Stars* is on. I always just miss it, but I love nature shows. God bless you."

Eric realized how very fortunate he was in his own life.

He made a commitment to himself and his future that he would make better choices from now on.

"Yeah," Eric mumbled to the man self-consciously. "God bless you, too."

Marybeth opened her mailbox.

Ever since finding the dead rat inside, she went out to get the mail with trepidation. She saw there was a note on top of the letters, and thought it might be from their mail carrier. Turning toward the house with the mail, she idly read the note, and realized it was from someone else entirely.

The hand printed note read: "I'm sorry for the graffiti—and for cutting all your flower buds—and for the dead rat. I won't bother you again. P.S. He was my friend."

Overwhelmed with relief, Marybeth realized the long ordeal was at an end.

And yet she knew that if she showed this note to Cabot, it would not exonerate her in his eyes. He would find a way to twist it around. He'd say she got someone to write it, trying to support her case that she was innocent.

She had never told him about the dead rat, knowing he'd turn it into a bigger drama than it was.

She folded the note and tucked it in her pocket, deciding to keep this private as well.

Gabriella and Andy sat on their favorite hilltop in Griffith Park.

"You've accomplished a lot," she said.

"Not enough yet. I want my mom to be happy."

"How do you think you can make that happen?"

"She needs to be with Mike. I know she does. But I'm afraid to meddle again."

"With that attitude, I know you will do a better job from now on. It is when we think we have all the answers and try to shove, instead of suggest, that we create chaos."

"Like I did."

"We all make mistakes, Andrew. And when we learn from them, we grow."

Marybeth went to the sandwich shop and bought a large sub, then went in search of the homeless man she had given the sleeping bag to.

It seemed a long time since she'd paid attention to people in need. She'd been far too absorbed in her own problems and worries, and now she decided to tithe her earnings from Cerise, and give the funds to the local mission.

The homeless man broke into a smile as she approached. "My angel! Thought you forgot about me."

She gave him the food, and some cash, knowing that in this small way, she was helping someone hopelessly confused and destitute lead a more comfortable life, even if only for a few hours.

When the shooting of "Seven Funerals" wrapped, Mike asked Marybeth what her plans were.

"I'm going to spend six months in the south of France. Provence. And I'm going to write a memoir and include vegetarian recipes and stories about my best friend Naomi. The trip was her idea originally...but she died before we could go."

"Send me a copy of the manuscript when you're done," he said. "Sounds like it's got a film in it."

Jemma dreamed she was trying to follow someone. A man. Dark hair. She kept trying to get far enough ahead to see his face. They'd been talking in the shadows and then he'd abruptly turned away. Now she was tripping after him.

A crowd kept pushing against her, creating a wall of people she had to break through.

She was walking against the direction of the crowd. And she was literally tripping because she wore platform flip-flops and the left one had something wrong with it. The three-inch-high sole was splitting apart into layers, coming undone.

She looked at her feet and saw she needed to fit her big toe under a loop, but her toe wouldn't stay there and her foot kept sliding askew as she ran. She tried to take the flip-flops off and go barefooted but couldn't get the right shoe off and was forced to leave both of them on or she'd be hobbled by the height difference.

She hurried around a corner, searching for the man, but couldn't see him. She felt sad in the dream but also felt confident she could find him, somehow.

When she woke up, she realized the dark-haired man hadn't been Andy. It was someone else she was looking for.

Mike? No, that's over. And I wasn't upset or frantic like in the other dreams when I was searching. I was...happy. And I was excited.

The dream stayed with Jemma.

It lingered throughout the day, and lifted her spirits.

Lulu phoned Jemma. "How are you sleeping lately, Jem? Dreaming okay?"

"What do you mean?"

"Nothing special. Like, are you having good dreams? Or scary ones, the kind where you wake up and your heart is pounding?"

Jemma frowned.

Into the silence, Lulu asked, "What did you dream last night?"

"Why?"

"I'm interested in how you're doing, Jemma! You were a wreck when I left after the funeral, and I want to know you're all right, or whether you'd like me to come back and hang with you for a few days. There's this book I'm reading, and I think that—"

"Oh great, you're getting into dream interpretation?"

"You don't have to tell me about your dreams," Lulu said, annoyed.

"Okay, so I had this dream I was trying to catch up with a guy–"

"Mike."

"Excuse me?"

"It was Mike, right? I dreamed last night that he came to the door at the old house. Like all the times when I was a kid and you guys were going together. He asked for you and I...I pointed."

"I see," Jemma said. "You pointed. Where? To L.A. because I moved from Phoenix?"

"Don't mock. This could be important."

"If your pointing to me led him directly into my dream, why was he walking away from me in it?"

"Well," Lulu said slowly, "Maybe he thinks you're still angry, and he wanted to let you know you can catch him, but you'll have to be the one to make the next move."

"Enough. I think you saw that on a soap opera. Dreams are the brain's way of sorting and storing images and information that pour into our mind all day."

But after they caught up on family activities and then hung up, Jemma thought about what her sister had said.

Jemma looked in her agenda book, found the number she needed, picked up the phone and dialed before she could talk herself out of it.

When the person she was calling answered, she said, "Hello, Rodney? I have a favor to ask...."

Finishing up post-production, Mike and the film editor were working on a rough cut of "Seven Funerals" when the door swung open and Rodney looked in.

He got Mike's attention, then held the door wider...for Jemma to enter.

At the sight of her, Mike's eyes lit up but he checked his reaction, and looked at her neutrally. He didn't dare let himself hope that she had come for anything other than a business reason. Otherwise, why not call him at home?

He glanced at the editor. "Let's take a break. Twenty minutes?"

The editor looked curiously at Jemma and they exchanged a "Hello" in passing. He left with Rodney, who shut the door behind them.

Once they were alone, Jemma said, "Don't be mad at Rodney. I was afraid you wouldn't see me if I tried to do it in private. So I talked Rodney into letting me know where you'd be today. I have to get back to Texas." Suddenly she felt nervous and unsure of her reception.

She glanced at the screen. The film was still running, almost over. She watched as Time Traveling Vale pulled a gun on Present Day Cerise. But Cerise was no fool, and she grabbed the gun. He tried to take it from her. In the struggle, it went off. The Time Traveler fell, wounded.

Mike watched her face.

"I'm sorry for the way I handled things," she said, still watching as Cerise sank to her knees and tried to revive Vale. "You deserved better."

He looked at her evenly, waiting.

Jemma turned to face him. "Twenty years ago," she said. "And now."

With a nod toward the screen, Mike said, as if afraid to infer too much from her reply, "Think Vale and Cerise deserve another chance?"

A smile slowly lit up her face.

She nodded, and moved into his arms.

He cupped her face in his hands and gently kissed her temples, then along the side of her jaw, teasing.

She sighed, wanting him, wanting more, wanting their love to last for eternity.

His lips reached her mouth and she clung to him.

They kissed.

After a timeless moment, Jemma broke away, leaning back so she could look up into his face.

She drank in every aspect of the man she loved heart and soul, allowing all the crustaceous matter around her heart to dissolve in the presence of love and simply disperse harmlessly into the air.

And then she took a step forward into his arms, and she knew she had come home at last.

Chapter 20

As night turned to morning, Qaletaqa stood on a deck at the Griffith Observatory and surveyed the City of Angels as it began waking up. He tossed a small tumbled quartz stone in his hand.

Gabriella joined him, her pink gown as rosy as the dawn, her new gold armband gleaming.

They looked out at The Big Sprawl together. Not speaking. Or needing to.

At the Kourou spaceport in French Guiana, on the Atlantic coast of South America five degrees north of the Equator, Jemma slept soundly in spite of being keyed up about tomorrow's launch.

She dreamed she was at home, sitting alone in the living room. Andy came to visit, and with him were other beings, whom she came to realize were beings who helped humans, just as he did. As they spoke, she realized Andy didn't belong at her side anymore. He was out of place, out of time. A visitor in a former home.

"I wrote a song for you," he told her. "It's called *Just Around the Corner*." He sat at the piano and she joined him on the bench.

He improvised a simple melody while singing:

I faded with the sunset on the day I left.

But I'm just around the corner,

Don't feel bereft.

I'm happy and I'm spinning dreams,

At home high in the sky.

We'll say hello again one day,

So please don't say goodbye.

Each sunbeam comes from me to you,

A message from above.

I'm just around the corner now,

Creating peace and love.

She heard Qaletaqa say, "Don't worry. He's doing great. He's with me now."

Jemma woke up, humming the tune Andy had played, feeling confident and calm.

As she dressed, she put on the buffalo nickel necklace, and then tucked pictures of Andy and of Mike into the bag she'd take on the launch.

Later, five spaceflyers strode to the space capsule--Commander Jemma Malotki and the four members of her international team. All five were women.

In Hart's bistro, Hart and his staff gathered around a TV monitor in the kitchen, watching Jemma on a pre-recorded interview that was being interspersed with live coverage of the launch.

"In the first twenty-five years of America's space program," Jemma said on TV, "women qualified to be part of it, in absolutely every single way except gender. Some people think too many years have passed to still care about the Mercury Thirteen--those women aviators who trained to be astronauts and were then pushed aside. But millions of others do care! My team is going for them. And for the Russian women cosmonauts who didn't get their special all-female launch in the early days of their own program. Actually–we're going for all women with adventure in their hearts and wings on their souls."

"I bet you're really proud of her," Tracey said to Hart.

"I am. Yes, I sure am." Hart smiled at her and then squeezed her hand affectionately.

Another pre-recorded segment aired on the television. In it, each surviving member of the Mercury 13 astronaut trainees held a captioned photo of herself from 1961. There were also captioned photos of the deceased members, on easel stands.

A reporter's voice informed the viewers, "Dr. Jemma Malotki, commander of history's first all-female astronaut crew, dedicates their fourteen-day mission to the International Space Station to these women aviators, dubbed the Mercury Thirteen, who never got a mission of their own."

In French Guiana, Mike watched the launch with other special guests and visitors, at a distant location for safety's sake. He knew it was easier on the astronauts' nerves to have their final goodbyes already taken care of, so that now they could focus on the job at hand.

When he had started to tell Jemma good luck and goodbye last night, she stopped him with her fingertips over his lips. "Let's not say goodbye, ever again."

He smiled into her eyes and drew her in for a tighter embrace. "You must have read that book I got you at the book fair—*No Good-Byes*."

She nodded. "No matter what happens in our lives–what lies ahead--I know now that we'll be together again."

"I'll love you forever, Jemmie."

She rested her head on his shoulder, contented. "Me too, you."

They kissed passionately, knowing that nothing would ever cause them to turn their back on the other, ever again.

Qaletaqa put a hand on Andy's shoulder. "Since you don't wish to reincarnate at this time, have you given thought to the direction you'd like to pursue? Teacher, guide, healer, greeter of new arrivals, or–"

"Dream Spinner. If that's all right with you, Qaletaqa."

Qaletaqa nodded. "Excellent choice. I have somewhere to go now. But we'll be in touch."

Inside the space capsule, Jemma and her team prepared for the launch.

Unseen, Qaletaqa entered, perched at Jemma's side and watched her face intently, ready to be of spiritual assistance if she asked for help.

The Air France flight to Paris boarded. It was a crowded flight, with all seats taken. Two passengers recognized "Cerise" from advance publicity for *Seven Funerals* and excitedly asked Marybeth for autographs.

She smilingly complied, thanked them for their support, and admitted the rumors were correct: she was on her way to Nice for six months after a week's vacation in Paris. She found her window seat and got settled.

Unseen by the humans, Andy approached Marybeth, radiating the healing energy of love and forgiveness. He touched her wrists with his fingertips. She wore bracelets over the scars from her two suicide attempts, but he knew that they were there.

Wistfully, Marybeth touched her wrists in the same places. After a moment's hesitation, she removed both cuff bracelets. She had never gone out in public without covering the scars. Now she studied her old faded scars and tentatively stroked one.

As the plane lifted with a surge into the air, she decided it was time to stop hiding her history of pain. So what if she had scars? They were the visible sign that she was stronger than her pain. She'd be writing about all of it in her memoir, anyway, so she might as well get used to curious stares.

With a sense of rueful self-acceptance, Marybeth flung the bracelets into her tote bag.

Her hands were bare. No wedding ring, because she'd mustered the courage to leave Cabot, with the encouragement and support of a new therapist who was trained in helping victims–no, survivors–of emotional and verbal abuse.

She looked out the window at Los Angeles as the sprawling city receded, and let out a small heartfelt sigh, finally at peace with herself.

During the flight, Marybeth got out the copy of *A Year in Provence* that Naomi had given her and began reading it, using the birthday card from Naomi as her bookmark.

When the two people next to her got up for the lavatory, she glanced across the aisle and saw a young woman about her own age at the opposite window.

As if sensing she was being stared at, the young woman turned her head. She noticed the book title, and said, as if with a confidential comment, "You'll love the book, except all the parts about meat. Totally disgusting. Poor animals."

"My cousin who gave me this already warned me," Marybeth said. "But thanks for the heads up. I appreciate it."

When the attendant came through with the meals trolley later, he said, "Vegetarian?" and both girls raised their hands. "Hey, what is this," he teased. "A veggie convention going to Paris and I didn't know about it?"

"We're not traveling together," Marybeth said, darting a friendly glance at the other young woman.

"Well, maybe that can be arranged," the steward said, looking meaningfully at other passengers with raised eyebrow and motioning a swap with his arms.

Laughing, people traded seats until Marybeth and the other woman were side by side.

"I'm Marybeth."

"And I'm Katherine but my friends call me Kitty."

Marybeth smiled at a her new friend, and they exchanged phone numbers. As they continued chatting about books, films and recipes they both loved, Marybeth sighed softly to herself, knowing in her heart that Naomi had brought about this meeting...this new friendship.

Thank you, Naomi—thank you, thank you. I'll love you forever.

Marybeth glanced out the window, reflecting on how far she'd come since Naomi's death, since her baby Stephanie's death, since the accident that took Andy Powell's life, and since her decision to end her marriage.

Enough history.

She happily turned her attention back to Kitty.

Andy gazed at Marybeth with affection and compassion. *I love you. I'm sorry. Please forgive me for the pain I caused by leaping out in front of your car without looking. Thank you.*

He brushed a kiss on the top of her head, satisfied that she would be all right now.

She was on her path and wouldn't look back too often at the lessons that had brought her to this higher and finer realization of who she really was and how much love she was capable of sharing.

With a smile, Andy realized he could finally say the same thing about himself.

Epilogue

Five months after Jemma's successful mission to the International Space Station, Mike drove her to a picnic area in Griffith Park.

When she got out of the car and glanced around curiously, he said, "Stand right there and close your eyes."

"What for?"

"Show patience, Birthday Girl," Mike said. "Wait here. And no peeking."

Smiling in anticipation of her gift, with no thought for what it might be, knowing only it would be something she would treasure because it was coming from the love of her life, she stood with her hands over her eyes.

On her left hand, her wedding band gleamed in the sun.

He hurried to a woman waiting in a parked car whose door signs advertised a dog rescue group. She got out and lifted a Golden Retriever puppy from a crate in the back seat. He gave her an envelope with the payment, and then put a leash on the blonde dog, a female. "Thanks," he whispered.

The woman drove off, waving goodbye.

Mike carried the puppy to Jemma. "Keep your eyes closed!" He held the dog up near her face.

It licked her nose.

Jemma's eyes flew open. She saw the puppy. Taking the dog in her arms, she said, "Oh, Mike! After Joker died I've always said I didn't want another dog.... But she's perfect. How did you think of this?"

Mike smiled, pleased by her reaction.

As they romped with the puppy, the shadows cast by the nearby oak and pine trees seemed to spin and shift and change.

Andy, Joker, Gabriella, Naomi and Qaletaqa watched them for a moment.

Gabriella cast Andy a suspicious look. "Did you spin Mike a dream about getting a puppy for your mother?"

Andy just smiled. "I'm taking a lesson from Qaletaqa," he said. "I elect the right to remain silent."

The invisible group turned and vanished into the depths of the park.

Joker lingered, playing with the puppy.

Andy whistled from within the shadows and Joker ran to his side.

On a beach in Malibu, Andy created an intricate miniature sand castle.

He held it up, displaying it in the palm of his hand, and decided that, objectively speaking, the castle deserved a first place ribbon.

He felt happy not only with the sand castle, but with his new way of life, being a Dream Spinner.

Getting up, his higher awareness signaled him that he needed to go somewhere and spin a dream for a person in need.

At once, he transported himself and his companion dog Joker into a small bedroom where a frightened old man lay dying alone, fretting in a twilight state of sleep.

Without being seen by the man, Andy looked at him a moment, radiating love and comfort. "Relax. It doesn't hurt to die. You're going home. Home, where love resides, where you'll experience the peace that passeth all understanding. Ready? Step out of your earth suit now...and soar."

THE END

"High Flight"

Oh, I have slipped the surly bonds of Earth
And danced the skies on laughter-silvered wings;
Sunward I've climbed and joined the tumbling mirth
Of sun-split clouds...and done a hundred things
You have not dreamed of...wheeled and soared and swung
High in the sunlit silence. Hov'ring there,
I've chased the shouting wind along, and flung
My eager craft through footless halls of air.
Up, up the long delirious burning blue
I've topped the windswept heights with easy grace
Where never lark, or even eagle flew.
And, while with silent lifting mind I've trod
The high untrespassed sanctity of space,
Put out my hand and touched the face of God.

John Gillespie Magee, Jr. (1922-1941)
(American aviator and poet)

About the Author

Evelyn Roberts Brooks is a writer, transformational healer, lightworker, and speaker. She's shared the stage with Bob Proctor ("The Secret"), Gay Hendricks, Peggy McColl, Arielle Ford, Misa Hopkins and other experts in personal growth.

She's the author of many fiction and nonfiction books. Keep up with her latest releases by visiting booksbyevelyn.com

Evelyn is passionate about helping others experience a transformational healing in their lives, reduce their stress, heal heartache from loss, divorce, grief and trauma, and be happier.

Her goal is to uplift, inspire and encourage, while showing people how to gain clarity and manifest more of what they really want in all areas of their lives.

Message From The Author

I hope you enjoyed *The Dream Spinners*. This novel took many years for me to write, as my own personal growth and long-delayed grief recovery from a series of childhood tragedies prompted me to keep revising it again and again, to tell the most "healing" story possible, one that would inspire and uplift you with a feeling of comfort and peace long after you finished the last page.

I wrote the first draft of this novel in 1997, and it was much longer than this final edition. In addition, it was written entirely in the format of email letters—I was determined to be the first novelist to create a book that would be the technically updated version of a book written in diary format. Email was a new phenomenon at that time, and to me it seemed perfect for an intricate novel.

In every revision from the start, it was always my intention to weave the subplots of love and second chances for several characters in and around the two main storylines of Jemma and her son Andy. And, of course, there were changes brewing at NASA that kept affecting my storyline and requiring revisions. Even so, I felt the book wasn't quite ready for the world, and so I kept putting it aside to work on other projects.

Jemma nagged me to finalize her story for publication, but there was something missing and I couldn't put my finger on it. I slowly came to the realization that it wasn't a story just about Andy and Jemma, it was about the triangle created by the intersection of those two people with Marybeth—this book needed to include her perspective as a main character and not simply the driver on the day of the accident.

At its heart, this novel is about a skeptical woman who learns to find joy in the midst of grief by accessing a greater understanding of our eternal, spiritual nature, and, as part of that same woman's story, we witness the launch of the first all-female space flight in honor of the American women aviators dubbed the "Mercury 13" who qualified to be astronauts in the 1960's but were not allowed to go into space due to gender discrimination in that era.

Although this is a novel, not a work of nonfiction, the story has been energized spiritually. The energy of peace, compassion and healing is within the vibrational frequency of the words themselves. That's what this 2019 revision is all about—showering you with love and happiness while you enjoy *The Dream Spinners* experience.

You don't have to do anything special to receive the good feelings, simply be open to knowing that we are all connected in a field of infinite possibilities and infinite joy.

In this edition, I've also added the Reader's Guide to provide a list of topics for group discussion.

I'd appreciate it if you would take a moment to leave a nice review at Amazon.com so others can find this book—a 4 or 5-star review would be wonderful, and I thank you in advance for it.

I love to hear from readers! Connect with me at evelynbrooks.com

All the best for your happiness,

Evelyn

P.S. Stop by my main site to claim your free serenity gift collection: evelynbrooks.com

Reader's Guide

Spoiler alert: Reading these 21 discussion topics before you finish the novel may disrupt the fullness of your experience by revealing major details and relationship outcomes out of context.

1. In the introduction, the author cites various themes that are interwoven throughout *The Dream Spinners,* including the motifs of love, second chances and forgiveness. While reading, did you discover themes that resonated with you? Did any of these feel uncomfortable, or bring attention to a situation in your life you've been avoiding?

2. Andy is determined to do whatever it takes to be accepted by the in-crowd for his senior year of high school, even though the hazing means going against his own values. Have you ever been confronted with a situation like that, perhaps at work or in a relationship where you were being asked to do something that felt wrong? How did you resolve it?

3. During the events surrounding Andy's arrest for shoplifting, which parent's side were you on, if either? How would you have handled this situation, from your own perspective rather than imagining yourself in Jemma's or Hart's shoes?

4. If you'd been an angel on Marybeth's shoulder after the accident, how would you guide her through the emotional devastation she feels over killing Andy?

5. Jemma has a lifelong goal related to space travel, and she is determined to make the best of changes at NASA and lead a crew into space. Her plan for an all-female crew is hinted at a few times before being fully revealed. Had you heard of the Mercury 13 aviators before this book? If so, did you relate to Jemma's drive to redress a wrong in history?

6. Have you ever survived a near-fatal accident or a serious illness or been close to someone who did? If so, did that experience color your emotional reaction to the events in *The Dream Spinners*? In what way?

7. Out of all the characters, was there one in particular whom you identified with or resonated with? If so, who? Is it because you have gone through a similar experience to theirs in your own life? Or because you've felt helpless when a friend or family member was going through something like that?

8. Although Jemma's experiences are at the heart of *The Dream Spinners,* was there a group dynamic that struck a chord with you, such as the relationship between Marybeth and Cabot, Hart and Andy, Andy and Eric, Andy, Qaletaqa and Gabriella, or others?

9. Have you ever thought about the synchronicity of coincidences? Was it interesting to witness all the near-misses before Mike and Jemma finally meet at the book fair? Did you feel that each of them was ready for that encounter, whereas earlier they would not have been in harmony yet?

10. Was the relationship between Marybeth and Cabot troubling to witness? Have you known someone who was trapped in an emotionally

abusive marriage? If you were Marybeth, with her belief she was meant to make others happy despite her own grief, would you have acted differently? If so, would you have made different choices than she did?

11. *The Dream Spinners* addresses the complex issue of suicide and the upheaval it creates in the lives of relatives and friends. Have you experienced the suicide of someone you knew? Did the story give insight into the troubled thoughts that might lead someone to consider taking their own life to end their pain?

12. When Cabot discovers graffiti on the house and then the decapitated rosebuds, who did you believe? Marybeth's protestations of innocence? Or Cabot's belief that she intends to plead insanity in the upcoming civil suit? Did you suspect Eric?

13. Brooks uses the metaphor of being trapped in "The Gray Zone" to indicate a state of confusion and lack of awareness. Are there times in your life when that state describes you or someone you know? What could you learn from this novel to heal that situation?

14. Hart is devastated by Andy's death, but he takes a different path than Jemma does. He journals his feelings, seeks grief support, and opens to healing. He accepts the opportunity to move forward with his television show, and later, a new relationship. Do you think he was wrong to leave Jemma?

15. When Marybeth reads for the role of Cerise, she decides this film will be her salvation. What do you think she means by that? Have you ever come across a project or creative outlet that you felt would uplift you to a higher expression of your true self? If not, are you willing to welcome the experience? How could you do that?

16. In Jemma's shoes, how would you handle the realization that the young woman called "bunnygirl" at the suicide support forum is actually the driver of the car that killed Andy? Further, Marybeth is playing the role of "Cerise"—a movie character based on Jemma herself. Would you go to Marybeth's house to confront her? If not, what do you think you would do?

17. In the prologue, set in 1998 during Jemma and Mike's college graduation weekend, Jemma tells Mike that she doesn't have "the right stuff" for marriage, although she does to be an astronaut. By the end of *The Dream Spinners*, do you feel that Jemma now has the right stuff—a higher awareness of her capacity for love and self-expression—for both career and love?

18. Jemma broke off her engagement with Mike to focus on graduate school and her intended career with NASA. How did her relationship with Hart differ from the one she had with Mike, both in their early years together and the reunion twenty years later?

19. Throughout *The Dream Spinners,* there are references to taking responsibility for your own choices. Which character is faced with the biggest challenge in this area?

20. As the story draws to a close, were you surprised to witness Jemma's forgiveness of Marybeth? What about Andy's relationship-in-spirit with Marybeth, where he forgives her and asks forgiveness for inadvertently causing the fatal accident by not looking where he was going? Do you think forgiveness is an important part of relationships? If so, why?

21. In the after-life, we see that enlightened people are involved with projects that create growth and expansion while helping others. Naomi

decides to become a "Greeter" and welcome people who have just died after a trauma similar to hers, so they can adjust to their transition from physical to non-physical. Andy, too, decides not to reincarnate right away, but to stay on the Dream Spinners team. Qaletaqa offers other choices as well: healer, teacher, guide, plus of course, the option to return for another lifetime on earth. What would you choose?

www.ingramcontent.com/pod-product-compliance
Lightning Source LLC
Chambersburg PA
CBHW050123030726
47505CB00007B/2002